I0712585

OF SHADOWS & FAE

USA TODAY BESTSELLING AUTHOR

JEN L. GREY

Forgotten Kingdoms Collection
Introduction

Forgotten Kingdoms Collection

Eight women.

One sacrifice to save their kingdoms.

A chance to reclaim the love they lost.

Collection notes:

Forgotten Kingdoms is a collection of full-length stand-alone fantasy romance novels with fated mates and a guaranteed happily ever after. With vampires, fae, shifters, and everything in between, each book features a unique heroine and her epic love story that can be read in any order. All relationship dynamics are strictly M/F.

Authors in this set include:

Chandelle LaVaun

G.K. DeRosa

Megan Montero

Jen L. Grey

Robin D. Mahle & Elle Madison

LJ Andrews

Jessica M. Butler

M. Sinclair

KINGDOM OF FUOCO
KINGDOM OF EYRE
KINGDOM OF TERRE
DRACONIA
KINGDOM OF AQUOS
THE NEVER C
KINGDOM OF NIGHTFALL
KINGDOM OF EVENTIDE
VARGR
ISLE OF WILDCREST
S
KINGDOM OF KROPELKI
KINGDOM OF OGNISKO
SEPEAZIA
COURT OF BLOOD
COU NIGH
ISRAMA
TER

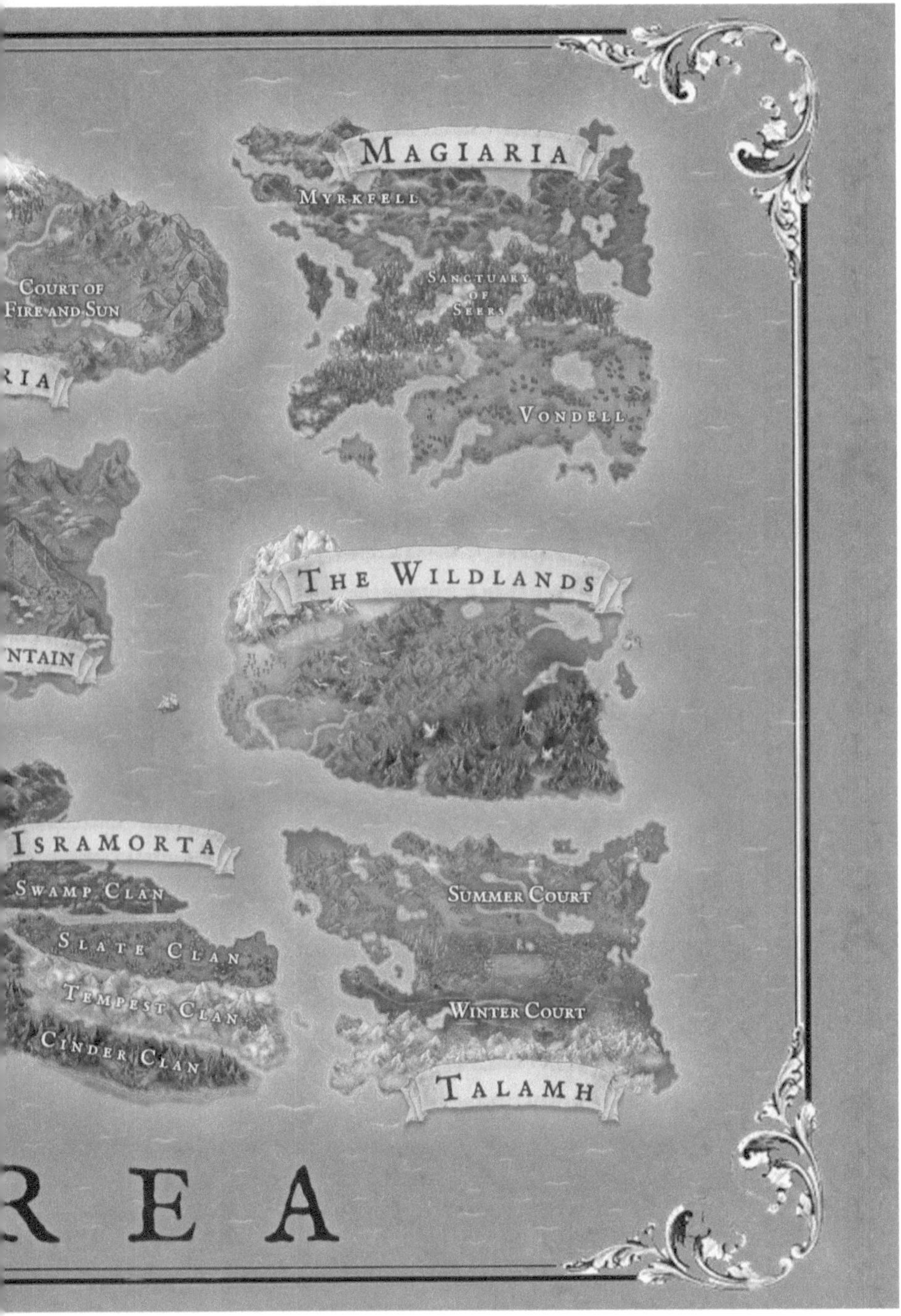

MAGIARIA
MYRKFELL
SANCTUARY OF SEERS
VONDELL
COURT OF FIRE AND SUN
RIA
NTAIN
THE WILDLANDS
ISRAMORTA
SWAMP CLAN
SLATE CLAN
TEMPEST CLAN
CINDER CLAN
SUMMER COURT
WINTER COURT
TALAMH
REA

Dath Falls
Beatha Mountain
Sambradh Castle
SUMMER COURT
Elon Village
Cath Arena
Sacred Temples
Scath Village
WINTER COURT
Geimhreadh Castle
Dergh Mountain
TALAMH
KINGDOM OF THE FAE

One

DESPITE THE HOT DESERT TEMPERATURE, a chill ran down my spine. The hairs on the nape of my neck rose. It'd been that way since I'd left my room at the Horseshoe Las Vegas hotel. Someone in the congested crowd on Las Vegas Boulevard this Halloween night was watching me. I scanned the Strip, the bright lights damn near blinding, for the culprit, the sensation confirming what I already knew.

I never should've come here.

Stan, my mentor and the closest thing I had to a father, always told me to trust my instincts. That if more people did, they'd avoid a lot of the bad shit that happened to them.

I hated being around this many people. Sweat pooled in my armpits, and every fiber of my being urged me to run away. I'd much rather be alone, wrestling with Stan or punching a damn beanbag instead of being out *here* in *this*.

A woman stumbled into me and spilled beer on the pig onesie costume I'd selected for the party. The liquid darkened the pink belly section, drenching me down to my underwear.

Lovely, now I was going to smell like sweat and stale yeast. This night was already a disaster, and I hadn't even made it to the hotel yet. Instead, I was caught in a cement hell with lights that were too harsh to be comforting and people who reeked of body odor and alcohol bumping into me. My head screamed at me to get away.

Everywhere I looked, I sensed an impending doom that threatened to swallow me whole. The sensation had started as an inkling when I'd received a random golden ticket to a casino Halloween party in the mail. The invitation had been sent to Stan's community gym as my address, which was correct ... except no one but Stan and I *knew* that.

To add more pieces to the ever-growing puzzle, my friend Ember, who worked out at the gym, had received one too. She'd brought her best friend Isa along since they were inseparable. If it hadn't been for their harassment, I wouldn't have agreed to come. But they'd gotten Stan on me, informing him of what we'd received. He'd encouraged me to go, saying, "This might be the only opportunity you have to get out of Nashville for a few days. And hell, Ivy, it's an all-expenses-paid trip."

I'd caught a later flight than Ember and Isa and decided I wouldn't stay in the hotel room at the casino, expenses paid or not, much to my friends' displeasure. Growing up, I'd learned if something sounded too good to be true, it was. This was no exception.

Something inside me had screamed at me not to go while another part of me couldn't wait. The "couldn't wait" part scared me. Being rash and doing things out of the ordinary was how people got into trouble, and trouble was one thing I always avoided. I'd rather stay at the gym and teach kids how to defend themselves so they'd never get into trouble like I had.

The glistening gold doors of the Portal Resort and Casino caught my attention just as my phone dinged a special tone. I didn't have to look to know who it was. Hell, she was the one who'd programmed her number and selected the ringtone when she'd pushed me to come.

Ember: Ho, where r u? Isa left me alone and drink. At farty bar.

My stomach clenched. A fucking *farty* bar? Not only was I somewhere I didn't feel comfortable, but now I had to deal with a drunk Ember and stench. That would be fun.

Not bothering to answer since she probably wouldn't be able to read the text anyway, I put the phone back into my pocket and removed my golden ticket, then forced myself to move forward. The hotel seemed almost familiar, though I couldn't say why.

Taking a deep breath, I clutched the door handle, and that prickly sensation of being watched washed over me again. I used to get this sensation in foster homes right before something went horribly wrong.

My phone dinged with the same tone, and my heartbeat quickened. What if Ember was in trouble and this was her way of calling me for help?

Exhaling, I opened the door, stepped into the lobby—and stopped in my tracks. I'd never been in a place so beautiful. Metallic golden tiles that reflected the twinkling lights and dazzled my senses covered the high ceiling. The lobby was packed, everyone in costumes, laughing with drinks in hand.

I searched for someone to show my ticket to, but no one was there. Everyone was laughing and having a good time, and people walked in from behind me without pause. Maybe the ticket was for the food and room here, not the actual party? Either way, I was in. Now, I needed to find Ember and Isa.

I homed in on the woman behind the hotel reception desk, trying to ignore the gorgeous stained-glass pyramid behind her that separated us from the casino. If Ember was in trouble, I needed to find her.

As I approached, the young woman lifted a brow and smirked before hiding her reaction. She cleared her throat. "How can I help you?" Humor was woven through her tone.

If she thought I looked funny in a beer-stained pig onesie, I couldn't wait to see her reaction to my question. Lifting my chin high to try to appear confident, I said, "I'm looking for the farty bar." I waved my ticket in front of her face, wanting this interaction over with quickly.

"Excuse me?" She blinked and coughed to cover up her laughter. She hadn't even blinked at my ticket.

Clearly, there was no farty bar. At least, that marginally improved the odds of this night not being a total disaster. "My friend is drunk and sent me a text." I showed her the message.

"Oh." She mashed her lips together. "She must mean the Fairy Bar. That's the closest thing to it. It's to the left, past the elevators. Go outside and follow the stone path."

"Thanks."

A few people glanced at me as I walked beneath an archway lined with glowing pink lights and past the elevators. A tall, stocky guy stood rigidly beside one elevator. His black suit, pressed and starched, made him look young. He was so still that I would've believed he was a wax statue if not for his warm cognac-brown eyes and thick hair, the rich color of tree bark.

When our gazes locked, a frigid chill of warning ran through me, and my legs almost gave out. His stare had my heart galloping against my ribs; it was the way a predator gleamed at its prey. Something was familiar about him, but that added to his creepy vibe.

Either this place was dangerous, or I was letting my paranoia get the best of me.

Facing forward, I ignored the urge to run. If I needed to protect myself, I had a knife strapped to my thigh.

A glass door led outside to a stone walkway, as the receptionist had promised. Lights lined the cobblestones, and plants and trees arched over the path. More lights hung from the trees, beckoning me through the darkness.

When I stepped onto the pathway, the fresh scents of dirt and trees loosened my shoulders. I was alone out here, and finally, I could breathe. Ten yards away was an archway of lights, and I headed toward it.

As I strolled under the calming lights, that damn shiver coursed through me once more. I picked up my pace and glanced over my shoulder, only to see no one behind me.

I couldn't shake the sensation of being watched. I needed to hurry and find Ember and Isa.

I heard the thudding bass and the laughter and knew I was

close. My legs moved faster and faster until I was jogging, and then a glistening silver dome-like structure appeared. The top was all glass, so I could probably see the skyline from within, and large arched windows offered more views from every angle of the building. It was gorgeous, but what was in front had me stumbling to a halt. Numerous pink roses lined the pathway, and a pool of water glimmered right in front, splitting the path into two. This place would have brought me peace ... if I didn't still feel like I was in danger.

I sucked in a breath, enjoying the scent of roses, then continued down one side of the path until I stepped into the bar, the loud music blaring "Low" by Flo Rida. A group of women, including Isa, was dancing in the center of the massive open floor, and others sat at tables around the edge. To the right was a wooden bar that almost blended into the background. I might not have seen it if not for the long-ass line of people waiting to get drinks.

Again, no one asked for my ticket. Strange.

I scanned the area for Ember, fighting the urge to run back outside to the roses. I found her in a dark corner with a red drink in hand, staring at two mirrors hanging on the wall. As I approached, I realized they were actually framed paintings.

Ember swirled her drink with a small red straw and tapped her black boots against the smooth tile floor. I beamed when I reached her side, but she was leaning toward one picture, oblivious to my arrival.

"Not drinking whiskey, huh?" I tilted my head, watching her face.

Her head snapped in my direction, and her eyes bulged. She bent down, no doubt going for the knife she kept in her boot, and damn near toppled over.

A rare snort escaped me as I grabbed her arm, steadying her.

"You *bish*," she gasped, attempting to clutch her chest but snagging her boob instead. "You scared me."

Yeah, she was drunk. "You did tell me to come join you at the farty bar, so, you know, shit happens." I was never going to let her live that one down.

"Ew." She wrinkled her nose. "No waaay. I sid Fairy Bar." She straightened and took a wobbly step back. "Wut's that smeel ... and wut are you weawing?"

"A costume. Unlike you." I gestured to her flattering little black dress that covered just enough to make her seem more mysterious and alluring.

"Don't celerberate." She shoved her glass into my hand and continued, "You know dat I'm gonna 'et a drunk. Be riiightt back."

Before I could tell her she still had half a glass, she swayed off, bumping into people on her way to the bar.

I took a sip of the fruity drink and downed more than I'd intended, enjoying the sweet taste as I watched her join the long line.

She'd be there for a while, and I was in the perfect spot—a somewhat dark corner with no one close by. The only annoyance was the blaring music.

Not interested in watching people dance, I examined the mirror paintings. They were side by side, both equally beautiful in different ways.

The one Ember had been staring at was an image of the night sky with glowing trees underneath. I wasn't surprised because Ember had always had an affinity for the sky, just like I did for the sun. Being in darkness had never felt natural to me unless I was trying to hide from a crowd.

When I moved to the next one, my lungs seized. The painting was exquisite. The sky was a bright blue with a few fluffy white clouds hovering over a thick field of wildflowers in an open section of the woods. I'd give almost anything to be there, lying in the flowers, glancing at the sun.

With my free hand, I reached out to touch the painting, but when my fingers should've touched the canvas, they disappeared inside the artwork.

I jerked my hand back. Damn. How strong was this drink? It hadn't tasted strong, maybe because it was full of sugar and fruit.

My body tensed just as someone ran into me *hard*.

I stumbled, trying to use the wall to catch my balance, and a strong arm wrapped around my waist and pulled me against a chest that could've been a damn brick wall.

"What the fuck!" I exclaimed, trying to wriggle out of the stranger's arms, but his hold was too strong. When I glanced up at his face, I froze.

It was the man I'd sensed watching me in the lobby.

This couldn't be a coincidence.

A scream lodged in my throat, but it was as if I'd forgotten how to make a noise.

The corners of his mouth tipped upward as if he enjoyed my fear. With his other hand, he brushed my arm then took my drink and released me. "Careful. You're going to spill your beverage."

I didn't like anyone I didn't know or trust touching me or my drink. I reached for it, and he countered my move, waving a hand along my front and taking a sip.

I wanted to punch him, but that might have been his intention, so I closed my eyes and took a deep breath. When I opened them, he was adjusting his jacket with his free hand.

"Interesting outfit." He tilted his head, a cocky smirk locked in place. Somehow, it made him more handsome despite the unease slamming through me.

Placing my hands on my hips, I leaned back on the heels of my sneakers. "At least I attempted to dress up. What are you supposed to be?"

"You call that dressing up?" He grinned and took another sip. "I think we have completely different definitions of the concept."

I didn't want his germs all over my glass, so I grabbed for it again. This time, he released it, and I clutched it to my chest.

I stepped away from him, needing distance. I would have left, but I didn't want Ember coming back to this creep.

"Is that all you wanted?" I managed to keep my voice steady. There was something both familiar and odd about him, like he didn't quite belong here and that was why he was focusing on me. "To insult my pig onesie?"

His brows furrowed. "Pig? That's what it's called?"

I rolled my eyes. He was pompous and a prick. "It's a fucking onesie made to fit an adult." I pulled up my hood so he could see the embroidered face and pink ears, cheeks, and nose. "You can tell this way."

He snickered. "Interesting."

If he didn't walk away, I'd stab him. Then I'd get thrown into jail, and Stan would have to drive all the way here from Nashville to bail me out. "Great conversation, but I need to find my friend who's waiting on me." Technically, it wasn't a lie, and even if it was, it didn't matter. I needed to get away from him, and the sooner the better.

He leaned forward, and the scent of fresh-cut grass swirled around me. "I'll see you soon, Alina."

"You have me mistaken for someone else." I spun around, unable to fight the urge to get away anymore.

I expected him to follow, but when I looked over my shoulder, he remained in front of the painting I'd been looking at before he ran into me. I wondered if it had been on purpose.

I had to get Ember and Isa, so I could talk them into moving to a different section of the casino, if not leaving altogether.

Throat parched, I put the glass to my lips and tilted my head back. The liquid soothed my raw throat, though it tasted slightly bitter. I placed the empty glass on a vacant table and strolled toward Ember.

After a few steps, the world spun, and I had to slow my pace.

That drink *was* strong. No wonder Ember was plastered.

I reached out and ran my hand along the smooth wall, needing it for balance.

Darkness blurred my vision.

My brain fogged, but one clear thought rang in my head. *I've been drugged.*

I never should've come here.

As my eyes closed, strong arms circled my waist. I wanted to punch or scream, but I couldn't move or make a sound. All this time, I'd made sure to never lose control. I always stayed aware and knew what was happening to me, unlike so many of my friends, but all that slipped away like water through fingers.

The strange man whispered in my ear, "It's time to take you home."

Two

THE SOOTHING SCENT of roses invaded my senses, providing relief from the pounding headache. What in the hell had I done last night?

Groaning, I rolled onto my back and sank into a soft mattress. A *way* too soft mattress that made me feel like I was lying on a big white, puffy cloud. Not the firm, thin one I slept on at the gym.

Several soft gasps caught my attention, and my eyes fluttered open.

Panic clawed at my chest as I took in my surroundings. An intricate chandelier made of vines and flowers of various pinks, blues, purples, and yellows hung over my head. Each flower looked different from anything I'd ever seen, the delicate bulbs and vibrant colors emanating warmth. The scene could have been part of a strange dream, except my head pounded as if it were splitting in two.

More disconcerting were the three gorgeous women hovering over me. They didn't budge, seeming unashamed of getting caught staring. That made my skin crawl even more.

"If I wasn't seeing her with my own two eyes, I wouldn't believe it." The woman to my right, whose long, dark, silky hair had the faintest hint of purple in it, shook her head. Her violet eyes, enhanced by her glowing bronze skin, sparkled. However, it wasn't her beauty that struck me. It was the way the tips of her ears pointed out from under her hair.

Something poked my side, and I flinched and kicked at the person to my left.

Large sky-blue eyes widened as the second woman moved back a few steps, and my leg caught air. Her caramel-blonde hair shifted around her like a cape then settled perfectly behind her back, not a strand hanging over the front of her cobalt dress. "What was that for?"

"Cara, maybe humans don't like to be touched," a hunter-green-haired woman with golden eyes answered, standing beside the dark-haired one. She tucked a piece of hair behind her ear and adjusted her vine headband. Her olive skin was flawless, and her cheeks held a faint rose color that anyone would envy. Her green strapless dress was made of leaves as if she were part of the woods.

They all had pointed ears. This had to be a dream. No one could be this gorgeous or have *ears* like theirs.

I sat up, and the world spun. I wasn't sure if the sensation came from my head or the view I had of the room. Large white columns rose at the end of the bed, creating an opening to a larger room with a high ceiling, the arched glass of the windows similar to the ones in the Fairy Bar back in Vegas. Two massive lilac-colored couches sat side by side across from the windows, and behind them stood two doors about twenty feet apart.

Had Ember set this up?

I wouldn't be fooled again. "*I* don't like people I don't know touching me." At least I could count on my mouth running without thought, like usual.

"What?" The dark-haired girl clutched her chest. "You don't *know* me? I'm Lilidh. I've worked for you for the past hundred complete cycles."

I snorted and promptly thought my head might implode. This *had* to be Ember's doing. She was getting me back for cutting the toes out of her socks while she was showering at the gym. Who knew how much she'd fucking saved to get even with me for the odd pranks I'd played on her over the years. She was vicious like that. "Yeah, and I'm, what? A hundred and fifty years old?"

"Don't be so chilly." Lilidh laughed, the noise sounding like bells. "You're only one hundred and five full cycles."

I wasn't sure what perplexed me more: her telling me I was over a hundred years old or what the hell *chilly* meant. I decided to focus on the latter since I was certain I was twenty-three. I could show them my birth certificate to prove it. "Chilly? Do you mean silly? And let's count years instead of cycles."

"Silly?" Her brows furrowed. "What's that? I was saying you're using cold humor like the Winter fae do. A full summer and winter season is one cycle. What do you mean by years?"

"*Fae*?" My high-pitched voice made my head throb. At least, that explained why they'd put on pointy ears. "Let me guess, you're Summer or Spring fae."

"Enid, something is wrong with her." Cara bent down and examined my face, her nose wrinkling. "Beyond smelling worse than rotting bark."

"She was drugged." Cara pursed her lips. "Maybe he gave her too high a dose."

That was enough to drive me out of bed. I opted to get out on Lilidh and Enid's side, not trusting Cara after she'd poked me. The green sheets I lay under tangled around my legs and nearly toppled me onto the floor.

Lilidh caught me and gagged, likely from the smell, while tossing me back onto the bed.

I bounced, the impact painless except for the jarring of my head.

I had to get out of here, joke or not. Drugging someone was taking things too far.

Memories of last night fluttered through my head, including the guy. He must have spiked my drink, and that's why he'd kept putting his hands into his pockets. The drink *had* been strong. Why hadn't I considered that before I'd taken it back and downed the rest of it?

Getting back up, Enid sighed and raised a hand, palm facing me.

I lifted my chin. "Do it. Hit me." That sort of pain I could handle. It was being unconscious and not knowing what they'd done to me that had taken the joke over the top.

Suddenly, something slithered over my arms and legs, although none of the women had moved toward me. My throat hurt, and I forgot to breathe, fear freezing me in place. I looked at my arms, only to find vines had snaked from the ivy growing on the wall to bind my forearms and ankles, anchoring me to the bed. A fucking *plant* was holding me captive.

"Don't panic." Enid rolled her eyes. "Once you calm down, I'll allow the vines to release you."

Cara bit her bottom, full pink lip. "Alina would never have let you hold her down like that."

Alina.

That was what that creep had called me.

"I'm Ivy. You guys are fucking with the wrong person." I tried to breathe steadily, needing to retain logic. Stan had taught me that fear and panic were my worst enemies, especially if I was restrained. I had to be able to think outside the box, which wasn't possible when emotions were guiding me.

"She doesn't remember." Lilidh took a step back and placed a hand on her chest, scrunching the fabric of her flowy pink dress.

"Oh, I remember perfectly." My breathing remained rapid. "Some tall, handsome, creepy man drugged me and brought me here so you three could make me feel like I've lost my mind. Just let me go home to Nashville and the gym."

Cara leaned over me, and I tensed, waiting for a poke or a smack. "She doesn't remember Dallas. Interesting."

"Forget that." Lilidh waved a hand. "What is this Nashville and gym?"

I wanted to scream, but that wouldn't accomplish anything. They'd likely make the vine cover my mouth and then drug me all over again. If I wanted to have a chance of getting free, I would have to play along.

"That's your question?" Enid shook her head. "I'm more curious about why she's wearing *that*"—she gestured at me—"and why she smells like decay."

At least Enid's questions were legitimate. I'd roll with that. "The costume's for Halloween, and Isa said that if Ember and I didn't dress up, she'd disown us. I opted for a comfortable look that could hide—" I cut myself off. The last thing I wanted to share was that I had a knife strapped to my thigh. "That I could move in more freely, so I opted for this pig onesie. On my way to the party, some drunk stumbled into me and spilled her cheap-ass beer on me. It doesn't smell like decay. It's just yeast."

"Pig?" Cara sat on the edge of the bed.

They were really playing up the fae angle. "A pig is a delicious animal us 'humans' eat. Or keep as pets."

Heels clacked somewhere outside the room, and all three women tensed. Enid flicked her wrist, and the vines receded.

They seemed nervous, and I dreaded whoever was coming. "What's going on?"

"Your sister is here. She's back from the meeting she was called to before Dallas brought you here." Lilidh hurried past the door closest to the bed and opened the second one, then disappeared inside.

Enid tossed the covers off me, and Cara moved quickly past the column on the left. She held out a hand, and I wanted to smack it away. But if they were acting this way about my "sister's" arrival, I had to act the part. Taking her hand, I let her help me to my feet.

The door closest to us opened.

If I'd thought these women were gorgeous, they had nothing on the woman who entered. Long red hair wove down her back, and a crown of golden vines adorned her head. Her dress was dark red, its neckline embroidered with gold and cut in a low *V*, revealing her ample cleavage, with a golden frayed belt that emphasized her tiny waist.

"Queen Orla." Enid curtsied. "I hope all is well."

"It will be." Orla nodded, her hazel eyes focused steadily on me.

The corners of her lips tipped upward. "Alina." She moved toward me, holding out her arms. "It's been too long. How I've missed you."

I stepped backward, and the back of my thighs hit the mattress. "My name is Ivy, not Alina." Hopefully, *she'd* listen.

Her smile fell, and her arms dropped. "Are you trying to be funny? Fifty complete cycles, and you're being icy?"

Based on what *chilly* meant, I had an idea of what she was getting at. If Winter fae had a dry sense of humor, I imagined they weren't very warm either. "I don't like touching people I don't know." I'd never had to explain this before. Everyone at the gym was the same as me. We touched during classes only because we were learning to defend ourselves. Outside of that, we respected each other's personal space.

"I'm your sister." She crossed her arms, pouting. "We know each other better than anyone."

I wasn't sure what to say, so for once, my mouth remained shut. I suspected anything I said would make this situation worse.

Her fair skin blanched at my nonanswer, disapproval evident in the rigid set of her jaw.

I'd opened my mouth, unsure what would come out, just as Lilidh sashayed back into the room, carrying a green and slightly orange off-the-shoulder dress.

"I was thinking this would be a strong look for Alina when she presents herself back to the High Court." Lilidh beamed.

Orla clasped her hands in front of her. "That's perfect. It's something she'd pick out for herself."

I never experienced fear like this before. Wearing that thing would be my worst nightmare. I stiffened and laughed, sounding like a hyena. "Okay, joke time is over. There's no way I'm wearing *that*."

Orla's head jerked toward me, and the tips of her fingers turned red. "You think that horrendous outfit you have on is what you should wear to meet the highest fae officials? Not even a Winter fae would wear that!"

"I'm not loving this outfit either. It reeks of beer, but if I could get a pair of jeans and a shirt, that would work great." I preferred flare or boot-cut jeans over shorts. I could hide weapons better that way. At this point, I'd even take skinny-leg jeans as long as I didn't have to wear that beautiful death trap.

Orla huffed. "It's like I don't even know you."

Finally, someone was on the same page as me. "That's because you've got the wrong person. I'm sure Alina is out there, looking for you and ready to wear that to meet the bougie fae."

"Bougie?" Enid scratched her head.

"Fancy." I hung my head. Though we were both speaking English, I wasn't sure it was the same language.

Orla straightened and tightened her lips. She closed the distance between us and put her face in mine. "You *will* bathe, get yourself together, and *wear* that dress. Whatever little joke you're playing is not funny. If you embarrass me in front of the High Court and the Winter King, there will be ice to pay."

Though she'd lost me with that last part, her message was clear. I was her captive, at least for the moment, and I had to obey.

I needed to find my way downstairs and *leave*. "Fine."

"Good." She straightened her shoulders, and then wings exploded from her back. "I'll see you downstairs at dinner."

I gasped and blinked. Each time I did, her red-feathered wings sparked with hints of fire. My lungs seized. This *had* to be a wild dream. I'd wake up soon.

Still, her wings were gorgeous. I was transfixed as she walked out the door until Enid sighed noisily.

"Come along." She made her way to the second door, the one Lilidh had used. "It's time to take a bath."

Bath.

That word alone had me obliging.

We stepped through the door, and I tried to take it all in. To the right was a closet holding so many clothes I couldn't see an end to them. Everything hung from large thorns on tree branches. To the left was a gorgeous bathroom with a pearl-like tub in the middle and large windows surrounding it. There were whimsical pink fabric curtains for privacy, and the same flowers that decorated the chandelier grew around the tub and along the bottom of the windows.

A golden faucet was running, filling the tub with crystal-blue water, and the fragrance of flowers surrounded me.

"You have five minutes to get clean." Enid went back to the wooden door and made to leave.

"Wait." I spun around. "I need soap and shampoo."

She tilted her head, staring at me.

"To get clean." Her confusion was too genuine to be part of a prank, especially with the beautiful room and flowers. But if this wasn't a prank, what did that mean?

"You don't need anything. The water does it for you." She left and shut the door, not wanting to answer any more questions.

Unable to think of anything else to do, I stripped off my onesie and hunted for somewhere to hide my knife, eventually settling on the plants under the windows. I gripped the wooden handle and stuffed it under the thickest section of flowers, then took a few steps back to see if the bronze blade glistened in the sun. Nothing happened.

Good. It was safe.

Satisfied, I slipped into the water. My skin tingled as I submerged my body, and suddenly, the faucet turned off.

None of this was normal.

Trying to enjoy the moment, I leaned my head back. I had to have been losing it because I could *feel* the water cleaning me. I'd never felt so refreshed. I held my breath and went under, and tingles prickled over my scalp. More strangely, I relaxed.

When I rose back up, Lilidh entered with the dress. "It's time to get out."

I crossed my legs and arms, covering my chest, then glanced around for a towel. "How do I dry off?"

"Just stand up, Your Highness."

Your *Highness*? That was something I'd never expected to be called in my life. "Do you mind turning around?"

She laughed and held the dress out, not budging. When I stayed submerged, she frowned and said, "Wait. You're serious."

"Uh. Yeah."

Lilidh's forehead creased. "That's so odd. Fae are proud of their bodies."

Yeah, I bet they were. Every one of them I'd seen so far was gorgeous. "I like privacy."

"I hate to tell you this, but I'll need to help you into this dress." She cringed. "So, you don't have an option this time."

Wanting to end the conversation, I sighed and did as I was told. The magic water disappeared from the tub and my body, leaving my skin glowing and smooth.

I wanted to retrieve my knife, but not with Lilidh standing there. I'd have to leave it behind.

I couldn't swallow around the lump in my throat.

The next few minutes were torture. The dress was more comfortable than I'd expected, fitting loosely. Its green material hung to midarm, the skirt done in a mermaid cut. The front of the skirt blended into a deep, beautiful orange with flowers at the hem. Enid and Cara joined us, and the women forced me to wear green heels made of vines, which were oddly comfortable. Cara worked on my hair.

When they were finished, they walked me to a corner of the bathroom, where a tall mirror stood next to a small vanity that housed hair supplies. My strawberry-blonde hair was piled onto my head, with tendrils curling around my face. My green eyes seemed brighter, and my lips were a deep red even though I had no makeup on.

And I had pointed ears.

What the actual fuck. I stroked the tip, expecting it to slice my finger, but it was soft and bendable, just like my ears back on Earth. Whew.

I didn't even look like the same person. That magic had done wonders.

"Now it's time for you to go." Enid went to the bathroom door. "Cara, prepare for her return, and Lilidh, clean up the mess."

I glanced around the bathroom, wondering what mess she meant.

We walked through the bedroom and down a hallway, and I truly felt like I was in another world. The walls were covered with grass and flowers, and trees lined the walk. Huge chandeliers hung every ten feet, their bright light making the space more magical.

"Are you coming?" Enid asked, her hands on her hips.

I hadn't realized I'd stopped walking.

A deep chuckle came from behind me. "Don't worry, Enid. I can take her from here."

The voice was all too familiar, and chills coursed down my back. I tensed, ready to fight the man I now hated most in the entire world.

Three

I SPUN around and nearly tripped on the damn three-inch heels, expecting to face Casino Guy. Forming a fist, I prepared to throw a punch ... and faltered.

The person in front of me resembled the man from the casino, but he was way more handsome. His face seemed more angular, and his ears were pointed and sticking out from underneath his hair. Even his grassy scent was more intoxicating.

I clenched my teeth. I wanted to make the bastard pay for what he'd done.

My plans for vengeance were brewing, and I wished I'd retrieved my knife so I could use it. It'd be nice to make him bleed for the shit he'd pulled.

My hands would get the point across.

A cocky grin spread across his mouth, resembling his smile at the bar.

Game on. This was *definitely* Drug Guy.

"Now this is the Alina I'm familiar with." He moved quickly, cupping my cheek with his abnormally soft hand. "That *pig* outfit was atrocious. Even Winter fae would rather be dead than caught in that."

What was it with them and the Winter fae?

Taking a step back, I twisted my ankle and winced at the jolt of pain. I gritted my teeth and adjusted myself, pretending I hadn't almost toppled over.

"And just like that, she's gone." He chuckled and closed the distance between us again. Mirth danced in his irises as he watched me squirm.

The bastard liked making me uncomfortable. Every cell in my body urged me to run from him, but I straightened and stood as tall as possible. In my heels, I had to be close to six feet tall. "Back off. I don't want to talk to you or be anywhere near you. You drugged and kidnapped me!"

"When did you get so dramatic?" He leaned forward, his face inches from mine. "I swear, if you didn't look almost identical and have the same voice, I would never believe you're the same girl."

I wanted to pull my hair out. I had to hold my own while playing along until they let their guard down. "Listen, Drug Boy." I poked him in the chest, already ruining my plan of compliance. My mouth had a mind of its own. "You got the wrong girl. In fact, why don't you take me back and fix your mistake? I'm sure Alina would be more than happy to be here instead of me."

Shame constricted my chest. Here I was, wishing some other girl had been taken. What type of person did that make me? "Better yet, take me back and leave all of us alone. If Alina wanted to be here, she would've come willingly." I stomped my foot since I was certain punching him in the face would be frowned upon.

He exhaled, his sandalwood-scented breath hitting my face. "Surely, your memories will return soon. Maybe when your magic settles in."

He must have selective hearing. I'd heard that most men were burdened with this particular flaw, though Stan was an exception. He was way too perceptive. "I hate to tell you this, but the only magic I possess is my ability to demolish a large sausage and pepperoni pizza in one sitting." My stomach rumbled at the thought of food. Damn, there was no telling how long it'd been since I last ate.

"I have no idea what you're referring to." When I opened my mouth to answer, he placed his finger on my lips and interjected, "And after seeing your choice of clothing last night, I'm confident I'd rather not know what you're talking about. Any sort of attraction I still feel for you could vanish."

Ew. Between the touch of his finger and that comment, I wanted to vomit.

I did the only logical thing and bit his finger, wanting to draw blood so he'd never touch me again.

Instead of yanking the digit away, his smirk bloomed into a full smile.

I was going to wipe that off his face really quickly, so I bit down harder. Blood entered my mouth, but it didn't taste like copper. My stomach roiled. The taste wasn't great, but there was something sweet in it that I could only describe as liquid sunshine. That last part was enough to make my jaws freeze.

"There she is," he cooed, his pupils dilating. "Bite harder."

I had no clue what that meant, and I didn't want to find out. My face heated, and I released his finger to find teeth marks deep in his skin. Instead of crimson, blue blood trickled from his finger, a faint sparkling brown mist wafting from it.

All I could do was stare. I'd never seen anything like that before.

"Though Orla and I are wed, our agreement doesn't prohibit us from sleeping with others. We'll just have to be careful that no heirs result from our sex." He winked and lowered his hands. He then extended his arm as if expecting me to slide my own through it.

The idea of sleeping with him made me queasy. Worse, he seemed to legitimately think it would occur. "I don't think heirs will be a problem since nothing will ever happen between us." I kept my arms close to my sides, not wanting to chance touching him again.

"My marriage to your sister is merely political." He puffed out his chest. "When I was betrothed to you, the expectation was that I'd become king. It was my duty to help strengthen your sister's claim since I never fathomed you'd be coming back to us."

Gag me. This Alina had been *engaged* to him? Poor girl. "So nice that you broke your promise to me to marry the person who came into power."

"Don't be such an icy draft. You know the only way a fae can get out of an agreement is by death. When you died, it nullified all agreements and bargains we had with each other."

Unable to hold it in, I laughed.

His expression twisted into disgust. "What's so funny?"

"That you actually believe I came back to life." If they were expecting me to walk on water, they'd soon learn otherwise *and fast*.

Orla's voice came from behind me. "Dallas, what are you two doing?" I didn't need to know her to hear the suspicion in her voice.

That right there showed me she would not be okay with me starting a sexual relationship with her *husband*. For him to even consider it a possibility was insulting, not only to me but to his *wife*. I had no clue how long they'd been married, although it couldn't be long since they appeared to be in their twenties, but I had no doubt he'd already cheated on her.

"Enid was taking me to wherever I needed to go." I turned around, expecting to find the woman there, but she was gone. How was that possible? She hadn't made a noise.

I took a step back, startled that she wasn't there, and ran into Dallas's chest. He placed his hands on my waist, steadying me.

Orla hovered in the air just a few feet away. Wings fluttering soundlessly, she moved toward us. The sparkling magical flames seemed bigger than they had in my room. "Seems convenient, given that Enid isn't here."

"Now, Orla," Dallas said. "When we entered into this arrangement, you were well aware that Alina and I were lovers. Unlike *you*, I didn't realize she would have a second life, or my decision might have been different. Besides, we both have other paramours."

My brain fogged and seemed to short-circuit. Everything he'd said was nonsense, but he'd said it with such conviction that he was either delusional or an amazing liar.

"None of mine are your *brother*," Orla sneered, taking my wrist and tugging me after her.

As I moved away, Dallas's hands dropped, brushing my ass along the way.

I yanked away from her grasp and turned back to him. I rasped, "I might be the one who was dressed like a pig last night, but you sure act like one."

Landing beside me, Orla's forehead creased. "What is she talking about?"

"The horrid outfit she was wearing was called Pig." He cringed. "It was unspeakable, so I didn't ask for clarification. I'm just glad she's dressed normally now."

Whoa. *Normally.* I didn't like the sound of that.

"You two have talked enough," she said as she looped her arm through mine. "You go on ahead and tell the Winter King and the High Fae that we'll be there shortly."

Her ginger scent reminded me of home, which bothered me. I didn't want to associate this strange place with anything familiar.

"Of course, My Queen." He bowed, his gaze lingering on me. When he rose, warm-brown feathers shot from the back of his chocolate suit. The feathers were gorgeous, but he lacked the magical flames that Orla had. He flapped his wings, his scent mixing with hers as he glided away toward our destination.

Pulling me tight to her side, Orla strolled me away from my room and down the gardenesque hallway. Our heels clicked on the clay floor, and I fought the urge to extend my hand and touch tree branches and flowers as we passed.

Once Dallas vanished from sight, Orla inhaled deeply. "I meant to tell you about him and me before he got the chance." Her lips tightened, and something that could only be described as a flame danced within her pupils. "After careful consideration, it was determined to be best for the kingdom if everyone thought you had perished that day on the sacred lands. Even better, they hailed you as not only a worthy royal fae but a heroine. When Mother passed, I ascended the throne to prevent our kingdom from falling into chaos. Talamh was still in ruins due to the former vampire king." Her body recoiled slightly. "Civil war could have easily brewed again, like the past Great War. Having a strong, reputable fae by my side as king helped secure my reign."

She'd thrown a whole lot of information at me at one time. "What's Talamh? And did you say *vampire?*" I hoped they had plenty of garlic and silver. Or wait, was silver for shifters? I hadn't read a lot of paranormal stories, which I was now regretting. I'd chosen to fight and train rather than sit and read.

She stopped us in our tracks. "You don't remember anything, do you? At first, I thought it was one of those tricks you like to play."

"I'm not lying. This is my first time *here.*" I waved my free arm around, emphasizing my point. "I can't remember somewhere I've never been."

"Fifty complete season cycles ago, you and a woman from each of the other eight kingdoms sacrificed yourselves to save our world from dying. Then you were reincarnated on Earth." She ran a hand down her gown, her fingers stopping on the gold belt. "I'd hoped you would return with your memories, but obviously, that was chilly."

This whole place was on some sort of drug—the one Dallas had dosed me with at the hotel. It had to be acid or something hallucinogenic. But I had boundaries, whether high or sober, and there was something I had to make clear. "I do know one thing. I'm not interested in him *at all,* and I would *never* sleep with a married man."

She laughed, but when she noticed my expression, her mouth dropped into an *O* of surprise. "Wait. That wasn't a joke?"

I blinked repeatedly, as if clearing my vision would change her implication. "No. Why would it be? Marriage is a commitment between two people. I have no desire to get in the way of that."

"Is that how humans think?" She tapped a finger against her lips. "So strange and terribly misguided."

"The vow is to have and to hold till death do us part."

She hummed. "Interesting. Our vows are nearly identical. Yes, Dallas and I hold each other from time to time." She grinned wickedly, making her more beautiful. "But the words aren't to have and to hold only one. We fae need variety and sexual freedom. And, of course, marriage for us is until death. Death is the only way to end any agreement or arrangement. If you try another way, the magic of the land kills you anyway, freeing the other party to make new deals with someone else."

I couldn't fathom it. The thought of sharing myself with one person alone terrified me. After spending years in the foster system, I had trust issues. Rightfully earned. I couldn't imagine sharing myself with multiple people. "I'll still pass."

"Good." She nodded. "Though he can sleep with anyone he chooses, I'd rather it not be my sister. Things with the crown will be difficult enough to navigate—the last thing we need is the king consort meddling in our precarious situation."

We resumed our walk, and I attempted to sort through everything she'd shared with me. I felt as if I were drowning. "Why would there be questions about the crown?"

"Because you are the oldest and strongest sibling." She giggled, but an edge of viciousness hid inside the sound. "Though, technically, you aren't anymore."

"We must be close to the same age." I lifted a brow, almost challengingly. "I'm twenty-three."

"And I'm eighty-seven cycles." She winked. "The problem is— when you add in your first life here, you are still older, so there will be numerous fae who will want you to ascend the throne. The Winter King and the five members of the High Court are waiting for us in the dining hall to meet you before we talk about making an announcement to the masses."

A lump formed in my throat. "A king and ... what is the High Court?"

"There are supposed to be six members, but one died while Dallas was away retrieving you. The High Court has the final say in any decision that affects the entire kingdom." Orla huffed. "They want to meet you, and we have to deal with what losing the sixth and oldest member of the court means."

We approached an archway, and I started, "What—"

She lifted a finger, cutting me off, and gestured to an archway on the right side of the hall where a massive room came into view.

Ten rectangular tables made of vines were placed strategically throughout the space. Large branches grew from each table into seats framed with large yellow cushions that resembled petals of flowers for the back and bottom. A large canopy of vines arched over the entire room, and more plants grew in the corners. Twinkle lights lit up the room, and again, this place felt magical. Especially this garden. Every inch of this place was bursting with plants and flowers, and the succulent scents were like the best perfume I'd ever smelled.

Six commanding figures sat at the first table, and Dallas was grinning as he leaned against a plant on one side of the room.

All six figures stood and turned toward us.

My first instinct, as always, was to size up a room quickly, but something inside me couldn't do it.

For the first time in my life, I had no control over my body, and my eyes fixed on a man on the far side of the table. He was tall, dark, and commanding, with ice-blue eyes that sliced straight through to my soul, making me feel naked.

His jaw clenched as he scanned me and pushed shaggy, dark, wavy hair out of his face. He frowned as he leaned over, placing both hands on the table. Intimidation laced every twitch of muscle as he practically vibrated, his presence chilling despite the warmth of the air.

His hands glowed a faint blue and sparks the same color as his irises flickered out of them, spurting from his *skin*. Then something even more ridiculous happened. A frosty glaze spread over the table from underneath his palms.

This man, both beautiful and terrifying, was furious with ... me. Or with Alina, who he likely believed me to be.

Something like ice chips and lightning flared in his eyes, and I hoped like hell I could convince him I *wasn't* Alina before he killed me. Because that look? That was a man on the edge of murder.

Four

"KING KIERAN," Orla snapped, body rigid. "Your magic isn't *allowed* in Summer territory."

"Unless provoked." His jaw clenched.

I didn't know how to describe his voice. The tone was icy, but his voice was deep and husky, and I wanted to close the distance between us.

I planted my feet firmly, refusing to be the type of woman who ran straight into danger. Listening to those red flags was important to avoid perilous situations.

Dallas chuckled from his place against the wall across from Kieran. The cocky prick said, "Don't try to justify your provocation as due to being in Summer territory. You came here of your own *free will.*"

Kieran's steely gaze moved from me to Dallas. If five other pairs of eyes hadn't been on me, I would've crossed my fingers, hoping Kieran would kick Dallas's ass. The prick deserved a severe beating, and if I couldn't give it to him, I'd settle for the Winter King doing it on my behalf. Kieran was twice the size of Dallas, and I had no doubt the Winter King could take him.

"No one has said anything to you or drawn a weapon on you."

The tall, elegant woman who'd spoken crossed her arms, bunching the silk of her white dress with its golden lace bodice at her waist. Though her gown was sleeveless, pieces of white silk draped her arms, contrasting with her light-brown skin. "After two thousand cycles, are you trying to negate the peace treaty and attack *my queen*?" She arched a perfectly shaped eyebrow and narrowed gray eyes the shade of a storm cloud.

At least she was aligned with my sister and her territory.

King Kieran stiffened, and his magic vanished, but the ice that had sprouted from his hands remained. He lifted both hands from the table and wiped them on his navy-blue suit, which had a silver snowflake etched on the pocket. "That wasn't a show of aggression, Kaley. I just can't believe they're trying to pass her off as Princess Alina."

He was the first person to agree with me.

"Don't be daft." Kaley ran a hand over her long, mahogany-brown ponytail. Her pointed ears bore gold hoop earrings.

A man sitting by King Kieran's side chuckled menacingly, bringing my attention to that section of the table. The woman sitting on the man's other side had to be his sibling if not twin. They both had long, snow-white hair that contrasted with their dark skin. The biggest difference between them was their eyes, his irises so pale they would have blended with the whites if not for a thick blue ring that outlined them, whereas the woman had navy-blue eyes that were almost black.

Still, neither of them was as terrifying as the Winter King.

"And calling my king *daft* is provocation enough." The man clenched his hands. "You must respect all royals, including the Winter King."

Based on that interaction, I assumed he supported King Kieran.

"Brother," the female beside him said, confirming my assumption about their relationship. "Don't be *summerheaded*." She smirked and ran a hand along her fishtail braid. The style gave her an Elsa-like look.

Why wasn't I surprised that the Winter fae used summer-themed words as insults? Apparently, both sides disliked each other equally.

"Leanna uses shadow insults while Caden is direct," the man in the middle across from Caden, the brother, observed. His shaggy, midnight-blue hair complemented his blazing teal eyes and olive skin. He bumped his arm into Kaley's. "However, he lacks the warmth that is a requirement for that attribute. He should leave that to us Summer Court members."

This was what I needed. If their insults continued to escalate, I could sneak out and get away from all this craziness. Either that, or I'd wake up from this dream ... or nightmare. I wasn't sure what to call it.

"Eamon, we're not here to be petty," the dazzling woman across from Leanna bit out. "We traveled to the Summer Court to see Alina with our own eyes before announcing her return to the kingdom and discussing the open seat on the court." Her turquoise gaze landed right on me.

Okay, no one was supposed to be reasonable. I already didn't like this nameless woman who, with her full peach lips and wavy butterscotch hair, could pass as otherworldly.

Orla sighed, loosening her grip on me and straightening her shoulders. She appeared very much the queen. "Quinley is right. Instead of meeting at Rioghail Tower, we agreed to meet here to decide how we will announce her return. We need to make sure there isn't a revolt, especially in the Summer Court, since many will want her to be queen."

Pressure squeezed my chest, and I became more eager to get away. Not only were they set on me being Alina, but they also wanted to introduce me to who knew how many people as this fae princess I most certainly wasn't. I had to find a way out before that happened. "Maybe we don't tell them."

And there went my mouth.

All seven of them turned to me and stared at me as if *I* was the strange one.

If I kept this up, I wouldn't be able to sneak away. I might as well have put a target on my back—or maybe the pig outfit they all found so disgusting and intriguing.

Orla's brows rose so comically high that it *had* to be magic. "You don't want our people to know of your return?"

Fuck no, I didn't. But my brain caught up quickly enough to keep those words from spewing out. Maybe my sense of self-preservation hadn't vanished. "I'm a little out of sorts. It could be best if we kept my return on the DL for a while." *For a while* was code for *forever*.

"DL?" Quinley asked, placing a hand on her bare chest just above her low-cut neckline. Her black dress was trimmed with gold thread that decorated the loose sleeves hanging on her arms. "What in summer is that?"

I wanted to pinch myself to see if I could startle myself awake. "Down low?"

"You want to keep the information that you're back on the floor?" Eamon scratched his head. "That's not possible unless I've missed something crucial in my six hundred and twenty-five cycles."

My jaw dropped, and I was surprised it didn't hit the floor. Come *on*. Now they were just seeing how far they could take this joke before I had a meltdown. Nope. I wouldn't let Ember get the best of me. "*Only* six hundred?" I scoffed.

"You're right." Eamon wrapped an arm around Quinley's shoulders. "It's nothing compared to the one hundred and seventy-five cycles Quinley has on me."

"Get your balmy arm off me before you make me thaw." Quinley's nose wrinkled, and she stepped sideways, her heels clanking.

Did every woman in this place wear heels? I needed to find my sneakers—stat—before they tossed them. I didn't care if they reeked of beer; my toes were already aching. Anything would be better than wearing these shoes.

My heart thudded, and my traitorous gaze landed back on the Winter King. He stared at me unabashedly, and his nostrils flared as if my mere presence offended him.

I hadn't done anything to offend him—I didn't think—but that look of disgust couldn't be misinterpreted. Worse, my heart ached from it.

I tried not to focus on that. I needed to pay attention to the one thing I could control: putting King Kieran in his place. That was the thing with bullies—if you didn't set boundaries, they would escalate things to the next level. "What's your problem, coldy?"

"*Alina*," Orla chastised, her eyes bulging. "Even though he's Winter Fae, he's the king. You can't call him *that*."

He stalked toward me. With each step he took, my blood chilled. I wasn't sure if it was fear or his magic working on me, but my flight instinct was coming in fast while another weird sensation that felt like longing slipped through me.

Yeah. I was becoming one of *those* girls. But I refused to be attracted to a toxic man.

I didn't know where the hell to go. I didn't know the layout of this ... castle? The only rooms I'd been in were the bedroom and here.

When he stalked up to me, my blood turned to ice, which had my anger brimming to life. I wasn't afraid of *anyone*.

"I don't know what in the summer you're trying to pass off here, but this is *not* Alina." King Kieran leaned into my face. His scent hit me—fresh winter snow.

Unfortunately, that was one of my favorite smells since we rarely got snow in Nashville.

He reached out and touched the ends of my hair, and my breath caught. A mixture of emotions churned in my chest. I wanted to push him away *and* pull him toward me. I wanted his arms wrapped around my body.

"This isn't even her hair." He tugged a piece back and stared at my ears then frowned. "Though she does have pointed ears, that doesn't mean she's your sister, especially given her atrocious behavior. She could be glamoured for all I know."

Why was he so upset? I'd merely used a winter term to describe him, same as some of the others had done.

"Your Highness, except for the ends of her hair and the dullness of her eyes, she looks exactly like Alina." Orla gestured to my figure. "She came from the human realm not too long ago. I'm sure her fae magic needs time to remanifest."

"In fairness, she already looks a lot better." Dallas finally strolled over to Orla's other side and continued, "The outfit she wore stank and looked like some sort of strange magical creature, one I've never seen before, so there's no telling what she worships."

My patience snapped, and I stepped back, needing distance from the Winter King. "If you call the animal that provides the most delicious feast in the world magical and me devouring parts of its body as worship, I could agree with that assessment."

Dallas grinned wickedly. "What sort of body parts do you devour in the name of worship?"

Cheeks heating, I wanted to vanish into thin air. He was not only flirting with me but also accusing me of doing things with an animal. "Nothing like that. We slaughter the pig and cook the meat, which is what I eat."

One day soon, I would punch Dallas, but I was already on thin ice with the Winter King. No pun intended. Dammit, these people were rubbing off on me.

King Kieran stepped in front of me, partially blocking me from Dallas's view.

I should've been annoyed. I didn't need this asshole protecting me, but I couldn't quite summon that anger. I did note that I could see the outlines of his muscles underneath his jacket.

Orla cut her eyes to Dallas. I didn't have to know her to understand what that look meant. *Shut it.* I supported her command.

"You're just letting this stranger—" King Kieran started.

"You met with Alina only a handful of times and briefly, so for you to accuse her of not being *my sister* when I'm vouching for her is insulting to me." Orla's eyes flashed. "I know better than *anyone* that this is her, or believe me, I wouldn't have brought her home. Her presence here complicates everything, which means Alina's right. We should put off informing the kingdom."

"First, you know that's impossible." Kaley shook her head. "Everyone will know she came back on Havestia. If you hide her, you'll only upset everyone more when the truth does come out."

"Not only that, but Muir died earlier this sun cycle. The Comortas will begin within a week. We have the announcement of Alina's return and the death of one of the oldest and most respected members of the High Court prompting a tournament that hasn't happened in two hundred and fifty complete season cycles. Not since Caden took the last seat." The corner of King Kieran's mouth tipped upward as if he were trying to hide a smile. "According to the High Court's doctrine, the tournament must begin within seven sun cycles."

They were throwing around so many terms I didn't understand that I didn't even know where to begin. "Havestia?"

Caden tilted his head, examining me. "The sun cycle that occurs every fifty complete season cycles—when the veil between Terrea and Earth is thin enough for us to travel between realms. That's today, seeing as you're standing here."

"You mean Halloween?"

"What the heat wave is Halloween?" King Kieran rasped.

Fine. Two could play this game. "On Earth, it's when we get naked and have group sex with each other."

"Oh." Leanna winked. "That's how we celebrate winter solstice here in honor of Mother Terrea."

Okay, that had backfired, and now I had more questions I was too terrified to ask. I wasn't a prude, but I had zero experience with men. I had stayed away from them and somehow miraculously avoided being abused while in the system, a far luckier fate than that of most of my friends and foster sisters. As soon as I'd aged out, I'd kept my walls high and impenetrable. There was no way in hell I would open myself up to a guy—not when I'd seen firsthand how horrible so many of them were.

Eamon frowned. "This is bad. Yes, she mostly looks and sounds like Alina, but she doesn't talk like her, nor does she seem to know anything about Talamh. If we introduce her like this to the kingdom ..." He trailed off and huffed.

My tongue stuck to the roof of my mouth as my muscles clenched. I was as much of a disappointment to them as I'd been to all my various foster parents. I hated that their reaction upset me. I felt like a worthless kid all over again, and I'd worked like hell to overcome that personal demon.

"We don't have a choice." Leanna pressed her lips together. "Someone from the royal line on each side must take part in the tournament. That's one of the rules. Unless Queen Orla wants to give her royal responsibilities to someone else and take part, we have to inform the kingdom of Alina's return."

That didn't sound horrible. "Why don't you hand over the kingdom to Dallas while you're in the Comortas?" She had married the prick, after all.

Dallas beamed. "That's a stunning idea."

"Absolutely *not*." Orla scowled. "There is only one solution. We will inform the kingdom of Alina's return but keep her at arm's distance from the people. It's not like we can make her *queen* like this, and for frozen sakes, I've already been crowned."

King Kieran's head jerked back. "You can't be serious. You're going to throw her into the griffin's den?"

"Why does it matter to you, Your Majesty?" Quinley shrugged. "There'll be one less formidable contender for your brother to slay."

I tried to breathe, but my lungs refused to suck in air. I choked as if I were drowning. She'd legit used the word *slay*, and I was certain she didn't mean it in a good way. Who the fuck was this guy's brother, and why did he want me dead?

"Don't discount my Summer Fae." Orla straightened, seeming taller. "We have just as good a chance of gaining the seat."

This felt important, and I wanted to understand. "What's the point of the tournament? Whoever gets first blood wins?"

Eamon laughed loudly, startling me.

When Kaley sliced a hand through the air, he stopped and

looked at me. Whatever he saw in my expression made his olive complexion turn almost as pale as King Kieran's.

"The point of the tournament is to decide who will fill the vacant seat on the High Court. It's doctrine that there must be six members at all times, so we can't go long without a sixth." Orla turned to me, her face tight. "The last person standing is the winner."

That was how most competitions worked. There was one winner unless everyone got a participation trophy. "And the losers go back to doing whatever they did before the tournament?"

"There is only one winner because they're the last one standing." King Kieran focused entirely on me, and I couldn't move. Under some sort of trance. "The last one standing is there because they have killed everyone else, proving they are worthy of being on the court."

I gulped because, surely to goodness, I'd heard him wrong. Still, I wasn't sure how I could've misunderstood his direct statement. "*Killed* killed? Like, no heartbeat?"

"Heart?" His forehead creased. "We aren't like elves. Our magic returns to Mother Terrea to be used and regenerated again."

Unable to stop myself, I placed a hand on my chest. My heart thumped against my ribs, and my eyes burned as relieved tears filled them.

"Nonetheless, the ending is the same." Orla nodded. "The losers cease to exist."

This was *barbaric*. Here they were, offering up people they loved to take part in this deadly tournament. "Why not just vote for someone?"

"Because the original council was forged from battle and bloodshed as every High Court member has been from that point on." Quinley lifted her nose. "It's an honor and a privilege to participate. We all did." She gestured at herself and the other four members sitting at the table—everyone besides King Kieran, Orla, Dallas, and me.

The five of them had killed no telling how many people to win their position. The thought made me sick.

"From the Winter royal line, Prince Nolan will be the contender." Quinley gestured to Orla at the front of the room. "Who will represent the Summer Court?"

My stomach roiled ... because I was certain I already knew.

Five

I WATCHED Orla's face shift from a grimace to a mask of indifference.

That was all the confirmation I needed.

"I'm queen, and Alina isn't herself. She can't lead, and since there are two members of the royal line, there's no reason for the king consort to become acting king." She wrung her hands together and hung her head. "Therefore, I must nominate Alina."

My vision blurred, but I blinked, refusing to let any tears fall. My supposed sister had approved of people ruthlessly killing me. I thought I'd seen the worst in people, but this was next level. She was trying to make it sound as if *she* were the victim, not me.

"You've got to be warming me," King Kieran growled, his hands clenching. "Do you want her to *die*? It would make keeping the crown easier for you."

His words punched me in the gut. He was right. If people believed I was Alina, sending me to die in the tournament would eliminate the issue of them wanting me to take the throne.

"Uh ... *King Kieran*." Quinley placed a hand on her hip, her face like a piece of ice. "This is a *Summer Court* decision."

If she wasn't telling the king to shut the fuck up somewhat nicely, then I was a pig's uncle ... since clearly pigs were my thing.

Orla's fingertips glowed red again, and she fisted her hands. "I don't *want* Alina to die, but my hands are tied. I *am* the crowned queen, and it would be chilly to cause turmoil among my people. Besides, her memories should come back soon, and we all know Alina was a fierce warrior. She may well win the seat. Until then, I'll make sure she's adequately trained for the Comortas."

"I can train her." Dallas stepped toward me. "*I* am the most qualified here in Summer to do it."

Frowning, Orla went unnaturally still.

"That's an excellent solution." Kaley placed her hands behind her back. "Dallas is the best swordsman in all of Summer, if not the entire kingdom."

King Kieran snorted, making his point without saying a word. A cocky grin spread across his face, but somehow, it was damn alluring. I stepped closer to him, his crisp scent both calming me and making my stomach flutter. Maybe I was coming down with a virus or something.

He glanced over his shoulder at me and glowered as if I were a rodent beneath him that needed to be squashed.

Talk about mixed vibes. One minute, he was protecting me, and the next, he was looking at me as if he couldn't wait for me to die.

Despite my head screaming at me to take a step back, my feet had a mind of their own, and I stayed in place. *This* was how people wound up hurt: They put themselves in dangerous situations.

"It's settled." Quinley steepled her hands. "Prince Nolan and Princess Alina will be the royal competitors. In the next sun cycle, you'll need to select another nine from each of your courts and submit them to the High Court so the list of competitors can be made official."

So there would be twenty contestants, including me.

I'd spent the past seven years of my life in Stan's gym, working out and training with him, but I'd never *killed* anyone, and the thought of doing so had acid burning my throat. How was I supposed to win if I couldn't bear the thought of killing someone?

"That's not the only decision that needs to be made," Orla said, avoiding my gaze. "We need to address informing the people about Alina's return. She should eventually look just like their *beloved* princess after she's had time to acclimate. She had the golden ticket, so that's the only thing that makes sense. The priestess wouldn't mess up something like that, so we have no choice but to trust her. To prevent civil unrest, we need to tell them immediately."

I couldn't help noticing the way she'd emphasized *beloved*. I didn't need to be "from here" to know she was worried they would usurp her and put me on the throne. Even if this world was real—not that I doubted it was all a dream—I would never want to be queen. I didn't like people, and I didn't want to worry about taking care of anyone but *myself*. I was certain that being queen required the complete opposite of that.

"I propose that when we leave here, we spread the word about Muir's death and Alina's return while she remains hidden here in Sambradh Castle." King Kieran strolled back to his spot at the table. "If she's present during the announcement, it could cause more turmoil."

Orla bristled. "I agree. We announce Muir first and allow a pause to mourn his death. Then we talk about the trials and Alina's return. We won't reveal she's joining the Comortas until we announce the other competitors. She won't make her first public appearance until she goes to Rioghail Tower for the duration of the tournament."

Caden snickered. "Another Summer Fae gone. I don't understand why anyone would mourn."

Head snapping toward him, Leanna bit her lip despite the corners of her mouth tipping upward as if to hide a smile, but she shook her head in disappointment.

"You're truly a drafty to even consider saying that in *our* castle." Dallas puffed out his chest, resembling a rooster before it squawked. "You'd best leave before I kick your ass for everyone to witness."

"No need." King Kieran ran a hand down his wrinkle-free

tunic, his biceps bulging through the thick material. "We have nothing left to discuss."

Drool might have pooled in the corner of my mouth, so I wiped quickly, not wanting anyone to see. Unfortunately, I found a bit of moisture, and I hated that he had that effect on me. He might be a king and a jackass, but he was also hot.

Quinley curtsied, staring directly at King Kieran, then rose and turned her gaze on Orla. "We should take our leave. All five members of the High Court will circulate the news of Muir's death. Right now, I suggest you help Alina remember something so she'll have a chance of surviving the first trial."

First? The urge to flee grew stronger, and I shuffled back, damn near tripping and spraining my ankle again because of these blasted heels. Whoever had invented these atrocities was either a sadist or had molded their feet into a whole new form to wear them. Hell, I bet if I shucked the shoes and hiked up the hem of my dress, I could outrun all of them in their bougie outfits.

But then I remembered Orla's wings. Dammit, she would definitely be able to catch me and was the most determined. If I didn't take part in the trial, Orla would be required—or mandated, whatever the fae term was—to participate.

"Something is wrong with her." Leanna's brows furrowed, and her dark irises turned ebony. "Who retrieved her from Earth? Did they poison her?"

Finally! Someone showing concern for me.

"*He*," I said and gestured to Dallas, "drugged me."

"She's being a smidge dramatic." Dallas shrugged. "I merely added spirits to her drink, but as you can see, none of her fae side was activated, so it knocked her out. Unfortunately, she was as ungraceful before I spiked her drink, so I'm not to blame for this." He motioned wildly at me as if that said enough.

Without thinking, I gave him the middle finger. I winced as soon as I'd shot him the bird. He was a prick, but knowing him, he'd take it as an offer.

All seven of them stared at me blankly.

"What is she *doing*?" Eamon smirked as if I were a comedian.

Orla tipped her head up at the vined rooftop, the vines coiled so tightly that not an ounce of sunlight filtered through. "I don't see anything peculiar."

I lowered my hand, my shoulders sagging. My attempt at an insult hadn't hit the mark, leaving me defeated. I lifted my chin, refusing to feel inferior to these pranksters. I could at least have a little dignity. "Made you look," came out without approval.

Quinley's brows furrowed together, and she leaned away from me, looking at me like I was the strangest creature she'd ever seen. She glanced at Kieran.

His steely gaze was locked on me, his lip curled, reinforcing exactly what he thought of me.

Worthless and odd.

I wanted to move closer to him and touch his sexy, tousled hair and muscular body, but survival skills kicked in. Thank *goodness*.

I had one disturbing thought, though, that I couldn't ignore anymore.

Ember would *never* do anything *cruel* to me. This wasn't her style. An innocent joke was one thing, but this situation had turned toxic.

"Is there anything else we need to decide?" Orla asked, snagging my arm and yanking me toward her. Though her face was smooth, she held herself stiffly. She was furious.

Worse, I somehow *knew* that about her. How was that possible when we'd never met before today?

"That's more than enough decisions at one time," Kaley said. "It's time for us to adjourn. We need to inform our people of the news. Otherwise, they'll assume we were withholding information." She stepped away from the table and headed toward a door at the back of the dining room.

Her concern meant they'd withheld information before. From the limited knowledge I'd picked up from a girl who loved to read and talk about books in the group home, fae couldn't lie, but they were master manipulators. That had led to one of the dumbass boys snorting and putting his own spin on it. He'd thought he was cute each time he corrected her, saying fae were expert masturbators. He and his equally dumbass friends had laughed about it until tears had run down their faces. *Boys.*

"For once, I can agree with a Summer Fae." Leanna waved a hand in front of her face. "It is time to go. It's way too warm here, and I'm certain I'm not far from melting."

"Ah. That would be a damn shame." I batted my eyes, trying to look innocent, but come on, these assholes had agreed to throw me into a tournament, hoping I'd *die.*

Dallas chuckled.

Quinley sighed. "There goes the last bit of lingering doubt I had that she's Alina. She may be clueless, but that was something Alina would say and exactly that way. I suspect her memories are returning." She *tsk*ed. "Such a shame."

That was it. High Court member or not, the bitch was going down. Punching her just once would make being here under more scrutiny worthwhile before I could slip away and get back home.

I'd *told* Stan that coming to Vegas was a horrible idea. And here I was, proving my past self right.

Orla's firm grip on my arm held me in place. I tried to yank out of her grasp, but her hand, despite its softness, was incredibly strong.

A cruel smirk flitted across King Kieran's face, but his forehead creased as if he, too, was concerned. I wanted to know what he was thinking, to remove the mystery around him that intrigued me. He'd been both protective of and seemingly disgusted by me at various times, and I wanted to know why.

I couldn't get free, and my body stiffened. I'd been trained, and I was strong, yet I was in her clutches, and the walls were closing in. Worse, the Winter King had noticed how weak I was; I didn't want the others to realize I couldn't get away from Orla, especially when all she was doing was holding my arm.

"The High Court members and I should head back to Rioghail Tower so we can get the message out and return home." King Kieran strolled toward me.

My heart raced, and my stomach churned. As he stepped toward me, I yearned to meet him halfway, just so it wouldn't take as long. Still, my head screamed at me to get farther away.

He stopped in front of me and leaned close as if bowing. For a moment, I thought his lips would touch my earlobe, but he stopped a breath away. He whispered, "I'm watching you, Princess Alina. We all are, but especially me. Don't underestimate me. I'll discover your secret."

His minty breath was as cold as a winter breeze, and a shiver ran down my spine. I wasn't certain if it was from his words, the sensation of his breath, or the weird feelings he brought out in me.

I looked at him, our faces inches apart. His blue eyes darkened a shade as if shrouded in desire. My body wanted to respond, but I shut it down. I wouldn't be attracted to someone who treated me like this.

Furthermore, I refused to cower. I wouldn't be anyone's punching bag. "When you discover what it is, please inform me. I'd like to know as well."

When I moved to place a hand on his chest and push him away, he recoiled, straightening and taking several steps back in a blur. He glowered as he rubbed the section of his suit that I'd almost touched. Loathing slid back into his expression.

He turned on his heel and marched toward the door. The other remaining High Court members followed him, and Kaley watched me as she held open the door.

"We'll make sure the announcements are handled accordingly, My Queen." Kaley curtseyed and smiled at me. "It'll be interesting to have you back, Princess Alina."

"Ivy." I hated them calling me Alina. I wasn't *her*. "That's my name."

Eamon rubbed his temples. "I hope she gets her memories back quickly." He placed a hand on Kaley's back and guided her out the door.

When the door shut, Orla snarled. "What in frozen winter were you thinking?" Her face turned a faint pink while her hands glimmered red again.

I'd heard the expression red as a tomato, but this was more extreme. The vibrant red reminded me of fire. "What part? Not wanting to be thrown into a tournament to the death, wanting to go home, or asking them to call me Ivy?" I was sure I'd done more stuff she wasn't happy with, but those were the first three points to pop into my mind.

"*This* is your *home, Alina*." She stomped her foot. "Besides, you can't return to the Earth realm. The veil is closed."

A lump formed, and my throat ached. "What do you mean? You brought me here. I should be able to get back."

She laughed, and the sound was high-pitched and warm but somehow scary. "If I didn't have to wait for you to be reborn and until Havestia for the veil to thin so we could traipse to Earth, I would've taken you the moment you were born so we wouldn't run into whatever *this* is. You're going to embarrass me and weaken our family if you don't get yourself in line."

I had to get *home*. The walls still wanted to close in on me, but I couldn't shut down. "Don't worry." I placed my hands on my hips. "I won't be alive long, according to your friends. And what do you mean, I can't go back ho—er—to Earth?"

Dallas answered, startling me. I'd forgotten he was there. "Caden explained this to you already. Stop feigning ignorance. The veil only opens for a short amount of time on Havestia— every fifty complete season cycles." He templed his hands. "Priestess Abba sent you and the other seven girls who sacrificed themselves a golden ticket to get you to that ridiculous ... *casino* so we would have an easy time locating you before the veil closed."

My stomach was now churning so much that, between this news and Dallas's presence, I was certain I would vomit. After everything I'd seen and heard, I couldn't help but think this horrible nightmare was, in fact, my new reality.

That damn golden ticket.

And Ember and Isa had gotten one too. Did that mean they'd also been kidnapped and brought here? Maybe I could find them.

"None of that matters now that you're here." Orla snapped her fingers. "Your name is *Alina*. That is what everyone will call you, so you need to get used to it."

She took my hand—hers almost as hot as a flame, though it didn't burn—and led me back down the hallway in the direction we'd come from.

As I passed Dallas, he winked and blew a kiss, causing my skin to crawl.

He was way too confident for his own good.

Wanting to get away from him, I didn't argue as she led me away. I was far more comfortable with her than him. "Where are we going?"

"I'm taking you back to your room. I don't want any additional castle servants to see you until the announcement has been circulated."

That was more than okay with me, so I didn't respond. The two of us marched down the hallways, and soon we were back in the bedroom I'd woken in.

Lilidh and Cara were there, and both of them bowed to Orla and her red glory.

"Leave *now*," Orla commanded, the faint scent of sulfur filling the air.

They hurried out, and I realized no one would help me if it went against their *queen*.

Once they'd gone, I waited for her to insult me or smack me.

Instead, Orla's chest heaved. "Get in bed and rest. Dinner will be brought to you. Until then, dream or do whatever you need to do to get your memories back. I need you to at least attempt to win the Comortas and not have me waste a competitor."

Crossing my arms, I didn't say a thing. She'd already decided to send me to my death, and I'd learned I couldn't get back home. Even though I wanted to continue to pretend this was a fucking nightmare, the chill in my body had already accepted this new reality as truth.

Whatever she saw on my face must have been enough because she turned and walked away.

Alone, I flopped onto the bed, my chest constricting uncomfortably. No one here liked me. I was stuck, and most importantly, the one person who was like a father to me wasn't around to help me figure out how to get home. But Ember might be here somewhere. Maybe I could find her, and the two of us could figure a way out of this mess.

I snorted. Like Orla would let me out of her sight now.

Hot tears gathered and spilled down my face, and I let the hopelessness weigh me down. This was real, and worse, in a few days, I'd be dead. There was no getting out of this situation, and I couldn't help but think about all the kids I wouldn't be able to help back home.

Eyes stinging and nose stuffy, I somehow managed to fall asleep.

* * *

My eyes opened, and for a moment, I didn't remember where I was. The light was dim, with only a faint glow, as if from the moon and stars, but it wasn't daytime anymore. A few lanterns were lit in the room, giving it a soft glow.

I sat up, taking in the shadowed room, and memories flooded back. *Dammit.* I was still here. I'd hoped it was a dream. I couldn't suppress a bitter laugh. Years of being passed from shit home to shit home should've taught me the futility of hoping a long time ago. When would I learn? The sheets, buttery soft linen, crinkled in my clenched fists, and I forced myself to relax, push down the anger, and tap into what I could use *on what was going right*.

That's what Stan would want.

I stood and found the cool floor comforting. No one was here. This could be my chance to escape.

I rushed into the bathroom, retrieved my foldable knife, and slid it into my cleavage—one of the few perks of the horrible dress I still wore was that it offered easy concealment and easy access for my knife. Then I scurried to the door to the hallway and placed my ear against it. I held my breath, trying to make sure I wouldn't miss a sound or sign of life on the other side.

Forcing myself to be patient, I waited several minutes. Then, with a steady hand, I grabbed the wooden branch doorknob and opened it slowly, hoping not to make a noise.

There was no one outside.

I stepped into the hallway, looking left and right.

Empty.

Sweet.

Following my gut, I turned in the opposite direction of where I'd gone earlier with Orla. There had to be another way out of this place.

I scurried down the hallway, passing a few doors and holding my breath, waiting for someone to burst outside so I could scream for them to catch me. No one appeared.

A faint glow lit the end of the hallway, and I picked up my pace until I reached a large, arched wooden door.

This had to be an exit.

I clutched the wooden handle and pulled it open, then cringed, waiting for a creak or groan. It never came.

But the view outside had me catching my breath.

A gorgeous garden boasted flowers of every color, vivid even in the moonlight. Their sweet scents filled my nostrils, giving me a sense of peace I'd never experienced before.

The purple flowers glimmered in the darkness, while the yellow flowers reminded me of mini suns. The blue bell-shaped flowers were the color of a summer sky, but the pink flowers, which seemed to have flames swirling from their petals, called to me the most.

They looked so magical. A tree that reminded me of a weeping willow rustled in a slight breeze.

Energy buzzed around me, blending with my soul and loosening the knot coiled in my stomach.

"I was wondering how long it would take you to come here," an unfamiliar female voice said from behind me. "You won't get very far."

I froze, my blood turning to ice.

Six

I TURNED, prepared to fight, but when I noticed the swords at her sides and the bow on her back, I knew there was no way I could win. Self-Defense 101—the best thing I could do was get the *hell* out of here while I could.

I raced deeper into the seemingly endless garden. If I could get enough of a lead, maybe I could escape her ... even though I didn't know where to go to even *try* to get home.

One objective at a time.

The person huffed behind me, her voice farther away. "That's what I figured."

I wanted to pump my fist in victory—I was actually making headway.

Lanterns lit the stone pathway bright enough that I could see without issue. Something blurred to my right, and my heart faltered. Before I could pivot, a person stood in front of me, feet set wide, blocking my path.

The swords were still sheathed at her hips, the bow wrapped around her arm the way I wore a purse, a quiver full of arrows sticking out above her back. She was beautiful in a different way than Orla and the others I'd met inside. Her long, dirty-blonde hair was twisted into braids, and her skin was fair with warm pink tones.

The biggest difference was the warmth in her brown eyes.

"Let me go. You don't have to tell anyone you saw me. I'll slip away quietly." I clung desperately to the hope damn near exploding in my chest that I could get through to her. I'd been around enough people to know when someone sincere crossed my path.

She sighed, and her shoulders drooped. The dark-gold metal of her armor clinked softly. "I can only imagine how this feels for you. I'm sure nothing makes sense, but letting you leave would be both futile and dangerous. Nothing good will result from your attempt to flee. The veil is closed."

A cold realization gut-punched me. Hearing that from *her* made me believe that trying to escape truly was unattainable. My eyes burned, but I refused to cry. I'd done enough of that for the night. "So, I'm just supposed to stay here and be forced into a tournament where I'll likely die."

The irony wasn't lost on me. I'd spent so much of my time keeping people at arm's length to protect myself, only to land in another fucking *world* and die. There was no way I could've prepared myself for that.

"If you want to, give up." She shrugged and took a step back, the lantern illuminating her front side and emphasizing the thorns and petals designed on her armor. "Or we could train together."

Though I didn't know her, I'd much rather train with her than Dallas, with all his inappropriate touches and flirting. "Dallas has been assigned to me." I rolled my eyes.

She laughed unexpectedly. "At least in this life, your taste has improved." She tipped her head, and the lantern's glow highlighted the freckles across her cheeks and nose. This woman smelled of fresh rain, and I realized I sort of wanted to stay around her to absorb some of that essence.

"I swear there was a mistake." I rubbed my arms to keep from shivering. "I'm not Alina. I'm *Ivy*. I just want to go home."

Some of that sympathy I'd seen vanished, and her expression tightened. "You can either whine and pity yourself or choose to do something productive." She lifted her chin, staring me right in the eyes as she continued, "Whether you believe it or not, you *are* the reincarnated princess. There's no denying your essence, so I suggest you prepare as much as you can for the Comortas. Unless you *want* to die. Again."

My bottom lip quivered, and I bit it. The more weakness I showed, the more of a target I'd be. Stan had coached me for seven years, emphasizing that bullies targeted those who seemed weak and defenseless. Unfortunately, that was already how people here saw me, and I was beginning to realize that my training hadn't prepared me for beings who could move so much faster than me.

Stan had also reinforced that I should surround myself with and learn from those stronger than me. I wanted to at least make the assholes struggle a bit before they kicked my ass. I'd die with some level of badassery. Maybe she was my chance.

I straightened. "Do you think they'll allow you to train me?"

A smirk flitted across her face. "Leave it to me." She winked, and unlike Dallas, it wasn't creepy. "But *Ivy*, you need to be careful and not offer information about yourself so freely. Mystery gives you power, and your life in the human world will have many fae wanting to know everything about that world. Use their curiosity to your advantage. That curiosity is the one thing you have over all of us."

I swallowed. In just a few minutes, this random guard had given me more advice than anyone else here, including my supposed sister. "Why are you helping me?" There had to be a catch.

The woman exhaled and shook her head. "And the second lesson of the night is never admit when someone is helping you. It means you owe them. One day, that person *will* come to collect."

"Noted," I gritted out. There were already so many different customs here. With my human upbringing, I was bound to mess up.

She blew out a breath and held out her hand. "Don't be so hard on yourself. You were tossed into a new world you weren't even aware existed. In time, things should begin to feel right."

I stared at her offered hand, unsure if this was another test. If I touched her, would I owe her something? "Clearly, I have a lot to learn, and quickly."

"If you're even half the person Alina was, you'll be fine." She stretched out her hand again. "Isn't this how humans introduce themselves to one another?"

There was that curiosity she'd mentioned, golden lines lightening her dark irises.

I shrugged. "Maybe. Is that something you'd like to know?"

Her mauve lips stretched into a full smile. "You're a fast learner."

Taking her hand, I shook it. I had to trust my instincts and listen to any advice she could spare. "Part of the interaction is stating our names. Mine is Ivy."

"Maeve," she replied without missing a beat, her grip nearly crushing the bones in my fingers.

"You aren't supposed to break my hand." I squeezed back, not wanting to seem intimidated.

Her mouth dropped. "Oh, Your Highness, I didn't mean to." Her grip went slack before releasing me completely.

"No problem." I lowered my hand and rubbed it against my dress.

She continued to stare at me, making me squirm inside. Even if I did feel more comfortable around her than the others, I didn't want to spend a lot of time with her, but I didn't want to go back to the room, either, and this garden brought me a sense of peace. Tilting my head upward, I took in the sky ... and my mouth dropped open.

I blinked, thinking it was an illusion, but each time I opened my eyes, the view was the same. There were two moons in the sky.

Just like on Earth, there was one silver moon that was completely full, but a second equally full, shimmery silver-pink moon peeked from behind the Earth-like one, almost like a blushing shadow.

As the light shone down on my face, my skin tingled. The warmth spreading through my body seemed like a high.

Faint turquoise flashes of light flew around me, and the buzzing I'd felt before Maeve had interrupted me thrummed through me, energizing something within me. There was no doubt this place contained magic.

"Princ—" Maeve stopped and cleared her throat. "Ivy, it's late, and if someone other than me finds you out here, they will notify Queen Orla. It's best she remains unaware of your foray. She doesn't need another reason to be unhappy with your return."

I hated that she was right. I suspected Orla had an entire list of how my presence here had complicated her life. Her primary concern seemed to be the risk of her people wanting me to take her spot on the throne. As if I'd ever want that to happen. I had a hard enough time taking care of myself, let alone who knows how many thousands—millions?—of people.

"Fine." I lowered my head, watching as the magical pink lights swirled around me, noting they didn't do the same to Maeve. So weird.

"Are you sure you won't let me try to run and hide?" I lifted a brow, my heart squeezing with hope but my stomach hardening with dread.

She adjusted the bow underneath her left arm. "Maybe, if you were actually near an exit." She gestured down the stone pathway that led to more colorful flowers. "But thick walls surround the entire garden, so unless you can sprout wings, you can't escape from here."

Any other time, I would've thought that was a joke, but not after seeing Orla with her wings earlier. I had so many questions, but Maeve's advice rang in my ears. If I wanted to remain mysterious, I shouldn't pepper anyone with questions unless I wanted to reciprocate with answers of my own. I needed to act as if I belonged in their world so they didn't have something to hold over me.

"Not only that, but there's a reason I waited for you within the castle. At the end of this pathway, guards are stationed to watch for you per Queen Orla's orders."

There it was. I was a prisoner even if this was supposedly my home.

Everything inside me wanted to stay in the garden for a little longer. Even though my room was comforting, something out here made me *feel* magical, but I knew it wasn't true. If Orla had people watching me, she wanted to see if I'd try to escape. I needed to go back to my room and be an obedient human in case I ever did get a chance to run away. "Good night."

Maeve didn't say a word, and I forced myself to walk back toward the castle door. As I drew closer, the lights swirling around me faded. I stepped back into the castle, and they vanished into thin air.

Even with the gorgeous flowers lining the hallway, I couldn't get past the sinking feeling that I would never get home.

* * *

Never in my life had I ever worn a dress before last night, but Lilidh waited for me in the middle of the bedroom to assist me into yet another one. "How am I supposed to train in that?"

Her brows furrowed. "What do you mean? This *is* for training. It's leather, and you'll be covered for protection." She lifted an all-black leather dress that was really a formfitting top and a long shirt with leggings and boots. It might be more comfortable than last night's dress, but it wasn't my jeans and shirt.

I gestured at the top, which was so low cut I feared a nipple would pop out. "There seems to be a huge piece of cloth missing if I'm supposed to be covered everywhere."

"You have lovely breasts, Your Highness." Cara rubbed her hands together. "There's no reason to be shy."

I wanted to laugh. I had so many reasons for not wanting to show off my chest, but the most important was that I'd like to keep both boobs and not have one accidentally cut off. "Isn't there another outfit?"

"No." Lilidh frowned. "I'm sorry. We had this one made

quickly last night for today. They're working on your outfits for the Comortas when you'll need better protection."

I wouldn't argue with that. I glanced at the bed, which she'd insisted on making while I washed my face in the bathroom this morning after dining on the most delicious muffins and breads I'd ever eaten in my life.

"I'll need to help you put this on." She pursed her lips and fidgeted.

She was the nicest of the three women who were apparently my attendants, yet I made her feel uncomfortable.

I forced myself to undress and let her pour the leather over my body. I was certain the clothes wouldn't fit, but the leather gave until, eventually, it fit me like a glove. I'd never worn anything so formfitting before.

"My turn." Cara slid in front of me, wiggled her fingers, and flicked her wrists in my face.

My skin buzzed, and I startled backward, thankful for the boots instead of the high heels from last night. I didn't know what she was doing to me, but I never wanted her to do it again.

"There," she exclaimed. "Perfect."

I spun around and looked into the mirror on top of the dresser in the corner of the bedroom. I couldn't believe what I saw. My skin was smooth and flawless, and my face had a natural look as if I'd spent hours on my makeup. I rubbed my face. "How the—"

"Glamour." Cara straightened her shoulders. "I've mastered it in the fifty complete season cycles you've been gone."

That was a handy gift, though I preferred not to wear makeup. At least it wasn't uncomfortable, except for the faint buzz left behind.

As if by clockwork, Enid entered the room with a small smile. Her hair was braided to one side, and she wore a simple gown, just like the other two girls. "Good sun cycle, Princess Alina. Dallas is waiting for you in the training room."

Dallas.

The last person or fae I wanted to see. I'd rather have a root canal than endure his presence, but if that was the only way I was going to get trained, I'd suck it up. In fact, training with him might give me better motivation since I'd do everything possible to keep him from touching me.

I nodded, not bothering with pleasantries. She'd left me alone with Dallas yesterday, and I wouldn't forgive that anytime soon. You didn't leave other people alone with predators.

The corners of her lips twitched downward, but she kept up the smile. "Come along."

The two of us turned down so many hallways that I lost all sense of direction. Even if I wanted to escape to my room, there was no way I could find it without help. Each hallway looked identical with the same flowers and vines—beautiful, vibrant, and all-encompassing.

We arrived at a set of doors similar to the one that led to the garden. This time, the door opened to reveal a huge canopy. The sun, which resembled Earth's, shone in the sky and radiated warmth. Since sparring was inevitable, I scanned the area to get a sense of it. Vines grew in the corners, and five men sat at a sizable table with wooden chairs and green satin seats. To the right, a gigantic weeping willow grew at the edge of a ginormous circle of stone. Instead of Dallas, Maeve stood in the center of the space that had to be our sparring area.

The sight of her would've been a relief if not for the way Maeve was glaring at me.

She wore the same sort of outfit as last night, her hair now pulled back and out of the way.

"Good sun cycle," she said as she walked toward me. Smaller weapons, like daggers, had replaced her swords, and her stern expression made me realize she hadn't been joking in the slightest last night. She was going to train me hard.

As she strolled over, I wanted to run away.

From the table where the men were sitting, she lifted a belt with two sheaths and daggers and handed it to me.

"I can't wait to watch your session," Dallas cooed, and I realized he was sitting the farthest from me but with the clearest view of the circle.

Wanting to look anywhere but at him, I took the belt from Maeve and buckled it around my waist.

The man closest to me chuckled, his lime-green eyes bright. "At least she's familiar with weapons. Maybe the princess is in there after all."

I didn't want to correct him and tell him I'd been trained by a former Marine for the past seven years.

A man with vibrant red hair sat across from Lime Eyes, body turned toward the training area. He tilted his head, scanning me. "She doesn't stand a chance against Maeve. She's the best fighter of us all."

Maeve strode into the stone circle.

I turned and saw Enid walking away, but all five men stayed in place, and Dallas leaned back with his hands behind his head.

"Uh...aren't they leaving?" Fighting her on my own would be bad enough. The last thing I wanted was anyone watching. I didn't want them to know I'd had professional training.

"You nervous, *Princess*?" a man with lavender streaks in his silver hair asked from his spot next to Dallas.

I hated how all these men knew who I was, but I didn't know a single one, and I didn't want to seem curious, not after what Maeve had said last night, so I tried to concentrate on the task at hand.

Maeve shrugged. "Thousands will be watching the Comortas. You might as well get used to it."

I swallowed. I wouldn't be able to get out of this.

"Let's train." She removed two daggers from her sides, handles made of vines.

Taking a deep breath, I took one of my daggers in hand. I'd trained with knives, and these blades were only slightly longer. Hopefully, that difference wouldn't bother me. I lifted them, ready to bring it.

Once I was set up, she charged.

Seven

EARS RINGING, I lifted my dagger, barely blocking her from piercing my left shoulder. She gritted her teeth and used all her weight to get the edge of the dagger to slice my leather and dig into my skin.

Pain stung me, and I sucked in a breath, refusing to make a noise. Her getting the best of me was bad enough.

I scurried backward, needing to gain a little distance.

The men watching us cheered while Lime Green exclaimed, "Next time, cut deeper!"

This place was totally insane. "What the *hell*? You're supposed to be *training* me."

"I *am*." Maeve wiped the edge of her dagger against her chest. "The Comortas is in six sun cycles, so our training time is rather limited. Do you expect the other competitors to take it easy on you because you were raised human?"

I hated that I already knew the answer. "They won't." Most of the competitors would ignore me, focusing on the more imminent threats, but when the numbers dwindled, they wouldn't hesitate to slit my throat...or whatever fae did. "I didn't realize you would try to kill me before I even made it to the tournament."

"Now you wish I was training you, don't you, love?" Dallas asked.

I turned around, and he winked, making me regret gracing him with any attention.

"I'd rather die." I wrinkled my nose, wanting him to feel how much I disliked him.

"Oh, Dallas." The redheaded man patted him on the back. "Even after Alina being gone for fifty complete cycles, your chemistry is still intact. I know what will happen tonight."

A gag lodged in the back of my throat. I was at a complete loss. I'd insulted him, and they were treating it as foreplay. These idiots needed to leave.

The only one who didn't seem to be a complete jerk was the quiet man beside Dallas, who hadn't said a word. But the way his forest-green eyes watched me made me uncomfortable, so I turned back to face Maeve.

She was right. I didn't need to act like a princess. I snorted, unable to hold back the noise at my random thought.

Maeve pretended not to notice as she lifted both daggers and commanded, "Again."

I rolled my shoulders, adjusted my grip, and watched her eyes lock on my side before she charged again.

With as much speed as possible, I dropped the dagger from my left hand and blocked her. I used a downward motion, knowing she was stronger than me and she'd wind up cutting me again. With the dagger in my right hand, I jabbed her shoulder, wanting to even the playing field.

The edge of my blade hit her armor and vibrated in my hand.

That didn't matter. I'd managed to hit her.

Before I could counter, Maeve swung out her leg and took mine out from under me. I crumpled to the stone but caught myself with my free hand. When I jumped back to my feet, Maeve kicked me in the stomach. I soared backward and landed hard on my ass. My body jolted as my tailbone throbbed, but I refused to quit after two small attacks.

"You surprised me," Maeve said, moving toward me and extending her hand. "The fact that you could tell where I was aiming was good. I figured you'd assume I'd go for your shoulder again."

I glanced at where she'd sliced me. The leather was damp from my blood, but the sting was already gone. She hadn't cut deep, but I'd expected it to sting for a little while.

Strange.

But I had more important things to focus on.

Taking her hand would be a sign of weakness, one I couldn't afford.

"I'm good." I couldn't hide the wince as I stood. My ass was literally on fire, and when I took a step, I wanted to groan. At least I managed to hold it in.

"Frozen sakes, this is worse than a conversation with a Winter fae," one of the dumbasses whined. "There's no blood, and despite Maeve's protest, she's taking it easy."

Maeve rolled her eyes. "I'm trying to help her, not kill her. I barely kicked her, and you see how far she went."

My face burned. She made me sound helpless, something I'd always feared back home. Helplessness got you hurt. I'd trained hard with Stan for seven years, and I was one of the strongest women in the gym, but that seemed like a different life. Here, I couldn't keep up with Maeve's strikes and blows.

"Let's get out of here," one of the men said.

I kept my back to them. I didn't have any reason to be ashamed. They'd kidnapped me and brought me to a strange world I'd never asked for or wanted to be a part of.

Gathering every ounce of self-control, I forced myself to face them, and the expressions on their faces confirmed what I already suspected.

They viewed me as weak.

The man with gray-and-purple hair strolled around the edge of the stone. "Let's head to the tower and make bets. I have a feeling I know who'll be the first to die." His gaze cut to me.

I flipped him off. I didn't give a damn that they didn't understand the gesture—it brought me joy.

"Uh..." He glanced at Dallas. "What does that mean?"

"No idea." Dallas shrugged and strolled toward me. "You all head inside. I'll be right behind you."

The four men obeyed their king, and resisting rolling my eyes was more painful than my throbbing tailbone.

Dallas watched the four of them leave. He didn't utter a word until the door shut and they were out of sight.

Then his shoulders drooped, and he sighed. "Why aren't her powers back yet? She'll wind up dead if they don't manifest before the trial. You should have the answers." He gestured at Maeve, his forehead lined with worry.

What the fuck was going on? The man before me wasn't the same Dallas I'd come to know in my short time here. He seemed ... different, almost like a human being.

He stared at me and said, "We need to figure out a way to get her through this."

"Your Highness, I don't have any answers either." Maeve licked her lips. "This is unprecedented. No one knows how reincarnation works, especially since she was born human. Maybe her powers won't come back, or maybe it'll take time."

"*She* is right *here*," I seethed. I hated when people talked about me as if I wasn't present. "Maybe I have no powers because you *kidnapped* the wrong person." I needed Dallas to become the cocky jackass I blamed and hated. This whole nice-guy act was threatening to crumble the one thing I was certain of: Dallas had dragged me into this mess. He wouldn't be excused because he was worried about me.

"You *really* need to stop saying that." He pivoted to face me, the arrogance sliding back into place. "It makes you look weaker, and denying that you're the princess will only make others despise you more."

I wanted to stomp and scream. I hadn't felt this out of control since I'd turned eighteen and began living in the back of Stan's community gym, away from the predators that had always surrounded me.

"There's no chance you aren't the princess." Dallas stepped forward, his gaze warming. "You *sound* like her. You *smell* like her. And you're even as *stubborn* as her." He reached out and tucked a strand of hair behind my ear. "If you let me kiss you, I bet I can confirm you even taste like her."

Ew. His normal demeanor was firmly back in place. *Thank goodness.* "I'll pass."

"Oh, love, we've always enjoyed this game." He chuckled.

Maeve cleared her throat. "She's supposed to be training. Flirting with her is a distraction. If you want her as prepared as possible, you need to let me do my job. I thought that was why you agreed to let me take over her training."

Dallas frowned and nodded. "Fine. I'll go inside so you two can focus, and I'll keep the idiot fae away, but I wanted them to see that, despite her current weakness, she is stubborn and won't give up."

I scoffed. "Are you serious? You want to make me a target for your people?" At home, people were afraid of things that were different ... things they couldn't understand or label. The fae people probably weren't much different. But if Orla was worried about my place in the kingdom, this was an easy way to make me a target before the trial.

"I wanted them to see that you are important enough for Maeve to be assigned to protect and train you." Dallas straightened. "Especially since you're so determined to undermine your place here. They might hesitate now that they've seen how resilient you are."

My head jerked back. I hadn't expected *him* to be concerned about protecting me.

"I've stayed out here too long." Dallas smoothed his warm-brown suit jacket. "I need to attend to my visitors. Next time you hit her, try to restore reason to her head." He pivoted and walked away, leaving me alone with Maeve.

I turned around, ready to spar again. "Let's go."

Maeve nodded and strolled into the stone circle, ready to fight.

* * *

Time passed way too quickly, with every free moment spent training, eating, or being squashed into a dress. Now, it was the night before the Comortas.

I made my way to the garden. Since I'd been behaving, I wasn't confined to my room, though I rarely left it. Orla kept her distance, and the few times she'd attended my training to see my progress, her expression had been cold and distant, with no hint of the woman I'd met the night I'd arrived.

My bare feet padded across the cold stone of the castle floor as my fingers brushed the flowers I passed. I tried not to overanalyze the fact that some pieces of this place felt like home.

As I approached the hallway that led to the garden, a warning flashed down my spine.

A hand reached out and clutched my arm, and my training kicked in. I whirled and punched the person in the face, and a sickening *crunch* filled the air.

"Shit," Dallas exclaimed, releasing me and jerking back. Ocean-blue blood poured down his nose, a faint mist swirling from it.

I blinked, trying to get used to the color of their blood. With Maeve's armor, I'd never been able to make her bleed, but I'd expected her blood to be crimson like mine. Seeing Dallas bleed blue seemed like further evidence I wasn't fae.

"You can't go around sneaking up on people," I snapped, feeling awful that I'd hurt him. Yes, he was a creep, but I didn't need to add assault to my ever-growing list of faults.

He pinched the bridge of his nose, seeming more human-like. "I didn't realize you wouldn't know it was me, but at least we know your training has improved your reflexes."

Prick. If he expected me to apologize, he'd be disappointed.

Beyond the window, both moons were high in the sky. It was late—even more reason for him not to be in the halls. "What are you doing out and about? Shouldn't you be with Orla?"

He waggled his brows. "Alina, are you jealous? That doesn't usually attract me, but for you, I'll make an exception."

I shook my head. "Don't. Find me appalling."

"One day, you'll beg me to make you scream Mother Terrea's name once more." He rubbed the blood from beneath his nostrils. "You used to say you didn't have to go to the temple to worship when I was inside you."

Was he being serious? I smacked him upside the head. "First off, gross. And second, are you hitting on me when blood is pouring out of your nose?"

"Blood is an aphrodisiac for us fae."

"No, bruh." I shook my head, finding his persistence kind of funny. I had to give him that.

His nose wrinkled, and he winced. "You didn't just call me your brother."

To see his disgust made using Earth slang worth it. "Well, you *are*. You're married to my sister."

"Frozen sakes, Alina. We're not blood."

"Technicalities." For some weird reason, his flirting didn't bother me as much anymore. Over the past few days, he'd seemed genuinely concerned about me. Maybe he wasn't a horrible guy— though still definitely one I would never be interested in *that* way. "You better go and clean that up."

He rolled his eyes. "Fine, but this conversation isn't over."

It never was with him.

Turning around, he marched off to who the hell knew where, and I continued to the garden.

As soon as I stepped outside, my gaze landed on Maeve. She was leaning against the stone arch, staring at the two moons, both slightly less than full.

"I figured you'd come out here," Maeve said. "Especially with tomorrow being the big day."

I sighed, my loose pale-pink dress whispering over my legs as I leaned against the arch across from her. "Yeah, I couldn't sleep and thought fresh air might do me good."

She nodded. "I'm the same way."

We gazed around the garden, the silence between us comforting.

I pushed off the wall and headed toward the flowers. My hand touched each bud, and the small pink lights swirled around me. It was odd that it was happening again, but something about them felt right.

"Got a lot on your mind?" she asked. "We can discuss strategy."

I had a ton of questions, but one had been lingering on the tip of my tongue since that first training lesson. "What did Dallas mean the other day when he asked about how fae magic revealed itself? He said, out of everyone, you'd know best." Everyone here was playing games and speaking in riddles. It'd be nice if someone spoke the truth.

She exhaled. "I'm only half fae. My mother was human."

My mouth dropped open, and I jerked my head in her direction. "How is that possible?"

A smirk slid across her face. "Fae women have the same body parts as Earth women, so my dad—"

I stuck out my tongue. "I don't need a sex lesson. I meant I thought there were no humans here. The whole veil thing."

"Your mannerisms are really odd." She snorted and walked over to me. "Like I told you, all fae are intrigued by the human world, and sometimes one will travel to Earth when the veil allows. My dad did that and became infatuated with a gorgeous woman, and he brought her back here."

"Wait. You *all* do that?" I wondered how many poor humans had been kidnapped and dragged here.

"It was love at first sight, or so Dad says." Maeve shrugged. "He swears they were fated mates, which hadn't happened in centuries."

I picked at my nails, trying not to make her uncomfortable. "What does your mom say?"

"Never got the chance to ask." She adjusted her bow. "She died giving birth to me."

"I'm sorry." Though I didn't know Maeve well, I felt like we were becoming friends. Maybe that was because she was half human.

She continued fidgeting with her bow, which wasn't like her. I'd made her uncomfortable.

I needed to change the subject. "What's my biggest weakness in the tournament? My lack of magic?"

"No." She looked up at me. "We've worked on that. Your greatest weakness is the one thing I can't prepare you for, but we'll train with Dallas on it in the morning."

My stomach dropped. "You haven't trained me on something? The tournament is tomorrow!"

"We had to get the basics down, and though they're still not perfect, you've gotten a lot better. Tomorrow, you'll fight Dallas while he flies and uses his magic against you."

My heart leaped into my throat. "How many fae can fly?" Here, I'd been feeling not *quite* as panicked, and now I'd learned that Orla wasn't the only one who could fucking fly.

"All the High Fae, which will be every person in the Comortas." Maeve stretched out her arms. "Only High Fae are eligible to enter the tournament. You should have wings too—that's one reason I keep kicking you like I have been—but they haven't appeared."

Could this get any worse? I was slower and unmagical. Now, we'd added wingless to the mix.

"Which is why you should go to bed and rest." Maeve walked over and placed a hand on my arm. "The odds *are* stacked against you, but when our land was dying, you faced worse odds and came out on top. I believe in you, and I'll be there every step of the way possible."

I started to get flustered, but then my vision went black.

Eight

AS THE DARKNESS *merged around me, light flashed like a strobe. Colors blended and swirled, and I found myself transported to a place I'd never visited before.*

A woman stood in front of a pond, her lavender gaze locked on mine as she held out a golden chalice. Her bright-violet curls contrasted with the magical blue glow of the water and the white gown she wore.

I moved toward her, my heels clicking against the stone floor, my lungs burning as if I were drowning. My heart pounded faster, and my mind screamed at me to run, but my legs carried me forward.

Taking the chalice from the woman, I said, "In gratitude for all you've done, I offer warmth and sun in return. Take my magic and balance our world." The words were foreign to me, but they hit deep within my soul.

As I lifted the chalice to my lips and sipped the cool, refreshing liquid, a rosy crystal on the chalice flashed. I took the crystal between my thumb and finger and tugged, removing a short dagger. I held it tightly, but before I could see beyond the priestess, darkness surrounded me once more.

"Ivy." Maeve's voice sounded thick with concern. "Alina."

My body jerked, and I blinked as the garden came back into

focus. Maeve was squatting in front of me, hands on my shoulders, shaking me.

I clutched my head, trying to understand what the hell had happened. As I straightened in my seat, my hand brushed against vines and leaves.

What the—

Glancing down, I found myself sitting on a seat of plants in the midst of flowers, vines, and dirt. My heart dropped into my stomach, and I jumped to my feet. When I turned to assess the damage to the flowers, my pulse skipped a beat.

It looked as if the plants had parted around me, protecting the flowers, but as I stepped back, vines with thick leaves shifted to where I'd been seconds ago. Right before my eyes, the plants moved, returning to their original places, and the seat disappeared.

"Did you do that?" I stared, trying to understand what I'd seen. Maeve had used her magic when we'd fought, but nothing to that degree. She must have been holding back.

"That was all you." Maeve moved up beside me, staring at the spot I'd been sitting in. "The plants wrapped around you when you ..." She sighed and shrugged. "When you did whatever the winter you just did, and then they eased you into the seat you made. Are you okay?"

I snorted. That was a loaded question with so many possible answers. "Let's see. A freaky vision hit me while I was wide awake, and I woke up with plants that created a seat for me. And the first thing I was concerned with was whether I'd injured a flower. I'm pretty sure that's the opposite of okay, but hey, I'm alive ... for now."

She arched a brow. "None of that is funny, and you use the strangest gestures and words sometimes." She waved at the plants as if I might have forgotten what had happened just *moments* ago. "And look, this is a good thing. Your magic must be returning."

"*Good*?" I flailed my hands. "I'm not sure that's the word I'd use. Even if I did do it, it happened while I was unconscious."

"You have to start somewhere, and at least it's *returning*." She crossed her arms and stared me down, challenging me to contradict her.

Stan popped into my head, and my chest ached. Had he been here, he'd tell me not to look a gift horse in the mouth. He loved dropping Southern aphorisms at every opportunity.

What scared me more than anything wasn't the magic. It was that, in the dream, I'd been the Alina everyone expected. I'd felt her resolve. Whatever she'd been doing, her action hadn't only been for the fae but for the entire realm. Now I wasn't so sure I was the wrong girl, not anymore. Which made my head want to implode.

"What happened?" she asked, bringing me back to the present. "Your eyes glazed over, and you wouldn't respond. The only reason I even knew you were somewhat conscious was that I watched the plants form a chair to prevent you from falling. You said you had a dream?"

"Yeah." Then I told her everything I'd seen. As my story progressed, her expression became more and more strained. Once I reached the end, I asked, "What's wrong?"

She rubbed her temples. "I don't think that was a dream. I think that was a memory of your life before. The violet-haired woman sounds like Abba, the priestess of Terrea, who speaks and acts on the instructions of Mother Terrea, the goddess of our world. The chalice sounds like part of the sacrifice you and one woman from each of the other lands in Terrea made to save all the realms."

The urge to run the fuck away soared through me again. Training had depleted my excess energy, but learning I could actually be *Alina* petrified me more than the thought of dying. I didn't want that responsibility or burden. I wanted to go back in time and not go to Vegas. I'd give anything to be at the community gym, teaching teenagers how to protect themselves.

"Ivy, I know that look." Maeve mashed her lips together. "Running away is the worst thing you could do. Believe me. All you'll find is trouble, especially when everyone hunts for you. You can't fly, and Talamh isn't huge. Besides, we've sparred every day, and you're getting better. Your speed and reflexes are improving, which will serve you well with everything we've gone over."

"Not good enough. And I never asked for *any* of this." I didn't want what they said to be true. It had to be a dream, maybe some sort of magic juju they'd done to make me believe. "I don't want to be a prisoner."

I'd hoped that maybe I could run away and be free. But Maeve was right. For whatever reason, the fae would hunt me. Orla because she viewed me as a threat—I could see it in the way she looked at me —and the High Court because they did not want to appear as if they weren't in control. Maybe that was why they forced people to kill one another to be part of their club.

Maeve hung her head. "You have no idea how many times we had this same conversation when you were here before, but unfortunately, the responsibility still falls on you. At least, in this life, the queenship doesn't depend on you."

Tensing, I tilted my head, observing her. "Wait. Are you saying you believe I'm her and that you were here to have those conversations with former me?"

She nodded. "Since I was half human and weak, Dad trained me to be a superior warrior. Over two hundred complete season cycles ago, I joined the guard here, and I was assigned to train you to protect yourself. Royals, especially the rightful ruling monarch, have many enemies and need to be prepared to defend themselves, even with guards. Fae are ruthless creatures when they covet power."

Here I'd thought humankind was the worst of the worst.

"We were friends, weren't we?" That had to be why she'd waited for me my first night here.

"Eh, more like we came to respect one another." She smiled sadly.

That I hadn't expected. "What do you mean?"

She adjusted her bow across her armor, a tic that revealed she was uncomfortable. I wasn't sure if messing with a weapon was an assertion of power that served as a reminder she was dangerous or if she needed a reason to avert her eyes without appearing passive.

"Summer Fae aren't big fans of halflings. They prefer purebreds and perfect powers, not diluted magic. However, my dad was respected here as a High Fae, and he got me a job as a guard. You didn't like me, but because I was the best, you accepted that I was your lead guard. Eventually, you saw beyond my human half and asked me for advice from time to time. We'd meet here in secret for those conversations, so I knew it was a place you favored to hide and take a breath without someone watching you." She shrugged. "When our training got tense, you were afraid you'd fail, and you couldn't bear the thought."

Lovely. I'd been arrogant. That had to be a trait all fae had. "I'm sorry." The words slipped from my mouth. If I hadn't known better, it would've sounded like I was admitting to being Alina. "Even if I'm not her, no one should ever make you feel unworthy." I touched her arm, and she looked into my eyes. "I know you said not to thank you, so I won't. But know that in our short time together, you've been the closest thing I've had to a friend here, and you're the only person I trust."

Her bottom lip quivered as she lifted her chin. "I think warmly of you as well, but *I'm sorry* is as detrimental as *thank you* here. Never say either phrase again." She cleared her throat. "We both should go to bed. Tomorrow is going to be a long day, and you'll need your rest. Even when you aren't fighting, you'll need to pay attention to your competitors and surroundings. You'll never be safe."

I hoped this wasn't her version of a pep talk. If so, we needed to work on her skills. "I'll see you in the morning?"

"At the stone circle." She patted my arm then left, going deeper into the garden.

When she vanished, the blue lights swirled around me. I could feel the energy of their buzzing deep within my soul. The concern inside me receded some, and I forced myself to go back to my bedroom.

* * *

The next morning, I hurried to the stone circle. Maeve always beat me there, and I questioned if she ever slept.

This morning, Lilidh dressed me in armor. I wasn't sure that I preferred it to the training leather. The armor was a dark gold, similar to Maeve's, but mine had leaves woven into it. When I breathed deeply, my chest pressed against the metal, and sweat was already pooling at the nape of my neck. Wearing it while the sun beamed on me heated my skin uncomfortably.

A *whooshing* startled me. It reminded me of a bird's flapping wings, but ... bigger.

A lump formed in my throat.

Maeve had mentioned I'd be fighting someone who could fly, so I looked skyward.

Sure enough, Dallas was there. Despite the distance, our eyes met. Then he wrapped his wings around himself and dropped toward me.

I had no clue how to fight *that*—which was the point—so I went with my gut. I removed my bow from my body and nocked an arrow. When I aimed at Dallas, he was about one hundred yards away from me and closing in fast, so I did my best and loosed the arrow.

As soon as the arrow left my fingertips, I grabbed another one, nocking it as I watched the first arrow hit him in the arm.

"Icy testicles!" he growled but continued his downward spiral.

I loosed another arrow but missed him completely. The arrow soared past the stone wall, landing who knew where.

He flapped his wings, slowing his descent, and hovered over me. He grabbed the sword at his side, and I dropped the bow and removed both daggers.

When he swung with his uninjured arm, I blocked him. I expected him to fight like Maeve, but instead of pressing down, he flapped over my head and landed behind me.

Before I could fully turn around, he kicked me in the back. I stumbled forward so brutally that I barely turned my daggers to the sides before my hands and knees hit the stone.

"See—" he started, but I jumped to my feet, spun, and round kicked him in the stomach.

He flew back and landed on the ground, and I rushed over to him, dropping my daggers. I didn't need them—I would make him hurt with my hands. I went to punch him, but he shifted and swiped my legs out from under me.

Worse, I fell on top of him.

He grinned. "If you wanted to roll around with me, all you had to do was ask, not pretend you wanted to train."

I grabbed the arrow protruding from his left arm and dug it in a little more. "Not funny."

"What in frozen summer is going on out here?" Orla's shrill voice almost busted my eardrum.

I winced, guessing what this looked like to her. Apparently, blood and roughness were foreplay. Of course they were. Climbing off Dallas, I rose and found her eyes narrowed and shooting daggers at me.

"We're sparring." I gestured at the arrow in his arm. "Dallas is training me to fight High Fae."

Orla's chest heaved, and her skin turned red, contrasting with her sky-blue gown. "You need to prepare for your introduction to the Summer Court. Now. We leave shortly."

Flames engulfed her fingers, making me pause. She had fire magic, which meant her ass could fry me.

I wanted to argue, but an hour more of training wouldn't get me far. I'd have to practice in my room at night. Instead of making more of an enemy out of my sister, I nodded. "Fine. I made him bleed anyway."

"You got lucky." Dallas chuckled, and I cringed. He was making things worse between Orla and me.

"Thanks for the quick lesson." I sheathed my daggers and grabbed my bow.

The whooshing sound came again, and I glanced at Maeve. Who else had she lined up to train me?

"Secure the palace!" Maeve shouted as I glanced skyward and saw bright-green smoke soaring toward us.

What the fuck was that?

Dallas and Maeve readied their swords, so I followed suit with my bow and arrows.

"Queen Orla, we mean you no harm. It's Lord Avalon from the demon kingdom of Isramorta." A deep voice rang through the open area as the smoke stalled. "Morgana and I have come to ask a favor of you. May we join you?"

I had no clue what any of this meant, but he didn't seem too threatening with that introduction.

"A favor, you say?" Orla chuckled. "Come. Join us, but at the first sign of a threat, we will kill you without remorse."

"I'd expect nothing less," he replied as the flames extinguished around him. All that was left was the bright-green smoke.

As he descended, his glowing blue eyes were the first thing I noticed. That and the girl in his arms. When his feet touched the ground, the smoke vanished, and his long black hair settled past his shoulders. He placed the woman, who was more than a foot shorter than him, on her feet.

Something about her seemed so familiar. I should remember— she had striking purple eyes and long, wild black hair with emerald tips.

Orla stepped toward them. "What is it you need? We are about to leave for the Comortas."

"This request won't take long." Lord Avalon licked his lips and stood protectively next to the woman. "King Dacio stole some land at the corner of the Winter Court territory and has used his earth magic to create his own personal armor that isn't permeable by any demon magic or weapon, so we cannot injure him."

Demons? Could this place get any wilder? Wait. Scratch that. I didn't want to know.

"Frost sparks from it with every blow, but if we obtained some soil from the Summer Court with its fire abilities and used it against him, we could pierce his armor and defeat the king, bringing peace to our lands. Instead of taking something that isn't ours to take, as the king did, we came as a show of good faith to get your permission."

Whoa. They even had evil kings. Now *that* sounded like a badass story.

"What do we get out of this?" Orla crossed her arms and arched a brow.

Wait. Was she serious? They were talking about taking down a fucking evil king.

"The satisfaction of knowing an evil tyrant will be eliminated and no longer a threat to your lands."

She laughed. "As if he would be a threat to us. Unless you can give us something of equal value, the answer is no."

I turned my head, hoping she was joking. She was not. Her lips were pressed into a thin line, and she was scowling.

"You've got to be kidding. They could've just taken the soil. They should now just because you're being stubborn." And there went my mouth. Excellent.

"Alina," Maeve warned just as Dallas shook his head at me.

Too late. The damage was done.

Orla snarled and glared at me. "You aren't queen, so keep your mouth shut."

I'd insulted her, which meant she would be even more unwilling to help these people out.

I lifted both hands. "Fine." I strolled over to the weeping willow tree and reached up, threading my fingers through the branches hanging just over my head. It might not be ground, but the tree was still part of our nature and rooted in the Summer Court earth. Maybe this would create the same sort of abilities for them.

"Like I said, the answer is no. This sounds like a Winter Court problem." Orla expanded her wings, making her status known. "My people will watch you leave to ensure you don't take anything with you."

"I told you," Morgana whispered to Avalon and frowned.

I pulled a few leaves from the branches and fisted them in my hand. This might not help much, but I couldn't do nothing and have people get hurt and die because my sister was a jerk.

"We must get ready." Orla pointed at me. "You should go to your room. You have a big afternoon ahead of you."

I pushed off the tree a little too eagerly, and just as Avalon lifted Morgana again, I stumbled and fell into them.

"Oh, excuse me," I muttered while putting my hand on top of Morgana's, which clutched Avalon's shoulder. I slipped the leaves into her hand and winked. "I've been training hard and must have overextended myself there."

Maeve marched to me just as Morgana mouthed, *Thank you.*

I didn't wait for them to depart. Just hurried back to my room, hoping like hell I'd get some time alone.

* * *

Two hours later, I was in my bedroom, preparing to leave for the Rioghail Tower.

"I think this is the perfect dress," Lilidh said, placing a hand over her heart.

I looked in the mirror, taking in the light-green dress with leaf sleeves that hung down my upper arms. The dress was a sweetheart cut, emphasizing my cleavage, with a bunch of small white roses and thorns bunched at my waist. The front of the skirt opened slightly, revealing a light-gold underskirt, giving it more dimension.

I almost didn't recognize the woman staring back at me in the mirror. Cara hadn't done my glamour yet, but I looked like a different person ... at least to myself. My strawberry-blonde hair had light-gold tips, my irises were darkening to forest green, and my skin seemed more sun-kissed.

"It is perfect." Cara clasped her hands. "She looks very much like Alina. Now, let me add a little bit of flair to complete her look." She waved her hands like before, and my skin buzzed as the glamour slipped over my face.

I watched in amazement as my lips turned pink and my cheeks

blushed. Her glamour added a polish that made me truly seem like another person. This had to be how movie stars felt every time they glammed up for a red carpet.

Enid beamed from her spot in the corner of the room. "There won't be a single doubt about who you are."

A shiver ran down my spine. I understood that everyone expected me to be Alina, but after my conversation with Maeve, even if I was Alina's reincarnation, I didn't want to be the same version of her.

I swallowed hard, but I'd learned not to protest. It only frustrated me and whoever had paid the "compliment." I still wanted to escape this prison, but I wasn't ready. Not really. "Shouldn't we be packing things for me to use while I'm gone?" *While I'm still alive* would've been the more accurate description.

"They'll have everything you need there." Enid pursed her lips. "You'll still live a life of comfort."

I barked a laugh. "Oh, so at least I can sleep in a bed that feels like clouds before dying. How reassuring."

The three women glanced at each other. Fae couldn't lie, so if nothing else, I had that going for me.

After donning this dress, I'd sneaked into the bathroom to grab my knife and added the dagger Maeve had given me to my other thigh. I had two weapons to defend myself with.

A knock sounded on the door. Maeve entered, keeping the door open. "It's time, Your Highness."

I flinched, not liking that honorific, but we were in front of others. I nodded at the women who had been kind enough to help me, though they asked tons of questions at every opportunity. "Thank you—" I started.

Maeve hissed, reminding me of my faux pas.

All three women's eyes widened, and the smiles that quickly followed chilled me.

Maeve hadn't been kidding when she'd said not to thank anyone. Lesson learned, but unfortunately, I'd already thanked all three women.

I held back a groan. I'd be dead soon, so I wouldn't have to worry about favors.

That thought didn't actually provide any comfort, and now my armpits were sweating.

"Come on," Maeve gritted out, taking my arm and tugging me through the door.

We walked toward the dining area where we'd met the High Court Fae the night of my arrival. I kept waiting for a lecture, but Maeve didn't do anything but scowl.

Somehow, that was worse.

"Where did you disappear to after training?" I rolled my eyes, remembering how Orla had interfered.

"I had to make sure your room in Rioghail Tower was secure. I left men there to ensure nothing happened between the inspection and your arrival."

My body tightened. What threats was she expecting? I wanted to chastise her for not warning me, but I kept my mouth shut. She'd done more than enough, and I didn't need to upset her since I was leaving and there was no telling if I'd make it back.

In the dining hall, we took a right, heading in the same direction as the sexy—er, I meant the Winter King had gone. The door led to an open foyer with curving white stone stairs that swirled up several levels from the floor. Colorful flowers lined the banister, their scent perfumed and fresh.

I wanted to gawk, but Maeve led me to a large door that took us outside to the front of the castle. A lavender carriage covered in matching roses waited for us with two unicorns—unicorns! What the hell?—hitched to the carriage. One was pure white with a mane and tail of light pink, sky blue, and a color that could only be called sunshine, matching the ends of my hair. Matching flowers were woven into its hair, and its horn looked like solid gold. The other unicorn was dark teal with a mane and tail of bright sunshine, purples, and blues that reminded me of peacock feathers. Its horn matched the ice-blue color in its mane. Both were gorgeous in a completely different way.

The unicorns watched as I stepped into the carriage, and magic buzzed stronger in the air. The carriage smelled of sunshine and roses, and I sat on a lavender-cushioned seat that molded to my body.

As soon as Maeve settled across from me, the carriage jerked into motion.

Gripping the sides, I caught myself before I fell over. "What about Orla? And who's driving the carriage?" I hadn't seen anyone up front.

"She's already there, along with the High Court and the other competitors. You'll be the last to arrive."

Of course I would.

"And the unicorns know where we need to go. Why would someone guide them?" Her brows furrowed.

I didn't have the energy to reply and explain how things worked on Earth.

She must have understood because she waved a hand. "You'd best take a moment to decompress. You won't be able to breathe freely again until the end of the trial."

Not up for conversation anyway, I settled into the seat and watched this strange new world flash by.

* * *

The journey to the tower was gorgeous. Leaving Sambradh Castle, the edge of the grassy mountain range had surrounded us with warmth. As we made our way south, we passed a pond full of glistening crystal-blue water. Then a land steeped in the warmth of summer appeared, filled with trees that reminded me of dogwoods blooming with flowers in blues, pinks, whites, and purples.

We passed through a few villages with hundreds of cottages, vines covering the houses as if the wood was alive. Fae mingled and went about their business wearing loose-fitting, comfortable-looking gowns, leather vests, and peasant-like shirts and pants. I'd never thought the day would come when I would covet a loose, flowy skirt, yet here we were. It would be better than tight leather or these gowns that made breathing hard.

As we passed another bustling village, I saw what looked like a natural arena connected to a majestic stone building. At the edge of the village, the tree leaves began to change from various greens to gold, orange, and red.

Signs of fall.

When the front of the stone building came into view, I gasped. Hundreds, if not thousands, of fae were lined up on the stony ground in front of the towering three-story building, which was bigger than any shopping mall I'd ever seen.

"I told her you should've arrived first," Maeve muttered, tensing in a way I'd never seen before. "They saw other competitors arrive, noted you weren't here yet, and now more people have had time to gather for your arrival."

"They can't possibly be here for me." I shook my head. There had to be another explanation.

As our carriage approached, fae of all different complexions and hair colors converged, blocking the road. Soon, the unicorns stopped.

"Frozen summer," Maeve growled. "They can't get the carriage any farther. We'll have to walk from here."

"I'm sure it'll be fine." Once they realized I wasn't the person they were hoping for, they'd surely go away.

Drawing both swords, Maeve glanced at me. "Stay close behind me. Do *not* get separated from me."

"Sounds easy enough." I smiled reassuringly.

Maeve stepped out first, and the crowd went silent.

See.

Disappointment.

More calmly, I followed suit.

Then chaos erupted.

Nine

AS SOON AS I stepped from the carriage, a woman with long auburn hair gasped, "There she is! It's Princess Alina!"

I froze, and every gaze homed in on me.

Maeve glanced over her shoulder, her jaw clenched. Her normal composure was gone, and in its place was concern. Feeding into my panic.

My knees locked as memories of the times I and several other foster kids had been locked in a dark attic flashed through my mind.

The world around me blurred, mixing past and present, and the sounds warbled as if I'd gone underwater.

"Alina," Maeve rasped, her familiar voice ripping me back to the present. "You need to move."

Right.

Flee.

I needed to get the fuck out of here and go *home*. Fuck the fae and all this magic shit. I needed to be back at the gym and smack a punching bag in my black workout clothes.

The crowd pressed in, blocking my way back to the carriage. Hands touched my back, shoulders, and arms, tugging me in so many directions that I didn't know how I was still standing in these wobbly heels.

My mind shut down, and my vision blurred.

Maeve cursed and began using the broadside of her sword to shove people away. She then clutched my hand and tugged me forward.

Bodies circled us, and my arms were pinched and yanked. My chest tightened, and terror clawed into me. More memories filtered in of being locked in that dark attic, unable to help the younger kids, breathing that stale, stagnant air.

All those times I'd rolled my eyes at celebrities whining about the paparazzi and fans—I took it all back. I'd thought they were being dramatic and ungrateful, but they weren't. This whole situation was terrifying.

Stan's voice rang in my head. *When you're panicking, remember to breathe. Panic makes things worse. No one here is trying to hurt you. We're trying to teach you how to protect yourself, to ensure you're equipped to handle whatever is thrown at you and survive.*

He'd said those words to me when I was sixteen and began attending classes at his community MMA gym. I'd been determined to learn to defend myself and others. The start had been rough, and I'd had a few meltdowns any time an adult came near to spar with me. It had triggered something dark within me. I thought I'd overcome the trauma.

I took deep breaths to center myself. Ignoring the way people were clinging to me, I focused on putting one foot in front of the other. These people weren't trying to hurt me; they were excited to see me.

"Princess Alina!" a woman shouted from close by. "We're so glad you're alive and back with us!"

A man several feet back shouted, "It's time to crown the *real* queen."

I lifted my chin and forged on, refusing to cower. I had to overcome this debilitating feeling and face my fears.

The cheers were deafening, and as Maeve and I made headway toward the tower's entrance, I started nodding and acknowledging the people around me. Each person was full of excitement.

The crowd, with people of varying complexions and features, including hair colors I'd never seen before, intrigued me. I detected a mixture of scents with lemongrass, sandalwood, and apples, reminding me of summer. And vanilla, grass, and blossoms, reminding me of spring. I didn't detect any notes of fall or winter.

That was strange.

Though it had been minutes at most, the journey felt like it took hours. I thought I was imagining things when the faint creak of huge doors opening echoed over the crowd, followed by shouts of, "Clear a way for Princess Alina!"

That had to be the guards Maeve had left behind earlier.

I smiled but kept my chest pressed to Maeve's back. The two of us moved in tandem, and the energy of the crowd shifted. People shouted my name like before, but boos blended with the cheers.

My stomach churned as panic sank in again.

The scents shifted, changing to amber, cinnamon, pumpkin and cloves.

Smells I associated with fall and winter.

As they became dominant, the heckling grew louder. Then something wet landed on my chest.

I flinched and looked down.

Someone had spat on me!

What kind of person *did* that?

"You're going to *die*," a woman with the coldest voice I'd ever heard hissed in my ear. My pulse thundered as the magnitude of the situation settled over me.

I gritted my teeth, hating that a stranger had any impact on me. But damn ... no one had ever wished *death* on me before.

"All hail King Kieran!" another person shouted. "Let the Summer Fae die and the Winter fae bow before his greatness!"

"Frozen summer," Maeve snarled, spinning and jabbing the edge of her sword into the stomach of a fae about to hawk more spit at me.

Blue blood spilled from the man's guts, but his sinister pale-gray eyes remained locked on me. "Long live the true fae king!"

The people closest to me cheered thunderously, the ground quaking under my feet. Walking in heels over the stone was hard enough, but add in the rolling ground, and sitting on the ground and scooting on my ass might've been the safest way to get to the front door.

"Alina is the true queen who will unite the lands," a Summer Fae yelled from behind us. Then I felt the crowd shift.

Fights broke out as the two sides clashed, and Maeve grabbed my hand and pulled me to her side. We'd been moving slow and steady, but now Maeve swung her sword at the people in front of us, and we pushed forward.

My chest heaved as I struggled to get enough oxygen, or whatever the hell I breathed now, my lungs straining against the tight dress that might as well have been a corset.

Bodies slammed into me, and I twisted my ankle, unable to stay upright in these stiletto heels. The guards hadn't reached us, and despite Maeve slicing at fae with her sword, more came through and blocked the way.

This was it. This was how I'd die. I wouldn't even make it to the Comortas.

A booming, ice-cold voice demanded, "Stop this!"

Something inside me *tugged* as if urging me to run to him.

The Winter King.

I hated that I recognized the sound of his voice and the way my body reacted to his deep baritone.

The Winter fae stilled, but the Summer Fae didn't freeze. After all, he wasn't their king.

This was completely ridiculous.

"My people, stop this madness as well," Orla commanded, but her voice lacked the ferocity of King Kieran's.

Nonetheless, it had a similar effect as the Summer Fae calmed as well.

I didn't understand how there could be such hatred between the two groups, but hell, I was only human. If I asked, they'd probably provide a dissertation.

"Sire, she should be dead." A woman with jet-black hair and the palest skin I'd ever seen wrinkled her nose and glared at me. "And she shouldn't be the reason our kingdom survived those awful golems and kept our lands from dying. It should've been you or Prince Nolan!"

I winced, wondering if I'd misunderstood. Were these people upset that a Summer Fae had sacrificed herself to save the realm and been reincarnated? They wanted their king or next in line to have sacrificed himself instead?

Orla flipped her fiery-red hair over her shoulder, the ends hitting her golden dress and reminding me of a candle. "Neither King Kieran nor Prince Nolan was strong enough to restore the balance. Not like the Summer Fae princess."

Nope. I hadn't misunderstood. They were upset because Alina was viewed as stronger. Yeah, well, they needed to take a hard look at me now. I didn't have magic, I couldn't fly, and I couldn't move as fast as any of them. I fit in on Earth, not here. This second life had been a horrible mistake on someone's part.

"Don't forget you weren't chosen." The pale woman bobbed her head from side to side, the hem of her black dress brushing the stone. "It was your *sister*. When our king slays her, it'll prove that Mother Terrea should've chosen him. He'll take down the chosen one."

I laughed. In the past few excruciatingly long minutes, I'd been treated like a celebrity, hated like a politician, and called the chosen one. If I hadn't been stuck here for a week already, I would've been certain this was a dream. Or a movie.

The Winter fae turned their frigid attention to me, their nearly translucent irises devoid of feeling.

Now some of the Summer Fae's curses made sense to me.

"You can't kill my *sister*." Orla crossed her arms, staring King Kieran down. "She's a competitor and protected now that she's arrived at the tower." She gestured for me to walk the final twenty feet to the stairs and stand beside her.

"She hasn't made it there yet," a Winter fae shouted.

Quinley marched out of the open doors and stopped beside King Kieran.

Kaley followed, taking the spot next to Orla, and Eamon stepped up to Kaley's other side. Two more Winter fae joined Quinley, flanking her, and Caden appeared on the Winter end.

Standing rigid, Quinley seemed like a goddess in the silver gown that complemented her flawless features. "Since Alina's return and Muir's magic became part of nature again, times have been trying for us. However, it's fae law not to hurt a royal even if they aren't your court's ruling family. The only exception is if they pose an active threat to you, your family, or our land."

Maeve placed a hand on the center of my back, guiding me forward toward the High Fae Court, Orla, and King Kieran. As soon as I began walking, I had to stop myself from running away from the crowd. I wasn't sure if the tournament would be as hard as getting here had been. Fewer people, even if they were trying to kill me, would be preferable to *this*.

"She *is* threatening me." The woman sneered, her inky, crystal-like eyes watching me. "Her mere presence is the problem." She smacked the back of her hand against her other palm.

Uh ... did she just threaten to spank me? I hoped that spanking would be considered hurting, but I didn't know with these people. They seemed to like pain.

Someone beside the woman gasped, and I realized I did *not* understand the meaning. Not wanting to be the only one without a secret code, I raised my middle finger high. *Take that, bitch.*

Everyone who saw the gesture stared up at the sky.

"What is she pointing to?" someone asked loudly. "I don't see a heated thing."

King Kieran cocked his head, his blue eyes searing my soul. I couldn't read the emotion behind them, but his body language indicated I intrigued him, which warmed my body very inappropriately.

I wrapped my arms around myself, and something cool trickled down between my breasts. I glanced down and wished I hadn't. As suspected, someone had spat on me.

Acid burned the back of my throat.

Schooling my expression, I kept my head high as Maeve and I joined the others on the platform. The worst thing I could do was react to the blatant sign of disrespect. That was one thing having foster parents had taught me—bullies loved to see their victims squirm.

I was done making people like that feel more powerful.

"She has reached the tower." King Kieran scanned the crowd, taking in each section slowly. "Not only is she now the Summer Court Princess but an official competitor in the Comortas. No one outside of the contestants can harm her from this point forward."

"We can't wait to see you kill her, my king," a man with luxurious pale-blue hair exclaimed.

My brows furrowed, and I stepped closer to Maeve. "They mean Prince Nolan, right?" That was the name of the man they all expected to beat me.

"That's part of what the early morning meeting was about," Maeve murmured. "Prince Nolan was injured last night during a training exercise. King Kieran is taking his place."

My breath caught. This had to be a joke. Even being close to him made me feel funny.

"The first trial begins tomorrow morning when the moons take their rest." Kaley spread her arms. "We will introduce the twenty contestants before the lute thrums."

I had no clue what that meant, but I would find out soon enough.

"Let's go inside and allow the contestants to meet formally and have sustenance before settling in for the night." Quinley gestured at the gigantic door.

King Kieran was the first to move, and when Orla took a step to walk beside him, he shook his head. He then extended his arm toward me.

My heart leaped into my throat at the thought of touching him. A part of me was desperate to feel each curve of his muscles, while the other side knew he posed an immense danger to me.

"Please, join me," he said and smiled.

My head went foggy.

"Don't trust him," Maeve whispered in my ear. "He's the most ruthless of them all and a competitor."

Unsure what to do without causing more issues, I slid my arm through his, and a weird energy churned inside me. I was fairly certain it wasn't magic, but I didn't know what else it could be.

The two of us stepped inside the building—fortress?—and I took in the golden walls and stairwell that circled the entire center space of the lobby to the two floors above us. At the top of the ceiling hung an enormous icicle chandelier that stopped at the bottom of the second floor. Four green couches surrounded the chandelier, and a large pink rose plant grew in the circle.

More modern than Orla's castle, the room seemed designed for royalty. But my chest ached. I missed the flowers that had surrounded me in the Sambradh Castle.

Out of the corner of my eye, I saw Kieran's hands slide under his charcoal black suit, and Maeve's warning replayed.

We were competitors … and he could kill me at any time.

Ten

MY BREATHING HITCHED as I reached under my skirt and removed the green-vine dagger. As I straightened, prepared to stab, he swung his sword under my chin, stopping with the blade against my neck. Not wanting to be the only casualty, I pressed the point of my dagger against his chest, ready to strike.

There was a faint sting where his blade had nicked my skin, and warmth trickled down my neck.

My blood.

His gaze homed in there, his brows furrowing as if he were debating how to end my life.

I needed to strike first.

But something prevented me from finishing him.

A low growl escaped me when his gaze locked with mine. For a moment, his icy irises thawed, and I became uncomfortably warm. Then, the corners of his mouth turned down.

Something coiled inside me, nearly springing me closer to him. The idea of rubbing my body all over him like a cat in heat popped into my mind. Luckily, his sword was at my neck, preventing me from following through.

Wait.

Did I legit think *luckily*?

Something was *very* wrong with me.

Orla's heels clicked against the smooth floor, but I refused to tear my attention away from him. If he struck, I'd take him with me. I had the dagger aimed at his heart, and I'd have enough time to finish him. We could be like fucking Romeo and Juliet, dying together ... but without the romance.

"What in summer's green grass is going on here?" Orla almost squeaked.

Lifting a brow, King Kieran answered, "I'm not sure. I was retrieving a handkerchief from my inside pocket when Princess Alina decided to draw her dagger." He raised the hand that wasn't holding his sword, and there he clutched a pale-blue handkerchief. "I thought she might want to wipe off the spit that's sliding between her breasts."

My face burned, and my heart skipped. The fact that he'd noticed the spit had reached my cleavage had me feeling all sorts of things, and I didn't want to analyze what any of it meant.

Despite wanting to hang my head, I refused. I recalled a time I'd thought I'd put a bully in her place, and when I'd turned to leave, she'd yanked my hair for not giving her my lunch. The stakes here were far higher, and I wouldn't make that mistake again.

"You can't kill each other yet," Quinley huffed and came to our side. She flicked her hands between King Kieran and me. "You have to wait until the first tournament begins—when everyone has been introduced."

I snorted, and King Kieran flinched. He stared at me as if I'd done something strange.

Clearly, snorting wasn't proper etiquette here, which made me do it again.

"What is she *doing*?" Leanna wrinkled her nose. "Is she dying before the trials even start? How would we handle that? We just formally announced her participation!"

"Maybe if the Winter King would remove the sword from her

neck, it would help her to breathe," Maeve said scathingly as she prepared to wield her own swords to protect me.

"I'll remove it once she drops her weapon." One side of his mouth tipped upward in a crooked grin.

That grin could easily be my undoing.

If I were interested in him, that was, which I wasn't. I was merely admiring his rugged good looks. They wouldn't make me lose my head ... more.

I lifted my chin. Though, with a blade at my neck, I doubted it showed confidence. "After you lower yours."

"Maybe you're smarter than I gave you credit for." He huffed. "Then let's do it together. After all, two royals should be able to *trust* each other. Right?"

The question held a hidden meaning. He had a look in his eye that some of my foster parents had had when trying to trick me. But I was clueless about what he meant. "We *should* be able to, but we both know that'll never happen."

"Alina!" Orla laughed a little too loudly. "There's no reason to be rude. All fae know the royals only have what's best for their people at heart in any decision they make."

I rolled my eyes. "I wasn't being rude. I was being honest and answering his question." I wouldn't call her out on her stupid last sentence, which pretty much said we couldn't trust each other, but in a more convoluted way. I preferred to be direct and simple, without fluff, especially when speaking to someone I didn't like or trust.

King Kieran winced, but his face smoothed so quickly that I might have imagined it.

"Shall we?" He tilted his head. "Or do you want to continue to stand like this?"

We had witnesses, and if I didn't oblige, this moment would become awkward. I sucked in a breath. "Fine. On the count of three?"

"Oh, we're counting?" His eyes twinkled. "Is that how humans handle such matters?"

"Most humans don't find themselves in situations like this. The ones who did, I stayed far away from, but unfortunately, I can't do that here." That was why I'd lived in the community gym, away from everything.

He leaned forward, pressing his chest harder against the tip of my dagger. He whispered, "It's not only here at the tournament. Everyone's like this in Talamh." He watched my face, searching for a reaction.

I forced my expression to remain neutral. I didn't want to give him what he wanted. But the only people in this realm who didn't seem interested in harming me were my three attendants, Maeve and Dallas, and I wasn't thrilled about that last name.

"One." I lifted a brow in challenge.

He smirked.

That reaction was good enough for me. "Two." My stomach clenched, and my heart pounded against my rib cage. I hoped I wasn't making a horrible decision. "Three."

We stepped away from each other and lowered our weapons. After all the grandstanding, I'd suspected he would step back, but I didn't trust him or anyone else here, for that matter, including *my sister*.

I hiked up my skirt and slid the weapon back in place while the king sheathed his sword. When both of us were settled, he held out the handkerchief again.

I considered snubbing him, but I really did want to wipe off the spit and now the blood. I reached for the cloth, our fingers almost touching, and he dropped the handkerchief and shuffled quickly away, desperate not to touch me.

I caught the handkerchief before it could hit the floor, then straightened, body taut, and allowed my words to drip with sarcasm. "*Tha—*"

"Princess *Alina*," Maeve interjected, her tone tense.

I flinched. She'd saved me from saying thanks. That was almost the second time I'd made the mistake *today*. If Kieran didn't kill me soon, Maeve would for my carelessness.

"Shouldn't you clean yourself?" she added. "Before you meet the others."

"No, please." King Kieran lifted a hand and stepped toward me. "Finish what you were going to say."

I raised his handkerchief. "That's clean, right?" Maybe not the smoothest transition, but it *could* be what I'd been about to say.

"Of course. Only the best for a *princess*," he said warmly, but I didn't miss the ice in his eyes.

"Perfect." I looked down, ready to wipe the spit away, then noticed blue liquid slowly dripping down my chest. My mouth tasted sour as I quickly wiped it and the spit away, not wanting to think about what the color meant.

"Easy," Maeve said, moving in front of me. She took the handkerchief and dabbed my neck. "You don't want to prevent your blood from clotting."

The world tilted under my feet, and I used Maeve's shoulder for balance. This couldn't be happening.

"Is something wrong?" Eamon asked with concern. "Did King Kieran poison his blade?"

"Don't be a hothead." King Kieran crossed his arms. "The tournament hasn't even officially started. I wouldn't cheat."

"You Winter fae think you're above the law." Orla strolled over and examined my wound. "Especially when you currently have a majority on the High Court. Not that you will for long. You're just lucky that it's in your favor. Otherwise, we wouldn't have accepted you as a substitute for Prince Nolan."

"Anyone from the royal line can enter," Quinley said as she sashayed over to stand by King Kieran. "He arrived before any other competitors joined us and made a last-minute change because of unforeseen circumstances. I'm not saying I agree with the change. The substitute should have been Princess Brianne, but the decision is ultimately his to make."

I was so sick of the bickering. Anytime these two sides came together, it was one pissing match after another. They were so focused on presenting themselves as more important or powerful than the other that nothing got accomplished. Politics here were just as convoluted as back on Earth.

"After being spat on and wounded, I'd love to get settled and bathed and into fresh clothes." I felt dirty, and I'd also love some time alone. I'd never been around people like this for so long.

Orla relaxed as if I'd said something right. "That's an excellent idea. We all need to go outside and ensure our people have listened then go back to our castles so the public knows all the competitors are situated and won't be seen until tomorrow."

"Since Prince Nolan can't be here, Leanna and I can handle it." Caden beamed, looking thrilled to be able to wield more power.

King Kieran nodded. "That's fine. Just get them to disperse. We don't need anything else to happen before the trial begins."

Lowering her hand from my neck, Maeve nodded toward the golden stairway. "Let's go to your room, and I'll check it one more time since we've all been distracted."

"Under the circumstances, we'll allow it, but after this check, she's on her own." Quinley tossed her hair over her shoulder.

I hadn't even considered that I might be rooming with other competitors. I was definitely relieved to learn I'd have the nights to myself.

"Understood." Maeve clutched the handkerchief and strode to the stairs. "I won't be longer than a few minutes."

Orla threw her arms around me and pulled me into a hug. She murmured, "Be safe, sister."

The gesture must have appeared sincere because Kaley placed a hand over her heart, but I wasn't fooled. Orla's arms were stiff, and I knew this game. I'd been raised by people who'd pretended to care about me in front of others when it benefited them.

I patted her back, playing along, but I had no doubt Orla wanted me dead, especially after my reception by the Summer Fae outside. I was a threat to her even if I didn't want the throne.

These people couldn't get past their own egos.

When Orla released me, my traitorous body had me glancing at King Kieran, and we locked gazes again.

He'd been watching me.

"I'll come get you when dinner is ready." Kaley bowed her head slightly to me. "Remember, it's a night of relaxation before the big day."

"Tha—t's nice." This time, I stopped myself, but damn, I had to break my particularly horrible habit of polite responses.

As I followed Maeve, I could feel the others' attention on me. I wasn't narcissistic; I could feel the hairs on the nape of my neck rise. All my life, I'd avoided being noticed. Now I had everyone's attention, and it was growing worse by the minute.

I ran my hand along the golden banister, needing to ground myself. When we reached the second floor, my jaw dropped. This hallway was *all* gold, much like downstairs, with five doors on each side, right across from each other. An archway bowed over each door, every arch covered with flowers that reminded me of summer and spring: begonias, amaryllis, clematis, roses, and impatiens of all colors. The sweet floral scent eased my stress and made it easier to breathe.

Maeve tromped all the way down to the last thick wooden door on the left. She removed a key made of vines with pink, green, and blue flowers intertwined within it and unlocked the door.

I stepped inside, taking in everything.

The room wasn't as large as the one at Orla's castle, but it was big enough for a bed and two sky-blue velvet chairs. Every inch of the space looked summery. I drew in a deep, calming breath.

"Keep this key on you at all times." Maeve shut the door and handed me the item. "The fae can glamour it and make a copy."

Any sense of comfort the surroundings had provided vanished. "You're acting like they'll try to kill me here and not wait for the trial."

"That's *exactly* what I'm telling you." Maeve closed my fingers around the key. "Once the trial begins, even killing someone in their sleep isn't off the table. That's why you *must* make sure you keep your door and windows locked and your blinds closed at all times."

I sat on the bed, which was just as soft as the one back at the castle. I ran my hands across the silky lilac blanket. "Don't worry. I want to survive for as long as possible."

She held my gaze. "You are a warrior, and you have it in you to win this. You've got to stop thinking you're human and embrace your magic side."

"I *am* human." I patted my chest. "Even if I have blue blood and can manipulate vines. I was raised on Earth, and one week of training won't change me."

"If you stop fighting your nature, everything will come back to you faster." Maeve placed her hands on my shoulders. "Trust me, I see the magic within you. It sparks off you when you're in the garden, and especially when you're alone. You just have to open yourself to it."

"You're desperate to see something that's not there. I fear that I'm going to disappoint you after you've invested so much in me."

Her brown eyes warmed. "Just promise me that, during the trial, you won't be so close-minded. That you'll do everything in your power to win. That's how you can repay me for helping you train. *That's* the favor I want in return."

After everything she'd done, how could I not promise her that? "I promise."

Her body relaxed. "Good, but make no more promises to anyone else. Death is the only way out." She nodded, dropping her hands and taking a step back. "I don't feel anyone's presence, but I'll take a quick look and then head downstairs. I'll be back to visit you as soon as I can, and I'll be there to watch the trial tomorrow."

"I'll see you then." I didn't want her to go, but it was better if she left. I'd only put her in more danger.

While she moved to the closet and glanced through it, I stared out the window next to the bed. She headed into the bathroom, and I took in the full, vibrant trees outside the window and noted some fae strolling through the parklike area and talking. The view was breathtaking but made me feel more like a prisoner.

When Maeve came back out, she went to the door. "Lock this behind me. And remember your promise."

"Yes, ma'am," I teased.

She gave me a tense smile and left.

For the first time since I'd arrived, I felt truly alone.

* * *

I didn't know how long I stayed in the bathtub, but the warmth was so comforting that I struggled to get out of the water, which resulted in me having to rush to get ready because I had no damn clue when dinner was. The sun was already setting, so I knew it had to be soon. The day had gotten away from me.

My closet was full of dresses and armor. I didn't even see any nightgowns, so bedtime would be interesting.

I'd sleep in my underwear if need be.

I donned a golden lace gown that was the most comfortable thing I'd worn since arriving in this world.

A knock sounded on my door. "Your Highness," a strange voice called. "Kaley sent me to retrieve you for dinner. She was detained for a discussion with the High Court, and they're waiting for your arrival."

I made sure my dagger and knife were secured to my thigh then snatched the key before strolling to the door. Maeve had said that no one could kill me until tomorrow, but at the first sign of something strange, I wouldn't hesitate to defend myself.

I opened the door to find a woman who appeared close to my age, although all the fae appeared to be in their twenties. Her long brown hair was pulled back, and she wore a simple green blouse and leather pants. Her cobalt eyes widened when she scanned me.

"I didn't mean to rush you." She gestured at my room behind me. "I can wait while you finish getting ready."

I turned and glanced in the mirror. I didn't look horrible and was wearing a dress instead of slacks. Maybe my resting bitch face was rearing its head? I'd trained my face to always have that expression to scare people away. "I'm ready. No worries."

"Oh, okay." She scratched the back of her neck as I locked the door and slid the key into my bra.

The two of us walked in silence, and soon we were back on the first floor, heading to a room next to the entrance.

As soon as she swung open the double doors, people looked our way. The conversation died instantly.

Eleven

BETWEEN THE GRANDEUR of the room and the two long rectangular tables that seated everyone, I wasn't sure where to focus: on the people staring at me or on the room, which was a mixture of ice sculptures and flowers.

The tug deep within my soul pulled my gaze to King Kieran, who sat at the head of the closest table with his back to me, a woman on either side of him. He glanced over his shoulder, his eyes capturing mine before slowly dipping to scan my body.

I flushed very inappropriately despite the chill from the ice sculptures of mountains and flowers in the middle of his table.

"All right, Princess Alina." The fae woman who'd led me here bowed. "Please take your seat. Dinner will be served soon." She scurried off, leaving me alone in front of all these strangers, my heart thudding.

"Oh, my sun." The woman sitting closest to me and next to Kieran smiled and quickly covered her luscious red lips with her hand. "This is very surprising."

"Well, Rowan, what did you expect from a human princess?" The other woman with hair as dark as the night sky chuckled. "She won't last beyond the first trial."

My jaw ached from how hard I gritted my teeth together. I

hated people making fun of me, most of all because I knew what that meant.

I was a target.

I should've known.

I'd hoped they'd disregard me completely.

Worse, I had no idea what they were ridiculing. Sure, my dress was more casual than theirs. They'd chosen to wear the constrictive corset style that I could barely breathe in.

King Kieran turned in his seat, and the warmth in his eyes ignited my blood.

"Princess Alina, maybe you should go back to your room and change?" He arched a brow, the corners of his lips tipping downward.

Just like that, it was as if I'd been dunked in cold water. My heart ached as if his words had been actual weapons that had hurt me.

Though his agreement with the women's ridicule did hurt, I shouldn't have been surprised. He was the *Winter King*, and I was a princess of *Summer*.

The other seven people at the table smirked. They must all be Winter fae.

As if confirming what I'd suspected, I noted that the table behind them had fresh flowers, the kind that grew throughout the Sambradh Castle. Seeing those flowers eased the knot in my stomach, and I realized how tense I'd been.

There was one seat open at the end of the table of flowers, which would give me a direct view of Kieran once I sat.

Lovely.

I had to force my feet to remain still instead of fleeing back to my room.

Leaving them after their insults would only make me appear weaker than they already considered me. Even though the tournament hadn't started, Maeve had been tense, meaning threats were all around. The way my skin crawled validated that, in all ways that counted, the Comortas had begun.

Knowing that the longer I stood there, the more gawking they'd do and the more insults they'd toss my way, I forced myself to go to the one vacant chair. With more distance between King Kieran and me, my lungs filled more easily. Being near him muddied my head and chased all reason away.

Before I could sit, the doors opened. Kaley entered and came to me. "Princess Alina, I need you to join me for a moment before you eat."

My mouth went dry, and my throat tightened. This couldn't be anything good, but at least it would get me away from all the stares so I could regain my composure.

Her brow arched, and her nose wrinkled as she scrutinized my appearance. I would have to own whatever was setting off all these reactions, or I'd never live it down.

Standing as straight as possible, I followed Kaley back into the entrance hall, where the other four High Court members were huddled. Quinley wore her classic scowl and had a round mirror in her hands.

Were they seriously going to force me to look in the mirror to make a point about my wardrobe or whatever the problem was?

Caden and Leanna glanced at one another, doing the weird communication thing they did, while Eamon beamed and said, "You're more exquisite than I ever dared imagine."

My face was now on fire.

An unfamiliar, deep, rumbly voice asked, "Is the girl finally here? For the love of Terrea, just put her in the mirror."

Mirror? Of course. They didn't have phones here.

Without hesitation, I hurried to Quinley and looked into the mirror. I gasped. Instead of my reflection, I saw a girl who vaguely looked like Ember and a handsome man with navy-blue hair and eyes and a strong jawline.

He looked me over and quirked his eyebrow faintly like he was attempting to hide his disgust. "Do you not provide clothing for your pets, or does she choose to wear her sleeping garments during the day?"

If possible, my face flamed hotter. I was wearing a nightgown? No wonder everyone was laughing and it was so damn comfortable.

Maybe-Ember glared at him. "Leave Ivy alone. She likes to be comfortable. Not all of us like to dress like an extra from *The Lord of the Rings* every time we leave our rooms."

Yeah, that was Ember, all right, yet it was hard to believe. Weight lifted from my shoulders from seeing her healthy and acting like herself. Her hair glowed like fire, and she had golden tattoos that I couldn't make out from here. Her black, flowy dress blended with what appeared to be dark shadows behind her.

Then, just like that, the man vanished as if he'd become a shadow himself.

Weird.

"Thank God you're all right," I gasped. "I've been worried ever since I realized this wasn't a prank you were playing on me. I *told* you and Isa we shouldn't have gone to that party!" I rolled my eyes, letting my frustration out, then stopped. "Wait. Isa. Is she okay?"

"As far as I know," she said sadly. "She wasn't with me."

My heart dropped into my stomach. Isa and Stan would search for us relentlessly. "She must be so worried. Stan, too. They'll blame themselves for what happened to us."

Ember's face fell. She glanced beside her, in the general direction of where the man had been, then turned back to face me, squaring her shoulders like she was bracing herself. "She doesn't remember us," she said with a rueful shake of her head. "None of them do. Not her or Stan or anyone. It's part of the *isos*—the magic surrounding who we are."

I rubbed my chest to ease my aching heart. I wasn't sure how I felt about Stan just forgetting about us, but it was better than the alternative, and I needed to focus on the most important part.

We were safe. Isa hadn't received a golden ticket; she'd come along with Ember for fun, so she was likely just fine. "Are *you* okay?"

"I'm okay. Better than being dead! Are you?" Ember bit her bottom lip. "I've been worried."

"About the same as you." I smirked, throwing her words back at her. "Maybe soon, the two of us could visit and remember *them*." Isa meant to Ember what Stan meant to me.

"Okay." Quinley jerked the mirror away and waved her hand over the glass, and Ember disappeared. "They got to see each other and know they're okay. Now we have High Court business to attend to."

I gritted my teeth, liking Quinley less and less. "You could've let me say goodbye."

"And have the elves learn we are down a High Court member? Not a chance." Quinley gestured to the dining hall doors. "Go eat."

I wanted to tell her what she could eat, but it was best not to piss off someone who was in charge of the trials that would lead to my death.

Spinning on my heels, I marched back into the dining hall, where snickers echoed through the room, bouncing off the golden walls and smooth stone. Despite my momentary absence, they were still laughing at my expense.

I didn't understand what was so funny about the nightgown. It was comfortable and pretty—all the things you wanted when preparing to devour a meal. I lifted my chin and stalked back to my seat as if I always dined in nightwear.

At my table, I couldn't help but notice that even my own people were giving me funny stares.

When my gaze landed on the man next to the empty chair at the head, I froze.

Forest-green eyes stared back at me, sending me back to my first fighting lesson with Maeve. He was one of Dallas's friends who'd watched me train.

My back went rigid, and I hurried to take the vacant seat.

"Good evening, Princess Alina," the man said cordially. "I hope your nap was refreshing, though I'm surprised you didn't bother to change."

I huffed out a breath and lifted my head. For a moment, I focused on the vine chandelier hanging over the Summer table. It was filled with gorgeous fae flowers. The icicle chandelier over the Winter fae table was twice as big as if they'd had to make theirs bigger.

That sounded about right.

Blowing out a breath, I kept my voice steady as I said, "I didn't take a nap."

"You purposely wore your nightgown to dinner?" a soft voice tinkled from a woman on the left side of the table.

A knot twisted in my stomach. Though she appeared to be my age, she was petite and small. Her large, innocent sky-blue eyes reminded me of a foster sister I'd known what felt like a lifetime ago. Beth was one of the girls I'd failed to help.

"Princess?" Dallas's friend said, bringing me back to the present.

I shook my head, trying to ground myself in the moment. "Of course." I stared down at my dress, which did look and feel similar to the dresses they'd given me for bedtime at the palace, but the skirt on this one was floor length and fuller. I'd thought it was a legitimate dress. Who slept in a fucking fluffy gown?

Fae. That was who.

What was wrong with these people?

Worse, I was the one they were making fun of, not the other way around. If I made it clear that this had been an accident, things would only get worse.

"I wanted to be comfortable," I told the woman. I had to fight to keep my shoulders from slumping, and it was a damn war. I couldn't believe I hadn't put that together on my own. There was only one way to throw off the ridicule—I needed to distract them with something they coveted. "We're going into battle tomorrow, so why not have a night of comfort? The clothes here are damn uncomfortable compared to clothes in *my* world." I emphasized *my*, hoping the implication that Earth clothing was superior to fae clothing would throw them off.

"Oh." The small girl clapped her hands. "I'd love to hear all about—"

"Moire," the woman across from the petite woman said with an adoring smile. "If the princess wishes to relax, pestering her with questions about Earth will do the opposite." She flipped her lavender locks over her shoulder, and her bright-violet eyes sparkled. Her gold dress clung to her curves and made her dark skin look radiant. "Take a deep breath, and then maybe we'll have a chance to ask about her time on Earth before she dies."

I visibly winced. The woman had said the words without malice, but to hear my death spoken about so flippantly had caught me off guard.

Moire pouted. "Fine, but if I don't get any answers, I'll haunt your magic when you pass back to nature, Catrina."

This feisty, petite woman had just proclaimed herself as the winner, and I liked her more for it. If only Beth had been the same. Maybe she wouldn't have ended up in prison.

"Princess, you have someone watching you," the woman on my other side whispered as she leaned toward me. Her hair reminded me of cinnamon, as did her scent. Under the table, she gestured toward the other end of the room.

Without thinking it through, I looked and locked eyes with none other than King Kieran.

I hated the way my body tensed in response. I didn't want to react to him.

I forced a smile, throwing Catrina's caution to the wind. "You know what? Let's talk about Earth."

Even the five Summer Fae who were silently watching shifted forward, so I launched into my story.

* * *

My throat hurt. That was how much I'd talked during dinner. The only break had been when Eamon and Kaley had stopped by to wish us each good luck. From then on, our whole table slowly became louder, everyone peppering me with questions. I'd scarcely had time to enjoy the sweet, amazing fruit juice and the breads, honey, and chocolate.

The Winter fae all stood up, but I had no intention of leaving. Not yet. This was the most fun I'd had since arriving in Talamh— since I could last remember if I was being honest.

I lifted my golden flute, my hand waving as the world tilted around me, signaling for Dallas's friend to refill it again since he'd placed the golden pitcher out of my reach.

"Of course, Your Highness," he cooed, lifting the pitcher.

Then, the most intoxicating smell swirled around me—crisp, clean snow.

"She's had enough," King Kieran said coldly. He took the flute from my hand and set it on the table. "We all need to be presentable in the morning."

"We're talking about Earth!" I reached for my flute, refusing to let him control me, but I missed it.

Huh. That was strange. He must have been using magic voodoo on me.

Refusing to admit defeat, I reached for it again, but it disappeared.

My head jerked toward him. He held it in his hand once more.

The prick.

"Stop using your fast fae juju on me." I exhaled, my stomach so full of drink and food that I feared someone might be forced to roll me out of here. "And just move like a damn person."

King Kieran sighed. "I don't know what juju is, so I can promise I did nothing of the sort. Now, let me help you to your room so you'll have time to sleep this off before tomorrow."

I snorted. "Like I would trust you. You're the *Winter King*."

"You're right. You shouldn't trust me, nor should you trust the people sitting before you." He set the flute back on the table and slid my seat out with me still in it. "Stand up and let's go."

Dallas's friend shot to his feet. "I can take her." He took my hand, pulling me to my feet.

The world tilted, and I realized I was drunk.

No.

Plastered.

How the fuck had that happened? I always stayed away from anything that dulled my senses ... well, except for the Halloween party drink, and look where that had landed me.

"There's no need, Curry," King Kieran said, shoving him into the window behind me. "I can take her from here."

"I'm fine." I needed to get to my room by myself. I didn't need them to see how bad off I was. "I'll go there myself." I took my first step, and I fell.

I braced myself for impact.

Instead, strong, muscular arms wrapped around my back and belly and pulled me against a brick-hard chest. Heat flooded my body, especially between my legs. *That* wasn't normal. It had to be due to the alcohol in my system.

A cool breath hit the back of my neck, followed by a low growl.

Holy shit. If I thought I'd been hot before, I was now a fucking inferno about to combust. And he wasn't even touching me inappropriately. Clearly, I needed to get laid and fast. And not by him ... unless—

"Are you going to try to stand again?" His breath hit my ear.

Oh, right. I was leaning into him, not even trying to move away. Enemies and competitors shouldn't want to touch each other. I needed to remember Maeve's words before it was too late.

With as much dignity as I could muster, I straightened and took slow, steady steps toward the door. It was tricky. The floor kept moving on me.

"You all should be ashamed of yourselves," King Kiernan muttered as he followed behind me.

"I ... I didn't do that to her," the woman with the cinnamon hair stuttered.

King Kieran's laugh was cruel. "By not stopping Curry, you're as guilty as he is."

Stopping Curry. He'd kept refilling my drink before it ever got empty, but I hadn't thought much about it because the juice was delicious. I hadn't realized it was alcohol. I couldn't believe how foolish I'd been. I *never* let my guard down, and the one time I did, it was with people I'd be fighting the next day. Being hungover would embarrass me more before I died publicly.

My eyes burned. I'd been so careless. Ever since I was sixteen and found Stan, I'd sworn I'd never become a victim. That I could be smarter than the bullies. But on my first night here and alone, I hadn't seen the signs. Hadn't even looked for them.

I'd stumbled into the hallway and was preparing to ascend the stairs when King Kieran caught up to walk beside me.

I waited for a condescending comment or a joke, but he didn't say a word. He merely kept the pace I set without one complaint. This was strange. No one here ever let me be. They were either warning me of things, talking strategy, or peppering me with questions about anything and everything.

Being with someone in silence was one of the nicest things I'd experienced since arriving here.

At the stairway, he gestured for me to go ahead of him.

"You'll be faster, and I'm sure you're in a hurry to head to your room," I said slowly to make sure I didn't slur a single word. I needed to retain some dignity.

"After what happened at dinner, I think it's best if I ensure you make it to your room before retiring to mine." He placed a hand on the center of my back and guided me forward. "I'll be right here, so don't worry about falling."

I shouldn't trust him, but I found myself obeying. I clutched the banister with one hand and took the steps one by one. Thankfully, we didn't pass anyone else. After what felt like hours of the hardest workout of my entire life, I made it to the top.

My head had cleared a little, and I wobbled to my door and started fishing the key out of my cleavage. When I glanced up, my jaw dropped because King Kieran had a smile on his face. It was breathtaking. If I'd thought he was handsome before, it was nothing compared to this moment. The frost was gone, and he showed no restraint.

Which meant I had to be plastered because I was seeing things.

"Are you always so ..." He trailed off, his brow furrowing as he searched for the right word. "Tasteful?"

I scoffed and lifted the key from my bra. "First off, this is a highly functional storage place. With a bra this tight, nothing will ever fall out of it. And second, if someone tries to get the key, I'll know."

"Even when they're refilling your spirits so generously?" He arched a brow, the smile still blinding.

"You're so hand—" I cut myself off, but not in time. I swallowed.

His brows arched higher.

I needed to shut this down and get in my room, stat. I cleared my throat. "You're so handy to have around to get me out of a pickle."

"Pickle?" His face fell. "What's that?"

"Just a delicious vegetable from Earth." Was it a vegetable? It was a cucumber, but it had seeds. From what I remembered, anything with seeds was technically a fruit. At this point, I was drunk and rambling. "Anyway, I didn't know the drink was spirits. I thought it was juice. It tasted like water but a little sweeter."

"I'm sure you won't forget the taste now." He leaned against the wall, studying me.

That strange tugging returned, urging me to close the distance. His gaze landed on my lips, and I licked them, giving in to the tug as I reached for his hand.

He jerked back, putting ten feet between us.

My face burned, and I wanted to die right then and there. I had totally misread the situation, and it wasn't completely the alcohol's fault. It wasn't my imagination—there was something sizzling between us.

"You need to get some rest." He gestured to the door then thrust his hands in his suit pockets. "I'll see you in the morning."

"Right." I clutched the key. "When we try to kill each other." That was the wake-up call I needed. Whatever was between us—

which was likely one-sided—it couldn't amount to anything. We wouldn't both be alive at the end of this competition.

He flinched before he smoothed his expression into a mask of indifference. "Yes. That. Get some rest. You're going to need it. There's no telling what tomorrow will bring."

I should've been offended, but his words were laced with care. He truly wanted me to do everything I could to be as prepared as possible. "Okay. Good night, King Kieran."

His breath caught, and he swallowed. His Adam's apple bobbing.

I slipped the key into my door and unlocked it. Just before I shut it behind me, he stepped toward the entry.

"Princess Alina, you need to remember something." His blue eyes blazed, reminding me of the pictures I'd seen of the northern lights. "The Winter fae are not your only enemies here. It's also those who proclaim to be your people. Yes, Winter fae are ruthless and cold, but don't doubt for a second that the Summer Fae are just as vicious."

I tensed as his words sank in.

"Get your rest. I need you ready to fight in the morning." He closed the door the rest of the way, and I locked it but remained standing there. I didn't know what had happened between us tonight, but one thing was clear.

I had to stay the fuck away from the Winter King.

* * *

Something slipped into the lock of my door and clicked, and I shot upright in bed. My ears rang as I reached for the dagger under my pillow and jumped to my feet just as the door opened and Maeve strolled in.

"What the *hell*?" I gasped, lowering the dagger to my side. "You scared the shit out of me."

Maeve's nose wrinkled as she raised the armor in her hands and a flask. "That is not royal-like, and I'm surprised you heard me after your night of drinking. Besides, it's not like I can warn you when I'm coming since it's at Queen Orla's discretion."

My stomach roiled at the sight of the flask. "If you're planning on making me drink again as punishment, it won't work."

She rolled her eyes, dropping the armor on the bed and tossing me the flask, which I caught with my free hand.

"It's a hangover cure. The last thing I want is to get you drunk for your first trial."

Out of everyone I'd met here, I trusted her the most, so I set down the dagger and downed the contents of the flask. I'd expected to have a headache and nausea, but I felt fine. Just thirsty. The faintly sweet taste of actual fae water slid down my throat. When I was done, I wiped my mouth with the back of my hand. "Thanks. I needed that."

"We don't have much time. We need to pull your hair back and get you into this." She pointed at the armor that was more golden with greener vines than what I'd worn before, along with matching sheaths for my weapons. "I let you sleep in as late as possible after what I heard."

I bathed quickly, and she helped me slide into the armor. She pulled my hair into a low ponytail and strapped on my dagger and bow, and then the two of us headed downstairs.

At the bottom, only King Kieran and Curry were there. The two of them were glaring at each other, except for the concerned glance King Kieran flicked to me.

"You got here just in time." Curry scowled. "The others have already been announced. I go next." He nodded toward the back of the entry hall, where Caden stood at a door that blended in with the wall.

"Curry, it's your time," Caden said as he opened the door.

The sound was deafening. People were screaming, and I caught a glimpse of what the trial was.

There was no way in hell I'd survive it.

Twelve

THE AREA beyond the door looked like a cave straight out of hell.

If I hadn't known the trial was taking place in an arena, I'd have had no clue, apart from the lustful screams for blood and death.

Sharp ice stalactites hung from above, and stone stalagmites jutted from below, but I couldn't see the ground, just darkness. Each formation looked capable of dealing a fatal blow.

I'd be dead in minutes.

After Curry strutted through the door, it shut, filling the entry hall with silence.

Somehow, that was worse than the screams. Hell had been hidden, yet I knew it was there. The room spun, and this time, I *knew* it wasn't from spirits.

Caden laughed and rubbed his hands together.

Fuck. I was so screwed.

"Ivy," Maeve said urgently, clutching my shoulder and forcing me to turn my back to Caden and the door to face her and King Kieran.

My chest heaved. I probably had mere seconds left to live. All the things I'd never done flashed through my head; I'd never fallen in love, sunk my feet into the sand while the ocean rolled over them, or grown my own garden.

Like I'd done in my childhood, I withdrew into myself and ignored the world around me. One of the group counselors had called it a survival tactic, but that wasn't the truth. It was a coward's way out of a threatening situation.

All this time, I'd thought I'd come so far, left all that trauma behind. Boy, had I been wrong.

"Alina." A deep, sexy rasp filtered through my senses, anchoring me to the present. I couldn't ignore the call, no matter how desperate I was to remain in my own world. "Heat wave. You're going to be the death of me," the voice spat, and strong, masculine hands cupped my cheeks.

Electricity shot from my face down through my body. Then, an intense, icy pain pulsed in my neck. The frigidness blasted from below my jawline down to my collarbones. The pain changed into something pleasurable and intense, and when I opened my eyes, all I saw was *him*.

King Kieran.

Something like pink mist swirled in the blue of his eyes, and I noticed a mark on his neck that hadn't been there before.

An odd white tattoo of half a sun with swirling rays of light and half a snowflake. The tattoo pulsed with a faint golden glow.

"Get your hands off her, coldy," Maeve snarled, and it sounded like she drew her sword.

But I couldn't take my eyes off him.

"You need to stay present," he murmured, his full lips captivating.

A warm tingle swirled down my neck, similar to how Cara's magic had felt when she'd glamoured my face. The sensation was comforting. The urge to lean forward and press my lips to his was damn near overpowering. If I was going to die, I'd at least like to know how he tasted. That wasn't an unreasonable request ... surely.

Maeve snarled, and then she had the blade of her sword pressed against his neck. Blue blood trickled from the edge of the blade, and a shady dark mist rose from it.

I turned to Maeve, ready to shove her away from him, when he dropped his hands.

He took a step back, the area around his eyes tightening as if he were in pain. The distance between us was mere feet, but it might as well have been worlds.

"There." He dropped his hands to his sides. "I was only trying to help her."

I hadn't even noticed his intricate armor. Where mine was golden with leaves, his was dark, like shadows, with a sizable ice-blue snowflake on his chest made of crystals that flickered in the light.

"I'm not drafty." Maeve lifted her chin. "She's got enough challenges without you adding more."

That was true. I didn't have wings like the others, so I couldn't fly through the obstacles. I wondered if they'd created this challenge just for me. I'd be the first and only fae to fall in the initial trial. I could hear the Winter fae now: *Yeah, what a strong and worthy chosen one.*

I waited for hysteria to close in again, but instead, my neck cooled, bringing a comforting chill that centered me.

King Kieran straightened, appearing every inch the royal he was. "This is the one pass I'll grant you for speaking to me in such a manner because you're worried about your ward. If I ever hear you say that to me again, there will be consequences."

I realized he was referring to her calling him *coldy*. It must be a curse word here. Interesting.

He'd also called me her ward.

He thought of me as a child.

"Excuse you." I shoved past Maeve and thrust my finger into his armor. The metal had no give under my fingertip, causing a slight ache, but I held my ground. "I'm not her *ward*. I'm twenty-three years old."

The edges of his lips tipped upward. I never thought such a

small movement could be that sexy, and for a moment, all rational thought vanished from my head.

"Years? Is that what humans call it?" He arched a brow, and his tone turned condescending. "Nonetheless, she is *training* you, so you're her ward."

Anger flooded through me. I'd show him *ward,* all right. It was a damn good thing his balls were covered, or he'd be in a whole world of hurt. I suspected that particular phrase fit no matter what realm we were in.

"Your Majesty." Caden cleared his throat. "It's time to announce you."

My heart fell, and I couldn't place why. I wasn't sure if it was because he was heading into the arena or that I was next. I wanted the two of us to stay out here where it was safe and closed off from the bloodthirsty people.

"Of course." King Kieran nodded, but his focus never strayed from me.

Maeve clasped my arm and pulled me aside so he could pass. I wanted to fight her, to throw myself into his arms. I'd felt an attraction to him from the start, but it had become so much more than that ... ever since he'd touched me.

None of this made sense.

He straightened his shoulders, not bothering to wipe the blood from his neck, and strolled to the door. Before he left, he paused and said, "Don't underestimate anyone. Do you understand me?" He tilted his head, towering over me.

I received the message loud and clear. *Don't make the same foolish mistake as last night.*

"I do." I straightened to my full height, refusing to let him intimidate me. "Believe me. I won't make that mistake again."

His shoulders relaxed marginally.

"Sire," Caden insisted again. "You're going to hold up the trial."

I watched King Kieran stride through the door. His armor highlighted the muscles I already knew were there, and the view of his ass was worthwhile.

"Ivy." Maeve sheathed her sword. "What was that about?" Concern oozed from every word.

The last thing I wanted to do was address this with her. Taking a deep breath, I squared my shoulders. "Nothing."

She lifted a brow, giving me an expression that made me feel like a child.

She'd *mommed* me.

And worse, it had worked.

Guilt settled heavily over my body like a weighted blanket, and I cracked. "I didn't realize they were serving spirits last night, and I drank too much, which you already knew. King Kieran escorted me to my room."

Her jaw dropped, almost comically so. Part of me wondered if I'd have to lift her chin off the floor.

She recovered. "You let him do *what*?"

"It wasn't my finest moment, but he didn't try to trick me." I exhaled. "Can we please focus on the cave of doom that I'm about to be forced into?" I gestured to the door. "I can't fly, so how the fuck do I get across?"

"Fuck?" Her brows furrowed. "I don't know what that is, but I'm more concerned about King Kieran. His being nice and concerned about you means he's trying to get you to trust him. You can't."

I hated that she was right. I didn't like thinking of King Kieran as my enemy, but now wasn't the time to focus on that. I needed to survive what happened next before I worried about his strategy.

I was *this close* to stomping my foot in frustration. Maybe I was her ward after all. "Maeve, *please*. Help me." I gestured again at the door to my impending doom.

She huffed. "Fine. All right. If you can't figure out how to get your wings to work, you'll have to climb across. Here, give me your bow. It'll cause problems otherwise."

I blinked. She had to be kidding me. That was her pearl of wisdom? "Ah, I see. That makes *complete* sense."

She sighed. "What do you want me to say? I'd have to do the same if I were in your place."

That must be what the first test was about. Proving to everyone we were High Fae and could fly our way through there. I shouldn't think everything was all about me, but I was the only one here without wings.

Caden beamed at me, not bothering to hide that he was listening to our conversation. I didn't know what it was with these fae, but they loved drama, blood, and death. There was no *way* I could be one of them.

"Focus on me, Ivy." Maeve snapped her fingers in front of my face. "You can do this. It won't be just about flying across—there'll for sure be something sneaky to overcome. None of these tasks will be easy. They want each person to suffer and show they can think fast, so you'll have just as much of a chance as anyone with wings in there."

Trying to squelch the nerves thrumming through my body, I took a deep breath and forced a smile. I needed to put on a brave face, at least for Maeve. She'd done so much for me, so I removed the bow and arrows from around me and said, "Climb across from rock to rock until I make it to the end or whatever the goal is?"

She nodded and took the weapons. "And be sure to keep an eye out for your competitors. Once you enter that arena, they can stab you in the back."

Focus on climbing so I didn't fall to my death while keeping my attention on everything around me. Yeah, that sounded super easy. "Got it."

"Princess *Alina*." Caden couldn't hide the excitement in his voice. "It's your turn."

My throat tightened, and acid crept up, burning. This was it.

Maeve threw her arms around me and whispered, "I believe in you. You're strong and a warrior. You'll win this."

At least one of us had faith. I was certain I'd plummet to my death.

"Now, *Princess*," Caden spat. He hadn't been rude to King Kieran, but he was his *king*.

Rolling my eyes, I channeled my annoyance into determination and prepared to meet my fate.

If I was going out, it was damn well going to be in a blaze of glory. I'd channel Bon Jovi and ensure I went down epically. After all, I knew all the words to that song since it was one of Stan's favorites to blare during training.

"Iv—Alina," Maeve called, her voice louder than normal.

For some reason, her showing her own nerves eased some of my worry. I wouldn't be letting her down by dying if she expected it.

Forcing my face to be expressionless, I spun around.

"Don't trust him." Maeve pointed at the door.

My brows furrowed. "Caden? Oh god, no. Don't worry."

"No. King Kieran." Maeve rubbed her arms. "He won't hesitate to hurt you. Trust me." She bit her bottom lip in a nervous tic.

There was something behind that statement, and I hated that I might not ever learn the full story, but the sincerity swirling from her had me nodding. "Understood."

Caden cleared his throat, and I suspected it would be mere seconds before he lost his shit. Part of me wanted to see it, but I had no doubt it would only screw me over more.

"I'll see you at the end." Somehow, I'd kept my voice light.

At the door, I noticed it had a small inset window. Through it, I saw Quinley and Eamon standing at the edge of a flat stone platform. Summer Fae stood to the right of Eamon and Winter fae to the left of Quinley. King Kieran stood closest to her, which meant I probably would stand in the same spot by Eamon.

The door opened, and half the stadium screamed, "*Alina!*" while the other half booed. The surrealness of the situation washed over me.

I'm going down in a blaze of glory, I sang in my head as I strode out the door.

Bullies wanted to see your fear. I wouldn't succumb to these assholes.

"Not only has Princess Alina been reincarnated after saving the entire kingdom, but she has agreed to represent the royal bloodline of the Summer Court!" Eamon's voice boomed without a microphone as if amplified by magic.

I scanned the crowd, noticing that the fae dressed in fall and wintery oranges, frosty blues and purples, and dark golds were on the left side, and the spring and summery people in greens, bright yellows, and other colors that reminded me of summer were to the right. Even in the stadium, there was a clear divide, and the significance wasn't lost on me.

Despite all the chaos, my head turned to *him*.

King Kieran had already homed in on me. His still body resembled a chiseled statue. Though he seemed confident and sure, I could feel the stress radiating from him.

Every cell within my body blazed, and I wanted to stand next to him. The irrational urge to be close to him nearly overpowered my mind.

He mouthed, *Move,* and nodded to Curry. *Be smart.*

"Princess Alina," Quinley murmured, her lips tight with disapproval. "Take your spot. You're going to make a spectacle of yourself ... *again.*"

I was standing frozen in the center between both sides, but luckily, Eamon kept talking, so I hurried to my spot beside Curry.

"What was *that* about?" Curry asked, his eyebrows raised.

I refused to acknowledge him and stared at the obstacle course. The arena was *gigantic*—at least twice the size of a football stadium, and above and below were all sharp edges. Luckily, the pieces I'd have to climb on were only about three feet apart. I'd been worried the gaps would be farther.

When *Kill!* was chanted over and over, I zapped back into the moment. All the fae faces were lit with joy as if this was the best thing they'd ever experienced.

"The competitor who reaches the end of the course with the most crystals collected from the top of the arena ceiling between the icicle pieces will get an early start on the next trial." Quinley raised her hands, pointing at the sharp stalactites, which weren't even two feet apart. They'd have to slide between those to get the crystals.

I'd be lucky to make it across.

Eamon stepped next to her, his sky-blue suit contrasting with her dark-purple dress. He said, "To make it to the next trial, you merely need to cross the finish line ... *alive,* where Kaley and Leanna await us." He pointed right across from us into the darkness.

The fae cheered, their hands lifted in excitement, similar to what I did every time I got mint chocolate chip ice cream.

Some might argue, but I believed my source of enjoyment was healthier. At least I was killing only myself when I enjoyed it.

But that confirmed I had one goal.

To reach the end ... with my heart still beating.

"Is everyone ready?" Quinley asked as she bent down and lifted something that resembled a weirdly shaped guitar. It had to be a lute.

The noise of the crowd rose ten decibels.

I was a little disappointed. I wanted to see something magical.

Quinley plucked the strings, and magic shot out of the instrument along with soothing music.

I stood there, transfixed, as the oranges, golds, pinks, and teals mixed together.

Then, something hit me in the back, and I stumbled and teetered on the edge of the platform.

My heart shot into my throat, but I pushed off with my legs and grabbed a stalagmite. I wrapped my legs and arms around it and held on for dear life.

Sickening screams echoed around me.

I glanced up and saw Curry, the two Winter fae women who'd made fun of me, and Catrina flying erratically overhead. Then, a dark mist drifted down from the icy stalactites and engulfed them.

I had no clue what the fuck was going on, but if the fae were struggling, I had little chance of surviving.

Then one of the Summer Fae women who'd been quiet at dinner flew past me, darted below the mist ... and didn't stop.

Thirteen

MY PULSE RACED SO hard that it pounded in my ears. The woman's saffron eyes widened in horror. Her green wings flapped haphazardly as she darted in all directions.

"No! Please!" she screamed, her voice carrying over the others due to her proximity to me. "Don't hurt *him*."

I searched frantically for the person in question, but all the others were still obscured in the mist and screaming. I had no clue who she was worried about, but she was flying away from him, not toward him.

"Wintery summer, no!" she screamed, tears shrouding her face. "I'll save you!"

My chest constricted. "Wait!"

Then the unthinkable happened. The woman barreled downward, away from the others and toward two jutting stones with her arms outreached. Her head hit one of them, blood spraying everywhere on impact, and her legs sailed into the other. Her body jolted and dropped, the feathers of her wings rippling in the wind.

This couldn't be happening. This had to be a trick they were using against me. She'd fly when she reached the bottom and come after me. I had to be ready.

Unsure how to do that while barely holding on to the stone, I watched as her body hit the dirt ground far beneath us ... the real arena floor.

The woman lay in a crumpled heap with dark blood seeping from more than her head.

I blinked, wishing this were a mirage, but when the crowd in the frosty section of the arena went wild, I couldn't deny it any longer.

She'd killed herself.

Winter fae jumped to their feet, shaking their hands in excitement, while the Summer Fae smiled and shook their heads. I wasn't sure which reaction was creepier.

What sort of hell did I now live in where violent death was celebrated?

Another shriek forced me to look skyward in time to see a Winter fae man impale himself on an icy stalactite above me. I could make him out only because he'd flown out of the thicker mist. His blood splashed me on the arm and dripped onto the ledge.

Holy shit.

I had to get the fuck out of here.

They'd all gone insane.

The first thing I had to do was climb this stalagmite and reach the thinner top section so I could easily hold one arm around it and grab the next one. Thankfully, Stan had trained me on climbing ropes, or I'd be screwed right about now.

I forced the screams from my mind, noting none of them sounded like King Kieran. I had to believe he was all right—a foolish sentiment since one of us had to die. It'd be easier if one of us died here.

Gritting my teeth, I nudged him to the back of my mind. Inch by inch, I climbed the stone. Unlike the rope, the stone wasn't rough, so gaining traction was hard, but I found ruts and divots in the side and used them to pull myself up.

Screams grew louder, and another body dropped. I had to get near the top and move before my strength vanished.

That would definitely result in my demise.

Time passed slowly, and the screams faded. But eventually, I made it near the top, where I could hold on and grab the stone beside me, pulling myself deeper into the arena.

My arms were screaming, a bad sign, but I had to keep going.

After about five stalagmites, I found my rhythm and increased the pace. It wasn't fast, but progress was progress ... that was what Stan liked to say.

I paused, noting I still had a fucking long way to go. I needed to take this in short goals so I could at least pretend it wasn't quite as daunting.

I could do that.

Not that I had an actual choice.

I locked onto the next stalagmite, and the air around it had a faint gray mist.

Whatever had been released at the top of the arena was floating down and about to obstruct my view.

Pushing forward, I'd just gripped a new rock when the air appeared to sparkle and shine, and the scene changed around me.

"Ivy!" Stan's strangled cry came from above. "Help!"

My lungs seized, and I tilted my head upward to see the man who was the closest thing to a father figure I'd ever known, gripping a stalactite high above.

Thicker gray mist swirled around him, and his teeth chattered as his hands slipped down an inch. "Ivy, I can't hang on much longer. I need you to save me."

"How?" The word raked against my throat. "I don't have wings. I can't reach you!" I glanced around. There had to be a way to help him. He'd saved my life with his guidance and through the safety of the gym. I had to repay the favor.

His bottom lip quivered. "Please, try. For *me*. I need you."

That wasn't something Stan would say. Something wasn't right.

I stared at him, taking in his familiar bald head and the gray stubble on his face. He looked like Stan, but the situation didn't sit right.

"Ivy!" he exclaimed. "I can't hold on much longer." His body lurched downward, and I coiled, ready to catch him.

Maeve's words from earlier repeated in my head. *There will be something more than making it across.* I didn't know why, but that warning seemed relevant.

I cleared my throat, my legs and one hand clutching stone while the other hung loose, ready to catch him. "How did you get here?"

"I was kidnapped." One hand slipped off the ice, and he grabbed frantically to regain his stability. "I woke up here this morning. They flew me here and put me on this icicle. Someone named Kieran?"

King Kieran.

My tongue stuck to the roof of my mouth. That *couldn't* be right. Kieran had helped me last night and this morning.

Had he done it so he could watch someone I cared about die? The Winter fae did like pain and torture.

Shit, I had to save Stan, especially if he'd been brought here because of me.

But wait. Maeve had told me that the veil had closed a week ago and there was no way for me to leave for the next fifty complete season cycles. I trusted her, which meant one thing.

Stan couldn't be here.

Damn, he looked so real ... and he could fall at any second.

Realization slammed into me, knocking my breath out from me. That was why the Summer woman had lost it. She'd been trying to save someone. Someone who might not have been here ... like Stan.

Maeve had mentioned that the fae could manipulate my room key by making a duplicate with magic. If that was possible, why wouldn't they do it with a person?

This *couldn't* be Stan.

I stared at him again, searching for something ... *anything* ... to validate my thoughts. A sound, a smell, something to prove he wasn't *my* Stan.

The problem was he looked identical to Stan. Maybe Maeve had been wrong about the veil, or maybe someone had brought him here on the same night as me and kept him asleep until now.

Doubt wiggled into my mind, making my head spin.

His other hand slipped, his fingers blanching from his grip on the ice.

A grip that should have been impossible.

"Ivy! Help me!" Stan's face turned red. "I'm going to die. You've got to save me."

I shook my head. "I ... I'm *sorry*." My throat was raw, and my heart shattered into pieces. But I had to hang on to the belief that this wasn't Stan. He wouldn't beg me for help. That wasn't like him. And he would never ask someone to risk their life for his. Though he appeared identical physically, his actions and words were playing to my fear.

My fear of letting someone else down ... of not protecting them, especially someone I cared about, like him and Beth.

"What?" He scoffed, his mouth opening and closing like a fish. "You won't even *try* after everything I've done for you?"

And Stan would *never* throw something like that in a person's face. He gave without expecting anything in return.

Now, he was dangling from one hand, and a tear trailed down his cheek. "Ivy!" he bellowed ... and his hand slipped.

"No!" I screamed, the sound ripping from my throat. I reached out, but my one arm and my legs remained tight around the stone.

He fell past me, legs kicking and arms flailing for something to hold on to. Then his body hit the dirt ground, and blood seeped from underneath him.

What if that *was* him?

Something wet dripped down my face, and I flinched. I swallowed vomit as I wiped the warm liquid from my cheeks. When I glanced at my fingertips, I saw it was clear liquid. I sniffed, noting my nose was stuffy. A sob racked my chest.

I was crying.

No.

I had to stop.

Shaking my head, I tried to put the horrific image behind me, but I couldn't help but glance toward Stan once more.

His body flickered and disappeared as if it were a hologram.

Thank God! Relief flooded my body, damn near making my grip go slack.

I didn't have time to dawdle. I'd already delayed moving as it was. Exhaling, I centered myself and continued forward.

Shrieks echoed through the arena ... or I thought they did. It was hard to tell over the crowd's cheers.

One thing was certain. The mist, smoke, shadow, or whatever the hell it was was still working its horrific magic. I suspected it revealed our greatest fears, and Stan had been the perfect candidate for that, signifying everything that could hurt me.

By the time I reached the halfway point, my arms and legs were jelly. I wasn't sure how I would make it to the end. I could still see competitors flying erratically ahead of me, so I wasn't the only one who hadn't crossed the finish line.

As I leaned against the stone, something dripped on top of my head.

Something that couldn't be *my* tears.

I looked up to find a woman with cranberry-red hair, a woman who had sat at the Winter fae table, dangling from a shard of ice, her body slowly sliding down as her warm blood melted the ice. My stomach roiled, threatening to spew. This place was worse than Earth, something I never thought I'd ever say. Beauty was an amazing disguise.

Warming frozen heaticles! That probably wasn't even the right way to curse here, but that was all I had because if I didn't move, she was going to fall on me.

Break time was over.

Adrenaline fueled me, giving me a much-needed second wind as I moved forward. I hated that the woman had died, but I didn't want her corpse falling on me.

Determined to get to the end of this nightmare as quickly as possible, I moved faster than before. I needed to capitalize on this adrenaline rush.

The mist thickened again. Trying not to panic, I kept my eyes on the next stone. A cold scream stopped me dead midtransfer, hanging between two stones. My body grew heavy as my arms and legs screamed from the pressure.

"You'll pay for that," the familiar frigid voice of the dark-haired Winter fae who'd sat next to King Kieran last night rasped. "You won't take him from me. No one will."

"Ginevra, it's not real," Rowan sniped. "We need to go. This mist is messing with you."

Ginevra snarled. "You're in on it too, and I won't let you have him!"

Ten yards from me, the two women hovered in the air. Rowan was facing me, her forehead creased, and Ginevra hovered underneath a gigantic stalactite.

Rowan lifted both hands. "I don't want *him*. I'm trying to help you. Like we agreed."

The crowd chanted, "Fight, fight, fight," indicating they could see everything.

"This is how our friendship ends!" Ginevra flew upward, her wing hitting the speared edge as she kicked Rowan in the stomach.

As Rowan flew back several feet, Ginevra's face twisted in a grimace, and she screamed in pain.

The sharp point dug into her emerald-feathered wing. A knot formed deep in the pit of my stomach as her body dropped and the right portion of her wing floated away as it dislodged from her body.

"Ginevra!" Rowan shouted, but she hadn't righted herself.

No one could help Ginevra.

Something exploded inside me. I hadn't helped Stan, and I couldn't stand by here and let someone else die needlessly for the fae's enjoyment.

Pain ripped through my back, and my body levitated. My back muscles bunched and spasmed like stealing my breath for a second, and then I was barreling toward Ginevra.

Wind blew through my hair, but seconds before I reached her, Ginevra's body wrapped around a stalagmite. She grunted and lurched, and as she began to roll, I slid my arms underneath her armpits and pulled her front side to my chest.

Our bodies jerked, shifting our momentum, and my back muscles bunched and strained again. We lifted several feet and hovered between the two death traps.

Boos were shouted from both sides, louder than they had been at any other point in the competition, and I knew it had to do with me helping Ginevra.

I gulped and glanced around then nearly let Ginevra go in shock. The cherry-blossom-colored wings flapping in my periphery were attached to *me*. The muscles in my back moved in a way I'd never experienced before, and hysteria lodged in my throat.

My back muscles trembled, already feeling the strain of flying. Not only was this my first time, but I was carrying someone else.

Of course, Rowan had gone.

I'd have to figure this out my-damn-self.

I tried to fly forward, but nothing happened. My wings flapped, keeping me in place. A scream built in my chest.

"Nolan?" Ginevra murmured. "Are you here? Did you come to save me?"

I swallowed my groan of annoyance. This was all over a prince. Why was I not surprised? "Hold on to me. You're hurt."

"What?" Ginevra moaned, but she threw her arms around my neck, which took the weight off my already tired arms.

I leaned forward, and my wings must have taken the hint.

We zigged and zagged, my wings not moving smoothly, but I made my way toward the finish line more quickly than when I'd been climbing. I kept my eyes focused on the end target, noting there were nine people at the finish line.

With each flap, my back ached more until agony was ripping through me. I wasn't sure how much more I could handle, but we were only fifty feet away.

I'd made it so damn far, and I'd make it the rest of the way.

Ginevra groaned and flinched.

"Hold on. We're almost there," I assured her, but I wasn't sure my wings would make it.

In fact, they stopped moving as rapidly, my back spasming hard. I gritted my teeth as we began to descend.

King Kieran ran to the middle of the finish platform. Though I was flying several feet above his head, I could see his expression was strained, making his cheeks look sharper than normal. He stood right where I should be landing, his attention locked on me. His hands twitched at his sides as if he wanted to help me.

My body dropped until I was level with his face and then his chest.

Then I was at eye level with his crotch before I dropped to his feet.

The edge of the platform was maybe five feet away, but it might as well have been a mile. My back convulsed, and I dropped even lower until I couldn't see the top of the platform.

As if anticipating my death, the crowd's boos changed to cheers. I couldn't give them the very thing they coveted without a fight, so I risked it all and flung one arm out.

My fingertips caught the edge of the platform, but my arms were going to give out.

A sinister laugh echoed from above. One that promised pain, blood, and death.

Fuck, I had to do *something*.

Anything.

I dug deep, pushing through my pain. I'd pay for this tomorrow, but at least I'd live one more night. I screamed, using the arm I had wrapped around Ginevra to thrust her body with all my might over the edge and onto the platform.

Rowan was there and dragged her friend away, and then Curry took her place. He smiled evilly as he stepped on my fingers and crushed them under his boot.

Pain exploded in my already exhausted hand, and I knew I couldn't hold on much longer.

Fourteen

CURRY PRESSED the tip of his boot harder on my fingers. I whimpered, unable to hold back the noise, and grabbed for the edge of the platform with my other hand.

"She's crossed the line," Kieran said frigidly.

Once again, he was trying to help me. I didn't see how doing so benefited him, but Maeve was certain he had ulterior motives.

"Are you serious?" Curry chuckled darkly. "She hasn't *crossed* it. She's touching it. Her heart has to cross the line."

Tears stung my eyes as everything inside me wanted to jerk my hand away from the platform to stop the pain, but my survival instincts kicked in to keep me hanging on.

I grasped for the ledge with my free arm, but my muscles ached, and I couldn't quite extend it.

Curry leaned over the edge, his lip curled over his teeth. "Wait until everyone witnesses me killing the *chosen one*." He then rolled his foot over my hand.

Bones cracked, and there was no way I could hold on.

The crowd roared as he lifted his shoe and released my hand. I dropped like a boulder, the wind blowing through my hair and wings. I rushed toward the dirt ground, but ten feet from it, my wings took on a life of their own and stretched out.

I glided. My back protested, but not like when I had flapped the wings. The soreness pulsed deep into my muscles, but I could handle it. I was still dropping, but not as fast.

I hit the ground on my front, and dirt filled my mouth and eyes. I felt like I was drowning.

Silence filled the arena, anticipation thick in the air. My body screamed, but I wasn't sure if it was from the obstacle course or the fall.

My lungs were still working.

I was alive, but I didn't know what that meant. I hadn't passed the finish line.

Slowly, I stood up. Every muscle ached. I took back all the times I'd told Stan that he'd broken me. *This* was worse than everything I'd experienced before.

However, I wouldn't allow these barbarians to believe they'd bested me.

Standing at my full height, I spun slowly to ensure I faced each section. I hated that all these people *wanted* me to die. Even those who'd been cheering when I'd arrived were on the edges of their seats, waiting for me to become mincemeat ... or fairy dust ... or whatever metaphor they used.

I hadn't accounted for what else I'd find.

The four dead bodies of my competitors lay haphazardly on the ground, blood pooling beneath them, their limbs strewn in unnatural positions.

My stomach jumped into my throat, and I feared I'd blow chunks everywhere.

Boos sounded again, and fae jumped to their feet, smacking the backs of their hands against their palms.

I glanced up to find King Kieran and Curry staring down at me. Curry's nose wrinkled while King Kieran's jaw twitched.

King Kieran waved a hand and said, "The trials are not over until you cross the finish line or die." His voice projected to me the way Quinley's and Eamon's had when they'd addressed the crowd.

Straining, I tried to spread my wings to fly, but they barely moved, and my muscles spasmed painfully. I groaned and relaxed my back. Trying was futile.

I had only one choice.

Climb.

Moving to the closest stalagmite, I studied my obstacle. The problem was getting up to the thinner part, where I could wrap my legs and arms around it to keep myself from falling.

One problem at a time, Ivy. Stan's calm voice echoed in my mind. *In war, there are times when you will want to lie down and die, but the key is to never stop. Try until you can't anymore. Focus on small goals.*

Though I'd never expected to go to war, he'd trained me as if I would. He'd said the Boy Scout motto had it right. *Be Prepared.* That was the key to survival.

I stood before the stalagmite, the width four times my size, and I foolishly looked up and realized it had to be at least one hundred feet tall.

Shit.

This was going to hurt, but it beat hanging around, listening to everyone boo me until I perished. I had no doubt they'd stick around and enjoy my slow demise.

My legs ached as I prepared myself to climb, but I couldn't find any purchase, which meant I'd have to make my own handholds and footholds.

I removed my dagger and hit the stone. I'd expected it not to work, but the stone chipped. I banged the same spot several more times and put the tip of my boot in the divot. It was just enough to give me leverage.

This could work as long as I could keep my strength up.

I made another four divots and began to climb, but when I attempted to grip the stone with my left hand, agony ripped through it, and I clutched it to my chest. It had to be broken.

Reaching the top just got more difficult.

Chest heaving, I gently wrapped my left arm around the stalagmite as much as I could and held the blade between my teeth. I climbed another step and forced myself not to think about how many more lay ahead.

I took the dagger again and made another divot above my right hand. When it was big enough, I leaned to the left and wrapped my top half around the column, then found spots for both feet to push myself upward.

I continued up, moving slowly, remaining methodical and trying not to rush. Rushing would make me careless, and I was already struggling. I breathed through my teeth as my legs and arms threatened to give out.

Every time I progressed, I wanted to glance up to see how much farther I had left, but I stopped myself. I didn't have any excess energy to spill on frustration.

Time dragged on, and I could feel the eyes of the fae on me. The noise had calmed to a low buzz, but they had to see how I was struggling.

My right arm was taking the brunt of my weight. Climbing was a full-body venture, and having one hand out of commission made things harder.

On my next step, my foot didn't hit the groove, and I slid downward.

"Fall, fall, fall!" the fae chanted.

My blood ran cold, and adrenaline pummeled my body, giving me another burst of energy. I wouldn't give these assholes the satisfaction.

My foot found a hold, and I continued to climb more slowly than before.

When the circumference of the stalagmite shrank to a size my arms and legs could wrap around, butterflies took flight in my stomach. Maybe I'd make it out of this.

I eagerly reached for the top ... and my hand slipped. My injured left hand also jerked with a sharp stabbing sensation. Salty saliva filled my mouth, making the nausea in my stomach roil.

"Princess Alina," King Kieran said in his deep, soothing voice. "Try flying again. Your back has had time to rest."

A shiver ran down my spine. I'd hoped the other competitors would've left by now, but he'd stayed to watch me. I didn't know how I felt about that, but I'd come way too far to die now.

I tried flapping my wings, anticipating my muscles cramping again. They were sore as fuck, and a deep ache rolled throughout my back, but they spread out again.

This time, I did look up, needing to take stock of how much farther I had to go. I prepared to be disappointed, but I only had about five more feet up and four feet over to go to make it onto the ledge.

I *had* to do this. I needed this trial to be over.

Gritting my teeth, I forced my wings to move.

With a shriek, I kept my eyes locked on my goal as my arms and legs gave out of their own accord. They couldn't hold my weight anymore.

My wings flapped harder, my full body weight straining them, and my back muscles spasmed again.

Excited chatter from the crowd rumbled in my ears, but when I looked into King Kieran's eyes, everything else disappeared.

I had to get to him.

Each beat of my wings hurt worse than the last, but my body was rising despite the jerky ascension. Someway. Somehow. I landed on the edge of the platform.

When my feet hit the ground, I dropped to my ass. My legs couldn't support my body anymore.

"Heat wave." King Kieran blew out a breath. "I didn't think you were going to make it."

"Nor did I." Curry didn't bother to hide his disappointment. "But you surprised us again, Your *Highness*."

I glared at him, but with the way my body was sagging, I doubted I'd managed the menacing look I was going for. "Your concern is noted." My voice was rough, like I'd smoked twenty packs of cigarettes. The dirt had dried my throat, and I desperately needed water. But there was one thing more important than that.

Ginevra.

My breath hitched, and I glanced back at King Kieran. The rest of the candidates were behind him, one in particular with dark hair spread around her and Rowan sitting next to her.

"What is she still doing here?" I shot to my feet, my knees almost giving out, but I remained standing. "She needs a doctor!"

"A doctor?" King Kieran's brows furrowed. "What's that?"

"Someone needs to help her." I took a few steps but stumbled. "She's seriously injured."

Curry scoffed. "We don't have healers. Besides, she's already gone."

My heart shattered. "No." I got her here so she could get help. She wasn't supposed to die. Helping her had somehow released my wings—she was part of the reason I'd survived. "I'm sure there's something we can do. Maeve brought me a medicine that's supposed to help hangovers—maybe it could help her too."

"Her magic is already gone, Princess Alina," King Kieran said slowly, a hint of confusion mixed in. "She died when you began your climb to make it back up here."

The last bit of energy left me, and my body crumpled.

Strong arms wrapped around me, and my legs were swept out from underneath me. I opened my eyes and saw King Kieran's face above mine.

He was carrying me.

His lips pressed into a line, and he shook his head. His expression showed confusion, disgust, or some combination of the two. But his eyes told a different story, and his crisp smell comforted me.

My eyes closed, and foolishly, I felt safe in his arms. Though it should have petrified me, I drifted out of consciousness.

* * *

"Is she up?" Orla's shrill voice made my head pound.

I sucked in a breath, my chest and back screaming. The trial flooded back into my mind.

"Frozen sake, Orla." Dallas moaned. "You *just* asked, and you get louder each time. If you're trying to wake her up, get on with it. Don't burst everyone's eardrums."

My eyes opened, and I found Maeve sitting on the edge of my bed between me and Orla. Orla was standing between the two chairs, her nostrils flaring. Despite the anger etched on her face and her clenched hands, she looked elegant and poised in her gold satin dress with her crown on her head.

"There you go." Dallas waved a hand at me from his spot in the chair closest to my head. "Mission accomplished." He wore a golden suit with a burnt-orange shirt, reminding me of a sunset. He also wore a crown similar to Orla's but smaller.

No doubt a way for Orla to emphasize she was the blood royal.

Maeve twisted toward me, shifting her knee on the bed.

When the mattress moved, my muscles twinged.

"Do you need something for the discomfort?" she asked gently.

If it hadn't hurt too much to laugh, I would've, but when my chest moved, all the air whooshed out of me. "No," I croaked, my throat so dry it felt like sandpaper. I didn't deserve medicine. I hadn't saved Ginevra. I was alive, and she was dead. The least I could do was feel a little bit of the pain she'd felt at the end.

"Good." Orla marched over to me, her wings exploding from her back, reminding me of fire. "After what you did out there, you deserve to feel every ounce of misery!"

I blinked. Luckily, that was the one movement that didn't hurt. "What?" I wasn't sure how I'd upset her other than, you know, not dying and all.

Maeve slowly stood and headed to the end table next to the window. In the distance, the moons were rising into the darkening sky.

"Saving that *Winter fae* and then collapsing." Orla lifted both hands. "Are you trying to ruin our name?"

I was so lost and confused. "She needed help." I winced. Talking essentially felt like a dagger stabbing me in the throat over and over again.

"Here." Maeve poured water into a cup and helped me sit up.

Hissing, I tried not to make more noise as my muscles burned, lighting my insides on fire.

Dallas jumped to his feet and rearranged the pillows behind me so I could lean back on them. When I finally got adjusted, he gave me a sad smile.

There was his nice side again.

"I think she's *fine* now," Orla snapped, her face turning pink. "You can sit down."

"Of course, *dear*," Dallas jeered, more like the cocky bastard I preferred.

Maeve brought the cup to my lips, and when I opened my mouth, the water hit. I groaned. The coolness eased my discomfort and washed away the grit of the dirt. Before I realized it, I'd downed the entire cup. I felt marginally better.

"I'm still *waiting* for an answer." Orla tapped her foot.

I had no clue what she wanted from me, but not speaking wasn't an option. "She needed help, and I couldn't help collapsing. I've never been through that type of physical challenge before. Would you rather I had died?"

She nodded, shocking me.

"Of course." She held out her hand. "You're now the joke of Talamh. You saved someone you're supposed to want dead. You made us look weak, and you were the last to cross the line. Then you fainted at the *Winter King's* feet!"

Every value in this world seemed the opposite of mine. I was built to protect people, not kill them. This competition went against everything I stood for. "I didn't ask to enter. *You* put me in this." I wouldn't let her blame me.

"I had no choice. You clearly aren't fit to rule." Orla's chest heaved. "You aren't even close to the sister I had before."

"This isn't accomplishing anything." Dallas rolled his eyes. "We need to handle the situation, not argue about it. The solution is simple."

"Oh, *really*." Orla crossed her arms and pivoted to him. "And what's that?"

"We say she tried to save Prince Nolan's betrothed to put the royal Winter family in our debt." Dallas flipped a hand. "Ta-da!"

Maeve tapped her finger on her lips. "That has merit."

"Did you know about her and Prince Nolan?" Orla asked me.

Jumping up to block my view of Orla, Dallas pointed at me and said, "Don't answer that. As far as we know, you did." He positioned himself so he could glance back and forth between Orla and me. "Do you understand?"

"Fine." Orla blew out a breath but narrowed her eyes at me. "But listen here—don't embarrass me again."

I didn't say anything because that wasn't something I could promise.

"Good. Don't answer that either." Dallas winked. "Orla and I are going downstairs while you get ready."

"Ready?" I squeaked. I could barely breathe, let alone handle the second trial.

"For the celebration ball." Orla tilted her head and smiled. "Take some medicine and make sure you don't let anyone see the amount of pain you're in."

So that was why she was wearing a fancier golden dress than usual.

"Come on." She held out her hand to Dallas. "We'll see you down there."

When the door shut, Maeve held my gaze and handed me a pink, frothy liquid. "Drink this and let's get you ready."

* * *

Getting dressed was just as bad as climbing the stalagmite, but the pink frothy drink worked wonders. Breathing didn't hurt as much —the worst part was standing on shaky, exhausted legs.

"See, I do as well as your handmaiden." Maeve chuckled.

I stared at myself in the bathroom mirror. The ends of my hair were so bright that they reminded me of sunlight. Maeve had curled my hair in waves down my back, and I was wearing the most gorgeous dress I'd ever seen with a deep, sweetheart neckline and flowy fabric decorated with pink flowers that resembled flames. My sleeves were sheer and flowy, and when I moved, they looked like wings, which was nice since mine were tucked securely in my back.

Everything about it screamed, *not me*.

The green in my eyes was so vibrant and my skin so golden that I barely believed I was the person in the mirror.

"You look gorgeous," Maeve added.

There was a knock on the door, and I flinched.

"I'll answer it." Maeve strolled out of the bathroom, leaving me alone.

But I was done being protected. It was silly now that I was in a tournament where people were actively trying to kill me.

I entered the bedroom as she opened the door and stared. She reached for her sword. "What are *you* doing here?"

My chest tightened, and I hurried toward the door. Rowan was there.

"I need to see Princess Alina alone," she gritted out as she fisted her hands at her sides.

Everything in my head screamed at me not to listen, but if I said no, Orla would no doubt scold me for appearing weak.

Maybe I'd die today after all.

Fifteen

"ABSO-FROZEN-LUTELY NOT," Maeve's hand tightened on the handle of her sword.

This was going to escalate if I didn't step in. When I straightened my back to look more authoritative, my muscles throbbed, but I swallowed my whimper. "It's fine."

The way Maeve's head swung toward me so quickly, a laugh lodged in my chest, but when I saw her glare, the urge left. She was *pissed*, and I never wanted to be on the receiving end of her wrath again.

"Seriously. If she has something important to say, it would be better to discuss it in here than out there in front of everyone." I might not like my sister, but that didn't mean I wanted to alienate myself from her. It was in her best interest to make sure I was somewhat safe, even if it was an illusion.

"I— Princess Alina." Maeve pursed her lips, her disapproval shining through in the way her body tightened and the sheer disgust on her face. It made me think she was considering all the ways she could kill me herself.

The irony of the situation washed over me. She was the only person who cared about me, besides—maybe—my fucking kidnapper. *Talk about a plot twist.*

Every fiber in my being shrank inside me as I prepared to say my next words. "It's not a request, Maeve." My voice sounded commanding and authoritative.

Maeve's head jerked back, and she said bitterly, "Yes, *Princess*."

Princess might as well have been a curse word.

I held firm. If Orla didn't have a field day with me not having a direct conversation with Rowan, she definitely would if I backed down to Maeve.

"If you decide you *need* me, scream. I'll be outside the door." Maeve kept her hands on the hilt of her weapon as she strolled past Rowan.

Rowan smiled, and a chill coursed down my spine as she shut the door behind her ... a little too hard.

Luckily, Maeve and I had secured the dagger to my thigh in case I needed it tonight. Getting it from underneath my skirt would be a sight, and graceful was one thing I wasn't.

I took a few steps back, putting more distance between us. Worst case, I could use my giant skirt to disorient her long enough to retrieve my weapon.

"If you're here to attack me ..." I hiked up the skirt, ready to attack.

Her fingertips darkened to a deep gray, similar to the color of the mist in the arena. "I'm *not*." Her deep frown was legitimately a smile turned upside down.

Here I'd thought that was a figure of speech.

I paused. "That's not the vibe I'm getting from you."

"Don't make this harder than it already is. *Please*." A shadowy substance danced over her fingertips like a flame. "I didn't want to come, but that doesn't matter. The result is the same, so I figured I should be frosty enough to admit it."

Unease pulsed through me. I didn't lower my skirt, but I wasn't alarmed enough to remove the weapon and potentially embarrass myself more. Whatever her goal was, I needed her to get to it. "Frost me."

She grimaced. "Yeah, this was a mistake." She spun on her heels and grabbed the door handle.

Shit! Apparently, whatever she had to say was a big deal, and I had to go try to speak like them. Every time I did, I insulted someone. "Wait." I stopped myself before the words *I'm sorry* came out. "I didn't mean to insult you. You said you had to be frosty enough to admit you didn't want to come here, so I was trying to encourage you to say what you came to say."

Pausing, she shook her head. "You really don't remember anything from your life before, do you?"

I studied her. Rowan's dark-purple dress molded to her body all the way to the floor, where a short train trailed behind her. She was beautiful, even scowling, but she didn't seem familiar.

I wanted to lie, but that wouldn't accomplish anything. "I don't. I mean, I had a flashback, I think, but it wasn't related to my former life here." I swallowed. Had I just admitted to believing I was Alina? I'd been so sure for so long that I wasn't, but ... dammit, I had motherfucking *wings*. How else could I explain that?

"For one, any time a Summer Fae uses winter or shadow terms, it's intended as an insult." She arched an eyebrow. "Even if you're trying to use them in a friendly way, *don't*."

I dropped my skirt, certain her demeanor was more annoyed than threatening. "Noted."

Silence descended between us and made my skin crawl. This wasn't the sort of comfortable silence I had with Stan. In fact, I couldn't handle it. "So, you dropped by to...?"

She rubbed her forehead. "You're not going to make this easy for me, are you?"

I wasn't sure how to respond, so I kept my mouth closed.

And it was hard.

Lifting her chin, she licked her lips. "I'm in your debt for helping Ginevra."

Now I really wasn't sure what to say because I was confused. "Not trying to get you to take it back or anything, but why? You left her behind, and she was also your competition. And she died anyway."

"She was my best friend, and we grew up together." She rubbed the back of her neck, and her eyes glistened. "We made an agreement when we were younger to always protect one another since it's not the typical fae way. Little did we know that both of us would become part of the Comortas. Because I'd given her my word, I would've *had* to help her, but when you stepped in, you removed that burden so I could finish the trial and survive. To be honest, I hoped you would die so I wouldn't have to owe you, but here we are."

Even though she was still cold, there was remorse there. She truly cared for her friend. "Then why did you come in here so aggressively?" I'd have thought she'd be more appreciative, especially if she owed me.

She laughed, the sound like an echo on a breezy day. "Because owing you is bad enough. Add in that we're competitors in this trial, and it's a death sentence. So tell me what you want me to do."

From the sound of it, she was expecting me to tell her to kill herself, but why would I do that when I'd tried to save someone in the trial? I'd never understand the way these fae thought. "I don't have anything to ask of you."

"At least I'll get to attend the ball." She forced a smile, but it fell flat. "Unless you're going to decide something there."

I hated that she felt this impending doom, but to be fair, we all had to be part of this tournament. "Do your best to enjoy the night. I won't be calling in any favors." I winked, trying to reassure her.

She rubbed a hand down the lacy material of her dress. Her face turned a shade paler as she nodded. "As you wish." She cleared her throat. "I'm heading downstairs. It's time for the ball, and I'd rather we not walk into the room together."

I placed a hand on my chest dramatically. "We wouldn't want that."

"Exactly." She turned, opened the door, and paused, missing the joke. "Uh ... see you downstairs."

She stepped from the room, and Maeve entered before the door even began to close.

She shut it and leaned against it with her arms crossed. "You're still in one piece. I'm not sure if that's reassuring."

Lucky for her, I found her concern endearing. Even Stan didn't worry over me as much as she did. "You'll be glad to know she owes me."

"What?" Her arms dropped. "How is that even possible?"

I filled her in on our discussion.

"That will validate Dallas's claim about the Winter King owing you." She pushed off the wall. "I've been concerned about that. We can say Nolan owes you, but that might not be the case. I'm not even sure if Ginevra and Nolan were officially promised—it was mere speculation. The only hint it was true was the fact that King Kieran carried you off the platform."

King Kieran.

The sexy Winter King, who was constantly renting space in my head even when I tried to pretend I wasn't thinking about him. His eyes were the last thing I'd seen before passing out. They'd been so full of concern, or that was what my injured brain had seen. But being in his arms—

"Ivy," Maeve said sternly. "Are you even listening to me?"

Hello, wake-up call. King Kieran's sculpted face disappeared and was replaced by Maeve's pinched expression. She was beautiful, but she didn't hold a candle to King Kieran.

"Well?" She tapped her foot expectantly.

"Sure." I had no clue what the right answer was, but I didn't want her asking why I'd been distracted.

She smirked. "Really? So that's a yes?"

This was a trap. *Mayday. Mayday.* Or was it SOS? I had no clue, but I needed help. "It depends, you know."

"On what?" she pressed, grinning wickedly. She knew she had me.

"Shouldn't we be going? Rowan said the ball started." I fluffed out my dress. "I'd hate to be too late."

"Uh-huh." She chuckled and opened the door. "You better be glad I've grown fond of you, or I'd be very annoyed."

We made our way down to the entrance hall, and Maeve turned to the door on the right, opposite the dining hall. A group of well-dressed fae stood outside the doorway, talking in hushed tones. They stopped when they noticed me. They wore bright greens, pinks, yellows, and blues, reminding me of summer flowers, but the way their noses wrinkled was more aligned with the disgust the Winter fae had for me.

A woman who reminded me of Salma Hayek but with hair the color of peacock feathers edged to the front of the group. "Good evening, *Princess Alina*. I'm surprised you're here."

I stopped. "Why wouldn't I be?"

"Can you even call yourself a contestant after your little stunt in the trial?" She sneered, her teal lips curling. "Saving another competitor, worst of all a *Winter* fae, should be grounds for elimination."

My heart stopped. "What?" *Elimination*. Although, why would the fae having an elimination policy surprise me? They were vicious. I feared to even consider the way they'd force me to go. They'd no doubt make sure it was very public and entertaining.

I glanced at Maeve, hurt she hadn't warned me that my death could be the punishment, but in fairness, did it matter? I'd barely survived the trial today—I seriously doubted I'd survive the next one.

Cold pulsed from the spot on my neck that had burned earlier before the trial, and then King Kieran's deep, commanding voice came from behind me. "Even though your point is valid, there aren't any rules regarding such a thing." He stepped off the last stair and strolled to my other side.

The woman's face puckered as if she'd eaten a lemon. "Probably because no *fae* would ever consider doing what she did today. The point is to kill your competitors or let them die, not *save* them."

A short, round man near her laughed. "She didn't even save Ginevra! She might have been reborn, but she's not our *Alina*."

They were trying to make that sound like a bad thing. "Damn straight I'm not."

Maeve's eyes bulged, and she shook her head, telling me to shut it down.

But I was just getting started. "This tournament is bar—"

"Barely started," King Kieran chimed in, placing his hand on the center of my back. "There is still plenty of time to kill tons of people in the next two challenges. Is there not, Princess?"

Despite the chill of his hand, even through my dress, heat flooded my body while my neck swirled with cold and heat. I hated that his presence had such an impact on me, and worse, I had no way of controlling it. I wanted to close the few feet of distance between us.

Frustrated with myself, I allowed my annoyance to simmer and emphasized each word: "I'm already getting an idea of who might be my first one." I glared at him ... and almost faltered.

The navy blue of his surcoat made his eyes glow, and I swore there was a faint, warm pinkish-yellow glow emanating from his neck. His pale-pink cravat complemented my dress—which couldn't be on purpose, could it?—and I noticed the white snowflake on the edge of his lapel. It was identical to the half of the white tattoo I'd seen on his neck.

He grinned, and I forgot how to breathe. He leaned closer, his minty breath hitting my face. "That's something I'd like to see."

The bastard reminded me of cocky Dallas, but unlike Dallas, I found King Kieran very alluring. A lump lodged in my throat, making me forget where we were and why.

Maeve cleared her throat loudly. "Princess Alina, you should join the other competitors and dance. I'm sure your sister would like to spend time with you before she leaves."

Yeah, that sounded *exactly* like something Orla would want to do.

I tried to move forward, but King Kieran tightened his hand on my back, unyielding.

"She's right." He tipped his head toward the doors. "We should join the others. Will you have your first dance with me?"

That was the worst possible thing I could do. Being close to him was dangerous, and Maeve would very likely kill me herself if I didn't keep my distance.

I nodded, unable to form words. My head screamed at me to stop, but I was at the mercy of something else entirely.

"Perfect."

Without removing his hand, he turned my body toward the door. The mouth of the Summer Fae who'd wanted me to die tipped down even more.

I stared each nearby fae in the eye, refusing to cower, but I avoided Maeve's gaze. I knew she was glaring at me from the way the nape of my neck tingled.

King Kieran's body brushed mine as we went to the entrance, and two tall men opened the double doors as we approached.

My first view of the ballroom made me stop. The floor was smooth and frost blue, similar to the tunic the Winter King wore under his surcoat. The walls and ceiling were lined in purple twilight flowers, giving it a romantic glow, and three fae dressed in opera-esque clothes were playing strange instruments I'd never seen before. The music was magical.

I'd never seen anything so glorious before.

When King Kieran and I stepped into the room, everyone stopped what they were doing and turned to stare at us.

My head spun. I wasn't used to attention, especially not like this.

"Come." King Kieran took my hand, leading me past Orla, Dallas, and several others to the dance floor.

My head screamed *no,* but I couldn't pull my hand away; not even my sister's stare landed on me.

I followed the king to the center of the room, where he placed his free hand on my waist and lifted our joined hands.

"What are you doing?" I fidgeted, sensing everyone's gaze on me.

He smiled. "I believe I was clear when I asked you for a dance."

My heart squeezed, my reaction to him scaring the shit out of me. Yet I didn't move, and my traitorous legs stepped closer to him. I murmured, "But everyone's watching, and I don't know how to dance."

"Then we'd better give them a good show, and you'll be fine if you follow my lead." He moved, confident and regal. The two words described him perfectly.

Without any input from me, my legs followed as if we'd danced together our whole lives.

He smirked. "See. I won't lead you astray. You just need to trust me."

I flinched, slowing our pace.

"What?" His brow arched. "Did I say something wrong?"

"This whole thing is wrong, and we're competitors. The worst thing I can do is trust you." The words were hard to say, but they were true. Maeve had been right to warn me away from him, but here I was, in the arms of an enemy for whom I felt *way* too many things. Things like not wanting to leave his embrace and the world tilting while he held me in his arms.

"No, the worst thing you can do is try to save someone from dying." He *tsk*ed as he twirled me around and tugged me closer to him.

The world spun, and I was certain it wasn't from the twirl. I had to get my legs securely under me, both literally and figuratively. "I won't apologize for that. And why do you care?"

"For one, your sister and the *king consort* are telling everyone that the Winter royal family owes you." The humor vanished from his face, his jaw clenching. "Which is not true, by the way. Nolan and Ginevra weren't betrothed, but they were close and might have gotten there once my brother was ready to have an heir."

"I didn't tell them to say anything like that, and that's not why I helped her." I needed to shut up, but I couldn't. For some reason, I wanted to tell him all my secrets. But even I wasn't that foolish. "She was scared, and I ... That's a horrible way to die."

Now he was the one who paused, and glancing around, I noticed he'd guided me into a corner where flowers surrounded us and darkness shrouded us as if we were in the shadows. Between him and the scent of the flowers, something inside me eased, even though all I should've sensed was danger.

"Death is inevitable, especially in the Comortas." He tilted his head, examining every inch of my face. "That still doesn't matter to you, does it? What's going to happen when someone attacks you? Will you stand there and let them?" His voice rose in what sounded like anger.

That was a good question, one I'd been pushing away, not wanting to think about it. The problem was that I didn't think I could take a life. It went against everything I stood for. "I ... I don't know."

"Therein lies our problem." He leaned forward, his face crowding mine. "I need you to know and to be willing to protect yourself. I almost thawed today, watching you struggle."

Sincerity wafted off him, and the way his face softened ... I didn't have the right words to describe him. Handsome wasn't right... it didn't do him justice. I breathed the word, not sure he could hear me: "Why?"

He homed in on my lips. "Because," he answered and lowered his mouth to mine.

Sixteen

MY HEART GALLOPED, and I clutched his suit jacket as I stepped back, tugging him with me. I didn't want anyone to see what was happening, but I also had to know what he tasted like.

When my back hit the wall and flower petals brushed my arms, excitement sizzled through my body. My head spun as his lips barely brushed mine, a jolt searing me straight to my soul. He paused, waiting for my reaction, but he didn't move away. His minty breath drifted over my face, mixing with his scent and the scent of flowers.

Stomach clenching, I pushed all rational thought away. I needed more; he wasn't close enough. I'd gripped his lapels to pull him flush against my body when he stumbled away from me.

What the—

Then I noticed Dallas's flushed face right behind him. The darkness that had shrouded us vanished, and the faint light of the room beyond the flowers trickled back into view.

Dallas let go of the back of King Kieran's suit jacket and shoved him away.

"What the frozen summer do you think you're doing?" Dallas seethed. His hands fisted, and the flowers around me moved as if under his command.

King Kieran's chest heaved, and his irises turned that frosty pale-blue once more. "That is none of your concern."

I needed to do something, but I was recovering from whatever Kieran and I had shared. My lips were still tingling.

"She's the princess of the Summer Court!" Dallas lifted his chin. "Anything concerning her extends to me."

When Kieran bared his teeth, revealing the ruthless and animalistic side to him, it both petrified me and made me want him to punish me.

What the *fuck* was wrong with me?

"You've been taking a lot of interest in Princess Alina. Are you asking as her king, brother-in-law, or *lover?*" Kieran snarled the last word.

Dallas smirked. "I don't have to choose just one of those options, do I?"

Oh, whoa. My body flinched, spurring life back into me. The shock of the words had snapped me out of whatever haze I'd been in.

Kieran's hands turned a faint blue as they had the first time I'd met him when he'd frozen the wood of the table. "It might be in your best interests to stick to the first two choices. The last one won't end well for you."

"So you *were* trying to harm her." Dallas reached into his coat pocket and removed a dagger. "That's low, even for the Winter King … picking off competitors when they're severely hurt."

My chest tightened, and my stomach soured. Surely that wasn't why Kieran had led me away from everyone. He wouldn't have kissed me if he was going to kill me, right?

The problem was that I wasn't so sure. I didn't understand any of the fae except for Maeve, and for some reason, I'd thought maybe Kieran too. But that was foolish. I was acting like one of the girls I'd grown up with. I'd sworn I'd never lose my mind and do stupid shit over a guy.

"Do you expect me to be afraid of *you?*" Kieran chuckled, not even lifting a hand or drawing a weapon to defend himself.

I was certain he had a dagger on him, just like everyone else here.

The fae were squirrelly people, though they wouldn't get the reference if I said it. Either way, I refused to be spoken about as if I weren't here. Not wanting to see which one had the biggest dick—I was pretty sure they were both underendowed, given how much posturing they were doing in front of me—I shoved between them.

I looked around to see if anyone had noticed the confrontation. Luckily, the musicians were still playing, and people were dancing ... except for Maeve and Orla, who were marching toward us.

This was getting worse by the second. At this point, I should have *Hot Mess* posted on my forehead. The fae would find a way to make it look bougie and match my dresses because, you know, that was how things worked here.

Maeve removed her sword from her side. The music stopped playing, and the fae who were dancing turned their avid gazes on me. Their eagerness to watch me make a fool of myself seemed to never end.

Dallas snatched my hand and swung me toward him. He pulled me to his side with an ironclad arm around my waist and rasped, "You're staying with me for the rest of the night. You can't be trusted on your own."

Aw, *hell* no. Hot rage bubbled within me. Everything faded as I focused on the immediate threat. "Heat wave, frozen summer, get your hands off me." I shoved him, refusing to let anyone manhandle me. The one time a foster dad had put his hands on me, I'd gotten a black eye, and I refused to let anything like that happen again.

Dallas stumbled back then regained his balance, but somehow, he didn't remove his arm from my waist, opting to take me with him.

Between the jerking around and my three-inch heels, I lost my balance and tumbled into his chest, where he wrapped both arms around me. I waited for his dagger to poke me, but he must have moved it to protect my back.

"Get your hands *off* her!" Kieran bellowed. From the corner of my eye, I noticed blue magic pulsing from his fingers and icing the floor.

I didn't need him fighting my battles for me. I had this one on my own.

I punched Dallas in the stomach, aiming for his gut ... or where the gut was on a human.

Luckily, it had a similar impact because Dallas's hold on me weakened, and he hunched over.

I shoved him away while he couldn't fight me, and then I spun, coming face to face with a livid Orla.

Flames danced from her fingertips as she lifted them. "What do you think you're *doing*? You just punched my husband and *your king*."

"I don't care if he's Liam Hemsworth! No one manhandles me like that." I needed to calm down and find my center. Stan had taught me that losing control gave the other person the advantage, but honestly, I was at my wits' end. I was powerless here. I had no say in what I did, what I wore, what I ate or drank—hell, I didn't even have a say in my own fucking *name*. They'd taken everything away from me, and the one person who'd made these awful feelings go away was plotting my demise. Add in the fact I'd failed to save Ginevra, and what was the point of playing along? None of it mattered. In the next trial, I'd die.

"Liam ... Hemsworth?" Kieran tilted his head, his hands turning back to their normal paleness. "Who in the hot winter is that? Is that yet another man who has your affections?"

I was certain my head spun around several times, and I felt an otherworldly presence enter my body. I had to be possessed because I wanted to kill Kieran right then and there. "Are you *slut shaming* me?" He didn't get to make women feel bad for having a healthy sexual appetite! Not that I had one since I was a virgin ... but that didn't matter!

"Slut shaming?" He placed his hands behind his head. "Are we speaking the same language? Because I'll be honest. Sometimes, I wonder."

"Let me make this very, *very* clear. It's none of your business how many men I have affections for." I wanted to flinch because, unfortunately, Kieran was the only one, but I had a point to prove. I placed my hands on my hips, ready to wield my dagger if it came to it. "If I want to sleep with *every person here*, that's my prerogative. You don't get to judge me."

His eyes narrowed, and he scowled. "I won't allow it."

I laughed, but when I realized he was serious, the sound turned bitter. He truly believed he had a vote in my life. "It's a good thing you aren't my king and I don't need your permission."

"She's right. You have no say in what any Summer Court member does." Orla moved to my side, straightening her shoulders. "You're growing too confident, King Kieran, especially when you're as likely to die as any other competitor in the Comortas."

"Is that a threat, *Queen Orla?*" Kieran said her name like the worst profanity available. "You only got to be queen because your sister died, and you—"

"Stop," I commanded, authority ringing through my voice. I'd channeled something raw and primal. He was trying to weaken my sister's position, and I wouldn't tolerate it. I had to protect her. "Tonight is about celebrating those who survived the first trial of the Comortas, not our two kingdoms fighting." I turned, searching for the five High Court members who should've interfered with this conflict.

Quinley, Leanna, and Caden stood at the edge of the dance floor, frowning at me. Each one wore colors that reminded me of winter and shadows. Quinley in an ice-blue dress, Leanna in a strapless black gown, and Caden in a suit that complemented his sister's dress.

Then there were Kaley and Eamon, who stood by the buffet of chocolates and spirits. Eamon lifted his glass, his suit almost the same color as his midnight-blue hair. I wasn't sure if he approved of what I'd said or was thanking me for the show. I couldn't read these people.

"Princess Alina's right." Moire's short form slipped through the crowd, and she stepped onto the dance floor. She wore a long teal dress that brushed the ground, with purple embroidery on her bust reaching down around her waist. "We should dance and be merry." She continued to weave through the crowd, moving to a song only she could hear. "Let's dance the night away and celebrate those who lived and our friends who died."

The way her cheeks flushed with excitement dissipated some of my anger. All eyes moved from us to her, and the music began once more.

Moire twirled her way to me and slipped her arm through mine. She leaned forward and whispered, "You're with me."

For some reason, I let her lead me away even though a large part of me wanted to stay behind with Kieran.

* * *

For the first time since I'd arrived in Talamh, I had fun. I stayed away from the spirits—because I'd learned my lesson that first night—and Moire and I danced. Unlike the other fae, she was kind and not as arrogant, and almost everyone here seemed to genuinely like her. There was something infectious about her, and I found myself warming to her.

"You and King Kieran always had a tense relationship." Moire laughed as we ate chocolate near the buffet. "I never understood what happened between the two of you."

I blew out a breath. Why was I not surprised? I'd felt something toward him from the start. Something intense and scary, but being with him and feeling his lips on mine had taken things further. "We're enemies." I shrugged. Even though I liked Moire, I didn't trust most people.

"Yes, but the way you two circle one another ... is odd." Moire lifted a hand. "I've never seen anything like it in all my years."

I blinked. "Should you be talking this way? How old are you?"

"There it is. The little girl jokes." She smacked the back of her hand against her palm. "You can go freeze yourself." She rolled her eyes, not amused. "You know I'm almost three hundred."

No, I most certainly did not. "Sorry, I'm still getting my memories back." I probably shouldn't have said that, but it wasn't a lie. I'd had one flashback, so that had to count for something.

"Oh, they aren't back." Her mouth opened, and she closed it. "I assumed you were poking fun like you used to do about my size. You used to say I had a big mouth to make up for my small size."

I flinched. That was so mean and sounded like something Orla or Curry would say. "I'm ..." I trailed off, catching myself before I finished that line. "Not quite the same person as before, and I think you're lovely." Especially for helping me when I'd been nasty to her in the past; she didn't have to do that. All the other fae here were tall, even by human standards, and she was barely five foot four. I understood her being sensitive about that—*this* me would never joke about it.

"Ah, good." She blew out a breath and added casually, "That's a very nice thing to hear before I die."

My lungs seized, and my smile vanished. "Don't say that. You could win."

"Don't. We both know it won't last." She ate another chocolate. "But I couldn't let them draft my little sister. She's only fifty and deserves a long life."

Another shiver ran down my spine, and my neck pulsed with cold. I didn't have to glance over my shoulder to know Kieran was watching me. Every few minutes, the sensation rolled through me.

I glanced around, only to meet his gaze as he danced with some gorgeous fae woman.

I inhaled. I knew what it felt like to have his hands on me, the way his lips had seared me with only a touch. I wanted to march over there, grab the woman by the hair, and yank her away from him. He was mine.

But that wasn't true. He wasn't, and the fact that I felt that way told me I needed to stay the hell away from him. He was messing with my mind.

"That's what my family gets," Moire said dejectedly. "So that's why I'm here."

Holy shit. Had she'd told me how she got here? I'd missed it all.

I was an official twatwaffle. "I could talk to Orla." I had no idea about what, and I doubted it would accomplish anything, but I could try.

"Didn't you hear what I said?" Moire blew out a breath. "My father told her she shouldn't have been crowned queen. This is our family's punishment for our disloyalty."

Yeah, there was no way I'd get her out of it. "Well, I wish there was something I could do."

"Just being here and hanging out with me like this is perfect." She smiled, sincerity flowing off her.

"Excuse me," Orla interjected, her words colder. "I need to speak to my sister. The ball is coming to an end, and we have to depart soon."

Moire curtseyed. "Of course, Your Majesty."

Taking my arm, Orla led me through the ball to the entrance, her hands firm on my arm but not tight like when she was upset with me. Maeve followed at our heels.

Another shiver ran down my neck and spine, no doubt from Kieran watching me leave. Either that or all night, it had been wishful thinking. It wasn't as if I could literally feel his gaze on me. That was ridiculous.

We walked in sync and strolled outside, leaving the loud music behind. She led me past a group of fae and into a more deserted area of the park.

When we were somewhat isolated, Maeve nodded at us.

Orla asked, "What happened back there?"

A lump formed in my throat. "King Kieran asked me to dance, and then he led me into the corner of the room. I didn't realize we were alone. Then Dallas interrupted us." I left out a lot of details as to why I hadn't realized and the fact that Kieran had kind of kissed me. I was certain that would only fuel more drama.

"I know that part." Orla rolled her eyes. "That's why I made Dallas leave. I didn't want another scene." Her jaw twitched, and her eyes hardened before they softened once more. "I meant, why did you cut off King Kieran instead of allowing him to soil my reputation further? Aren't you angry that I took the throne? Isn't that why you've been trying to embarrass me and come between Dallas and me?"

Clearly, that was something she thought my old self would do. "I'm not interested in Dallas *at all*. And you were right about needing to remain queen. I'm not upset about it. I don't know what I'm doing, and, Orla, I don't have even a quarter of my memories back. The only thing I resent is being pushed into this tournament."

"My hands were tied." Orla frowned, resembling an actual person and not someone who hated me. "But you sounded like my sister back there."

The doors opened, and all the fae began to leave. The sounds of the music were absent.

Maeve moved closer to us and murmured, "It's no longer safe to talk. We should go."

"You're right." Orla ran a hand down her stomach and patted my arm. "I'll see you soon. Let me say goodbye to Kaley and Eamon. I'll be right back." She walked over to the doors where the two High Court members stood, watching the guests leave.

"Ivy," Maeve whispered. "I sure hope you know what you're doing. You shouldn't let the Winter King hurt you again. This time, it won't just be your heart he destroys. He'll kill you without hesitation, and if you don't get yourself together, you won't stand a chance against him."

That was the second time she'd said he'd kill me without pause, and I wanted to ask what she meant, but the scenery around me morphed, and a memory flashed into my mind.

* * *

Kieran and I stood at the base of a long stone staircase before a towering white mansion. Snow fell from the sky, and I shivered, but I refused to show weakness to the Winter King, especially while in his kingdom...especially after what he'd done to me.

Tall, dark, ice-capped mountains rose in jagged peaks behind the castle, making me feel small. I hated feeling inferior. I touched my throat, where something cold pulsed beneath my fingertips.

"Stop doing that," Kieran snapped. "That doesn't change anything, and you know it. Did you insist on coming here to make things harder on us?"

I looked at the storage carriers that Maeve, ten other guard members, and the unicorns had brought. There was at least a month's worth of food for the people of the Winter Court. My guards were removing the food from the carriages, and his guards were replacing it with coal and gems.

"No, King Kieran." I stood tall, my golden dress flowing in the breeze. "I did not. Mother asked me to come on her behalf. I would rather not see you." That was only a half-truth. As much as I wanted to see him, each time I did, I left with a broken heart. He'd made it clear that he, his family, and his people would never accept me. That our union would cause civil unrest, no matter what Fate had forged between us.

Each time I saw him, my heart hurt worse, and the only solace I found was sleeping with my best friend and future husband, Dallas. Although what I felt for Dallas was nothing like what I felt for Kieran, Dallas was at least good in bed. Better than the lovers I'd had in the past.

"So, is this going to be a permanent thing?" Kieran grimaced as if the very sight of me disgusted him.

My heart wanted to shatter, but I let my magic swirl through me. The magic eased the edge of the suffering. "I'll find another arrangement." I curtseyed, needing to leave before I said something foolish. I needed anger and hate to fuel me, which always happened on my way home.

"Please do." His jaw clenched, and his eyes darkened.

I had to turn away. The regret would soon flash in his eyes, and it would make leaving that much harder. I had to be strong. I couldn't ruin my family's name.

I turned on my heels and let my wings explode from my back.

Maeve glanced at me with concern, but I ignored her. I didn't need some guard to see how much Kieran affected me. She was way too nosy.

* * *

Someone shook my shoulders, forcing me back into the present. I rubbed my heart, my vision cloudy.

Those emotions had been so strong and real. Kieran had rejected me in my previous incarnation. Could that be why he was being nicer to me now? Guilt?

Maeve touched my arm, scanning me. "Stay away from him, Ivy."

I nodded, trying to swallow. My mouth was too dry, making it impossible. Whatever was brewing between Kieran and me had been simmering for a while. What the hell was going on? "I will." I had to. I'd seen what he would do to me.

"Good." She gestured to the stairs. "You should head to your room before the others return. And you might want to take more of the painkilling medicine. It should've worn off by now, but you seem fine."

The urge to flee churned within me. I didn't want to see Kieran again. I rolled my shoulders and shrugged. "I'm not hurting, but okay."

"Be safe." She waved a hand. "I must leave with my king and queen."

After nodding good night, I headed up the stairs to my room. My feet and body were exhausted from the long, hard day.

Upstairs by my bedroom door, something dark shifted in the shadows near the stairs.

I shivered and peered around, but the spot had disappeared. My neck cooled, similar to how it had in the memory.

Someone was watching me.

Seventeen

MY BLOOD HEATED IN WARNING. I hadn't removed the key from its spot between my breasts, and I didn't want to with someone potentially watching. I didn't want them to know where I stored it— not that it was an original place.

My eyes searched every corner, but I didn't see anyone. The cool, prickling sensation pulsed through me, making me determined to find the source. The sensation reminded me of wariness and longing, identical to my feelings toward Kieran in the memory.

Oh, *hell* no. This wasn't okay. I didn't need to be thinking about him in *any* way. He'd broken Alina's heart, and I refused to let him break mine as well. I wanted to die with my dignity intact.

I tensed, preparing to grab my dagger. "Who's there? I know it's not a Summer Fae, or they wouldn't be hiding from me." A Summer Fae wouldn't hide in the shadows. The Summer Court liked to be flashy. This stalker scenario had Winter fae written all over it.

From the shadows at the end of the long hallway, Kieran stepped into the light and faced me.

The fact that I had sensed him had me questioning everything. I wanted to wrap my arms around my waist to protect myself from his presence. Maybe Alina wasn't the exact opposite of me.

I refused to allow him to see the power he had over me. "What do you want? I figured you'd be with one of the ladies you danced with."

As soon as the last sentence had left my mouth, I wished I could take it back. The point had been to appear unaffected by him, but instead, I'd acted jealous. I gritted my teeth, so damn annoyed with myself.

"You could have cut in at any time." He strolled toward me ... so confident ... so self-assured. His hair framed his sculpted features, and my traitorous hand wanted to reach up and caress his cheek.

"I didn't want to ruin your fun," I said. Thankfully, my voice was steady. He needed to leave before I did something I'd regret. "The other Summer Fae will be here soon. You should go."

"Watching you was the highlight of my night, but I made the first move. I need you to make the next one." Head tilting, he examined me and asked, "Do you *want* me to leave?"

That was a loaded question, and he knew it. This had to be a test. "If you're waiting for me to make a move, you'll be waiting for the rest of my or your life, whichever one is shorter." Enough people had hurt me already—the memory of how he'd made Alina feel was a sort of pain that would debilitate me. No one, especially this man, would ever break me. "And, yes, I want you to leave. I don't know what your intention is, but nothing good can come of it."

He licked his lips, drawing my attention to them.

My own lips prickled at the memory of the way his had felt on mine, and again, the urge to taste him flooded me. I wanted to feel that buzz like it was a hit of some illicit drug.

"That's only a half-truth." He stepped closer, his chest brushing against mine. "I can see the hunger in your eyes."

Body humming, I swayed toward him, a knot of desire twisting within me. If I acted on these emotions, it would only cause more problems. More pain. "Maybe, but we both know it's a bad idea. We're enemies and competitors." I took a step back, needing distance. "We both know your people would never approve of us ... not even temporarily."

His brows furrowed, and the cocky smirk disappeared. "Why would you say that? You haven't been here long, nor do you know how the Winter fae would react. I am their king."

I wondered if this was how Alina had fallen—an implied promise that they'd be together, only for him to yank the rug out from under her. "As tempting as that is ..." And boy, that offer was way more tempting than I wanted to acknowledge. "I'll have to pass. I'd hate for us to be the cause of any civil unrest." I let the words he'd told me so many years ago float between us.

He scoffed, and his mirth and arrogance vanished. "I see you're getting your memories back."

I nodded. "Not many, but a memory resurfaced tonight. I remembered the reasons you rejected me."

"Alina—" His face twisted in agony as his forehead creased.

"No." To drive the point home, I shook my head hard. "I don't want to hear it. You had concerns about us being together when I was born and raised here. Now, there are even more reasons to keep us apart. I don't have magic. I just got my wings, and one of us, if not both, is going to die in a matter of days. I don't need you to be more of a distraction than you already are. So please, Kieran, leave me be. The Summer Fae will be coming to their rooms, and after what happened at the ball, the last thing I want is for them to see us together."

He hung his head, looking broken. "You're right."

The wind whooshed out of my lungs. I *knew* I was right, but dammit, he wasn't supposed to agree with me. Despite my determination, I was officially becoming one of those girls. The kind who said one thing but wanted the guy to do another. The type I swore I'd never become, yet I was standing here, eating my words. Oh boy, were they bitter. "Yeah. I am," I said, a little defeated. I needed to get into my room, secret place for my key be damned.

I reached down my top, and Kieran shook his head as I fished out the key.

"Hey, it works." I was surprised no one else had come upstairs yet, but it was only a matter of time before my luck ran out. I showed him the key since he was acting as if I'd gone pervy. "So I can get away from you." *Before I do something stupid*, I almost added, but luckily, I kept that part quiet.

"You know you could carry a purse." King Kieran bit his bottom lip. "That's what most women do."

"I'm not most women." I slid the key into the lock.

A low growl emanated from him, the noise completely animalistic.

It should've disgusted me, but instead, my head clouded.

"Nobody better put their hands down your dress." His eyes darkened to a grayish blue. "If they do, I'll kill them, whether it's during a trial or not."

My heart fluttered. Officially, my body had a mind of its own, and it was very problematic. I hated how obvious my attraction to him was. The thought of him trying to take my key sent desire coursing straight between my legs.

Shaking my head, I turned to the door and slid the key into the lock. I needed to get inside and away from him before I did something foolish ... like invite him in or jump him right here. Even the thought of doing that had my legs wanting to run straight at him.

When the lock clicked, I pushed the door open, but he caught my hand. The jolt between us nearly stole my breath.

Nothing horrible could happen if we slept together, right? We could get rid of our pent-up sexual frustration, relieve the tension brimming between us. It couldn't make things worse.

Just as I'd talked myself into jumping his bones, Kieran dropped my hand and took several steps back.

Talk about mixed signals. But his drastic change in demeanor had my loins girded once more.

"You're right." He cleared his throat and adjusted his collar. "This won't end well for us, so we should be careful and not strengthen our connection."

"Right." My voice cracked.

He rubbed his hands together, not looking like the confident man I'd known. He exhaled and said, "Since you're at a disadvantage with flying and haven't been able to master your magic, maybe I could offer you some training before the second trial."

I glanced around, checking whether someone was watching us. Did they even have video recorders in Talamh? If they did, was I getting the fae equivalent of being punked right now?

Kieran tensed and spun to search the stairs. "What's wrong? The fae should be down there talking a little while longer. Everyone was tipsy and having a good time, so they won't be rushing here anytime soon."

That explained why no one had come to their rooms yet. I'd been all too eager to retire. Maybe I wouldn't have been so ready if I'd known Kieran would be waiting for me. I'd almost done something so stupid I would never have recovered. "I thought someone might be watching our exchange since you can clearly hide in the shadows."

They called him the Winter King, but he had cloaking abilities to shroud himself in darkness ... similar to the mist that had attacked us in the trial.

"My brother and I are the only Winter fae who can control shadows." He rolled his shoulders. "And Nolan isn't as good at it as me. But why do you think someone is watching us?"

"Why else would you offer to train me if not to humiliate me in front of someone?" We were enemies, and when I'd been in Alina's memory, she'd been concerned about her reputation and keeping her family name untarnished, except for her desire to be with Kieran.

"What in the warm winter are you talking about?" His jaw clenched. "I would never do something like that to you."

"Then why would you want to help me?" I stood tall, watching his expression, and finished, "You're supposed to kill me." My eyes widened. That was why. I could die under the ruse of a training accident.

"You have severe trust issues." He ran a hand down his face. "Even for a fae. I thought humans were trusting."

I rolled my eyes. "You clearly don't know many humans. And

between the few memories I have of who I used to be and how I grew up in *this* life, let's say I don't have many reasons to trust anyone, especially not the man who rejected me in the name of his people."

He flinched. "Yet you won't let me explain."

"It's irrelevant." Even if he gave me a good excuse, I wouldn't know if it was true or not. Not without all my memories.

"Fine." He pressed his lips together. "But I do want to help you. I care about your survival, and you were sent here to die. Let's at least give the other competitors a bit of a surprise." He winked.

Dammit, now he was breaking down my defenses. And if he killed me while training, maybe it wouldn't be so gruesome as the trial. I was so unprepared, even with Maeve's guidance. Letting him help me wouldn't be the end of the world. "But I wouldn't owe you a favor if we did this, right?" The last thing I needed was to be tricked into something else.

He smiled, pride shining in his eyes.

I wanted to puff out my chest, and I hated that his approval made me happy.

"Let's say this, mo fhlùr, that multiple people have already formed alliances. I suggest, for the second trial, we work together." He took a step toward me. "No one will expect that."

Working with him sounded so damn appealing. Against my better judgment, my legs carried me closer to him. "How do I know you won't betray me?"

"I give you my word." He placed a hand over his heart. "Princess *Alina*, I offer to ally with you until the end of the second trial. If you accept my offer, then training together would be in our best interest. A fae *cannot* break their promise." He extended his hand.

Rowan had said the same thing when she'd begrudgingly come to my room. She owed me because of a promise she'd made to Ginevra. In fact, she'd avoided me tonight.

I nodded, placing my hand in his large one.

The electric jolt shot into my soul.

The two of us stepped toward one another, drawn like magnets.

Our chests brushed, and I was completely at the mercy of whatever this was between us.

A loud giggle sounded from the stairwell, and Kieran scowled.

"They're coming sooner than I expected." He gritted his teeth and released his hold.

The coolness of his hands left me, and a deep ache settled within, missing the thrum of his touch.

"Meet me at the bottom of the stairs in the morning after breakfast." He brushed the back of his hand against my cheek. "I have a place we can use."

My eyes closed, and I focused on his touch and murmured, "But what about the trial?"

"They give us a respite in between so we can recuperate. The next trial won't be for a few more days."

That would've been nice to know before now. I kept coming in blind, whereas everyone else was aware of the rules.

"Rest." He inched away. "You need it after your day. Sweet dreams, mo fhlùr."

The edges of darkness surrounded him, and I didn't want him to go, but there was one more thing I needed to know before he vanished. "What does that m—?"

Before I could finish, he'd disappeared, and Moire and another contestant laughed loudly from the top of the stairs.

I didn't want them to see me. I pivoted and hurried into my room, but when I turned to close the door, I noticed the door across and one over from mine was wedged open. My gaze landed on Curry, who had clearly been listening to my entire conversation with Kieran.

I wanted to be embarrassed, but that wouldn't do any good. I had no clue how long he'd been there, but I saw a dark circle around his eye. He hadn't had it when we'd left the arena.

How strange.

Not wanting to worry about anything else, I shut the door and locked it. I leaned my back against the door and breathed shallowly.

One thing was certain.

King Kieran of the Winter Court would be the death of me.

* * *

Surprisingly, I slept well, but breakfast was loud. As usual, the Summer Court sat at the table decorated with flowers while the Winter Court sat at the icy table closest to the door. Unlike yesterday, only about half of each group appeared at each table.

Each person seemed joyful after the night of dancing, but I couldn't help but focus on the ten missing people. They'd died so horrifically and needlessly. I understood that this group needed to prove their worth, but why was *death* the price? With these fae, failing would be a worse punishment than death—oh, maybe that was the point.

I was surprised that both groups had lost an equal number, but had I saved Ginevra as intended, the Winter side would've had one more competitor on their end.

Curry sat next to me, his eye still black but not as bad as it had been last night.

Moire asked him what happened, but he refused to answer, choosing to glare at me instead.

From his reaction, I figured Dallas was involved. He was being protective of me, which was still hard for me to wrap my head around. He'd kidnapped me, after all.

I focused on eating the bread, honey, and jam, wanting to fill up since I hoped to burn a ton of calories in training.

I also couldn't help glancing at Kieran's back every few minutes.

Even the back of his head was sexy. How was that possible? It took every ounce of control I had not to jump up and run to him. Rowan and a woman who could pass as a young Cameron Diaz flanked him. I'd never wanted to harm those two people like I did at this moment.

"So ... how much pain medicine did you take?" Moire asked then took a huge bite of her grape jam and bread. "Because with how easily you're moving, you might have overdosed."

Shit. I'd forgotten to take the pain medicine last night and this morning ... but nothing ached. I felt completely normal.

Maybe it would be best if no one knew.

I could feel Curry waiting for my answer, his focus locked on his flute of water.

Maybe it'd be better if they thought I was still injured. I opened my mouth to lie, but no words came out despite my trying.

Something was wrong with me.

"Are you okay?" Moire dropped her piece of toast on the wooden plate. "Is something wrong?"

"I'm fine." When those words left me, I sighed in relief. I could still speak. "Just couldn't speak for some reason."

Curry chuckled bitterly. "That means you were trying to lie. You aren't human anymore, so you can't tell lies."

My face burned. I hated being called out. "I'm not sure of the dose."

"Oh, I can help you with that," Moire offered, patting my hand while glaring at Curry. "No one must have thought to share with you how much one dose is. It's just common knowledge for us."

That wasn't the only thing they hadn't shared.

Kieran glanced over his shoulder at me, a deep frown on his face.

Butterflies took flight in my stomach. Had he been listening to our conversation the entire time? I noticed he wasn't engaged in the conversations at his table, which was probably the only reason I hadn't gotten up and yanked his neighbors' hair out.

"I'll be fine." I took the last bite of food on my plate and stood, eager to get away. I hated the way Curry was focused on me, listening to everything I said. "Thanks for your concern. I'm going to get some air."

Rushing to the door, I hoped to get away before someone chased me down. The last thing I wanted was for Kieran to come find me while we had an audience. That would raise more questions than I wanted to answer, especially if I couldn't lie.

I could feel eyes on me as I marched to the door. I added a little limp to give the perception I was still injured.

When I strode into the entrance hall, Kaley and Quinley were walking toward the door to enter the room.

Kaley curtseyed. "Princess Alina."

Quinley remained upright with a smirk on her face.

She probably thought she would get a rise out of me, but I didn't even want Kaley to bow. I preferred them to address me like anyone else.

Clasping her hands, Quinley hiked up her charcoal dress slightly in front. "Where do you think you're going?"

My body tightened. Kieran had said we could leave, but now I feared he was the exception. "I'm finished with breakfast and want to find somewhere safe to breathe. Are we not free to move around the tower?"

"Yes, you are, but you can't leave the tower," Kayley interjected, cutting her eyes at Quinley. "You must be back in the dining hall for dinner; otherwise, you're disqualified, and the death sentence is immediate."

Of course it was. Death and blood were the only ways to get the fae to listen here. There was no positive reinforcement. "Understood." I nodded, needing to walk in the park outside or somewhere else to get a little solace.

Knowing there were flowers in the ballroom, I headed that way. It might not be outside, but at least it was some sort of nature.

Luckily, I heard Kaley and Quinley open the dining room door. Quinley said, "King Kieran. Are you already done with breakfast?"

I paused at the foot of the staircase to eavesdrop.

"Yes, and I have commitments for the day, so we can speak tonight," he said gruffly.

The door shut, and I turned around to see him strolling toward me. His expression was stern, and I couldn't help but take in his muscles underneath his surcoat. Even during the day, we had to wear uncomfortable clothing, but my dress was a little looser and easier to breathe in.

"Come," he said, taking my hand and leading me up the stairs. "We need to reach my room before anyone else comes out."

I froze. Did he just say what I thought he did?

Oh, hell no. That wasn't training, and I was definitely not safe alone with him in his room. "No."

He stopped dead in his tracks and turned to me. "What do you mean, no? You gave me your word."

Eighteen

HE'D LOST his damn mind. Worse, part of me was thrilled at the idea of the two of us alone in his room. I could take out some frustrations on him in pure physical form.

I had to shut this shit down before I convinced myself it was a good idea. "I agreed to train with you, not spend time with you *alone* in your *room.*" I took a much-needed step back from him and wrapped my arms around my chest.

He smirked, and heat swirled deep within me. "As much as I'd like what you're thinking to be the reason we're going to my room alone, that's not why I'm taking you there." He countered the distance I'd put between us and traced his fingertips along my arm. "Where else can we train that people won't see us together and learn about our fighting strategies?"

Goose bumps pebbled my skin, and the jolt that only his touch brought followed each brush of his hand.

He watched my skin respond to him, and my face heated. He was calling me out on every damn thing.

"There's not a private training area we can use?" I glanced around the entrance hall, unsure of the tower's full layout. The competitors' rooms took up the upper floors, and I'd seen only the ballroom and dining hall beyond that, but they were on opposite sides. The second and third floors held only bedrooms, so I hadn't considered there might be more rooms down here. But there had to be someplace to train.

One clear winner popped into my head. "Can we use the arena, or is that considered leaving the tower?" It would be ideal to get used to the space and practice while people weren't gawking at us.

"Alina, that's where everyone will go to train, and it's considered part of the tower, so we *could*." He took my hand again, his thumb rubbing the bottom of my wrist. "But I promise to behave when we're alone in my room."

That was the problem. I wasn't worried about him behaving. The problem was *me* due to all the things I felt around him. But he was right. If I didn't want the others to have more of an advantage over me, I needed to keep them in the dark about the little I could do to protect myself. "Fine." My hands shook, so I removed them from his and clasped them to hide how nervous I was.

His irises warmed to sky blue. "Alina, I promise I won't do anything to harm you in any sort of capacity." His deep voice washed over me, reminding me of a cool breeze on a hot, sunny day.

The perfect balance.

His intent was clear, weighing me down as my chest expanded until it throbbed like never before. I couldn't analyze that response too deeply, or I would be in a shit ton more trouble. "Okay, but if I'm uncomfortable, we stop."

He bowed his head. "Of course, mo fhlùr."

"What does that mean?" I breathed. Those words sounded so intimate.

He winked. "I'll tell you sometime soon. Just not now."

Voices murmured from behind the doors to the dining hall. Taking my hand, Kieran tugged me up the stairs, moving faster than before. I kept pace with him, not wanting anyone to see me go to his room with him alone.

I shivered. If someone did see and Maeve found out, I could imagine the disappointment in her eyes. Maybe Alina hadn't cared about Maeve's good opinion, but Ivy did. She had the most sincere intentions toward me, and I'd be foolish to drive her away. I needed a friend.

On the third floor, where the Winter fae were housed, the hallways felt different with their deep-cranberry walls. I kept glancing over my shoulder. Even though he'd said that no one else could use shadow magic, what if someone could and he didn't know?

I realized how foolish I was being. If anyone was using that magic, I wouldn't be able to see them.

Kieran removed a key in the shape of an icicle from his pants pocket and opened the door then tugged me inside.

The room was spectacular.

It was twice the size of mine, with walls the color of his eyes—a frosty blue. An icicle chandelier hung over his bed, which had a matching blue comforter and white sheets. His window overlooked the Winter section of the parkland, and the fall leaves were gorgeous.

I snorted. Of course he'd get a huge-ass room.

He walked across the smooth white floor between two burgundy couches and tossed his key on the white wooden end table beside his bed. "What's so funny?"

"Your room. It's like three times the size of mine." I spun around, taking in every inch and looking for personal items to learn more about him despite my desperate attempts not to. My gaze landed on a frozen statue on the floor behind the couch. It was a woman from the shoulders up with long hair and a nose that was very much like mine. My heart dropped into my stomach. That couldn't be me. It was ice with no color; it could be a coincidence. I jerked my gaze away, not wanting to be caught examining his room too closely.

Clearing his throat, he pulled my attention back to him. "I'm sure there's an explanation for that. There's no reason to be upset." He removed his jacket, tossing it onto his bed.

I blinked and forgot how to speak. All this time, I'd thought I knew how muscular he was, but with his jacket and armor off, in just a linen shirt, he was even sexier. His muscles strained against the fabric, and my stomach felt funny again.

But when he rolled up his sleeves to his elbows, something snapped inside me. My legs had a mind of their own, and I stepped toward him with fire igniting inside me.

He tilted his head, his forehead lined. "Are you okay?"

Taking a deep, steadying breath, I forced my legs to halt. "Sorry. I'm just taking it all in." That was one way of putting it, and looking away from his body was one of the hardest things I'd ever had to do. I focused on the end table where his key sat. That was when I noticed an iced purple flower that had decorated the ballroom last night.

How strange. It was a Summer Court flower.

"Once we start training, you'll be okay." He winked.

He brushed past me, his scent swirling around me and his muscles rippling under his shirt, causing me to think more indecent thoughts.

Something had to give.

He moved the couches to the side where the sculpture sat, completely hiding it. Needing to expend some energy before I got close to him, I strolled around the bed and noted another ice figurine on the other end table. I wondered how these things stayed frozen. Then I noticed the design, and alarms screamed in my head.

It was just like his tattoo, a half sun with rays swirling around and a half snowflake.

How was that possible? I spun around and looked at his neck. His skin looked untouched and smooth. My own neck cooled in the same spot I'd felt before, but that had to be a mental thing because there was nothing on my neck.

"You have that look on your face again." He lifted a brow. "As if you've seen a ghost. If you're that uncomfortable—"

I snatched the figurine from the table and studied it. The coldness of the ice cooled my skin, comforting me. The design was so beautiful and intricate. "What's this?"

His eyes darkened before he blew out a breath and smiled. "An ice carving. Something I do to pass the time. About fifty years ago, I became sun-bent on fine-tuning that talent. It's a hard skill to master."

His vague answer made me think there was nothing significant about the symbol. But if I'd seen this symbol on him and he'd designed it, the answer had to be significant. I couldn't be losing my mind, right? "But why *this* design?"

He unbuttoned the top of his shirt. "It's something I dream about from time to time."

"You dream about this design?" I didn't know why, but that made me feel more balanced. I wasn't the only one seeing this around. "I keep seeing it too."

The corners of his mouth twitched upward before settling back into a blank expression. "Well, that makes sense. It includes the sun, and you're the rightful heir to the Summer throne just as I am the ruler of Winter."

Huh. Even though Orla was queen, technically, I was the rightful heir. If the emblem represented Talamh, then it made sense for it to represent half of each court. I'd been trying to make it mean more than it did. "Right." I dropped the subject so I wouldn't sound deranged.

I placed the sculpture back on the end table, my fingers tracing the base. The symbol called to me, and my neck pulsed again.

I had to clear my head and focus. When I let go and turned to Kieran, I found a gentle smile on his face.

My heart pounded against my ribs, those weird feelings fluttering through me again. If he kept looking at me that way, especially in his more relaxed state, I'd jump him. "So, are you ready? I thought we came here to train, not to stare at each other."

He chuckled, sounding nothing like the angry, cold king I'd met on my first day here. "First, we need to address the amount of medicine you took this morning. How much was it? I don't want you feeling better than you actually are and wind up hurting you."

I lifted a brow. "You should take advantage. You'd be hurting me without meaning to and thus not breaking your promise."

"If I knew you overdosed, that would still be a broken promise, and we fae don't break our promises." He placed a hand over his heart as if the gesture added more sincerity to his words.

They all kept saying they couldn't break a promise. I'd learned this morning that they—we—couldn't tell a lie … figuratively. But I don't see how your body can *prevent* you from breaking a promise. "Everyone keeps saying that, but what does that mean? Is it like telling a lie—your body forces you to do something even if you don't want to?"

He went to the ice-blue dresser across from the bed and opened the top middle drawer. "No, it's not like trying to lie and having your voice stop working. If you break a promise, you lose your magic, including your wings if you're High Fae."

I ran a hand over the comforter, thin and smooth as silk. I swallowed hard. "How is that possible?"

"Your magic leaves you. The thing about our species is we're bound to the truth by word and action." He removed a long sword from the drawer. The blade was dark like a shadow, and the hilt was pale blue with a white snowflake etched into it. "Our magic prevents us from lying, but actions are different."

I snorted. "The saying 'actions speak louder than words' has a whole different meaning here."

"That saying comes from this kingdom." He tilted his head. "Humans must have learned it from our kind when a fae visited Earth." He took a belt from the drawer and placed it around his waist. Then he put the sword in the sheathe at his side.

Great. He had a long sword, and I had a dagger. Honestly, it was something I'd have to face at some point with the others. Might as well be now while I could learn a defense.

He removed another sword, identical to the first but with a thinner blade. "I need you to answer me about the medicine."

Here I thought I'd deflected quite well. I huffed, not wanting to reveal my secret. "I didn't take any medicine this morning." But if he was going to train me, revealing I wasn't injured was the better alternative.

His arm dropped, the tip of the sword hitting the floor.

I grimaced, hoping he hadn't messed up the tile.

"How is that possible?" He scanned me from top to bottom. His brows pulled together like he was solving the biggest puzzle in the world.

Yesterday, during the trial, the pain had been excruciating, and I'd believed I was near death. Given how quickly I'd healed, I must have been acting melodramatic. "I must have looked worse than I was." That was all I could come up with despite not believing it myself.

He stalked toward me and grabbed my arm, tugging so hard I thought he was going to pop my arm out of its socket.

"What are you doing?" I jerked away, glaring. "That's not training. That's manhandling, and if that's the shit you're going to pull, I'll see myself out."

His jaw dropped. "You aren't in pain."

I rolled my eyes. "I told you I'm fine."

"No, you said you didn't take the medicine." He shook his head. "I wanted to see if you were hurt, but you really are healed."

"Next time, just ask." I placed my hands on my hips, ignoring the way I wanted his touch. Each time he touched me, I became more desperate for him to do it again. That wasn't the sort of addiction I needed, especially when I was supposed to fight him. "Since I can't lie."

"That doesn't mean you can't skate around the truth." He held out the second sword to me.

He had me there. I glanced at his sword and back at him, arching a brow.

"Here." He turned his hand so I could reach the hilt. "Take it. I have a belt you can use."

I'd trained with a bow, daggers, knives, and guns. The one thing I'd never used was a sword. "Uh ... I have a dagger." I clutched the end of my sunflower-yellow skirt, wishing I could wear my pig onesie. At least in that, I could kick without worrying about my skirt flying up.

"No, you need to use this." He nodded to the sword again. "We'll work on flight too, but that will be harder in this room. Since you can't yet access your magic well or fly competently, you need a weapon that can reach farther to prevent the enemy from getting close."

I gritted my teeth, trying to keep calm. "Fair point, but I don't have my own sword, so there's no point in training with yours. It's best if I stick with my dagger. Besides, I can use my bow and arrows in a pinch."

"You do have a sword." He tossed the belt at me and grabbed my hand, placing the sword into my palm. "This one. It's yours."

I must have misunderstood him. "This has a snowflake decoration."

"And I'm giving it to you. We're allies, and no, there's nothing wrong with it." He winked as if that explained everything. "Come on. Time to train."

He moved to the center of the room and lifted his sword. "Let's fight."

After fastening the belt, I followed suit, hoping like hell I wasn't falling into a trap. I never knew with him. "We don't have armor."

"You won't get me. You'll see. And I won't strike you. I need you to get comfortable with the weapon first. Lift your sword and wield it like a dagger. The moves still work, but you'll need to adjust to the longer blade." He readied, waiting for me to engage.

I readied myself and lunged. I jerked forward, aiming the edge of the blade at his shoulder. The motion was bumpy and not even, as the sword was heavier than my dagger. He countered, knocking the sword out of my hand, and the weapon clanged on the floor.

Gritting my teeth, I retrieved it, watching him.

"Again." He raised his sword again.

Determined to get one good strike in, I slashed downward, aiming for his side. He pivoted, and my sword caught only air. I stumbled forward. I managed to catch myself and spin back toward him, striking again.

* * *

I tried, time after time, my body slick with sweat. No matter what I did, he managed to counter, and my competitive side hated that I couldn't get a lick in.

Time seemed to go still as I attacked him again and again. The awkwardness between us was gone, and fighting with him felt natural. When I lunged at him and he swatted the blade away, the impact forcing my arm across my body, I glanced outside and noticed that the sky was dark, but I focused back on him and swung again.

Our swords clashed for once at a standstill. My heart leaped— maybe I'd finally get a strike in. I didn't want to make him bleed, but I wanted to feel as if I had the upper hand. I moved my sword to the side and up, then swiped down when he moved his to the side. When I thrust down to catch the edge of his chest, he spun away, grabbed my wrist, and placed the sword to my neck.

He'd won.

That made my blood boil, and I took a step back. "You couldn't even pretend to let me get one hit in?" We'd been at this all fucking day, and he'd deflected me every damn time. I hadn't gotten close once.

A crooked grin stretched across his face as he lowered his sword. "Princess, what good would that accomplish? It would give you a false sense of how far you'd come."

I hated that he was right. I sheathed my sword. "Confidence. And please, I haven't improved at all."

"You have." He placed his sword at his waist. "You went from jabbing to swiping. You've gotten a lot more comfortable with your weapon. Tomorrow, you need to bring armor."

A lump formed in my throat. "You think?"

"I do. You're a natural and a fast learner."

I hated that his praise had me standing taller. I cleared my throat, needing to get out of here before I did something foolish. "Isn't it time to eat?"

"Yes, it is. Everyone should already be down there. Why don't you go first? I'll get my coat back on and head down a few minutes after you."

"Good idea." I removed the belt and handed it to him. It wasn't as if I could go down there with it on me. "Do you mind if I wash off quickly?" I didn't want to have dinner drenched in sweat. I at least wanted to dab myself clean.

He gestured to the door next to the dresser. "Of course."

Hurrying into the bathroom, I took in the charcoal walls and tub that looked carved out of frosted ice. I walked around the tub to the white sink and turned on the water. Next to the sink was a rack of gray towels, and I took one and dabbed it in the water. I wiped off my face and chest, the water rejuvenating me. I didn't know how water worked here, but it was magic.

I finished and set the towel on the sink, then went back into the bedroom to find him slipping on his black jacket.

I already missed seeing him in only the shirt, sleeves rolled up. He looked like a different person. With his entire suit on, he screamed sexy, dangerous Winter King once more.

I licked my lips. "I'll see you down there," I murmured as I slipped out his door.

Tiptoeing down the hallway, I heard voices in the entry hall drifting up the stairs, so I paused.

"That's what I'm saying," Curry murmured, but since he was the only one talking in the large room, I could make out every word. "We need to agree to this."

"I ... can't," Moire answered. "This is wrong."

What the fuck was going on?

Nineteen

I HELD MY BREATH, afraid if I breathed too loudly, Curry would hear me. Moire, feeling uncomfortable with his request, spoke volumes. He was up to no good.

My lungs screamed, but I tried to ignore their need for air as I tiptoed to the edge of the stairs, close enough so I could see over the banister.

Four heads came into view. Two I was familiar with, and the other two were the Summer Fae women in the tournament—the very two competitors who hadn't bothered talking to me except on the first night when I'd answered questions about the human realm.

The woman with long, pale-pink hair ran a hand through it. "Curry's right, Moire. She may look like Alina, but she's not. She has the mannerisms of a wild beast. Look how she tromps around in those heels, and she even saved a Winter fae in the trial! Something is wrong with her!"

Tromps? I crossed my arms, the urge to confront her over that comment making me move another step forward. I'd been working hard at being more graceful, and I resented her cotton candy head for saying that.

"Let's not forget the things she says that even a drafty knows about." The fae with hair similar to sunshine scoffed. "She called

King Kieran a *coldy* to his face. Then had him and Dallas almost fighting over *her* in front of the queen."

Hadn't been here a month and my reputation already preceded me. All my life, I'd tried to be invisible, but one night had changed that. My stomach churned. My own people were ready to turn on me. They didn't care that I'd been raised on Earth and needed to adjust to life here while fighting for my life. All they saw was that I was different ... that I didn't fit in.

"She hasn't been here long, and she's young." Moire huffed. "This isn't right."

"Frozen sakes," Curry spat, the venom heavy in his voice. "She's the royal representing us in this tournament, and she's shamed us all. She needs to go during the next trial before she can make our court look worse, so we need to work together."

"Then you three will have to do it without me," Moire snapped back just as strongly. "I won't team up with you to hurt her. She may be different, but who are you three to decide it's a bad thing? I'm going inside and joining her at our table. There's no reason for her to be sitting in there alone." As she moved to the door, more of her body came into view.

My head went light, and I couldn't hold my breath any longer. Making sure I didn't make a loud noise, I slowly filled my lungs, but even as the oxygen hit my bloodstream, I felt off balance. I suspected it had to do with the unexpected loyalty Moire had shown, even when it put her at a disadvantage.

Curry growled, "You better not warn her." He snagged her arm and jerked her small form toward him. "Promise me you won't tell her."

Even though all I could see was the back of his head, Moire quivered visibly. She was scared, and Curry knew it.

"Promise me *now*." He pushed, his voice turning more strained.

That asshole needed to learn a lesson, but rushing down there and breaking up their gathering would make them aware that I was listening to them. I glanced behind me, expecting Kieran to appear any moment. Luckily, he was still in his room, but he wouldn't be for long.

I clenched my hands so tightly that blood pooled under my fingertips. If Curry didn't remove his hands from Moire, I'd go down there and handle the task myself. No one hurt a friend of mine.

No one.

She just needed to make that promise because I didn't want her to become a target. I'd much rather they focus on me.

"Fine," her voice shook. "I promise, but what you're doing is *wrong*."

Though I hated that he'd forced her, my hands loosened now that she'd made the vow.

"Good." He clapped. "Now let's all go in and join her. We don't need to make her more suspicious."

Moire opened the door, hurrying inside with the three of them hanging outside the door together.

"I told you it was a bad idea to ask her," the pink-haired woman murmured and shook her head. "She avoided us every time we tried talking to her in the arena, and she tried to wait so we'd go to dinner before her."

"That's why we had to grab her." Curry scowled. "I thought we could pressure her and have a few days to train together. But it doesn't matter—we know where her loyalty stands."

Shit. Even her promise hadn't made a difference. I should've known. By not agreeing to team up with them, she'd insulted them, and boy, had I learned how vain all these fae were.

The blonde woman sighed. "We better go in and watch her."

The three of them walked toward the dining room, and when the doors shut, I exhaled. I had three High Fae competitors teaming up against me. Great. The last trial had kicked my ass enough without anyone directly attacking me. There was no way I would survive the next trial unless my fighting skills drastically improved. My chest tightened, and something that felt like claws dug into my gut.

"Alina?" Kieran asked from behind me.

Shit. I hadn't heard him open the door. I spun around and wished I hadn't. The way he stared at me so intently said he could read my thoughts and secrets. The feeling unsettled me. I tugged at my dress, needing something to do with my hands.

"Is that blood?" His forehead creased as he hurried over to me. He took my hands, flipping them over. In each palm, four nail marks had broken through the skin. He pressed, "What happened?" He glanced around the halls for a culprit to blame.

I opened my mouth to say it was nothing, but the words wouldn't come. Ugh. Had I known that one day I wouldn't be able to lie, I would've enjoyed doing it a lot more during my time on Earth. "I did it to myself." I had to settle on something that wasn't a lie without telling him what I'd overheard downstairs. For some odd reason, I knew better than to tell him. That he wouldn't take the news well, despite the fact that, at some point, the two of us would be fighting one another with the intent to kill.

My skin buzzed from where he touched me, and then he wiped his thumb over my cuts, smearing the blood. That should've disgusted me, but my body pulsed toward him.

"Why? What happened?" Concern tightened the corners of his eyes as he examined me again. "I thought you were heading to the dining room."

"Curry was outside the doors talking, and he has a knack for bringing out the worst in me." I pulled my hands away before I forgot all the reasons why we shouldn't be close to each other. "It's bad enough sitting at the table with him, let alone being stuck talking to him one on one."

"You need to be careful with him." Kieran pursed his lips as if hiding his true reaction. "He's ruthless when it comes to getting things he wants."

That wasn't shocking. "Then why is Dallas friends with him?"

He shrugged. "I don't have any answers for you, seeing as I'm not from that court."

That was fair. He was king and must have a list of duties that needed his attention. I'd have to ask Dallas about Curry ... if I had the chance.

"Let's get something to eat." He placed his hand on the center of my back. "You trained hard. Food will make you feel better."

Even through my dress, I could feel a slight buzz from his touch. Was it a mental reaction due to how damn attracted I was to him? His kindness toward me was also making it difficult to think about him as anything other than a good, sexy man.

But I didn't have time for a distraction, especially with Curry and his friends plotting together. "I thought we shouldn't enter at the same time."

"Go on, and I'll wait right here until I see you walk through the door."

I didn't want to leave his side, but survival instincts kicked in. Yes, the two of us were allies, but the longer we kept that secret, the bigger of an advantage we'd have. And I needed any sort of surprise I could muster.

Moving my legs was damn near impossible. Every fiber in my being wanted to stay right next to him, but knowing that someone could come out of a room was enough of a push that I managed to descend the stairs alone.

The nape of my neck tingled as if I could feel his gaze on me, and when I reached the door to the dining room, I glanced back up to where he stood at the edge of the stairs. Our eyes locked, and my neck pulsed cold.

He nodded, encouraging me to enter.

Facing the door, I inhaled and barged through. I didn't want any of the fae to think I was trying to hide or be quiet. If they wanted a fae royal, they'd damn sure get one.

I stalked into the room, keeping my footsteps light. Not because I wanted to please them but because I wanted to prove every last one of them wrong.

When I slid into my seat, Curry arched a brow, and the two women fidgeted in their seats. Moire glanced at her plate, avoiding my gaze ... and I realized that maybe I'd go down, but

I'd go down fighting like hell. I'd die with dignity in my own way.

Curry and the women didn't bother trying to talk to me, and Moire also remained quiet. That was more than fine with me.

Snatching some bread, chocolate, and honey, I filled my plate, getting ready for the hardest days to come—when I'd fight them all.

* * *

For four complete sun cycles, Kieran and I trained in his room. The day after our first training session, I snuck armor in with me, and we made use of the area as best we could. When I wasn't eating or sleeping, I was training with him.

"Pull out your wings," Kieran commanded as he jabbed at me with his sword.

I blocked his sword and kicked him in the stomach, then flexed my back muscles. That was the part I was struggling with the most —getting my wings out and back in. Luckily, the clothes that were made for High Fae accounted for this very thing; a small slit was fitted for each wing. Once the wings were out, I was fine, at least in the small area of his room where we practiced.

He didn't budge, just grunted as he swung the sword at my side. I pivoted, and our blades clashed as I flexed my back again, and then my wings exploded.

We circled each other as I blocked his blows. We'd gotten into a natural rhythm, which was bittersweet since we could read each other now.

"Attack me," he gritted out as he increased the pace of his swings. "You haven't tried that yet."

I'd hoped he wouldn't notice, but of course he had. He fucking noticed everything, and that was a problem.

Instead of obeying, I continued to block his blows. He picked up the pace, moving faster than ever before.

Clenching my jaw, I kept up with his moves. Each clang of our swords vibrated through my entire body.

"Stop holding back," he rasped. "Since they aren't allowing us into the arena today, I suspect the second trial will be tomorrow, and you need to unleash your strength out there. Holding back will get you killed."

Our bodies were slick with sweat, and the room was bright, indicating it was midday. We still had hours to practice.

When he lifted his sword over his head and swung it down, I gripped my blade at the tip and hilt, using it as a block, being careful not to cut myself. His sword slammed against it, forcing me to use every ounce of my strength to prevent the sharp blade from hitting me. Then he kicked me in the stomach.

My body flew across the room, and I tried to retract my wings, but I couldn't before my back slammed into the wall. My head hit hard, and I crumpled to the floor.

He'd kicked the shit out of me. Thank goodness it wasn't literally.

He stood in front of me with his hands at his side and growled, "I *told* you to attack."

Was he fucking serious right now? I jumped to my feet, and the floor tilted underneath me, but I managed to keep my balance. Probably just to spite him. I glared. "That wouldn't have prevented that from happening."

"Yes, it would've." His chest heaved, and I tried to ignore the way his annoyance had my body revving. "You were so focused on blocking my blows that you forgot I could also attack you with my body or another weapon."

Shit. He was right, but dammit, I refused to admit that. He had a big enough head already. So, I had to settle for the truth. "I don't want to learn to attack."

He sighed and sheathed his sword. "That's what I thought. Alina, it's either you or them, and it better fucking well be *them.*"

Though he didn't know about the conversation I'd overheard, he was right. Curry, the pink-haired girl—who I'd learned was named Lesli—and the blonde-haired woman named Mackenna would be after me as soon as the second trial started. I had no doubt about that. "All my life, I've wanted to *protect* people, not hurt them." I doubted he understood that being a fae and all, but the truth fell from my lips before I could stop it.

His face twisted into what looked like agony. "Believe it or not, I understand. I've always done what I thought was best for my people, but something I learned recently is that, when you worry only about protecting others, the decisions you make may come at too high a cost to bear. And you may actually weaken your people because of it."

Something twisted in my chest, right where my heart beat. Whatever he'd done haunted him, and I didn't like to see guilt and pain weighing on him. When everyone else turned their back on me, he'd allied with me and trained me to defend myself. "Attacking someone isn't protecting my people, and not attacking is protecting myself from becoming like Curry and the others."

"You could *never* be like them." He closed the distance between us, placing his hand on my cheek. His next words were almost a whisper. "You're amazing, kind, brave, and too damn good for this world. This world needs you, which means you have to protect yourself."

Something around my heart trembled, and I decided one thing right then and there: I couldn't die without knowing what kissing him was like. I dropped my sword, letting it clank to the floor, and wrapped my arms around his neck.

His eyes widened as my lips touched his, but I pressed on and kissed him.

When he didn't respond, my heart almost stopped. I inched away. "I'm sorry. I—"

"Don't," he groaned as his arms circled my body, and his hot, eager mouth met mine.

He tasted of cinnamon and chai, two of my favorite flavors that I missed from Earth, and I couldn't get enough.

I'd kissed only one person before. When I was sixteen. And it was nothing compared to *this*. My tongue stroked his lips, and his breath caught. Something warm swirled inside me as my neck pulsed cold, cooling off my body. When his mouth opened to mine and our tongues intertwined, I never wanted to stop kissing him.

He grabbed my ass, lifting me up, and my legs wrapped around him. Our armor rubbed together, making the position harder to navigate, but we were determined to make it work.

Fisting my hands in his hair, I tilted his head back so I could taste more of him. My head grew foggy, and my body brimmed with heat that might make me implode. I needed him with no barriers, especially not his armor.

He matched each stroke of my tongue, and before I realized what was going on, he'd laid me down on something as soft as a cloud.

His bed.

He pressed some of his body weight on me, inflaming my body further. I'd never understood desire, but I ached to feel his skin on mine. It wasn't rational.

A loud knock sounded on his door, followed by a loud voice as if the speaker were using a microphone.

"Trial two starts in twenty minutes." Caden's voice projected down the hallway. "All contestants have ten minutes to gather their weapons and armor and come downstairs to be let in."

Kieran froze on top of me, panting. Then he suddenly stood with wide eyes. "You need to go gather your things."

He was right. We didn't have time to waste, but my body hadn't gotten the memo because it wanted to carry on with Kieran.

Taking my hand, he helped me stand. He tucked a piece of hair behind my ear and said, "Keep this sword, change into your strongest armor, and bring your dagger and bow. It's time we go to war. Together."

Together.

That was the only part of the sentence I liked.

But now wasn't the time to be a girl with a crush. Kieran was counting on me to help him survive. I nodded and said, "I'll meet you downstairs." Then I hurried to my room.

Luckily, I reached it undetected, mostly because everyone was in their rooms preparing for the trial. I dressed quickly, putting on the golden armor Maeve had brought me. My blood buzzed as if the armor were connected to me and my magic.

Right at the ten-minute mark, I was the last person to make it downstairs.

Kieran and I locked eyes, and he motioned for me to come stand with him right in the middle, where the Summer and Winter fae divided.

As I passed the back line, Rowan glanced at me from her spot beside her king. She bit her lip nervously.

I took my spot, and Curry smirked, his glare turning more malicious. He moved toward me in his golden armor and chuckled. "I hope you don't expect to make it out alive."

I'd lifted my chin to respond when Kieran stepped between Curry and me.

Jaw clenched, Kieran sneered. "*What* did you say?"

Twenty

MY LUNGS SEIZED, but I somehow held my body still. I understood it was possible that everyone would learn Kieran and I had allied, but I'd hoped we wouldn't need to follow through on that vow. That way, no one would be the wiser.

With Kieran's reaction, everyone would soon be aware.

Curry lifted his chin, not bothering to hide his scowl. "It's none of your concern, *Winter King*. I was talking to a Summer Fae."

"The Summer Fae who is your princess and my ally in this trial." Kieran's chest heaved, his body more tense within his armor.

There went keeping that a secret, but my body warmed, knowing he had done it to protect me. Not that I needed it, but the thought was genuine.

"And no one insults and threatens those to whom I have sworn my allegiance, so let me return the favor." His nostrils flared, and he stepped into Curry's space. "I hope you don't expect to make it out alive either." He smirked, the threat hanging between the two men.

"Of course you'd ally with a *Winter* fae." Curry glared at me and spat as if *Winter* was the worst curse that anyone could ever mutter. "You're just a Winter lover."

If he thought I'd be insulted by that, he'd be greatly disappointed.

I batted my eyes and smiled, making it clear I wasn't offended. "I actually do love a good snow. In Nashville, we only get snow once a year if we're lucky, and each time, it's one of the best days of the entire year." Some of the foster kids and I would sneak away for a fun field day, building itty-bitty snowmen and having snowball fights. At one point, I'd thought about moving north to experience more winter weather, but my Southern heart enjoyed the warmer climate too much to ever make the leap.

"You're the princess of the Summer Court," Lesli scoffed from beside Curry, placing a hand on her silver armor, which didn't have any intricate designs like mine or Curry's. "You should hate everything winter stands for. Your sister must be ashamed."

Mackenna shook her head. "Please, ashamed probably doesn't even cut it."

At least they weren't hiding that they didn't like me. That made me respect them a little. I hated two-faced people who pretended to be my friend while secretly plotting my death behind my back.

Moving forward, Moire caught my eye and nodded her head behind us.

I glanced over my shoulder and saw Kaley and Leanna. Kaley wore a bright-yellow dress that reminded me of Mackenna's hair, but her arched brow pulled my gaze away from her outfit to her face.

Leanna's expression wasn't much better. She was dressed in all white, and her crimson lips were mashed into a hard line.

Both of them must have heard most, if not all, of the exchange.

Following my gaze, Kieran didn't flinch. Instead, he turned and scooted me into the spot between himself and Rowan.

I waited for my anger at him manhandling me to surface, but it didn't.

What the fuck is wrong with me?

I'd never let anyone fight my battles before, and I sure as hell wouldn't start now. Finally, the anger I'd hoped for came swirling into me, and I channeled it toward Kieran, not wanting to consider that I might be more mad at myself than at him.

"You're in my spot," I said loudly, the commanding tone from the night of the ball seeping into my voice.

Kieran cut his eyes at me. Though he had a blank expression, the past several days of training with him had taught me to read him better. When he was pretending he didn't care, he had a tell.

He tapped his fingers on his leg. Barely any movement, just enough for me to notice.

My heart ached. I didn't like that I'd upset him, but if I didn't stand up for myself, it would make things worse between me and the other contestants.

In fairness, they were already planning to kill me.

Still, I didn't want them to view me as weak. I took his hand, the buzz springing to life, and tugged him back to his spot. At first, his feet held strong, but I softened my expression, begging him to yield without saying the words.

He moved back to his place between me and Rowan. I didn't want to draw more attention to us, so I stood tall and stared straight ahead.

Kaley laughed a little too loudly. "With whatever *that* was behind us, let's move on with the trial."

The two women walked in front of us without a sound.

Odd.

When Kaley moved to stand in front of me and Leanna stopped in front of Kieran, I looked at the floor. Their bare toes peeked from the hems of their dresses.

They were barefoot, not in heels. That was why we hadn't heard them.

Kaley clasped her hands. "The last tournament was inspired by the terrain of Deigh Mountain of the Winter Court. Today's trial will embrace the terrain of the Summer Court!"

Loud groans came from the Winter side while Curry, Lesli, and Mackenna snickered.

"During the last trial, five Winter fae died." Leanna grimaced. "That proves that the people from a particular court may not be strong enough to endure their own elements."

The fact disgusted her. She wasn't even trying to hide it.

"I hope the competitors of the Summer Court won't succumb to similar issues in this trial, especially since the winner of the last trial is entering the maze as I speak." Kaley started with Moire and gave each of us a long stare before stopping at me. "Even with a head start and their royal bloodline, some of us might be too untrained to survive, but we shall see."

She'd just given me the middle finger, or what I suspected was the fae equivalent, reminding me of Southern parents threatening their kids with a whoopin'.

Kieran grunted and curled his upper lip, revealing the top row of his white teeth.

Never in my life had I found that expression sexy, but dammit, it was now right up there with the vision of him rolling up his sleeves the other day. I wanted to bite his bottom lip and taste him all over again.

Whoa. Down, girl.

I was about to fight for my life and face whatever hell the High Court thought would be entertaining, and here I was thinking I wanted to jump Kieran?

This was why I'd been determined to stay away from him.

"When the door opens, the five Winter Court members will follow me." Leanna gestured to her left.

Kaley then gestured to her right. "And I will guide the Summer Court members."

A lump formed in my throat. They were splitting us up. Of course. I should've known that our alliance wouldn't work. That would've boded too well for me.

I forced myself not to react, as if they'd just told me about the weather.

To my right, Kieran's fingers tapped gently on his legs again. He wasn't happy either, and that reassured me.

The two High Court members watched Kieran and me, and after a moment, Kaley spun around and knocked on the door before opening it.

A circular maze made of thick green brush and vines wove through the middle of the arena floor. Stone stairways led to the earthen floor of the area. The place was lit with sunlight so bright that it had to be magnified, though I wasn't sure how.

"Let's begin!" Kaley flipped her hair and pointed at me. "Please, *Princess* Alina, follow me first. Since we're Summer, we'll enter before the Winter competitors."

Everything inside me demanded I say something to Kieran, but I swallowed hard and moved ahead. I needed to at least pretend to be confident.

My legs were so leaden they must have doubled in weight in the last few minutes. I stepped forward, the urge to kiss Kieran one last time damn near making me spin and do exactly that. There was no way I was getting out of this alive. I'd be stuck on my own with Curry and his gang. They'd attack me as soon as we started.

The crowd jumped to its feet, and the loud boos began. At the last trial, I'd had some supporters, but this time, every single person wanted me dead. I'd not only embarrassed my sister but the entire Summer Court by trying to save Ginevra.

They can all suck my left toe.

Ginevra might not have survived, but at least she had died without traumatizing fear. That had to count for something other than me being a complete and utter failure.

Curry walked close behind me, and I expected him to push me down the stairs. That seemed like something he'd do. Maybe, in this instance, he wanted to make sure he killed me viciously in front of everyone.

Halfway down, the crowd members closest to me spat at the stairs as if their feelings about me weren't already clear. The worst part was that they were dressed in Summer colors of blues, pinks, yellows, and oranges. My people.

I straightened my back, refusing to cower. When I died today, I would with my pride.

On the dirt floor, my boots kicked up dust while Kaley seemed to glide over it. The heat of the sun poured over us. I looked skyward, noting the glass overhead as it nearly blinded me. It had to be magnifying the sun from outside.

Sweat pooled underneath my low ponytail, and I faced straight ahead as dots blurred my vision. I didn't understand the point of the maze. We could all fly over it.

No doubt they had something in place to debilitate us, like the nightmare mist from the previous trial.

The brush and vines of the maze stood twenty feet tall, making me feel extremely small. A cutout about midway down the maze appeared, and Kaley stopped. "Everyone, spread out here."

The chants of the crowd blended together, and only one word stood out.

Die!

I loved starting a bloodthirsty trial on such a positive note.

Kaley faced the entrance to the maze. Moire and Curry flanked me.

Turning my head, I watched as the last of the Winter fae stepped off the stairs. It wouldn't be long until they were in position.

From the corner where we stood, Quinley stepped forward, wearing a burgundy dress that contrasted with the light of the arena. "As the oldest High Court member, it's again my duty to inform all of you spectators and contestants about what this trial represents. The High Court attends to the concerns of both the Winter and Summer Courts to bridge the differences between our people. The best way to do that is to seek a new member who can survive the harshness of both winter and summer. The last trial frosted out those who couldn't rise above winter. This one will show us who can thrive without melting down in the heat of summer."

Eamon stepped forward with the magic lute in hand. The sunlight revealed lighter blue highlights in his hair, and he wore a green suit, likely as a tribute to summer. "In this trial, there is one simple rule: no flying. Anyone who flies will be killed immediately without honor, bringing shame to their court and the realm." He looked directly at me and added, "Not that it matters to some of you."

Laughter erupted from the stands, proving me wrong once again. I'd thought I'd rather hear anything but the boos, but laughter directed at me had just taken the top spot.

Even Quinley smiled.

Oh well. Who'd said I couldn't bring people together? I'd bet before today, no one would've thought that Winter and Summer would laugh over the same thing. At least I'd accomplished that before I died.

"Though the next note isn't a rule, it's something to remember." Quinley rubbed her hands together and paused for dramatic purposes. "If you don't reach the center of the maze by sunset, you'll be locked in overnight, and we've retrieved night screamers from the wildlands to end your life."

Moire gasped and inched closer to me.

I glanced at her, my brows furrowing, and whispered, "What is that?"

"An animal that looks like death and kills you with its scream." She shivered. "To avoid death, you require ear protection, which I'm sure they won't provide."

"Shh," Kaley hissed, glaring at us.

Great, now I felt like we were in grade school.

"If you reach the center of the maze, you're safe. No one can harm you. Until you get there, nothing is off the table. Caden will be in the center, ensuring no one cheats." Quinley raised both hands, and the crowd went wild.

When Eamon lifted the lute, my stomach churned. This was it. The last day of my life. I had to put some distance between myself and Curry and his followers and hope like hell I could find Kieran.

Eamon thrummed the lute.

I grabbed the hilt of my sword and rushed inside, Curry, Lesli, and Mackenna right behind me. I heard them unsheathe their weapons, and I could feel a sense of the attack to come.

As I stepped into the maze, the trail split and fog misted from the vines on the path, thickening in seconds. I didn't want to hang around to find out if this fog was anything like the one in the cave trial.

Betting that they would put the fog in the direction we needed to go, I pivoted right just as Curry, Lesli, and Mackenna blocked my way.

Curry had his sword in hand while Lesli and Mackenna held daggers. At least they weren't all using swords. I wondered if Kieran had trained me with a sword to put me on more equal ground with Curry.

I lifted my sword, the sun glinting off the white snowflake that signified Winter. "What do you want?" I already knew, but I wanted to hear them say it.

"You need to run," Moire whispered, appearing at my side.

Any doubt I'd held toward Moire shattered completely. She reminded me of Maeve. She was different and not as cutthroat as the rest.

"Stop being frosty," Mackenna seethed as the fog drifted toward them, thick as a cloud. "You're going to die alongside her."

"Don't pretend you didn't plan it that way anyway," Moire shot back, removing a knife with shaky hands. "At least this way, I go down protecting my princess, the rightful queen."

Oh damn. She wasn't pulling punches. I refused to let something happen to her. She was a good person, and she didn't know I didn't want to be queen. "If you want to hurt her, you have to go through me." I stepped forward and whispered, "Run. If you see Kieran, send him this way."

Moire's eyes became the size of saucers, and she nodded and spun on her heels, going to the left. I hoped she found the center before these three idiots killed me and came searching for her.

The white cloud blanketed the three of them and moved toward me.

Mackenna whimpered. "Something's wrong."

My heart raced. Whatever was in the fog would come for me next. I spun and ran after Moire. I didn't give a damn if it was the wrong direction as long as I got away from the fog, but then the mist swirled around me too.

I stumbled and fell to my knees. I lowered my hands, making sure the sword didn't stab me as I crawled after Moire.

Curry coughed somewhere behind me, and I turned to see if he was close, but all I saw was white. The cloud had taken them.

"I can't breathe," Lesli croaked behind me, and I knew I had to get the fuck out of here.

My chest tightened, and I tried to breathe slowly, but as the mist thickened around me, the end had to be near. I couldn't see, smell, or hear a damn thing except for my heartbeat hammering in my ears.

Small goals, I chanted in my head. I had to channel Stan; he'd been on battlefields, which was exactly what this was.

I crawled forward, inch by inch. That was my one goal.

My eyes burned, and dirt kicked up around me. Time seemed to go on forever.

"Princess Alina?" I thought I heard, though it had to be my imagination. Still, it was enough to keep me powering on.

One more foot, I kept repeating, pushing myself onward. Then something amazing happened.

The fog didn't seem as opaque.

My heart rate picked up. Had I made it to the center already? That seemed too easy. And how could others have died when no one could see them clearly?

Stomach fluttering, I pushed forward, and some of my sight came back to me. After fifty more crawling steps, the fog thinned and revealed a blurry person standing before me.

I stood up, shaking, and took a huge gulp of hot, dry air while leaning the sword against my legs. I rubbed my eyes. If this person was a threat, I had to defend myself, but I needed to see to fight them.

"Princess Alina, please help me," Moire begged.

When I opened my eyes, my vision cleared, and my throat ached.

The person was Moire, and even though she was standing, the

ground appeared to be swallowing her. She was hip-deep and sinking fast. If I didn't help her, she'd be gone.

Twenty-One

I DIDN'T HAVE any time to think. Moire gritted her teeth, crying as she struggled to get free of what appeared to be quicksand.

"Stop fighting," I said urgently, which only caused her to shriek and yank harder. I sheathed my sword, readying to help her.

She sank deeper, the sand at her waist.

Stan had warned me about the perilous situations he'd been in; he'd had to exude calm when he didn't feel it because he was the commanding officer. I'd never imagined that his war stories would become as relevant as they had since I'd arrived in Talamh.

Taking a deep breath, I hurried to the edge of where the dirt gave way between two willowy trees. The pathway's edges were fine, but not in the center where most of us would travel. She must have gotten stuck and tried to turn around to head back in this direction.

Still, she was about five feet away from me, and I couldn't reach her without falling in myself. I inhaled and forced my voice to come out measured. "Moire, if this is anything like quicksand back home, fighting it and trying to get out will only make you sink faster."

"What?" She froze. "This is gainmheach luath? I'd only heard about it in nighttime terrors from when the ponds formed a long time ago. The sand that eats you whole." She jerked harder, trying to free herself.

I wasn't sure if it was true here, but I could speak to how it worked on Earth. "In my world, it's not the sand eating you. It's sand that gets disrupted somehow and mixes with air and water. My mentor, Stan, used to tell me stories about his time in war, and one of them involved quicksand." I racked my brain to remember everything he's said. At the time, I'd only halfway listened, thinking this information would never be helpful.

Her bottom lip quivered. "It doesn't eat you there?"

For someone her age, she reminded me of a young girl. "It doesn't, so maybe it's the same here. If you don't know how to get out of it, it does look like it's eating you." I could only hope that some of the rules applied here. "The number one rule is to stop fighting it. It causes you to sink faster."

"I'm supposed to stand here and let it take me under?" Moire's mouth dropped. "And here I thought you were going to save me, not let me drown or be eaten."

That was like a punch in the gut, but I held in the pain. She was scared, and her fear was talking.

"I am trying to save you, Moire," I said clearly, wanting her to hear I wasn't lying. "From the gainmheach luath," I added, attempting to make it clear that I was being specific so she didn't think I was twisting my words. Not fighting against being pulled downward didn't make sense, but that was what it took ... at least on Earth. I was putting a whole lot of hope that things here worked the same way, but even with two moons and magic, there was a similarity to gravity, the seasons, and daylight and darkness—the fundamentals.

She chewed on her bottom lip before huffing. "Fine, but I don't see how that's going to get me out of here."

That was the catch. If she was having a hard time staying still, she wouldn't like what I suggested next. "Have you ever swum in water?" I tried not to flinch, but hell, I didn't know how things worked here.

"What?" She stared at me as if I had two heads. "Of course. I've swum in the ponds and under the waterfalls."

Waterfalls? That sounded badass. I wanted to see them. I could only imagine how beautiful they were here.

My heart dropped. I wouldn't make it out of this trial alive whether I died by the screaming things or at the hands of Curry and his minions. For now, I needed to focus on helping Moire while I could. I was certain Curry and the others would soon be behind us. "When I was younger, I liked to lean back and float. That's what I need you to do."

"But I can't use my wings." She shook her head. "I'll be eliminated."

Technically, the High Council said no flying, but I didn't want to argue semantics. "Take a deep breath and lean back. You don't need your wings to float. Humans do it all the time."

Her mouth dropped. "They do?"

"Don't the non–High Fae swim here?" They'd have to float using the same methods.

Moire pursed her lips. "I ... I've never seen them swim before, so I'm not sure."

I'd ask more about that later if ever given the chance. "Okay, I need you to listen and try it. I'm going to walk around to the other side so when you lie back, you can extend your hand, and I'll pull you toward me."

Her sinking had slowed, but she clasped her hands in front of her chest.

I didn't want to rush her—that would only make her freak out again—but I needed her to move. She was waist-deep, and it would only get worse from here.

I hurried to the side and pushed myself into the hedge to get around. A vine wrapped itself around my finger, sniffing me like a dog. I pushed away the strangeness and tapped my foot on the edge of the sand, where it appeared solid. Even though I was certain I could get out if I slid in, I didn't want to risk it. Curry and the others could come and cut off my head.

The crowd would love it.

My boot met solid sand, so I crossed, moving close. With my

back pressed against the hedges, something inside me stirred, giving my blood a kick. It felt similar to when I'd manipulated the vines around me. It must be my magic, and I wished like hell I could channel it.

I made it to the other side and damn near cried. Finding the edge where the ground started to sink, I realized that, from this side, she was farther than five feet away, but this was our best bet, especially if Curry and the others showed up any second, as I expected.

I removed the bow from my back. "Lie back, and I'm going to lean over with my bow. Grab it, and I'll pull you to me slowly." Any jerky movements would risk the sand suctioning her under.

She nodded and closed her eyes as she leaned back. Then she exhaled so her body didn't have the trapped air to help her float.

Bloody summer icecaps. "Inhale deep," I commanded. I got on all fours and held out the bow, but missed her hand. The top half of my body tumbled forward, and my hand slid into the sand. Dirt circled it. With my knees, I pulled myself out while maintaining my grip on the bow.

Moire's top half had already begun to sink, and she gulped a breath.

We were running out of time, and I could see the fear taking hold once more.

I gritted my teeth, keeping a firm hold on the bow, and inched closer to the loose dirt. With as much calm as I could muster, I slowly extended my hand and the bow toward her. The quicksand was already at her ears—she'd go under in seconds.

Her hand reached out again, and she missed the wood but clasped the wire. It would have to do.

Curling my legs underneath me, I used them for leverage as I reached out my other hand, snaked it around the bow, and began pulling her toward me.

When her head lifted from the water, my eyes burned with tears of relief until I noted blue liquid dripping from her fingers into the sand.

Blood.

The wire had cut into her hand.

"Readjust your grip real fast," I ordered and leaned forward. She had enough give in the weapon to grasp the wood on the other end.

Then she started to sink again. "Alina!"

I tugged harder, needing her to feel me reeling her in. Despite my arms screaming, I groaned, "I've got you."

The light brightened around me, and the heat intensified as I continued to pull her toward me. Sweat slicked my body, and beads of it rolled down my face into my eyes. I'd hit two obstacles within minutes of coming here, and part of me wanted to lie down and rest. But I couldn't give up. Not with Moire so close to death.

"You're doing it," Moire sighed, her relief evident, but my arms trembled harder between the strain and the heat.

I gritted my teeth as Curry shouted, "We're almost out!"

Of course, they'd be coming right when I almost had her freed. My head swam as my arms struggled to keep pulling. When I had her within two feet of safety, my legs gave out, and I tumbled forward.

My face hit the ground, and sand filled my mouth and nose with a grotesque, earthy taste. I hadn't taken a breath since I'd been winded from exertion, and my lungs were screaming.

This was it. The way I'd die. For some reason, I thought it'd be less melodramatic.

Not wanting Moire to be the last person I remembered, I conjured Kieran's face in my mind. I focused on his sculpted cheeks, full lips, and commanding presence, and the way he tasted of cinnamon and chai. The one regret I had was not throwing caution to the wind and enjoying his body. My heart broke in a way I didn't understand how to describe, even worse than it had in my memory as Alina.

My blood burned and came alive.

Something hoisted my legs, and my lower half was tugged backward. Suddenly, my body emerged from the sand. I inhaled deeply, and sand filled my mouth, but oxygen mixed within it and filled my lungs. My blood pulsed, and I realized I still had the bow in my hands.

Moire.

Whatever had pulled me out had dragged me far enough that Moire was half out of the quicksand and crawling the rest of the way out. Her top half dropped onto the hard dirt, and she took shallow, rasping breaths.

We'd almost died.

"What in the heat cycle," Kieran rasped as he dropped beside me. He gripped my shoulders, turning me toward him as he scanned my face and asked, "What happened?"

He was somehow more handsome than before despite the cut on his cheek. I reached out, touching it and getting dirt on his face. The buzz between us jolted, and I winced. "Sorry. I didn't mean to get you dirty."

I went to remove my hand, but he grasped it and murmured, "Don't you dare apologize."

"Of course she's touching the *Winter King*," Curry spat from across the quicksand.

I tore my attention from Kieran and glanced at Curry, Lesli, and Mackenna, who were standing in front of the quicksand.

I hoped like hell the three of them fell in. For the first time, I believed I might be able to kill someone ... and that terrified me.

Something raked across the dirt behind me, and I spun around to see vines heading back into the hedges. I shook my head, wondering if I was imagining things. I'd been oxygen deprived.

I connected to my magic by accident but couldn't do it when I was trying. That sounded like my luck.

Moire heaved herself up, and I stood to help her. We needed to get away, and I wasn't sure she could walk. She was still gasping while hunched over, and Curry and the others were behind us.

Sighing loudly, Kieran rasped, "Go help her. I'll hold them off."

My steps faltered. Had I heard the king right? He was protecting two Summer Fae from their own kind?

I decided not to question it and to trust him since he'd vowed to be my ally.

When I reached Moire, I watched Lesli move forward to walk into the quicksand, but Curry caught her arm and said, "Look at them. It has to be gainmheach luath."

"That's not just a horror story they tell the young?" Mackenna tilted her head and dipped the tip of her toe into the sand. It sank. "Frozen waterfalls. It's real."

"Go. I'll catch up to you," Kieran said as he moved forward.

The jackass truly thought I would leave him. I helped Moire to the side by the hedge to sit and said, "Stay here and yell if you need me."

She nodded, leaning against the hedge as I turned to find Curry moving around on one edge like I'd done while the women went on the other side.

"Fight them," I commanded, rushing to Curry. "I got this jackass."

"Jackass?" Kieran's brows furrowed, but he shook his head as if he'd decided it didn't matter what I meant. "You are hurt."

"I'm fine." My lungs had been screaming, but with the last several breaths, my energy had returned. "I promise."

He nodded, though his jaw clenched. We drew our swords, and he ran to fight the women as I focused on Curry.

Curry lunged, and I lifted my sword. Our blades clanged as he moved toward me. He swung his blade hard, not holding back like Kieran had, but he wasn't as strong as the Winter King.

I blocked each blow, and from Kieran's side, I heard the sickening sound of a blade cutting skin.

The crowd near us went wild, and the heat intensified as a body thudded to the ground. Lesli. She clutched her throat, and blood spilled between her fingers.

Something hard crashed into my chest, and I stumbled back. I caught myself and lifted my sword, staring at Curry again. He'd used my distraction against me.

I knew better.

He swung, aiming for my head, and I ducked. His sword whooshed inches above my head. While I was down, I kicked him in the knee, and he fell backward ... into the quicksand.

I froze.

Mackenna's body was tossed into the quicksand next to Curry.

What the—

They fought one another, trying to use the other as leverage to get out, which only caused them to sink faster.

I glanced at Kieran, who shrugged.

"You threw her in there?" I snorted. I was both amused—which bothered me—and disgusted.

"Seems fitting that they die together. They had every intention of doing that to you *or worse*." He grinned. "This is what they deserve. No one tries to hurt you and gets away with it."

My heartbeat quickened. Part of me liked hearing that. What sort of person was I becoming?

"Alina," Moire rasped as she stood, still leaning against the hedges. "We need to go. We have until sundown, and they didn't put us in here until half the sun cycle was already past."

Ugh. The High Court was trying to screw us in every way they could. I hated everything they stood for. Sheathing my sword, I tried to wipe some of the crusted sand from my face, but all that did was get it in my eyes.

"She's right. Let's go." Kieran jerked his head in the direction he'd come from.

That reminded me. "How did you find us?" He'd been let in on the other side, and it seemed suspicious that he'd found us over here.

"We made an alliance." Kieran sheathed his sword and lifted his chin. "I needed to find you."

My stomach did a somersault at his words, but I didn't want him to know how much of an impact he had on me, so I merely nodded. "Okay. Do you have any idea how to get out of here?"

"No. Shall we go that way?" He nodded toward the white mist.

That was still what my gut said, but as I scanned our surroundings, trying to block out Curry's and Mackenna's screams, I noticed something. "The branches." I observed both sides. "Are they all pointing one way?"

It was in the direction Kieran had come from.

The route was subtle, just slightly tilted that way.

"It's a clue." Kieran waved a hand back in that direction. "Let's follow."

"I'll follow wherever you go." Moire placed a hand on her heart as she continued to pant. "As long as you let me."

I smiled. I didn't want to think about the next trial, but for this one, the three of us could work together.

We took slow, measured steps, the heat sapping our energy. Kieran stayed next to me, sweat dripping down his face and onto his armor. His cheeks had a hint of pink, proof he was impacted by the heat despite his Winter power.

Screams echoed from other parts of the maze, and a shiver ran down my spine despite the heat. Each noise was a reminder that we weren't safe and another attack could happen at any moment.

"Are you okay?" Kieran asked, his forehead creased.

I wanted to answer him, but my mouth was so dry that my tongue stuck to the roof, so I nodded.

The edges of his lips tipped downward, but he didn't say anything else, likely because he realized he couldn't solve the problem.

As we continued to walk, the path inclined, and the trees vanished. There wasn't any shade, but the pathway turned to grass instead of dirt, and the kinds of flowers that hung over my bed back at the castle blended into the hedges.

"This area must represent the mountains of the Summer Court." Moire ran a hand over the pink, blue, purple, and yellow bulbs that reminded me of wildflowers. "Back there, it had to be the ponds with the trees, fog, and quicksand."

I wanted to roll my eyes. They sure did go through a lot to challenge us. "What else is left?"

She pursed her lips. "Forest."

"Is that all?" I feared there would be a lot more themes, but this maze could only be so big in the arena.

Kieran scowled. "Questions like those are why other Summer Court members target you."

Okay, I didn't like this broody version of him. I clenched my hands, trying not to throw a punch. "Excuse me if I was raised on Earth. We didn't do crazy shit like this."

We turned a few times, and I expected something to pop out at us. Then we stumbled on a pool of water. Moire gasped, dropping to her knees on the bank. "Oh, thank the heat of summer."

Kieran grabbed my shoulder, holding me back as if he thought I'd go after her, just as I said, "Moire, wait."

Blind with thirst, she didn't listen and took a huge gulp of water.

My stomach churned.

I waited for something bad to happen, but it didn't. She continued to gulp water.

If it was safe, I wanted some, too. I moved to join her, but Kieran stopped me.

"Don't," he murmured, his irises darkening. "We need to wait until the trial is over."

I could tell he was worried, so I nodded and grimaced. I could deal with my thirst for a little longer.

"Here," he said and reached out, brushing his finger against my lip. "Open."

My breath caught, and my lips moved of their own accord. He slipped his finger inside my mouth. After a second, ice gathered on my lips, and the heat of my mouth melted it so cool water ran over my tongue and down my throat. Our eyes connected as something warm surged through me that had nothing to do with the heat. Soon, my thirst was quenched enough that I wasn't desperate to drink the water, and he removed his hand as Moire stood and wiped her mouth with the back of her hand.

"You should have some. It's good, and I feel so much better." She nodded.

"Let's get moving." Kieran gestured to the path, ending the conversation.

As the three of us walked, following the branches, more screams echoed around us. Then we took a sharp turn and saw mirrors that lay against the hedges and flowers.

They reminded me of the pictures I'd seen at the Fairy Bar, where I'd met Ember.

I hurried to them, thinking maybe I'd see Ember, just as Kieran said, "Alina, don't—"

When I saw my reflection, I was suddenly transfixed.

Twenty-Two

IN THE MIRROR, the image changed from a reflection of me to the inside of the carriage that had brought me here. A younger version of me that looked like a prepubescent child sat in the forward-facing seat with a woman who appeared to be in her thirties sitting across from me. She looked like what I could only describe as nature ... and very familiar.

Mom.

My forest-green eyes widened. I glanced out the window and saw a garden where hundreds of fae were hunched over, harvesting various fruits and wheats.

"You know what a good idea would be, Mother?" I flung my braided strawberry-blonde hair over my shoulder. The ends were just becoming lighter ... like sunlight. "When these fae are done, they should swim in the warm waters of the falls. We could bring carriages to take them there. It would relieve their tired muscles."

My heart squeezed. Everything else I'd remembered had made my prior version seem unkind, but that right there proved I had cared about our people. Maybe it wasn't such a burden to be what everyone thought I should be.

Mother's nose wrinkled, and her gray eyes filled with disappointment. She leaned over, her champagne dress gaping, exposing more of her cleavage. "Alina, *no*. They need to go home and rest to be prepared for tomorrow. We can't have them staying out late and dragging the next day. They can rest at their homes."

The version of me in the mirror pouted and stared out the window again. "But Mother, one visit can't hurt anything."

She huffed, her face turning pink and contrasting with her wavy green hair. "Giving them access to the falls once is all it would take for them to want to go again. Sometimes, ignorance is bliss. You'd best remember that since you're to inherit this kingdom."

I rubbed my hands on my sparkly pink dress, and the current version of me remembered that it had been one of my favorites. I'd always been partial to the sunfire blossoms of our kingdom. The radiant pink flowers that bloomed in the mountains had petals that glistened like flames, emitting a golden glow.

"I know, Mother, but—"

"Not another word, Alina." Mom *tsk*ed and scowled. "Our harvest has been dwindling, and we must ensure our kingdom doesn't starve."

"I'm sure if we cut back a little on prod—" the younger version of myself tried again.

Mom flicked her wrist, and vines from the carriage wrapped around my mouth, cutting me off. My eyes widened as I grasped at the vines, trying to remove them.

"Nothing is more important than ensuring the Summer Court is strong and our family's reign is respected and never challenged." She leaned forward with a glint in her eye. "You care for our people, but only to the extent that we can maintain our lifestyle. The last thing we need is for the Winter Court—especially Prince Kieran— to get ideas and think they can conquer us once he takes the throne. Do I make myself clear?"

I didn't understand why the young version of myself didn't fight her. I could control the vines and flowers, too, but then the reason popped into my brain. Fae didn't get their magic until sixteen complete season cycles. My mother had total control over me.

Now, my dry throat had nothing to do with the heat and everything to do with the treatment this first version of myself had received. My mother reminded me of some of the foster moms I'd encountered, trying to control her child and mold her into whatever she wanted.

The image in the mirror changed, the carriage vanishing. In its place, teenage versions of me, Orla, and Dallas appeared in the garden back at Sambradh Castle. Orla was the age I'd been in the previous vision, and Dallas and I stood before one another. Maeve stood several feet away, giving us privacy but staying close enough in the case of an emergency.

Dallas grinned flirtatiously. "So, now that you're coming into your magic, are you going to go against your mother to help the less fortunate fae?"

I laughed hard, turning toward the flowers. "Mother would kill me." The edge in my voice made it clear that what I'd said wasn't a joke. "Even though that's what I wanted to do when I was younger, Mother has shown me that doing so will put all the Summer Court fae at risk, especially my family. I can't do that to Mother and Orla." I nodded as if trying to convince myself. "I *won't* do that to them." I leaned over and cupped one of the sunfire blossoms. Azurebell, sky-blue, bell-shaped flowers surrounded them, and together, the two flowers reminded me of the summer sky.

Dallas touched my arm. "I'm glad you understand the risk of doing what you dreamed of when we were children. Though I see the merit in what you want to accomplish, it would have severe consequences for us all, especially your family and the summer High Fae. But if you ever decide to pursue that dream, I'll have your back. You're my best friend, and I want you to be happy. Come frozen summer or fall."

His words unlocked more memories of my life. Dallas and I, as kids, swimming in a waterfall. The two of us, flying above the trees, swearing one day we'd not only tame Talamh but the wildlands too. He'd been beside me all my life, and his father was a High Fae who presided over the closest village to the castle.

I wanted to see more. Remember more. So I stepped toward the mirror. I needed to understand why I'd changed my mind about helping people and understand everything my mother had done.

Kieran blocked me. His expression was strained with concern, but I needed to see more ... learn more ... understand who I was and what had led me to sacrifice myself for my people. I hadn't learned the specifics, just that I had saved the world from mud monsters.

I tried to pass him, but he followed, remaining in my way.

I gritted my teeth. "Move," I commanded.

He sighed and hung his head. "I can't, mo fhlùr. We've already wasted too much time here. We need to go. Others will either find us, or you'll stay here until sunset."

"Fine. I just need one more minute." I needed more answers, and I'd say anything to get him to move out of my way. I was always at a disadvantage; maybe if I learned more about the past, I'd understand things here without someone either laughing at me or judging me.

I placed my hands on his chest, ready to shove him aside, but he gripped my wrists. He held them firmly and lowered his head so we were eye to eye. "We don't have a minute. We're in a trial, and our time is limited. I need you to move."

Kneeing him in the stomach, I tried to shove him backward, but he didn't budge. He was like a fucking brick wall, and I doubted his armor had anything to do with it. Tears of frustration burned my eyes. The one thing I wanted more than life at this point was to learn more about my past.

A sob racked my chest. "Please. I'm tired of not knowing things ... not understanding this world. I need it to make sense, and the mirror has answers."

"Hey," he said gently and moved so one hand clasped my wrists. With his free hand, he placed his knuckle under my chin, raising my head so I looked into his eyes. The jolt of our connection grounded me. "If you work with me and we both live, I'll tell you everything you want to know. If there's something you don't understand, I'll make sure you get an answer. I don't care who I have to ask or what favor I need to call in, but you won't learn what you want if you stand here and die. That's what the mirror does—it makes you want to stand here and learn about whatever your heart desires."

His tenderness stirred something in me, and after a request like that, how could I say no? I sniffed. "Okay."

His entire body sagged as if the weight of the world had been lifted from his shoulders. "Good." He released my hands and wiped the tears from my eyes. "For a second, I didn't think you'd listen to me."

Moire cleared her throat, and I remembered we were most definitely not alone and had thousands of people watching us. Still, Kieran had taken the time to help me despite how his people would react.

Blowing out a breath, I straightened my shoulders. I had to get myself together. I rarely cried. In fact, I couldn't remember the last time I had. "Sorry. I should've known it wasn't just a mirror. The last time I got enamored by one, I wound up here."

"That was likely the portal." Kieran scanned the area, avoiding the mirrors. "Mirrors here have magical abilities that depend on the type of glass they are cut from."

I swallowed, trying not to focus on the flutters going on inside me. He was taking the time to share information ... like he'd promised.

Moire's eyebrows rose higher to the point they were hidden under her bangs. I was certain she'd be bombarding me with questions later. Questions I wouldn't want to answer. Not solely because I didn't know how to answer them but because I had the same questions regarding Kieran's and my relationship.

"Which way do we go, Princess?" Kieran strolled toward the hedges, squinting at the branches. "I can't tell."

Was he serious? I could tell even from my spot several feet away from them. "We continue to follow this path and take the sharp turn." Of course, the route would take the Summer Fae across the mirrors. Had they put them there to target me? Everyone knew I didn't have all my memories and I didn't fit in. Out of everyone here, I'd want answers the most.

I spun in the direction we needed to go, and Kieran hurried beside me, keeping himself between the mirrors and me. His size prevented me from seeing them as he matched his pace to mine.

"Don't look at the mirrors," he instructed Moire behind him. "You'll be tempted the same as Alina was."

I glanced over my shoulder as Moire stared straight ahead and marched right past us. As soon as she took the lead, I followed her, content she hadn't fallen for the High Court's trick.

The sun beamed on us as the pathway continued to slope upward. Sweat dripped down all parts of my body, even from my forehead into my eyes. Nearby moans almost had me missing a step. People were close by, and everyone but the three of us was a foe.

Once more, my tongue stuck to the top of my mouth, and my throat ached from how parched it was. I'd be surprised if we didn't die of dehydration.

"Do you need more?" Kieran asked as he touched my arm, slowing me further. Sweat slicked his face, yet he was asking me if I needed something. He lifted his finger like he'd done when Moire had been drinking from the pond.

I nodded, not caring that I wanted him to use his magic on me.

Before he did, Moire's steps slowed.

"You should help her too." I hated the thought of him placing his finger in her mouth, but she had to be suffering as well.

His jaw twitched, but he nodded. "Moire, let's take a quick break."

"We need …" She exhaled and faced us. Her skin was pale, and her eyes were black.

She didn't look like herself.

"Warming icicles," Kieran gritted and lifted his hands. Ice flakes formed on the fingertips of one hand, and the other sent out a breeze, picking them up.

The wind carried the heat of the maze but gusted into a wide circle of ice. The ice melted into cool droplets as the air churned between the three of us. The water splashed my face and cooled me by several degrees.

I opened my mouth, allowing it to coat my throat. The sensation was similar to a winter rain in Nashville and rejuvenated me.

"Something isn't right," Moire whimpered and fell to her knees.

The cool water coated her face, but she'd grown paler.

"Blood's dripping from her nose." I squatted. If it was from the heat, the cool water should have helped, but blood wasn't usually a sign of overheating unless her nose was dried out. "Is your nose dry?"

She whimpered, wiggling underneath me. "Hurts."

"Where?"

"Everywhere." Her chest heaved as she grunted. Then blood trickled from the corner of her mouth.

"Shit, Kieran." I didn't bother to use his formal title. "More blood." I looked skyward, the sun so bright it was damn near blinding. "Something is very wrong."

His mouth mashed into a line. "The water she drank had a purple hue. It wasn't normal water. The High Court may have poisoned it."

No. This couldn't be happening. He had to be wrong.

I took Moire's hand in mine, clutching it hard as if that alone would force her to hang on to life. I understood that death was part of the trial, but it didn't have to be her. She was the most innocent of us all, having joined to protect her sister, knowing this was the end she'd have.

Blood seeped from her mouth, eyes, and nose, and she writhed in agony. Tears burned my eyes. I hated that she was dying like this.

"Don't ..." Despite her labored breathing and a sickening rattle in the back of her throat, Moire stared into my eyes and murmured, "Change." Then her chest stopped moving.

Cheers rose from the crowd as hot tears streamed down my face, plopping onto the arm I still clutched. I could see the mist of her magic pulsing from her skin and vaporizing into the air. Her death had been in vain, arranged by the High Court for pure entertainment.

"Alina, we need to go." Kieran leaned over Moire's body and touched my hands, which still clutched hers. "She's gone. We need to keep moving."

He was right. If I didn't leave, he'd stay here with me and succumb to his own death. I knew it. I had to move ... for him. "Okay, but I need to do something first." Moire deserved a send-off ... some sort of goodbye.

I didn't have anything but the bow, dagger, and sword at my disposal. I couldn't give her the sword because Kieran had gifted it to me, so I removed the dagger from the sheath on my left side. The vines twirled around the handle, feeling very Summer Court. I would leave her with something that represented her home.

I placed her hands over her chest and put the dagger in them.

"What are you doing?" Kieran's voice rose.

"She deserves respect. I want to leave something of mine behind with her," I explained as I moved her hands to clasp the dagger. I looked at her ravaged face. "You will be missed and thought of each day." I leaned over and kissed the top of her forehead, hoping that in some way, somehow, she'd realize how much I'd grown to care for her in such a short amount of time. "Thank you for being my first real friend here."

I didn't want to leave, but I had to think of Kieran, so I stood and waited for the boos to come.

The arena was eerily quiet.

Kieran swallowed and waved. "Let's go. The sun will be going down soon."

He didn't insult or criticize me. He was just ready to go.

We took off running.

Willowy trees overhead offered some shade as we followed the path. With every step we took and didn't run into trouble, my stomach shuddered. The willowy trees thickened, providing better coverage from the heat. Things were going too well. We kept moving inward, toward the circle, and I kept expecting something horrible to strike at us.

"Look," Kieran shouted excitedly. "It's the center."

My heart stopped. He was right. We'd found the center, but we couldn't just walk into it. A large canopy of vines began at the bottom of the hedge and grew over the central circle. A sign said that to reach the center, everyone had to climb over the wall.

There had to be a catch, but I had no clue what it was.

"Come on." Kieran rushed to the limbs, but as soon as he touched one, he hissed and stumbled back.

Twenty-Three

I SCRUTINIZED the hedges and canopy for something that could harm him. There were no thorns or anything threatening that I could see. I hurried to him and studied the palm he was examining. There was nothing there.

My brows furrowed. I looked up to ask what had happened, but his face was pale.

I swallowed, feeling as if knives were stabbing my throat. "Did you drink the same water as Moire?" This was how she'd looked not five minutes ago before she'd started bleeding.

He blinked and exhaled. "No, I didn't. You saw me the entire time. Why would you ask that?"

"Because you're pale ... well, paler than usual." My body tightened. What if the vines were poisoned and he was in the beginning stages? Maybe he'd gotten a tiny cut I couldn't see. I held his hand closer to my face, trying to find an injury. "Did you get pricked? If we get the poison out before it circulates, you might stand a chance." Maybe I could find something to suck the poison out like some humans did on Earth.

"I didn't get pricked," he said, cupping my cheek with his free hand. "I'm not poisoned. I promise."

Between the buzz of his hand on my cheek and his minty

breath, I wanted to taste him again. Once was most definitely not enough.

His hand closed around mine, and the world stopped.

A dark laugh came from close by.

"At least the traitor died," Curry croaked. He must be back where Moire's body lay.

My breath caught and white-hot rage swirled inside me. That prick not only had the audacity to laugh at her death but to actually show gratitude for it. No one celebrated the death of someone I cared about.

No one.

I released Kieran's hand. Not even the buzz of our connection would distract me from what I had to do. I'd felt this sort of rage before and buried it, not wanting to become the type of person who acted out the same horrors I'd witnessed in foster care and detested. I'd run away and found Stan, then channeled my rage into training kids who'd been victims of the system. I'd tried desperately not to become this vengeful person, but all that changed today.

Today might be the first time I killed someone and maybe, just maybe, danced over his dead body.

I grimaced. Okay, I'd taken that too far. I hated how callous and vindictive the prick was.

Kieran blocked my way. He arched a brow. "Where do you think you're going?"

"To kick Curry's ass once and for all." In fairness, I wasn't sure I could, but I'd handled him earlier. As long as I got in a few licks and made him bleed, I'd die happy.

"He's not worth it." Kieran nodded at the canopy. "We need to focus on getting over that and reaching safety." He gestured at the roof between the trees. "Sunset isn't long from now, and getting over that won't be easy."

My heart dropped into my stomach. "What do you mean?"

"Let's just say this is the hardest test we'll face." He pressed his lips into a line. "Trust me. That's why I jerked back. I didn't expect to hear your—" He cut himself off and cleared his throat. "*A* voice."

He hadn't stopped himself in time, and now I knew that, for whatever reason, I was part of this trial for him.

I sighed. He didn't want to talk about it, and we were running out of time. "Okay." I tried to put aside my rage. If this final challenge was that horrible, maybe Curry would die by the screaming monster. "Let's do this."

His head tilted as he exhaled. "You're listening to me?"

I placed a hand on my hip. "Not if we don't get moving. If we're going to stand here and stare at each other, I might as well use that time to kick Curry's ass."

"Like you said." His nose wrinkled. "Let's do *this*."

A laugh escaped me, catching me off guard. I felt like Jekyll and Hyde, one minute angry and the next laughing. Something inside me was changing fundamentally.

The corner of his mouth tipped upward, and we turned to climb the canopy. This time, Kieran's jaw was set as if he was ready to face whatever version of me he'd heard.

Unsure what to expect, I touched some of the branches of the canopy, preparing to hoist myself up.

"Ivy?" A way-too-familiar whisper brushed my ears. "Where are you?"

I released the branches and turned to search for the owner of the voice.

Beth.

My chest heaved. How had she gotten here?

"Alina, it's okay," Kieran assured me. "It's just the canopy."

I shook my head. "No, it's not the voice of a competitor here. It's someone I know from Earth. I've got to help her." The one girl I'd let down more than anyone else in both worlds.

"She's *not* here," he insisted, touching my shoulder and forcing me to turn toward him. A vein pulsed between his brows. "I'm pretty sure this obstacle will make us face our biggest regret in order to cross over."

I clasped my hands to my chest to prevent myself from falling over. Her voice sounded so real. As if she were here. But cold realization poured over me. Her voice had sounded the same as when she was eight years old, not the eighteen-year-old woman she was today. "How is that possible?" I rasped, hating that they could pull something from me that was so fucking real.

"It's an illusion spell of Quinley's." He blew out a breath. "Only a few people can do it, and she's one of the best. It's how she won the Comortas seven hundred years ago."

I didn't know who to thank since I had no idea who people worshiped here. But some entity had to be looking out for us because Curry didn't share that particular skill.

"This way," Mackenna said. From the sound of it, they were about to round the final turn to reach the hedge where we were.

Kieran and I nodded to each other and reached for the canopy of plants again.

Just like the last time, Beth's faint whisper swirled around me. "You're going to be back by seven, right? I don't want to be alone with her when she comes home from work."

I already knew where this was heading. The night I'd failed her.

Gritting my teeth, I reminded myself this was an illusion and continued to climb. It wasn't actually happening. The damage was already done, and I'd live with the regret of failing her for the rest of my entire fucking life, however long that might be.

"She said she'd be here." Beth sniffled quietly. "Why isn't she here?" The heartbreak in her voice was evident, and it sounded as if she was going through the experience all over again.

I'd been working on a school assignment at the local public library with some other of the foster kids. I should've been able to get back in time.

I climbed another branch, focusing on maintaining a decent speed so we would reach the top before Curry and Mackenna could stop us.

Kieran groaned beside me, his own agony coming through. I looked at him to find that he was several branches below me, his face twisted in agony and his hands shaking on the canopy.

What in the world could I be saying to him to make him react that way?

"There they are!" Curry exclaimed. "We need to end them now!"

Not being as careful, I quickened my pace just as a ghostlike Beth appeared beside me. Even in her ghostly form, I could see a tear in her eye.

"Why didn't you come home like you promised?" she whispered, her bottom lip trembling.

I froze. This wasn't real. She was alive and on Earth. This was another trick. But no matter how many times I told myself that, my legs stiffened.

Something grabbed my ankles, and before I could kick, I was yanked from the canopy. I fell to the ground, and my back twinged as my wings tried to open. For the first time, I had to fight the urge to let them loose, not wanting to chance the High Court proclaiming I'd cheated.

Mackenna stood over me.

Commotion between Kieran and Curry rang in my ears, but I couldn't take my eyes off Mackenna.

She raised her dagger to stab me in the chest, and I rolled to the left, away from Kieran and Curry. She swung down, and her dagger stabbed the grassy floor where I'd been a millisecond ago. I kicked her in the side and sent her stumbling into Curry.

Curry sidestepped and tried to regain his balance as Kieran swung his sword at the jackass. Curry raised his sword to block Kieran's blow as he shoved Mackenna away from him and onto her knees.

Why she followed someone who disrespected her so much, I'd never understand, but I was tired of them threatening me. I aimed a kick at her face, but she grabbed my foot and lifted it. I crashed onto my back again, the wind knocked out of me. Luckily, I had my sword in hand, and when she charged, I swung.

She jumped back, my blade catching air, and stumbled five feet before catching her balance. I forced my lungs to fill and started to climb to my feet, but before I could stand, she dashed toward me again and threw her dagger. The blade and handle rotated one over the other, and I didn't have time to think. I swung my sword like a bat. Somehow, I hit the dagger, and the blade flew to my left and hit Kieran's armor.

He flinched, and Curry aimed a blow at his neck.

"No!" I shouted, and my magic thrummed within me.

Kieran ducked, escaping Curry's attack. A vine snaked around the Winter King's body and smashed into Curry's chest. Curry flew back several feet and dropped his sword as Kieran's eyes widened in fear.

I jerked my head around just as Mackenna swung her dagger at my throat.

No.

I twisted, but suddenly, Mackenna's head dropped forward, and her dagger slammed into the armor on my shoulder as her body crashed into me.

"Alina!" Kieran shouted as I stumbled back into the canopy. Soft leaves brushed my head as Beth's faint whispers called to me, but I couldn't focus on them.

Not now.

Mackenna's heavy body lay on me, and something warm trickled down my arm and chest. I pushed her away, expecting her to continue to fight. Then I noticed the arrow in her temple.

Someone had killed her.

"Thank Mother Terrea," Kieran rasped as Curry's face turned red as a tomato.

Curry attacked with more vehemence, and the clanging of their swords rang out as Rowan stepped out of the maze, holding her bow. She pointed at me and said, "My favor has been fulfilled. Next trial, I'll kill you."

When I nodded, she raced past me and began scaling the canopy wall.

"Go," Kieran gritted out as he and Curry clashed swords. Kieran had strength on his side, but Curry had anger, and with the childhood I'd had, I understood that anger was a powerful motivator.

There was no way I was leaving Kieran behind after everything he'd done for me. I looked inward for the root of my magic. There had to be a way to connect with it after using it twice when I'd needed it.

I glanced at the top of the arena. The sun was nearing the horizon. We were running out of time, and we still had to climb the canopy.

Something clicked inside me. I remembered how to use my connection with the earth. When I didn't think about my magic, it came naturally. All the other times I'd tried, I'd been over-thinking.

I channeled energy from the ground, letting it absorb through my feet and up through my body. My blood thrummed, and I locked eyes with Curry. I didn't want him to die quickly—that was too easy for him. I wanted him to know he'd lost and dread his inevitable death.

Vines from the hedges snaked toward Curry, and when Kieran started driving him toward the wall, I realized he knew what I was doing. Swinging his sword harder, he pushed Curry back.

The vines wrapped around Curry's ankles. I jerked my hand up, and the vines followed, stringing him from his feet and hanging his head several feet above the ground.

"What—" he rasped and lifted his head, eyes locking with me. "You did this?" he asked, surprise in every word.

"She might have strung you up, but I'll kill you," Kieran vowed, raising his sword.

"Don't." I lifted a hand. "Don't give him an easy death. Allow him to watch us climb over the canopy and know we made it to the next trial."

Kieran smirked, pure delight dancing in his eyes. "That's ruthless, Princess. I love it."

My heart fluttered, but another part of me nagged that I should be ashamed.

For Moire, Curry deserved to spend the last moments of his life embarrassed and knowing he'd die.

"Come on." I sheathed my sword. "We're running out of time."

Surprising me, Kieran nodded, but he didn't sheath his sword. Instead, he sliced Curry's throat and watched the blood spill down his face and into the earth.

"What the *hell*?" I gasped. We'd agreed to let him hang there.

"It's not deep." Kieran put his sword away. "With his blood spilling, his magic will drain, and he won't be able to use it."

That was sick, but it worked. I nodded, and we headed for the canopy.

"Get back here and kill me!" Curry shouted. "I deserve to die like a warrior."

We ignored him.

Kieran tensed. He reached for the vines but hesitated.

"We'll do this together." I brushed his hand. "I'll be right beside you."

He glanced at me and nodded then began to climb.

Wanting to keep my promise, I followed him, and Beth's whispers haunted me again. I focused on the canopy top and found the best vines to climb, one thing at a time.

Kieran's breathing was steady, but I sometimes sensed him flinch beside me. The two of us climbed almost in sync.

"Why do you keep ignoring me, Ivy?" Beth asked, her voice as loud as if she were right beside me.

My head jerked toward the voice ... and there she was. I paused, unable to believe what I was seeing. Her eye was black and swollen shut, and she wrapped an arm around her stomach. "You told me you'd be here." The hurt in her voice was the same as the night when one of the other foster girls had stolen her teddy bear and left for good, leaving Beth with a black eye, broken nose, and split lip. "You were supposed to protect me." Beth's bottom lip quivered.

"I'm sorry." My vision blurred as I pressed on. "We missed the bus. When the study group got outside, it was already pulling away.

We had to walk home." I was back at the house by eight, Beth's bedtime. The altercation had gone down just fifteen minutes earlier.

Fifteen minutes, and Beth had lost the one thing that had helped her remember she was loved. She'd also lost her trust in the one person she'd let in—me. Eleven years old, and that one night had changed her. Then I was moved to another home, a place all the way across town, after I'd angrily confronted the last family. I'd meant to check on Beth, but each time, something had happened to prevent it, which meant I'd abandoned her completely.

"Why didn't you leave earlier? You promised me. You liked the other kids more than me." Tears spilled down her cheeks and onto her stained pink shirt. "You should've been here."

Those were the words she'd told me when I'd used that very explanation.

A sob racked me as I muttered, "I'm sorry." I had to get to the top. I had to end this trial. This was worse than seeing Stan because this moment had actually happened.

"Alina," Kieran rasped beside me, pulling me back to the here and now. I'd forgotten he was next to me. "I shouldn't have told you all that. I didn't mean it."

Tears trickled down his face. His expression was twisted in the worst agony I'd seen.

"I loved you then, and I never stopped." His chest shook. "You died thinking I wanted nothing to do with you, but you were all I thought about. Hell, even after you passed, you've been constantly in my thoughts. My kingdom wasn't worth losing you."

My heart pounded against my ribs, and I took a shaky breath. "Kieran, I'm here. It wasn't your fault."

"But abandoning me was your fault." Beth appeared between us with eyes so sharp they could cut through my armor. "Why tell him it wasn't his fault when you should be focused on me?"

Clarity crashed through me. She was right. How could I tell him it wasn't his fault when I blamed myself for what had happened to Beth? I'd been sixteen and trying to balance school and my own issues while also trying to help an eleven-year-old. I'd tried my damnedest to make it back like I'd promised, but something beyond my control had gotten in my way.

Stan had tried to tell me that, but I hadn't understood ... maybe because I couldn't. Not like now when I was trying to tell Kieran the same thing. I'd been beating myself up over something that shouldn't have been put on me in the first place. "Beth, I hate you got hurt like that and lost your stuffed animal, but it's not my fault. I tried to be there, and I'm sorry I wasn't. But you chose to hurt that girl. Not me." Years later, she'd found the girl who'd taken her bear and beaten her to a pulp. She'd been arrested for assault and sentenced to time in jail. "I helped you every time I could."

"But—" Beth started.

I shook my head and growled, "Stop."

Just like that, she vanished.

I glanced around for her, but she was nowhere to be found.

Rowan climbed over the top, and I realized we were close. The waning sun slanted through the glass ceiling.

"I know. I should die." Kieran whimpered. "You're right. It's the only suitable punishment for abandoning you." One of his hands let go.

Oh, frozen summer, this wasn't happening. I leaned over and smacked him in the face.

It was enough for him to groan and jerk his head toward me.

"Stop acting all martyr-y and move your ass. I'm right here and alive." I pointed at my face. "And I forgive you. Let's go." I didn't have to be a genius to know what his biggest regret was.

Rejecting me.

He wiped his face and grimaced. Luckily, he didn't dwell on it. "Let's go."

We climbed together, and I started rambling, telling him about the gym and things I did on Earth, wanting to remind him I was, in fact, alive and with him.

Groans and moans sounded from below us, but I didn't look down. I didn't need any more distractions.

At the top, we threw ourselves over the hedge and landed on the ground. In the center, there was a door set in an earth mound like a storm cellar. That had to be our exit. Kieran hurried and opened the door. Stairs descended underneath the mountain section of the maze. Wherever they led, that's where we needed to go.

He gestured me inside, and I led the way down the stairs with him right behind me.

"Alina?"

I stopped and glanced over my shoulder.

He scratched the back of his neck and shrugged. "Thanks for that."

He'd thanked me. He owed me yet another favor. "Don't think a thing of it." I didn't like this enclosed stairway, and I wanted to get the hell out of here before the High Court decided to throw in another obstacle. I moved once more.

"Not everyone would've done that." He followed me and took my hand in his.

The jolt between us strengthened, and I didn't know how or why. "You helped me with the mirrors. We're even."

He tugged me to a stop. I turned to him, knowing better, and his gaze went straight to my lips. He murmured, "I never want to be done owing you favors."

My legs betrayed me, stepping closer to him. As he lowered his head to mine, the door behind us opened.

My knees went weak when I saw who was there.

Twenty-Four

THIS HAD to be another damn illusion. Maybe we hadn't finished the trial. But the fae couldn't lie, and the High Court had been very specific about the rules.

But I'd hung Curry by his feet. How the hell was he here, standing in front of me?

Kieran dropped my hand and stepped between me and Curry, blocking me from his view. He snarled. "I should've killed you there."

Curry released a peal of manic laughter, and I didn't need to see him to know he was thoroughly enjoying this moment. Even as he spoke, laughter laced his words. "You failed to cut deep enough, Kieran. She's making you soft. And the two of you should never underestimate me. If Alina had taken the time to remember her past life or done her research in the present, she'd know this."

Even through the armor, I could see Kieran stiffen.

"That's *Princess* Alina to you," Kieran growled.

"Is *Quinley* aware of your growing affection for the *Summer* princess?" Curry's tone held a mean edge. "I'm sure she wouldn't be thrilled with this arrangement. Not that it'll be a problem since you'll both be dead after the next trial."

Quinley?

Why name her specifically and not the entire High Court? Granted, she did seem to be the head of the Winter members and a leader to the Summer members as well. From what I'd gathered, she was the oldest.

"None of that is your concern." Kieran clenched his hands. "And don't worry. Next time, I won't leave you to dread your fate. I'll kill you and watch every drop of life drain from you."

My body heated at the threat as if he'd whispered promises of all the ways he'd protect me. Ivy wouldn't have liked the sound of that, but I was beginning to realize that, maybe, I was turning into Alina. I sort of wanted to jump Kieran right here in the stairway.

"Don't plan on it. I will admit I underestimated *Princess* Alina, but I won't make that mistake again." Curry's boots hit the stairs, and he shoved past Kieran.

I leaned against the stone wall, not wanting to be near him. Curry paused, crowding me. He whispered, "You will pay for what you did back there and regret not ending me."

I regretted it now. I shouldn't have interfered with Kieran.

My chin lifted, and I met his glare head-on. "No, I gave you only a taste of what I have in store for you." I smiled, and my body strummed with magic. I needed to shut up, not antagonize the bully. But some new part of me was taking over and overpowering the person I'd been.

His smirk faltered, and something unreadable passed across his face. He set his jaw. "We'll see about that." He then continued his trek forward, leaving Kieran and me behind.

Kieran leaned forward and murmured in my ear, "That was damn sexy."

My annoyance vanished, and the heat of his breath on my neck had my body warming in the armor, already drenched with sweat. He and I were both gross, but that didn't matter.

"Let's head out. We shouldn't risk being stuck in here when the screamers come."

Those words were like a cold bath and got my feet moving. We hurried down the stairs.

A bright light glowed from the end of the hallway, and I quickened my steps. I didn't feel Kieran's presence as close to my back, and when I glanced over my shoulder, I noted he'd put several feet between us.

Curry's words repeated in my head. Kieran had to be giving me space because he wanted to play down how close we were in front of the High Court. We'd probably caused enough of a commotion by helping each other.

My heart squeezed uncomfortably. Were we more than allies? I wasn't sure. He'd said he loved me, but he'd been talking about the previous version of Alina, not me. That meant he regretted his decision from then ... not now.

This was why I needed to keep my distance. My momentary lapse in judgment had gotten me attached to a man I couldn't have. One of us, if not both, would be dead after the next trial, so what kind of future could we have?

Great, I was asking myself rhetorical questions I already knew the answers to. This day continued to be super.

I had to bury the hurt like I had my entire childhood, but *this* was harder to hide. The indifferent expression I'd perfected didn't want to slip back into place.

My entire body felt weighted down, but I kept up my confident strides. Kieran might have influence over me, but he wouldn't break me. I'd survived a childhood of abandonment—I'd be damned if I let a man I'd known for only a couple of weeks break me.

When I marched out of the tunnel and back into the arena, the entire place was quiet. I thought the crowd must have cleared out, but when I glanced into the stands, everyone was still there.

The hairs on the nape of my neck rose. Almost everyone had their eyes on me, including the High Court members standing in front of me.

The passage exit ended at the steps to the platform that would take us back inside the tower. Curry and Rowan were already gone, and there was no sign of the other competitors.

Quinley looked down her nose at me, her disgust evident. Kaley tilted her head, staring at me as if she wasn't sure what she was seeing. Eamon had a grin on his face like he was privy to a joke I wasn't a part of, while the Winter siblings flicked their eyes from me and back to each other, coming across as if they were talking telepathically.

Skin crawling, I stared straight ahead, pretending their assessment didn't bother me. I'd made it out alive. That was what mattered.

Kieran—no, *King* Kieran. I needed to reinstate that formality between us. He walked out behind me, and the cool spot on my neck pulsed. It hadn't bothered me in the maze, but now that we were around other people, it reminded me that something was off with me.

"It seems you are one of the last to make it back." Quinley ran a hand over her flawless wavy hair. "Five contestants will take part in the next trial. One contestant squeaked through and is coming down the way now."

My breath hitched. We'd started with twenty contestants, and within a week, fifteen had died. I swallowed the sour taste in my mouth over so much needless death. I already knew that only two Summer Fae had completed this trial—Curry and myself—and I'd seen only Rowan and Kieran on the Winter fae side, which meant someone had gotten out before Kieran and I had made it to the canopy.

I gritted my teeth. I'd never been super competitive when it came to tests and things, but knowing someone had outsmarted us annoyed me.

"Come," Kaley said, looping an arm with mine. "You should go to your room and rest. We have a huge celebration tonight."

My feet stopped. "A celebration? I'm caked in dirt, I've seen multiple people die, and I had to face my biggest regret. All I want to do is take a bath and sleep." What exactly were we celebrating? That we'd survived, only to die the next time? Even though the thought of killing didn't bother me as much anymore, the whole concept of the Comortas did.

"Princess Alina." Kaley laughed awkwardly. "You made it to the final round. You're one of the strongest fae in Talamh."

"She's tired." *King* Kieran's voice boomed behind me, sounding condescending, and he snorted. "She'll be fine once she freshens up and has some time on her own."

Now he was speaking on my behalf and poking fun at me. He was sending all sorts of mixed signals, but I refused to react. My opinions wouldn't end this tournament; they would only make my time here less bearable with all the nasty expressions tossed my way.

I felt like I was losing a part of myself, which infuriated me more than anything.

Forcing myself not to glance back, even to glare at him, I marched up the stairs. My boots thudded gracelessly on the stone.

Kieran distancing himself from me was the main reason for my foul mood, and that pissed me off. I should have been more upset over everything I'd had to do and what might have happened if Rowan hadn't been there to help me.

I marched to the door, threw it open, and continued into the lobby. Curry, Rowan, and another Winter fae competitor I had barely noticed stood at the base of the stairs. The man arched a brow, observing me, his overly rosy cheeks reminding me of a clown.

Curry sneered, and the corners of his mouth tipped up maliciously when his gaze landed on Kaley.

I didn't have to be a mind reader to know what he was thinking. He'd seen Kieran and me in the stairwell, and he was enjoying the fact we'd distanced ourselves in front of the others.

Maybe that had been Kieran's plan. He'd promised to protect me, and he had. But at what cost? I feared it was the largest price of them all.

My heart.

The one thing I tried to protect.

A cold void formed inside me. I felt more alone than I had ever before.

My skin tingled, and I knew that Kieran had entered the room as well and was watching me. I hated how attuned I was to him. If Quinley could create the illusion spells, maybe that whole canopy experience had been an act ... another way to lure me in.

Kaley guided me to turn toward Kieran and the High Court members.

Kieran took the spot next to me, catching me off guard.

Releasing my arm, Kaley went to stand next to Quinley, with Eamon on her other side, while the siblings flanked Quinley. Caden was at the end, and I realized the lineup was separated by courts, with the oldest in the center and the youngest at the ends.

"Well done." Quinley clasped her hands. "All of you have proven yourselves to be the strongest of the fae and worthy of the final trial, even our reincarnated princess." She gestured to me as if no one wouldn't know who she meant.

Holding her stare, I didn't flinch. I was tired of every single one of them acting like there was something wrong with me. These trials not only turned people into ruthless monsters, but they also built animosity between the courts. No wonder the two courts despised one another.

"Everyone, go to your room. Clean up and rest." Kaley stepped forward, her smile so warm it almost made me forget that so many of us had killed our peers as if they were nothing. "Tonight, your families will dine with you in celebration of your monumental victory and, in most cases, to say goodbye."

A goodbye dinner. Even better.

Kieran shook his head. "Prince Nolan is injured and needs to stay at Geimhreadh Castle, and my sister should remain behind to tend to him. Don't make them feel obligated to come to this."

"Prince Nolan and Princess Brianne have already accepted." Leanna clasped her hands at her waist. "They must not feel that the threat is dire, and since you haven't been home in a week, they must be in better spirits than you assume. Don't you agree, my king?"

He swallowed, his Adam's apple bobbing. "Of course. How foolish of me. I'm glad to hear that Nolan has recovered enough to feel comfortable traveling." He tapped his fingers on his thigh.

Interesting. He didn't want them here.

"Your families will arrive in two hours, so please hurry to your rooms." Eamon waved his hand with a flourish. "Clean up, pick out something lovely to wear, and take the time to rejuvenate with a quick nap if you dare. When the moons are halfway to full height in the sky, come down and join your family at the meal. A few snacks have been placed in your room to get you by since you've had such a strenuous day."

That was all I needed to hear. Bath, food, and alone time.

We all turned and headed to the stairs.

"Alina, I need to talk with you," Kieran murmured as he leaned closer to me and pretended to check his sword. "I need to explain to you—"

"King Kieran," Quinley said. "I would like a word with you—if you're willing, of course."

I guessed Curry had called it in the stairwell.

"What is it?" I whispered. It would be helpful to know what he had to say so I'd have time to process it while getting ready.

Jaw tensing, Kieran paused, and I watched as his face slid into that look of indifference. "It'll have to be later when I have time," he answered before turning and heading back to Quinley.

If I hadn't been so angry, I'd have laughed at his audacity. He'd talk to me when *he* had time? Clearly, my schedule didn't matter ... not that I had one, but that wasn't the point.

I marched forward, not bothering to respond, and headed to my room.

Curry paused outside his room and watched me go to my door. I wasn't about to remove the key from my cleavage while he was watching, so I leaned against the wall and yawned. "Dammit, where did I put my key? I hope it isn't lost."

He grunted and rolled his eyes, then removed a key attached to a chain around his neck. Now that would be smarter than sticking it between my boobs, especially during trials where I got drenched in sweat.

After he entered his room and shut the door, I removed my key.

The moment I entered my room and locked the door, the tears I'd been holding back broke free. Between Moire dying, facing my regret with Beth, feeling as if I wasn't the same person and all my strong emotions toward Kieran, I felt like one raw nerve. I'd guarded myself for so long, and here I was, in the worst time of my life, literally fighting for said life, and everything was crumbling around me. My heart was shattered, and I wasn't sure I could pick up all the pieces. Even if I could, I wouldn't have the energy.

Chest shaking, I crumpled to the floor. I wrapped my arms around my knees, leaned my head on the cool metal of the armor, and let myself cry. I didn't know how long I did, but eventually, I ran out of tears. The pain was still a deep, unfading ache, but I picked myself up and went to the bathroom.

After turning on the water, I removed my armor and slipped into the tub. My skin tingled as the water's magical properties swirled around me, caressing the tension away.

When the tub was filled, I held my breath, submerged my entire body, and enjoyed the sensation of the dirt, sweat, and blood washing away, leaving my skin clean. All too soon, it was time to get ready.

I opened my closet, and one dress tugged at me: a white chiffon gown with pale-green vines and leaves decorating the top of the bodice. The leaves continued up to frame my collarbone and flow into the long, off-the-shoulder sleeves—the very thing I wanted to wear tonight.

I slipped it on and found matching pale-green two-inch heels. I took my time fixing my hair into a French twist. Staring into the mirror, I lifted a hand to do my makeup. I didn't overthink it, just let my magic work, and felt the warm tingling that happened when Enid had done this for me. My eyelids turned a light pink like the tips of my favorite flowers, and my lips turned crimson, reminiscent of a rose.

I glanced at the sky. It wasn't quite time to head downstairs. I had a little while to lie down.

I'd taken a step toward my bed when there was a faint knock on my door. My stomach churned.

Marching to the door, I asked, "Who's there?"

Kieran replied, "Alina, hurry. Let me in."

I wanted to let him stand out there, but I also didn't want Curry to see him.

I opened the door, and Kieran slipped in, the shadows hanging around him.

Well, that was drafty of me. I'd let him in without even grabbing Stan's knife or my sword. He was wearing a navy suit with a snowflake on his pocket, and his shaggy, dark hair framed his face, emphasizing his stupid sculpted features.

"I'm sorry about earlier," he started.

I wasn't going to accept that. "Now doesn't work for me."

His forehead wrinkled. "What do you mean?"

"We talk at your convenience, and I'm tired of it." I pointed my finger at him. "You could have told Quinley that you needed a moment, but you didn't. You brushed me off after telling me you had things to explain to me."

"I had to." He held out his arms. "She's the head Winter High Court member. The worst thing I could do was brush her off, especially when she wasn't happy with me."

"I helped you during the trial." I refused to allow him to ignore what I'd done for him as if it wasn't important. "You might not have gotten up the canopy in time if not for me."

He laughed, but it was dark and devoid of humor. "You think I don't know that?"

"You said we were allies." He was making it out to be more than it was. "Just tell her that. It's not a lie."

"It's not just that, and we both know it." His nostrils flared, and his voice grew louder. "I talked to her for *you*."

Now, it was my turn to laugh. If he thought I would fall for that logic, I'd make him be the one to squirm. "Please, tell me. How was that conversation for me?"

He stepped toward me, his eyes blazing. "I'll tell you, but you won't like the answer."

Twenty-Five

I SNORTED. Part of me winced at how classless the noise sounded, but I pushed that aside. He needed to know I was disgusted and wouldn't be placated … to see my real self and not some version I pretended to be for him.

I squared my shoulders, facing him, and said, "I pretty much figured that I wouldn't like it. Ever since I arrived in Talamh, it's been bad news followed by worse news."

The shadows hovered near him, not blanketing him but staying close as if a threat could appear at any moment. "If I could change things—"

Here we went with all the flowery words that would make my heart sputter. "I don't need pretty words—I need the truth. I'm so tired of dancing around the truth and everything that comes with it. So *please*, tell me how that conversation was for my benefit." I didn't give a frozen summer if *please* would make me owe him. I'd be dead soon, so it didn't matter. "I need to hear the truth from you, Kieran."

"You want the truth?" He laughed bitterly. His handsome face was striking as he stalked toward me.

My heart quickened with what should've been fear, but I knew it wasn't. I *wanted* to be his prey and let him do all sorts of things to me.

"When you died, it broke me. I hated that I'd pushed you away … that *I* was the reason we weren't together." He grimaced and ran a hand through his hair, his fingertips gray from the shadow magic within him. "You were willing to risk everything to be with me, *asking who we were to fight the connection between us*. And I accused you of being selfish."

The more I learned about my past life, the more I connected with that version of myself. My heart ached with the sensation from the memory. The intense feeling of being broken and unworthy of his love. I repeated words I'd said one lifetime ago. "Selfish is *not* being together. Playing it safe so our kingdoms aren't uncomfortable was selfish. Not doing the hard thing to merge a fractured realm was selfish."

"That's exactly what you said then." He winced, and his forehead creased. "I thought you were just saying that until I lost you. When you died, I realized you were right. I was afraid of upsetting my people and not being recognized as their rightful new king. That was such a foolish concern because I'd already been crowned and anointed, but I thought it would be less painful to stay apart. I was wrong, but there wasn't a thing I could do about it then other than live with crippling regret as my punishment."

His punishment. Bitterness filled my mouth. I refused to let him play the victim. Not with this. "You think you were punished? I died, and let's not forget that, in this life, I grew up in the foster care system, so forgive me if I don't feel much empathy for you!"

"Foster care system?" Kieran tilted his head. "What's that?"

I wanted to smack myself. I didn't know why I'd added that last part—voluntary death seemed awful enough, but I didn't remember that part well. My childhood in *this* life was crystal clear, and I didn't want to explain it to anyone … especially *him*. Yet … "It's where kids who have lost both parents and have no one to take them in or are abandoned by their parents go. I lived in a group home where kids like me lived with caregivers." I didn't want to go into specifics. There were just as many workers who'd cared about us as there were who hadn't. "They tried to place us with foster parents, who they paid to let us live with them, and let's just say that doesn't always go well for us kids." That was it. That was all I had to say on the matter. "It wasn't the easiest upbringing, so don't act like you were the only person who suffered."

"What do you mean by 'it wasn't the easiest upbringing'?" His hands clenched at his sides, icy blue mixing with the gray as if he were brewing a storm of shadows and frost.

"A few homes I was placed in were with foster parents who did it for the money and not out of the kindness of their hearts." I hated that he wouldn't drop it, but in fairness, if he'd ever revealed something like this to me, I'd want to know more. I didn't understand the relationship we once had, but it sounded *very* toxic. All we'd done was hurt one another, and in this tournament, that was the last thing I needed.

"Give me a list of names, and at the next Havestia, they will be hunted and gutted for treating you maliciously. If I can't be the one who guts them, I'll make sure Nolan finishes my last request." His irises turned navy, and the stone floor underneath his feet glistened with ice.

He was about to lose it and damn if that didn't thrill me. He wanted to seek justice for any wrongs done to me and my foster siblings. "They'll be dead by then, so it would be in vain."

His hands shook, and his chest heaved. He didn't bother to hide his rage. "This is what I mean. If I hadn't rejected you—"

"Then nothing would've changed." Though I didn't appreciate him playing the victim, I didn't want him to live with regret. I suspected he would win the tournament, and on the canopy, I'd seen what that regret had done to him. I didn't want him to backtrack. "If I had to be sacrificed to save the realm, I doubt our being together would have changed the outcome. I get that you're a king and everything, but if it was my destiny to die, it would've happened, regardless."

"What if it did change, Alina?" My name rolled off his tongue in ways that should've been outlawed. He growled, the sound coming from deep within his chest. "I'll never know, and I always swore if I had a chance to do things differently, I would. I'd make this right between us come warm winter or frozen summer. I'd make sure the two of us would be together."

I sighed, but at least my reaction to his vow felt normal ... like I was still the same person. I wanted to help him deal with the trauma that had plagued him for the past fifty years. Maybe then he'd let it go and not be haunted by me again. He wasn't playing the victim like I'd thought. Rather, he saw himself as the antagonist in our love story. "My death wasn't your fault."

"Maybe not, but that doesn't matter." He shrugged. "Because, no matter how different I wish our story could be this time, the circumstances are such that it can't be different. That was what Quinley talked to me about—our working together will cause more conflict between our kingdoms when one of us dies, especially if it's by the other's hand. It will send the message that the one time a Winter royal and a Summer royal worked together, it led to a vicious death. We're in the Comortas, and whoever survives won't be strong enough to face the torment of how Talamh will react."

An ache worse than that in my memory squeezed my heart and intensified into excruciating agony. He'd come here and proclaimed he'd made a mistake, only to tell me that his original decision stood. What sort of mind games was he playing? "What's the point of you telling me all these things?" My voice cracked.

He sighed and reached out to touch my face, but he stopped a few inches shy. He licked his lips, and his mouth tipped downward. "To make sure you understand that it was a mistake for us to ally together today. I wanted to ensure you had proper training, but it might have come at too high a cost."

This had to do with Curry threatening us—that was when his entire demeanor had changed. I crossed my arms and put pressure on my chest, hoping to relieve the agony. "Okay. So you've decided, again, for the two of us." It took every ounce of self-control I had to ensure my voice didn't break, but I refused to reveal how badly he was hurting me *again*. Both he and my mother had been willing to sacrifice my needs and wants for their own vision of what needed to be done with no input from me. "Got it. Makes *perfect* sense. You can leave." I needed him to go. I wasn't sure how much longer I could hold myself together.

"Alina, I need you to understand. I'm doing this for *you*."

"Understood." Several foster parents had said the same thing when they'd informed me I was going back to the group home. The message was always so similar, but that was a lie they told themselves to sleep better at night. "Now leave."

His head sagged. "Don't do this. Don't shut me out."

Coolness swirled through that spot on my neck as hot rage boiled in my blood. It had been a long day, and I was exhausted. I wanted to get dinner over with so I could crawl into bed. I didn't have the energy to be around anyone, especially after what Kieran had said. "I'm not the one shutting you out, Kieran. You told me we shouldn't have allied and we shouldn't be seen working together in any capacity. I won't beg you to change your mind—I have more pride than that—but being around you hurts, so ... I need you to *leave*." Being alone with him when the only thing I wanted to do was touch and kiss him was making this situation more torturous. If he stayed, I didn't trust myself not to beg him to change his mind.

"Mo—"

"Don't," I spat. I didn't know what the nickname meant, but I didn't want him to use it ever again. "*Please* leave."

He nodded. "Fine. You're right. We shouldn't be alone with each other like this." He took a step back. "I wish things were different, but I have to put distance between us ... for you."

I wanted to call him out again, but I didn't want to argue with him anymore. All my words were gone.

Shadows flickered from his body, engulfing him. He stepped back, blending in with the shadows of my room. The door opened as if a ghost had done it, but I could sense him. The cool pulses in my neck announced his presence.

So strange.

Especially since I felt the coolness only around him.

When the door finally closed, I went to the window. The moons were nearing their peak, which meant I was expected in the ballroom. The trees reminded me of fall, with their leaves of gold, orange, and red glinting in the twilight. I took a deep breath to center myself.

Once upon a time, I'd never dreamed I could suffer more than I already had. That I'd already been hurt by the people I should have been able to trust. But coming here had challenged everything.

Memories of my first life were returning, and I'd felt a connection with Kieran in an instant. No amount of distancing could've prevented that; our attraction was like gravity. We wanted to revolve around each other, but if we got too close, we clashed, knocking each other away.

A faint knock sounded on my door, and Maeve called, "Ivy?"

When the knob turned, my stomach clenched.

The door flung open, revealing Maeve. Her eyes narrowed. "What in the icicles is this?"

Doing the very thing I hated, I chose my words carefully. Telling her it was unlocked because I'd let Kieran in would make her angrier than having the door unlocked without a reason. "I was about to leave."

"You're across the room." She scanned the space. "You have to be more careful. Dallas was sure Kieran called the shadows around you two that night at the ball. If that's true, and the Winter royal family still has shadow magic, that will be very bad for us all ... especially in the Comortas."

"If Kieran wanted me dead, he could've killed me during the trial today." A knot formed in my chest because, in the final trial, he and I might have to fight to the death. I tensed, feeling as if bricks were weighing me down.

She placed a hand on the hilt of her sword, ready to draw it. "You got lucky. It was foolish to trust him."

If she'd said that before Kieran had shown up here tonight, I would have disagreed with her. But the misery swimming through my body made me think she was right. I wouldn't be thinking clearly if we had to fight.

I shrugged, feigning indifference. "Maybe, but he helped me with the quicksand and the mirrors."

She scowled. "Queen Orla and King Dallas asked me to come up and retrieve you. They are waiting for you downstairs."

I wanted to roll my eyes. She could never admit she was wrong. In my past life, I'd tried to get her to admit I was right once, and she'd clammed up, making me not want to trust her. I blinked and shook my head, more memories from my former life coming back and merging with mine. It was the strangest sensation.

"Are you okay?" Maeve removed her sword, lifting it as if she thought Kieran was behind me, holding me hostage.

"I'm fine." The warmth I felt for her returned, taking away the annoyance that had caught me off guard. Even if she couldn't admit she was wrong, she did care about me. And *that* counted for something. "It's been a long day."

Her lips tightened. "It has, but we need to go downstairs. The other competitors may think you are weak if you don't join them soon."

My body tensed as two parts of me went to war. One part hated the thought of the other competitors thinking I was weak, while another equal-sized part liked the idea of them thinking that so they would underestimate me. But Orla would be pissed if I waited too long, and there was enough tension between us that I didn't want to add more.

I clasped the key in my hand and went to the door, Maeve following. I locked the room, and we headed downstairs.

I managed to keep my heels from clacking like they had when I'd first arrived. Walking in them wasn't actually painful anymore, and I didn't hate the dress, though I still would've preferred to wear pants and a shirt, so at least I hadn't completely changed.

We strode into the dining hall, and it looked more glamorous than before. Candles sat in the center of the tables, and the overhead chandeliers were dimmed. The effect was intimate, but with all the people there, it didn't pass for romantic. A buffet had been laid out against one wall with loads of spirits, water, chocolates, breads, jams, honey, and something I swore looked like cinnamon rolls.

I salivated as the sweet aromas washed over me, but my heart nearly stopped when I glanced at the one place I shouldn't have.

Kieran sat at his usual place at the Winter table with a man who looked similar to him and had to be his brother, Prince Nolan, on his right and a gorgeous woman on his left. That had to be their sister, Princess Brianne. But what caught my attention was how she contrasted with her royal brothers. It was marked, especially with the three of them sitting together. Both brothers had the same hair color, Nolan's shorter and styled in messy upward spikes. The princess's hair was a dark blonde that waved to the floor. Both men had blue eyes, with Kieran's as pale as ice and Nolan's a cobalt blue. The princess's eyes were a warm honey brown that reminded me of the sun on a winter day.

As I examined them, Kieran caught my eye, forcing me to look away. I didn't want him to think I was pining for him.

Rowan sat on the right side of the table next to a man with short brown hair while the quiet Winter fae sat alone on the other side of the table.

Interesting.

"Alina," Maeve murmured.

Lovely. I'd stopped at the edge of the table and was staring at the Winter fae. All six had stopped their conversations to stare back at me.

I smiled, wanting to make them uncomfortable. Ivy would never have done this, but Alina was taking root under my skin. "Good evening," I nodded. "You all performed amazingly out there."

Flinching, Rowan bit her bottom lip while the silent man arched a brow. King Kieran bowed his head slightly. "Princess Alina." His response was the kindest out of everyone, which made me feel funny before the hurt settled in again.

I nodded and made my way to the Summer table. My usual spot

was vacant, with Dallas seated on my left and Orla on my right. I'd expected Orla to sit at the head, but I didn't want to challenge her authority. I took my seat, locking eyes with Curry next to Dallas.

As I sat down, Dallas smiled. "You don't know how happy I am to see you."

Instead of the disgust that usually accompanied my interactions with him, a sense of ease spread through my chest. I placed a hand on top of his and replied, "I'm full of warmth at seeing you."

He blinked before his face transformed into a smile as bright as the sun. "You finally remember."

"What?" Orla gasped. "Is that true?"

I released Dallas's hand and touched my sister's shoulder. "I don't remember everything, but more is coming back to me, including memories of our time together with you lying under the weeping willow in the garden."

"Thank the rising sun." She placed a hand on her chest. "You reminded me of Alina at the ball, and when I was told you had used your magic in the arena, I hoped you were returning to your previous self."

They were both getting their hopes too high. "I'm remembering things, but I'm still not the same person you remember. I lived a separate life on Earth, and I won't ever be just like her."

"Isn't that sweet, son?" a man with dark eyes interjected. He sat between my sister and Curry. "Too bad she wasn't her former self. She'd have made sure she killed you."

The insinuation that I was weak slammed into me. No one talked to me that way and got away with it. "It wasn't a moment of weakness. I wanted your son to hang in torment, awaiting his death. Unfortunately, I underestimated him." My attention landed on Curry, whose sneer took up half his face. I continued, making sure he felt each word, "That won't happen again."

Orla grinned as the table fell silent, and then we all got up and filled our plates with food.

* * *

I hadn't realized how hungry I was, so I overate tremendously. Most people were enjoying spirits. But not me, not after that one night when I'd learned an important lesson.

After everyone finished eating, we all headed out to the lobby. The family members would be leaving soon, and the rest of us would go to bed.

In the entrance hall, the High Court lined up together.

Quinley stepped forward. "We would like to speak to Kieran, Orla, Dallas, and Nolan."

Kieran tensed. "Princess Brianne should join us."

Quinley shook her head. "She's not an acting royal."

Curry and his father stopped next to me and glanced back and forth between the Winter King and his sister, intrigued.

Princess Brianne hugged her brother and said, "I'll be fine. You won't be gone long."

Kieran and Nolan frowned, but soon, they went back into the dining area, leaving the rest of us in the hall.

I spotted Maeve and took a step to join her, but someone grabbed my arm and held me firmly.

Twenty-Six

BODY TENSING, I watched as Maeve's hand went for her sword. My heart pounded harder as I glanced over my shoulder.

I didn't know who I expected to see, but it wasn't her.

Princess Brianne dropped her white-gloved hand from my arm and bit her lower lip. "Hello, Princess Alina. I was hoping we could talk for a quick moment."

Her voice was soft, and her demeanor screamed that she was uncomfortable, which I understood all too well. That had been my body language for the past twenty-three years of my life, wanting to fly under the radar and stay invisible. Immediately, my guard lowered, which never happened. "Sure."

She nodded toward an empty corner of the entrance hall.

She wanted to speak to me alone. My earlier conversation with Kieran slipped back into my head. Was her meek and mild temperament a front?

Curiosity got the best of me, and we headed for the back of the hall, close to the ballroom doors.

The silence between us was a tad uncomfortable but not excruciating. Her presence was soothing, and even though that should have worried me, it didn't.

Reaching the corner, I faced the other fae and the front door.

Of course, Curry's and his father's attention was locked on us. A shiver ran down my spine, not because I feared him but because I knew he was a malicious person.

"Are you all right?" Princess Brianne narrowed her eyes and turned to see what held my attention so thoroughly. "Oh, yes. Curry Gall. He's one of the most vicious competitors, from what Nolan has told me."

That was fitting, but the last thing I wanted was to talk about Curry. If she had something she wanted to discuss, I'd much rather we talk before Kieran came back. "Is that what you wanted to talk about?"

Facing me, she pressed her lips together. "No. Not at all. I ..." She smoothed her blonde hair, which was draped over the shoulder of her glimmering purple-gray gown. "I ... I wanted to take the opportunity to say you seem like a nice person."

My head tilted back. I hadn't expected that. "What makes you say that?" I waited for the punch line. To become the butt of some joke she was making.

"Helping my brother." She wrapped her arms around her stomach. "Not many people would have done that even if they were from our kingdom."

I didn't know why, but I *liked* that she had said her kingdom instead of Winter fae. The divide didn't seem as wide that way. "He helped me too. It wasn't one-sided." For some reason, those words felt relevant. It wasn't as if I'd done something and he hadn't returned the favor. Although, in so many ways, I still owed him.

A lump formed in my throat as I remembered how I'd spoken to him earlier. But what did he expect me to do when he kept saying we couldn't be together? Hearing those words—again—had been harder than should have been possible.

"I know, but that doesn't surprise me." She shook her head, an adoring smile spreading across her face. "That's my brother. He doesn't tolerate injustice, especially not after the war fifty complete season cycles ago. He does everything in his power to protect those who need it, and when he learned that Queen Orla planned to put you in the Comortas even though you had been back in Talamh for a mere seven sun cycles, he was livid and beside himself."

He hadn't told her why. That sounded right. He hadn't believed it was me until the tournament started. "He sounds like a very good man."

"To a fault." Her smile literally turned upside down. "He always makes sacrifices so no one else has to. It's like he thinks he should be punished, but I've never been able to figure out why. Even with the tournament, after Nolan got hurt, he refused to even consider me com—" She slapped her hands over her mouth.

She didn't have to finish. I already knew the end of the sentence. Everyone had wondered why she hadn't been the one to compete, and it had everything to do with Kieran. With her timidity, I could see why he would be afraid to let her fight, but I saw a strength in her that most wouldn't. She was a survivor, but she was also a royal. What had she already suffered?

"Please don't tell anyone." Her face turned a shade pink. "I didn't mean to—"

"Your secret is safe with me." I reached over and touched her arm. "I promise." The last thing I would ever want to do was cause problems between Kieran and Brianne. She had a genuineness that I'd only seen in Maeve. It seemed rare in the upper-class citizens of Talamh.

Dropping her arms, she examined me and said, "My brother said you were different, but I didn't expect you to be like this."

I chuckled. "Like what? Promising to keep my mouth shut and not use that information as leverage over you?" Even if Kieran died, the knowledge that he hadn't thought his sister strong enough for the tournament would damage their family's reputation. Unfortunately, with my returning memories, I understood how things worked here. I didn't agree with that any more than I had when I'd arrived, and I'd sensed that Alina hadn't liked the way things were, but back then, I hadn't realized that things could be different. My time on Earth had shown me that sometimes, those who appeared weak were actually the strongest people out there.

"That's exactly what I mean." She pressed her lips together. "If Kieran doesn't win this tournament, I hope it's you." She winced. "That sounded bad. I don't want you to die. It's just that I don't want to lose my brother."

"That's fine. You didn't upset me. If someone I loved were in this tournament, I'd feel the same way." I grimaced, but I pushed the thought away of what was to come. I didn't want her to regret hoping that her brother survived. Part of me hoped he did too, even if it came at my expense, a paradox that didn't sit well with me. I refused to let myself die for a guy, even Kieran.

The sound of footsteps on stone caught my attention, and I tore my gaze from Princess Brianne to see Maeve moving toward us. She was very protective of me, and she hadn't been thrilled about me walking off with the Winter Princess.

"Is everything all right here?" Maeve's body was coiled tight as if Brianne was the biggest threat she'd ever encountered. At least she wasn't underestimating the princess like everyone else was.

Brianne's demeanor changed. She averted her gaze to the stone floor.

A sense of protectiveness surged within me, but I gritted my teeth and held it back, keeping my aggravation from seeping out. Maeve was only trying to protect me. "Yeah, we were talking. She was telling me how she heard about the trial earlier today and she was happy Kieran made it through."

"I'm sure she is," Maeve said and kept a hand near her sword as if someone might strike me dead here.

Maybe someone would, but the more likely culprit out of everyone was Curry, a fellow Summer Fae.

The doors to the dining hall opened, and King Kieran and Prince Nolan marched out. The two of them scanned the area until they found Brianne. When Kieran's gaze landed on me, his face hardened.

A deep ache pulsed in my heart. I didn't understand why he'd be upset that she'd been talking to me. He hurried over to us and stepped between Brianne and me. He touched his sister on her arm and glanced at Nolan while he said, "You two should head home."

Refusing to stand there and let him ignore my presence, I touched his sister's shoulder. "It was nice talking with you." Then I strolled toward Orla and Dallas, who'd just exited the dining hall. They met me halfway, in front of the stairs. I'd expected some tension in their expressions, but their faces were smooth with no trace of concern.

"Is everything okay?" I asked, taking Orla's hands in mine. I hadn't meant to make the gesture, but it felt as natural as breathing.

"Everything is fine. It was a discussion about what would happen if King Kieran died tomorrow." Orla squeezed my hand. "Quinley wanted a formal note of what King Kieran wants done if the throne becomes vacant. It was no surprise when he said that Prince Nolan should be crowned king as the rightful heir since Kieran was still childless. It will make the transition easier, especially if random people rise up and proclaim that Kieran is their father."

I blew out a breath. "How is that possible? Fae can't lie."

"That doesn't mean they can't spread a lot of innuendo and start turmoil." Orla pressed her lips together. "I know you weren't here when Mom passed, and she was already queen when we were born, but when I took over the throne forty complete season cycles ago, the situation got ugly because I was considered the spare, and everyone had hoped you would be the ruler of Summer."

I flinched, hating that I hadn't been able to help her. "I wish—"

"Don't you dare." Orla pointed at me, cutting me off. "You sacrificed yourself not only to save our kingdom but Terrea as a whole. You and the seven royals from the other continents. Your sacrifice balanced the power that was drained from the land, and if you hadn't done it, *none* of us would be here today."

"That was one reason Orla and I were wed. Everyone knew you and I were betrothed, so they always expected me to be king." Dallas bumped shoulders with Orla. "By marrying and with me standing beside her as I was supposed to do with you, we helped solidify Orla's reign."

Orla's bottom lip quivered. "It was the best choice. If we had left the throne open in case of your return, there were some who would've taken advantage." She glanced at Curry. "I'd been dreading you coming home for so long, and when you did and you didn't seem like yourself, it set me off. And Alina—er, Ivy, if this is the last time I see you ... I need you to know—"

"You can call me Alina." I could do that for her, give her a chance to see me like the sister she obviously thought highly of and mourned. "And you don't need to say anything. The two of you kept the Summer Court stable and safe and healed the damage of the war." Flashes of how the ground had cracked and crumbled, our people dying at the hands of monsters, ran through my mind. "Not only did you have to deal with taking over the throne while rebuilding our kingdom from ruins, but you did an amazing job. That alone proves you're the rightful queen, and I would never dream of fighting you for that honor."

Her entire body sagged while Dallas chuckled and said, "I told you that you didn't need to worry. Granted, I thought I'd have to eat my words, but there she is."

I rolled my eyes as Dallas spread his arms. He used to always demand a hug before he left me.

When I jumped into them, I surprised myself. And the moment his sweet grass smell overwhelmed me, memories of our times together came pouring back, including why and how we'd become lovers. After Kieran had rejected me, I needed support to hold myself together. Dallas had been that for me. Even though the first time I'd asked him to make me forget my heartbreak, he'd been hesitant. Then, something had shifted between us, and I realized he'd developed feelings for me. At the time, I hadn't cared, and I hated that I'd been so selfish. But the person I'd been in my previous life hadn't been as confident as so many believed because she'd bent herself in any way needed to keep the people she cared about happy with her. To be the person Mother had expected her to be despite her heart wanting to help her people in ways Mother disapproved of, despite wanting to be with Kieran.

Dallas buried his face in my hair and murmured, "Frozen summer, Alina. You don't know how much the two of us missed you."

The nape of my neck began to tingle, and that spot on my throat cooled. Kieran was watching.

I hated how much I loved that I had his attention. Something ruthless blossomed in me; I wanted Dallas's touch to drive him insane. My gaze landed on Orla, and I froze. Pain lined her face.

She'd always had a crush on Dallas, even as a child. I hadn't remembered that until now. No wonder she didn't want Dallas to even consider sleeping with me again—not that I would. He was committed to someone else, my sister, and that was a line I'd never cross. I didn't give a damn if it was the fae way.

"Isn't it time for everyone to depart?" Kieran asked icily from his spot several feet away. "We should all get some sleep. We've had a long day."

I removed myself from Dallas's embrace, only for Orla. The last thing I wanted to do was hurt her; however, Kieran could kiss my warm ass. He could pout all he damn well wanted.

Without missing a beat, I pulled Orla in for a hug. At first, she stiffened, but she relented and wrapped her arms around me. Her scent of flowers with a hint of sulfur from her fire magic was like coming home. I couldn't believe it had taken me so long to remember her. I pulled back and cupped her face like when she was a little girl and said, "If I make it out of this, we fly over the waterfalls together."

Eyes glistening, she sniffled. "I'd really love that."

"King Kieran is right." Quinley clapped her hands. "Everyone should take their leave. The contestants have today and tomorrow to rest and prepare for the final trial, which begins the following sun cycle morning."

Last time, we'd had almost a week between trials, but this time, we had one complete day before four of us faced our deaths. Reality crashed over me as I thought of how little time I had left, but I had to be strong, especially in front of Dallas and Orla.

Silence descended along with the cold realization that this was the last time four of us would see the ones we loved. The bitterness I'd felt about the Comortas surged once again. The unjust cruelty made the situation horrible. Why did anyone have to die? Why not compete until all but one contestant yielded? But that wasn't how the fae worked. It was either kill or die instead of facing the shame of failing.

"Well, son, I have no doubt I'll see you again," Curry's father taunted. "I don't need to drag out our goodbye."

Dallas growled and rasped, "Why do I need to pretend to be friends with that drafty again?"

"Because his father is a High Fae and respected by his peers." Orla glared and focused on me. "No matter what, I need you to kill Curry. We need him to die so his father has no heir. They were a large source of the unrest in the kingdom when I took the throne."

That didn't surprise me. "Done," I said before realizing what I'd agreed to without much regard. I'd committed to taking a life, and the worst part was that it didn't bother me. It was a means to an end for my sister and our kingdom.

"More than that." Dallas pulled me into his arms again. "We need you to win. I'm not ready to lose you again."

Suddenly, a strong hand gripped my arm and removed me from Dallas's grasp. The buzzing of my skin informed me of exactly who it was, and Kieran's mask of indifference slipped slightly as his eyes met mine. His tone held an edge of anger. "My sister would like to say goodbye to you. Apparently, she enjoyed your conversation."

I wasn't stupid. This was a ploy to get me away from Dallas, but at least I'd gotten a reaction out of him for a change instead of him always taking control of our relationship.

The request made saying goodbye to Orla and Dallas a little easier. I wasn't sure I could walk away if left to my own devices. Now that I'd mostly remembered them again, thinking this was the last time I'd see them made me want to hug them and never let go.

"Of course I'll tell her goodbye." I turned back to Dallas and said, "You treat her well." I looked at my sister. "And you make sure to keep his troubling ass in line."

Orla snickered. "Oh, I do, but it's never-ending work."

Dallas winked at me. "She just thinks she does. I have my ways."

And there was the flirt, but I understood it was innocent. If I told him no, he wouldn't push. He loved me too much to ever do that.

Maeve walked over, bowing her head slightly at Orla and Dallas. Then she touched my arm, whispering, "You'd better stay safe."

"Please look after them and yourself."

She swallowed hard, trying to school her expression.

Kieran tugged on my arm to lead me to his family, but I stayed firmly in place and waited until Dallas, Orla, and Maeve reached the front door. Maeve opened it for them, and Dallas glanced over his shoulder and blew me a kiss.

A low snarl came from Kieran, and when he tugged on me, I followed him to his family.

"I didn't mean to interrupt your family's goodbye, but I wanted to say farewell to you as well as my brother." Princess Brianne tucked a piece of hair behind her ear. "It was an honor to meet you, the chosen princess who saved our realm."

Prince Nolan arched a brow but nodded. "Please don't let Kieran do anything stupid."

I shook my head. "Impossible. Kieran decides his own fate. In his mind, no one but him has a say in these matters."

Throwing his head back, Prince Nolan laughed. "Oh, the ice mountains must have thawed. For the first time ever, I think I found a Summer Fae I like." He leaned forward, touched my arm, and whispered, "Ginevra was a good friend, and the risk and sacrifice you made for her was noticed by me and several of our court. You have a few admirers and will never be forgotten."

I couldn't believe it when the corners of Kieran's lips inched upward, but he mashed his lips together.

Kaley and Eamon marched to the front door. Kaley said,

"Everyone has left but the prince and princess of the Winter Court."

The High Court siblings leaned against the doorway to the dining hall while Leanna scoffed. "They are talking to a Summer Fae as well."

Kieran stiffened and nodded at his siblings. "You two better go."

Wanting to give them privacy, I made my way up the stairs. At the top of the second floor, I glanced down to see Nolan and Brianne leaving. Kieran wasn't in view.

My heart ached, and I rubbed it, trying not to think about the person who caused it.

When I reached my door, I removed the key from my bra. Before I slipped the key into the lock, I glanced behind me to find Curry's door shut. I exhaled.

My eyes were starting to close, and I was ready to crawl into bed and let exhaustion take over.

As I turned to shut the door, the cold against my neck flashed, and within seconds, Kieran stood in front of me, kicking the door shut with his foot. His eyes scanned my body.

Before I could take a breath, he'd closed the distance between us and was pressing his lips to mine.

His tongue slipped into my mouth, and his cinnamon taste filled me. I opened my lips wider, wanting more of him, as my hands reached between us and fisted his suit. Skin buzzing, I wanted *more*.

Then, the memory of everything he'd said crashed over me. Instead of pulling him closer like I wanted, I pushed him away.

He stumbled back, his eyes opening, and he frowned. "Are you rejecting me because of *him*?"

Twenty-Seven

I SAW RED. Or maybe his face was turning scarlet from his anger. Either way, none of this sat well with me.

I pushed my finger into his chest, hitting hard muscle while a jolt shot through me. "Are you fucking *serious*?"

"I don't know what *fucking* means, but I'm deadly serious." His nostrils flared as his jaw clenched. "I saw the way you two hugged one another."

"Let's say you're right." He wasn't, but I refused to back down. *He* had decided we shouldn't be together with no consideration of what I wanted. "Why does it matter to *you*? You said we couldn't be together."

"Why are you being so summerheaded? Especially after *everything*." His jaw clenched, his muscles working.

I hated that he was so damn sexy. My draw to him had me stepping closer when I should've pulled away. "*You said* we couldn't be together! *You* decided that without any input from me. Am I supposed to die in two days without looking for some happiness?" I hated how vulnerable he made me feel. Everything inside me was laid bare in front of him, and he had the power to ruin me worse than death ever could.

"Alina," he growled, the sound angry and sensual. "You're pushing me."

"Me?" I laughed bitterly. "You've been in control of whatever this is between us since I came here. You knew what we felt for each other in my past life, and I had no clue what was going on. I still don't understand how I'm so in tune with you, Kieran, but stop playing head games with me. All my life—at least this one—I made sure to stay away from people who can hurt me, and you threaten everything I've worked hard to protect myself from."

He exhaled, his shoulders slumping. "I'm trying to protect you from when this ends. I need you—"

"I don't want your *protection*!" The words flew from my mouth before my brain understood what I was saying. "All I want is *you*. Even if it's just for the next day."

His face twisted in agony, but his icy eyes burned hot. "Those are dangerous words. You don't know how much I want it as well."

"Then why fight it?" I was ready to throw caution to the wind. Though I'd fight like hell to win the next trial, I wanted to be with him. Our time was running out, and desperation had my heart clenching tightly, making me feel as if I could break so damn easily. "Haven't we done that enough?"

"If we complete this bond ... we'll be hurt worse during the final trial," he gritted. "I don't want you to have to experience that. Losing your fated mate—"

"Fated what now?" I'd never heard that term before, but something inside me tugged *hard*, and I stepped closer to him, our chests brushing.

He cupped my face, and my body moved of its own accord, pressing against him. I tilted my head, wanting every inch of his skin to touch me. He whispered, "You don't remember that?"

"I remember how strongly I felt about you, and I know what I feel for you is stronger this time." I placed a hand on his chest, the sensation changing from a buzz to a jolt. "I don't understand it. Though I'm not certain what a fated mate is, fated is exactly what this feels like." I'd denied that it felt as if we were meant to be together because it was hard enough to accept how intensely I'd been drawn to him before I'd seen the good and protective side of him.

"It means we're two halves of the same soul." His thumb brushed my bottom lip, and the spot on my neck pulsed coolness through me. "Fate chose us for each other, knowing we balance each other and make the other stronger when we're together. Why she would choose us—a Summer and a Winter Court royal—baffles me, but that is what we are to one another."

I closed my eyes, enjoying the soothing sizzle between us. His words solidified and made me understand our connection, but I was terrified. There was no way to get out of this unscathed. "Is that why this place on my neck always cools when you're near?"

His gaze lowered to the spot the sensation came from. He swallowed. "It's our fated-mate mark."

The memory of his tattoo—half sun and half snowflake—popped into my mind. Then I remembered how, after it had appeared, Kieran had placed his hand over it, and I'd felt a warm magical buzz. "You glamoured our marks. Didn't you?"

He winced, sliding his hand down my face to my neck while placing his other hand on his own. The coolness pulsed between us, mixing with the warmth that resided inside me. The sensation was delectable, similar to a warm brownie with ice cream on top. When the glamour slid away, my eyes widened as the white tattoo I remembered reappeared.

My breath caught as I reached out and touched it. The mark flashed a bright pink that reminded me of a sunrise.

His eyes closed, and he moaned. "You don't know how many times I've imagined what that would feel like."

That sound had me wanting to press myself against him, but I had come to my senses enough to keep my distance and remain firm. I couldn't let him come and go as he pleased.

That was one thing I'd learned during this second life. You taught people how to treat you. If you let them walk all over you, they would. If I wanted Kieran's respect and, more importantly, my own, I would set boundaries and stick with them. "Maybe if you stopped pushing me away and then deciding you can't stand to see me with someone else, you'd have experienced it sooner."

"It's not wise for us to be like this." Kieran wrapped his free arm around me as his eyes stayed locked on the hand over my mark. He pulled me close, and my own hand put more pressure on his mark. The pink sparked brighter, lighting up the room, and an icy blue light that matched Kieran's eyes glowed from my neck. The pink and blue collided and swirled together like cotton candy.

"If you kiss me again, you don't get to walk away." I let the words hang between us, setting those damn boundaries. "For the next sun cycle, I want to be with you, future consequences be damned."

His brows pulled together. "You're making this very hard for me."

"Then leave." I lifted my chin, meeting his gaze. "You've been good at that in both my lives."

He groaned like I'd kicked him in the stomach. "Fine, but I need you to answer two things."

He removed his hand from my neck, and I whimpered in protest. He grinned and fisted my hair, tipping my head upward to him. He growled, "Do you have feelings for him?"

"He was my best friend in my first life, so yes, I care about him." If he was trying to make me feel bad for having Dallas as a friend, it wouldn't work. I'd had to see Kieran talk to Quinley more than enough times to know they had some sort of friendship and respect for one another, which meant a lot in this world. "We grew up together, and he always supported my dreams even when he didn't agree with them."

Yanking my hair harder, he frowned. "Wrong answer."

"Maybe for you." I arched a brow, ignoring the knot of need twisting inside me. "But I'm being honest and not burying the truth. I'd like the same respect from you as well, so don't ask anything you don't want an answer to."

"Did you have *sex* with him?" he snarled, his fingers on the back of my dress pressing into my skin.

Dread pooled inside me as I answered the question the best way I knew how. "Not in this lifetime."

Gray shadows flashed through his eyes as he bent down and lifted me to his hips. My legs wrapped around him before I thought it through, and his hardness pressed against me through my dress.

In a moment, he had me laid out on the bed as he hovered over me. He nipped at the bottom of my earlobe, causing me to gasp, and murmured, "Wrong answer." He sucked on my earlobe, and my body shuddered. Then he rasped, "Now I have no choice but to make love to you so you can forget about all the lovers before me in both your lives and yearn only for me until the day you die."

"You don't have to worry about this life … only my last."

He stilled.

Okay, I'd meant that as encouragement, not to make him stop.

"How many men do I have to kill?" He raised himself, staring at me. "I'll make sure they die even if it can't be by my hands."

I grew light-headed. I loved that the thought of me with someone else made him want to hurt them.

Whoa. Whatever was brewing between us couldn't be healthy. "Then you'll have to return the favor with a list of names. I'm sure you haven't been abstaining all these sun cycles."

"During the first visit you ever made to my kingdom to handle the trades, we touched, marking one another. I haven't touched anyone since. To list everyone before then, I'll need some pen and paper, but I'll gladly provide it." He grinned wickedly, probably enjoying that I wanted to hurt anyone who'd ever touched him.

Instead of finding him paper, I shoved him so he fell onto the bed, and I straddled him. Unfortunately, my dress was way too long and bunched up, ruining the moment.

"This is a problem." He glanced at the fluff of material piled on his chest up to his chin. "We need to fix that." He rose and pulled me against him, pressing my breasts to his chest. He ripped my dress down the back and growled, "That was in the way."

I nodded, not wanting to talk. "Kiss me."

His lips were on mine, his tongue demanding entrance.

I opened my mouth and moaned at the taste of him.

My dress loosened, and he pulled away long enough to slide the dress lower, revealing my strapless white bra underneath. Kissing his way down my neck, he unfastened my bra, and when he undid the clasp, he removed the bra with one hand and found my nipple with his tongue.

I threw my head back, and he shifted underneath me and laid me on the bed again. He removed my dress and underwear, and I lay sprawled before him, completely naked.

"You're so beautiful," he rasped, taking in every inch of my body.

I should've been embarrassed, but as his eyes darkened and I saw how hard he was even through his pants, I felt only exhilaration.

But it wasn't enough. At least, not for me.

He leaned over me, and I greedily yanked his jacket, but in my desperation, I couldn't get it off. He chuckled. "Here. Let me help." Within a second, he had tossed the jacket aside, and my fingers lifted the hem of his shirt. Each inch revealed his chiseled chest, and once I'd tugged the shirt over his head, he captured my lips again.

His fingers dug into my sides in a way that drove me wild. My heart pounded as I responded to each stroke of his tongue.

He lowered his head and sucked a nipple into his mouth, his tongue flicking against the sensitive skin, causing my back to arch. He sighed. "You taste exquisite. Better than anything I ever imagined."

"Same," I gasped as his fingers rolled over the other peak. "I imagined it so many times in my head," I panted.

"Don't worry. You won't have to imagine all the times we'll have tonight."

I tugged on the waist of his slacks and almost growled over how long it was taking him to get rid of them. Once they were gone, I ogled every inch of him, my vision blurry with insatiable need.

Leaning back over me, he kissed my breast again. "I want to

touch you, Alina. Can I?" He then slipped my other nipple into his mouth.

"Oh yes. *Please*," I begged, something inside me urging me toward him, coolness and heat mixing and surging within me.

He slipped a hand between my thighs, and I nearly combusted, but I tried to control my breathing.

His tongue flicked my nipple, and his fingers circled between my legs. I gasped.

Friction coiled inside me, and heat churned through my body. "Can I touch you too?"

Moaning, he nodded, not missing a stroke on my nipple, so I wrapped my fingers around his arousal.

A deep, throaty groan left him, giving me courage. I stroked him, enjoying the weight of him in my hand. But when he slipped his fingers inside me and began to move them in and out, my vision hazed over.

My breath stuttered, and he quickened his movements. I matched his speed, wanting to make him feel just as good as I felt. Need building within me as he drove me closer to completion. I had to be doing the same to him because his hips swiveled and bucked, increasing our frantic rhythm.

He moved his fingers quicker and harder, and it wouldn't be long until I was pushed over the edge. With my free hand, I stopped him, and he pulled back and looked into my eyes.

I wanted him inside me. "I need you," I moaned. I tried to move his hand, but he shook his head. To make myself clear, I said, "Make love to me, please."

"I will." His fingers grew a little rougher, but not so much that it hurt. It was the exact pressure I needed to bring me to release.

"Kieran," I gasped and stroked him faster as an orgasm exploded within me.

My breath caught as my body clenched, and I melted under his touch. As soon as the pleasure subsided, I was more desperate for something else ... him inside me. "Kieran. Sex. Please."

"I love hearing you say my name, especially like this." He slid between my legs and pressed against my entrance, his eyes on mine. When I thought he'd push inside me, he paused.

I blinked. "What's wrong?"

"If we do this, our connection will be complete. Our souls will be fully linked." He slid a little more inside me, only his tip. He moaned, his body shuddering. "I'm not letting you go ever again. You're mine until death."

My stomach fluttered, and I nodded. "That sounds perfect to me." I'd gladly take a lifetime of pain to have this moment between us. Knowing that in less than two days, we wouldn't have this ever again made me determined not to waste the little time we had.

"Okay." He thrust inside me ... and stilled.

Pain cut through me, and I winced as he stretched and filled me.

"Are you—" A blinding smile filled his face.

"I am." I nodded. I didn't add *in this life*, certain it would take away from the moment.

He inched in slowly, giving my body time to adjust, and soon, he was completely inside me.

I'd never felt so full and complete. For the first time since I could remember, I didn't feel a void inside me.

He kissed me and moved slowly, then faster, and soon, all the discomfort vanished as my hips thrust against his. He growled and increased the pace, and I panted and wrapped my legs around him. He slid his hands under my legs and lifted them so he could slide even deeper. Our bodies quickened the pace, each of us desperate to bring the other's release.

He caressed my breasts as he slid in and out of me. Friction knotted in my core, and before I realized what was happening, ecstasy pulsed through me. My head dropped back as he kept a steady and fast movement, watching as I succumbed to the sensations.

"Mo fhlùr," he groaned, pumping faster. "I've never seen anything as beautiful as you at this moment." He removed his hand from my breast and settled it between my legs, circling my core as he continued his rhythm.

I wasn't sure how it was possible, but my body was already tensing again. The desperate need for another release took control as his fingers pressed harder and more insistently.

"Are you close again?" he gritted out.

I nodded, at a loss for words.

"Good." He threw his head back, and his body jerked and arched into mine.

Moments after his orgasm, a third one pulsed through me. I whimpered as we rode out our pleasures together. Our bodies writhed slowly, completely in sync, and something snapped inside my chest. A liquid sensation flowed out of me as buzzing swarmed within me, and my ecstasy intensified as if I was experiencing twice as much.

When the pleasure subsided, Kieran lay beside me and pulled me into his arms. I nestled into his chest, smelling the crisp, clean first-snow scent I treasured. The sizzle of our bond simmered everywhere we touched, even as the coolness flowing from the tattoo eased the heat inside me.

Kieran's voice popped into my head. *I love you.*

I stilled. Had he just …

I pressed up and stared at his face. He *must* have said it out loud —that was the only explanation.

"What's wrong?" He tensed, looking into my eyes.

"I thought I heard you—in my mind." I shook my head, trying to knock the weirdness out. In a fit of fancy, I thought at him, *You must have pleasured me into oblivion. Not that I'll ever tell you that.*

"I pleasured you that much, did I?" He waggled his brows. "I'm very proud of that." He booped my nose.

A lump formed in my throat. "What are you talking about?" I hadn't spoken aloud. I was certain.

"Pleasuring you into oblivion."

I sat up, not bothered that I was still naked. "I thought that in my mind, Kieran. How did you hear me? Did you … did you say that you love me earlier?" My heart pounded. If he hadn't actually thought that, things would get super awkward really fast.

"Uh ..." His face turned a slight pink. "Yes, but in my thoughts."

Something uneasy swirled through me, adding to my discomfort. Then I remembered the feeling of something snapping in my chest and the strange intensity as the pleasure surrounded me. "Can fated mates talk telepathically and ... *feel* one another?"

He bit his bottom lip. "Fated mates are rare. It's more usual for shifters ... I don't know how it works for us, but now that you say that, I remember hearing rumors that fated mates have a connection that no one else can understand. They know what the other person is thinking and feeling."

There was only one way to test this. So, I said the one thing that made sense. *I love you, too.*

A huge smile spread across his face. "I had no doubt you did." He pulled me on top of him, and I straddled him.

He hardened underneath me.

"I want you to show me how much you love me," he said as he pressed against my core.

I shivered on command. "I can do that. I can't believe you abstained from physical relationships for me." He had no clue how much that meant to me, especially when he thought I'd died with no chance of returning. "You gave up having a direct heir to the throne." I knew things like that were important in this land. I leaned down to kiss him, but his kiss lacked luster.

Something strangled me, but it wasn't from my own happy emotions.

I tensed at the sudden change. Something was wrong.

Straightening, I examined his face, only to see him force a smile.

What would've changed his demeanor like that so suddenly?

I froze. *No.* "If you haven't had a physical relationship since I was gone, how were you going to have an heir, Kieran?"

"It's not important, Alina. It won't happen anyway, so there's nothing to worry about." He leaned forward, trying to kiss my breast.

I scrambled off him and the bed and stood. "Who were you

planning to have an heir with?" I hoped like hell he didn't give me a name. If he did, that would make this person more real.

"You died, and I was losing my magic." He sat up, rubbing a hand through his hair. "Nolan thought that if I took a queen and had an heir, the magic would return to the Winter Court. The line of inheritance from the active king would then be fully intact as intended. She doesn't mean anything to me, so it doesn't matter."

My mouth dropped, and my heart ripped open, agony slicing me in two. "You're *married?*"

"What? No!" He shook his head vehemently. "I'm not."

I exhaled, my knees nearly giving out. My heart raced from fear that he was with someone else. "Why did you say it like you had promised to wed someone?"

He flinched. "Because I did. But Alina, it doesn't matter. You and I are lovers. She's just to be my wife. That's all."

Vomit burned my throat. "You're engaged." Every principle I stood for was based on trust and faithfulness, and I'd lost my human virginity to someone promised to another. "And you slept with me."

"I made the promise six months ago to be wed in the next complete seasonal cycle. She agreed to sit on the throne and bear me one heir. After that, I don't have any commitments to fulfill toward her."

I placed a hand on my chest, wondering if my heart was still in it. "You promised to have an *heir* with her. And that's not *important?*"

"Alina, this discussion is becoming pointlessly heated." He stood.

I hated that even as my lungs seemed crushed inside me, I noticed his bare chest and craved to be held in his arms. Worse, I could feel his frustration. I couldn't change how I felt, and I knew that the first incarnation of me wouldn't have liked this either. Sharing him wasn't possible. "You're right. It is pointless. Because one, if not both of us, will die in the next trial. Well, that might be true, but it doesn't change the issue. What if the trial hadn't happened? Not only are you *marrying* someone else, but you expect me to be fine with you impregnating her?"

He flinched, and guilt swirled from him. "I thought you were dead. And fae can't break a promise."

"Who is it?" As much as I didn't want to know the answer, I needed to. "Do I know her?"

When he averted his gaze, that made it worse.

I didn't know many people here, but clearly, I *did* know her. And the problem was I only knew four female Winter fae, and one of them was his sister. That left Leanna, Rowan, and Quinley.

Twenty-Eight

THE NAME LODGED in my throat, and I wanted to choke. "It's Quinley. Isn't it?"

His gaze darted back to my face, and he bit his lower lip. "Yes."

I was certain I *was* going to vomit. I stumbled to my dresser, no longer comfortable being naked in front of him even though I longed to close the distance between us.

I refused to be *that* girl. The other woman, the mistress, the *lover*. The girl who was second choice. I'd grown up around people who didn't want me, and now my fated mate had promised himself to another. Yes, he'd thought I was dead, and he'd done it because of his weakening power, but that didn't keep the situation from dredging up a lifetime of baggage. "You need to go." I grabbed a gown and threw it over my head.

"Mo fhlùr." He stood and reached for me. "She means *nothing* to me. You're the most important person in my life."

"Mo fhlùr, my ass," I spat, struggling under the fabric and trying to yank the gown over my body. I wasn't being elegant, but if I didn't do something, I'd throw myself into his arms.

"What?" he said. "That makes no sense. My flower, my ass?"

My head popped out of the top of the dress, and I, unfortunately, noticed that Kieran was still naked ... I resented even more how much I wanted to stand here and peruse his entire body.

Wait. Had he been calling me his flower this whole time? My heart sputtered.

Fuck no. He was *engaged* to someone else, and worse, if one of us wasn't guaranteed to die, he would have expected me to be fine with him banging her and having a child with her. My stomach churned again as I remembered how incredible I'd felt when he'd been inside my body.

Then it hit me. "If you won't leave, I will. I'm going to find Curry."

His nostrils flared. "Why would you go searching for that hothead?"

"You obviously thought I'd be fine with you sexing it up with Quinley. Since you'll likely be doing that after I die tomorrow, I should go experience some variety as well. After all, it's not *important*." I was being a bitch, but I suspected this was the only way he'd understand even a sliver of my agony.

Hot rage and sharp pain that weren't mine flooded me. Light-blue magic sparked at his fingertips, and his whole body tensed as if he were ready to fight me. He snarled, "If he even *looks* at you, I'll kill him. If *anyone* looks at you in any way I don't like, I will end their life. Make sure you understand the ramifications of your decisions."

There it was. The understanding. But I *hated* that it came only after he'd considered the possibility of someone else being inside me. "It hurts, doesn't it, even thinking about the possibility?"

He froze, the anger morphing into deep regret. His breath caught. "Alina—"

"No." I pushed my arms through the armholes of the dress, finally clothed. "Don't *Alina* me. You made love to me and didn't consider how I'd feel afterward, knowing you don't belong to me."

"Don't *belong* to you?" He scoffed, marching toward me, eliminating the distance I so desperately needed. He gestured to the mark on his neck, which was back to its white color. "The fated-mate mark proves I belong to you more than anyone in this world! Not even a wife can claim such a deep connection."

My soul tugged at me, trying to agree with him. Maybe the supernatural part of me did agree, but the human part I'd been raised with couldn't accept it, so I let that part respond. "If you have a wife, can I sit next to you on the throne? Would *our* child be considered legitimate and an heir to the throne in the eyes of the fae?"

He flinched. "I want to have everything with *you*. That's one reason that losing you the first time haunted me so much. If I hadn't been so stubborn, we'd have had a chance to be together. This time, it seems Fate has been more cruel, bringing us together just for you to be part of the Comortas. If I hadn't been so scared for my people and Brianne ..." He ran his hands through his hair.

"Brianne?" When we'd talked before, he'd insinuated there was a reason he hadn't wanted to be with me, and now he was throwing his sister into the mix. "What does she have to do with anything?"

"She's not a full Winter fae, Alina. Honestly, that was the true reason I chose not to be with you before." His shoulders sagged. "Her father was from the Summer Court, and if you and I had gotten together and your *mother* had learned of her heritage, I feared—"

That she would use that information against Winter. Even without all my memories, I remembered she'd been warm and fun to play with but emotionally unavailable. She was all about appearances and making sure every decision strengthened Summer's rule. "None of that matters now." He kept going back to the past and reliving his decisions. "The past can't be changed, but *this* lifetime, *these* moments, can."

He exhaled. "I agree." He touched my shoulders and continued, "So let's enjoy every last moment we have together since they will be our last."

Chest throbbing, I forced my legs to move backward, and his hands dropped from me. I already missed the sizzle between us. I shook my head. "Not with you promised to someone else. I can't let that go, Kieran."

"She means *nothing* to me. A mere means to an end. I can't get out of my promise, no matter what I'd be willing to do to change it." His forehead creased. "I thought you were *dead*. Had I known there was the faintest chance of you returning—" The regret and guilt emanating from him tightened my chest.

All the anger whooshed from me, leaving me exhausted. "I know." I went back to him, cupping his cheek with my hand. The tingles zapped between us. He hadn't been trying to be unfaithful. The fae couldn't break a promise without losing their magic. If he lost his magic, what sort of life would be left for him? Our magic was part of us, part of what made us whole. "And I get that." Without my righteous anger, my agony was more debilitating. I wanted to crumple to the floor and lie in the fetal position. "But that doesn't change how I feel."

"Summer's sake, Alina. The tournament resumes in a little more than a day." He wrapped an arm around me, pulling our bodies close. "And one of us is going to die. Why are we wasting our last bit of time together fighting? You said we were all in."

He was right. I had. "Had I known about your promise, I would never have agreed to be all in." I licked my lips, which still tasted of his cinnamon essence. "We can't be together, not like this, and I'm sorry." Letting my hand fall to my side had my stomach in knots. "I can't share you, Kieran, and whether you understand or not, that's exactly what you're asking me to do." I swallowed, preparing myself to say the next words. "Now, please leave."

"Is that what you really want?" He lowered his head, staring into my eyes.

"No." I couldn't lie. "But it doesn't matter what I *want*. I *need* you to tell me goodbye."

His jaw twitched, and he snatched his clothes from the floor. I looked away, not wanting to see him dress. I could feel agony radiating from him, and unfortunately, it was as potent as mine. My chest ached so much that a jolt of pain shot through me with every breath. I wasn't sure how I would survive this ... survive losing him.

But I refused to fall apart because of a man. Loving and approving of myself was more important than a moment of pleasure, and surprisingly, it was my first life that taught me this lesson.

Even though I wasn't watching him, I could feel each movement. Through our bond, I could sense his thoughts, feelings, and even his location in conjunction with me. I'd thought I'd been aware of him before, but that didn't come close to the way I sensed him now.

I heard his belt fasten, and he moved toward the door. Beside me, he paused, and I could feel his gaze on my face.

Alina, he said in my head.

I shook my head. If he tried to convince me to let him stay, the situation would only escalate. We'd said everything we needed to say. I replied, *I'm not mad anymore, nor do I hate you. I just can't be with you like this.* It'd be better if I was mad. I could hang on to rage to numb the pain. But the thing was that he hadn't meant to do me wrong. In his mind, in this culture, he hadn't. But when I'd flipped the situation, he'd understood where I was coming from and had felt just as awful about it. *I'm sorry, but put yourself in my place. How would you feel?*

I'd kill the person standing between us, he snarled. *Hell, if I could, I'd do it now, but that would break the promise and mean losing not only my magic but my kingdom's respect, and it would put Nolan and Brianne at risk of being slaughtered so a new family could ascend the throne.*

My mouth dropped open. *Are you asking me to kill Quinley?* Worse, the idea sounded damn tempting. But that would be murder in cold blood. I blinked hard and shook my head. "Don't answer that. I can't kill someone over something that wasn't wrong." I couldn't fault her for agreeing to marry Kieran. He was an amazing and protective man.

He exhaled and went to the door, and I swiped the key from the nightstand and followed him. When I brushed past him to unlock it, I took a deep breath to memorize his scent. I couldn't chance getting too close to him again.

His fresh winter scent filled my nostrils as I opened the door.

As he stepped through into the hallway, I fisted my hands, trying like hell to prevent them from grabbing him.

I moved to shut the door, eyes stinging and vision blurred, but his hand stopped it from closing. He popped his head inside, our eyes locking, a tear of his own trailing down his cheek. His voice was deeper than normal and raspy. "I will *always* love you. You will own my heart even in death. And I hope you have the happy life you deserve."

"If you win, I wish you the same thing." Warm tears trickled down my cheeks, and my nose became stuffy. "And … I love you too. That will never change." I pushed on the door, and he stepped back. I shut and locked it, then dropped to my knees.

Even as the magic inside me grew hotter, I'd never felt so broken.

* * *

I tossed and turned, dream after dream assaulting me. No matter how hard I tried to wake up, it was one flashback after another. I didn't know how long I'd been asleep. It could've been hours, or it could've been minutes, but my mind was reeling.

Finally, my eyes popped open, and I jolted upright in bed. I glanced around the room to get my bearings. I couldn't remember where I was, and I expected to find myself in Stan's office or my bedroom back at Sambradh Castle.

Alina? Kieran's voice entered my mind, and some of my dread faded. *Are you all right? I've been trying to get through to you all day.*

My stomach fluttered at the sound of his voice in my head. I blinked, and the room came into focus. That was right. I was at Rioghail Tower because of the Comortas. Muir had died, even though he must have been only nine hundred complete cycles. He should have lived at least seventy-five more—wait. I'd died fifty complete cycles ago, so that would make him ... nine hundred and fifty. Here I'd thought the funny, crude coldy would live to be a million.

Head spinning, I put my hands on the bed to keep myself upright. How did I know Muir? I was only twenty-three years old. Except I wasn't.

The walls crept in on me. I remembered *everything* from my former life.

The two time lines merged, and it was as if I had two different sets of memories inside me ... two different versions of myself that had lived in two vastly different worlds.

I'm on my way down, but you'll need to let me in, he said, his concern quickening my already rapid heartbeat.

I rubbed an arm over my forehead, feeling uncomfortably hot. I needed to take a bath. *I'm fine.* There was one thing Alina and Ivy agreed on: Kieran complicated matters. He'd hurt both versions of me, and both refused to share him with anyone ... even in name. *I just remembered everything.* I swallowed and swung my legs over the side of the bed.

When I stood, I almost stumbled into the window. I was so off balance.

Unable to do anything else, I lay back down on the bed. *I'm going to take a nap,* I told him, not wanting him to worry. Then my eyes closed, and darkness blanketed me.

* * *

My head pounded so hard I could actually hear the noise. I opened my eyes, but this time, I wasn't confused. I knew exactly where I was ... and the noise stopped.

"Open the door, or I'll do whatever it takes to get in," Kieran's voice boomed, and there was another round of pounding.

I sat up, and the world didn't spin. Instead, everything seemed ... *more.* I could feel energy ... magic swirling around me, stronger than I remembered from my first life.

There was a crack, and Curry shouted, "What the frozen summer are you doing?"

"She hasn't left her room in over a day, and the trial starts in an hour."

I'd been asleep for over a sun cycle? How was that possible?

Not wanting a fight to break out, I snatched the key from the nightstand and rushed to the door. Slipping the key into the lock, I opened the door and came face to face with Kieran.

His eyes went to my mark.

You need to cover—

No. I lifted my head high. I was tired of hiding who I was, which included being his fated mate. *I'm not glamouring it anymore.* I noticed he'd hidden his.

"You look different." Curry's voice grated on my nerves. I remembered him now and how he'd tried to force his way into being my husband. His father had become my mother's lover and had been whispering in my ear about the arrangement, which was why Dallas and I had promised ourselves to one another. Obviously, Orla had to keep Curry and his father happy so they wouldn't cause more problems than they already had.

At least I didn't have to pretend anymore. Either he or I would be dead by the end of the day. "And you still look like an ugly coldy. The complete cycles haven't aged you well."

Kieran laughed but covered it with a cough while Curry's eyes narrowed.

Lips pressed into a line, Curry clasped his hands until his knuckles blanched.

I tried not to smile. I'd learned that meant I'd gotten under his magic. "If the two of you are done, I should get dressed for the trial."

And you should eat since it's been over a full cycle. Kieran's irises warmed as he glanced at me. *You need all your strength to make it through today.*

Seeing him like this when we both cared for each other so completely was hard, but I wanted to cherish the memories of our time together before reality crashed over us. We were always meant to be kingdom-crossed, never getting our happy ending. Everything inside me wanted to reach out and touch him, but Curry was still glaring at us.

I nodded, not wanting Curry to be more curious about our relationship. If Kieran won, I didn't want his people or Quinley to turn against him. She had much influence over the Winter fae, especially considering how long she'd been on the High Court. That must be why Kieran had chosen her.

Acid burned my throat, but I was pragmatic enough to understand his reasoning, and his promise hadn't been made for love.

"Well, gentlemen." I curtseyed, the cycles of etiquette falling into the forefront of my mind. "I'll see you shortly." I shut the door, watching as Kieran's face disappeared, and locked it.

I spun around and went to my bathroom. I had to hurry.

A short while later, I had bathed, put on my golden armor with vines—which was my favorite—and placed my dagger in its sheath, my quiver on my back, and the bow around my body. I didn't bother to glamour my face, but I braided my hair and pushed it into the back of the armor, wanting to limit what the other competitors could use against me.

I glanced at the room. Kieran's sword lay on the bed, and with our mate mark showing, it was the last thing I needed to bring with me. It would draw attention to the half snowflake on my neck.

I fought the urge to sniff the sheets for Kieran's scent to remember the only time Kieran and I would be together. Instead, I went to the door, threw it open, and strode out, not bothering to lock it behind me.

If I came out of this alive, I'd be going home to mourn Kieran. If I didn't win, no one would be waiting for me here to kill me.

When I made it downstairs, Kaley's and Eamon's eyes widened. The two of them bowed their heads, which they hadn't done for me since I'd come back from Earth.

"Princess Alina," they murmured.

My gaze landed on Kieran, who was talking to Quinley.

If I thought I'd understood pain before, I'd been *so* wrong. Seeing them together, knowing what their future held if Kieran won, nearly dropped me to my knees.

The only thing keeping me upright was that I refused to allow the others to see me fall.

We're discussing what happens to her if I die. Kieran's voice popped into my head. *She wants to know if my promise extends to my brother. I informed her no. I won't make that decision on his behalf. For heated sake, I wish I hadn't made that decision for myself.* His regret and pain were so powerful that I had to lock my knees.

Curry, Rowan, and the quiet Winter fae man, who was still nameless despite my memories returning to me, stood in the corner.

Leanna and Caden strolled out of the dining hall, both wearing crimson. The color of blood and war. Leanna waved a hand. "All the fae are inside, and it's time to start the trial. The only thing missing is our competitors."

Quinley had a deep frown on her face, but when she looked away from Kieran, her expression smoothed. "Very well. Kaley and I will go out and prime the audience. Eamon and Caden can stay here and make sure the competitors don't begin fighting too early while you, Leanna, can get the main attractions ready."

Main attractions.

I didn't like the sound of that.

Kaley and Quinley headed to the doors of the arena while Leanna went to where the ball had been held several nights before.

Here. Kieran came to my side, looking delectable in a black suit that reminded me of his shadow magic. He held out a piece of bread and jam. *Eat this.*

I shoved it into my mouth in one bite, not wanting the others to notice.

How are you still so sexy when you're shoving an entire piece of bread into your mouth? Kieran chuckled, his expression carefree. *It shouldn't be possible. I'd be disgusted by anyone else.*

He was flirting with me in front of everyone ... and worse, I liked it.

He's promised to someone else, I reminded myself.

Obviously, you haven't been with the right person, I teased, but the joke fell flat. I hadn't meant to take a dig at him like that. *I'm sorry. I just meant—*

It's fair and true. He smiled sadly. *But I am determined to rectify that.* His gaze went to my mark, and the coolness pulsed through me.

There was a knock on the arena door, and Eamon and Caden marched to it. "The time has come." Eamon sounded jolly.

My stomach roiled.

Everything will happen as it should. Kieran brushed his hand against mine as we walked behind everyone else to the door. *Fate must know what she's doing.*

I almost laughed until the doors opened ... and I stared into a dense forest. We'd be fighting each other, but knowing the High Court as I now did, I knew there would be something extra. Leanna was likely releasing something terrible from the cells in the basement.

As if conjured by my thought, monster after monster flapped its wings, flying over the trees.

Twenty-Nine

WITH A HEAD THAT RESEMBLED AN OLD, grouchy, balding man from Earth, a body covered in reddish fur in the shape of a lion, a tail that was long and scorpion-like, and leathery wings, there was no doubt what these monsters were.

Manticores.

They were some of the most vicious creatures in this realm, and there were only three ways to kill them: behead them, which was damn near impossible with their claws and razor-sharp teeth; strike them through their sensitive stomachs, which was about as likely as beheading them; or burn them to death because their skin and fur were highly flammable.

Only two competitors might have firepower—Curry and me. I had magic linked to the trees, flowers, and plants, while he was more attuned to controlling water.

That must be why the High Court had chosen the manticores. None of us naturally had an easy way to kill them.

Stay beside me, Kieran's voice popped into my head. *No matter what.* His fear slammed into me, chilling me further.

My heart did a quick pitter-patter. He sounded as if he still wanted to protect me, and that wasn't wise. Not here in the final trial of the Comortas. It was kill or be killed, and our fated-mate connection would make this trial damn near impossible for us ... and perhaps get us both killed. But even if I'd wanted to, I wouldn't separate from him, especially when he'd made it clear that he wanted me near. *Okay, I will.*

There was no way either of us could win. Even if one of us was the last one standing, the cost would be too high. My stomach gurgled, and I wished I hadn't eaten that frigid piece of bread.

Everything will be fine. Kieran brushed my hand as we walked past Eamon and Caden. Caden held the door on the left, Kieran's side, and Eamon the one on the right. Eamon's brows furrowed as if he'd noticed Kieran's touch, but when his eyes met mine, I lifted my head in challenge. I refused to be questioned about my choices, especially when I was facing my death.

He had enough sense to glance away.

As we stepped into the arena, I fought the urge to cover my ears. The audience was loud and unruly, their various chants blending into a chaotic roar. They knew four of us would die today and a "winner" would be decided, so watching us battle each other and these almost indestructible monsters would be the highlight of their lives for who knew how long.

The seats were packed, with even little ones in attendance, despite the ten monsters flying overhead. As we stepped onto the platform, I tensed, preparing to fight for my life so I could live and entertain the audience, but the manticores didn't seem to notice any of us.

I noted a slight shimmer in the air where the steps went down to the trees. The five of us would be safe until we descended. They must have performed the same illusion spell on the audience; otherwise, the manticores wouldn't have been oblivious to everyone's presence.

Kaley came to my side. "Princess Alina, I'm glad to see you are yourself once more." She smiled and placed a hand on my shoulder. "Now you have a real chance at winning this trial."

I lifted a brow, trying to hide my annoyance. "Even without all my memories, I made it through the first two trials. Maybe you should remember that." My voice held a slight edge. I wanted to punch her and put her in her place, but that would accomplish nothing. Once again, my younger and more reactive side and my first incarnation were at odds, but instead of resorting to violence, which I'd soon have my fill of, I clenched my hands into fists.

Her mouth dropped open, and her cheeks turned a shade of pink. "Yes, Your Highness."

Quinley cleared her throat, and her voice boomed, echoing off the massive walls of the arena. "Today is the final day where the strongest fae of Talamh will take a seat on the High Court. The manticores will continuously attack, and the competitors won't be able to leave the center until only one remains alive. Until then, they will fight one another as well as the manticores."

Lovely. That pitted us against each other even more.

I hated everything this competition stood for.

In the front, Curry, Rowan, and the silent Winter man stood as still as statues. I didn't have to see their faces to know that concern, if not fear, was there. Most of us hadn't seen these beasts, but we'd all heard the stories handed down over the complete cycles. They lived in the wildest part of the wildlands. Mother had given me a book that contained pictures and information about all the animals in Terrea.

Leanna leaned into Kieran, and I took a step toward the gorgeous woman, ready to grab her by the nape of her neck and yank her away from him. No one but me was allowed that close to him.

He took a slight step toward me, putting more distance between them. I waited for him to say something since I was the one who was adamant we couldn't be together while acting jealous of someone trying to talk to him. He didn't speak, but I could sense his happiness and humor. I kept my gaze forward, refusing to act curious about what was going on with him.

"Your Majesty, I wanted only to wish you the best of winter out there." Leanna's voice rose at the end of the sentence, making it sound like a question. His reaction must have concerned or confused her.

Quinley continued. "Bring out the lute to begin the trial."

Without permission, my eyes cut sideways to see how Kieran responded to Leanna.

"I'll make sure the right person wins." He winked.

My blood heated at his flirty response, so I forced my legs to take another step away from him.

The edges of his lips tipped upward. *Is something wrong, Alina?*

A deep snarl emanated from my chest, something I'd never experienced in this body—my ruthless fae side coming out. *Ask one more time, and I'll make sure the manticore doesn't get the first blow.*

Now that, my love, sounds like you're trying to seduce me.

My body warmed, clearly disagreeing that we couldn't be together. The fact we were around a ton of people made it easier to restrain myself. Maybe I'd been foolish to decree that we couldn't still sleep together, but Ivy wasn't the only one who thought that way; Alina did as well. Something about our fated-mate connection made the thought of sharing him in *any* way too painful.

Eamon strummed the lute, the sound like taking a bath in frigid water. My magic thrummed inside me as natural as breathing, and we prepared for the battle ahead.

When the music stopped, the audience went deathly quiet. Everyone stood, all eyes on us with various expressions of excitement.

My skin crawled. Both my old and new memories were disgusted by such acceptance of violence, and I realized maybe the two versions of me weren't so different overall.

Curry drew his sword, lifted it high, and yelled a battle cry. Then he charged down the stairs, rushing toward the manticores.

The audience went wild as Rowan and the silent man followed him, eagerly racing toward their death. I wanted to roll my eyes, but that wouldn't change a frozen thing.

The manticore closest to the edge of the forest roared as its head jerked toward the three newcomers. The other nine jolted to attention, and they all flapped their black wings and dove toward them.

"What are you doing?" Quinley turned and glared at the two of us, her gaze landing on Kieran. "Get out *there*."

Shall we? Kieran asked and took a step toward the stairs.

We needed to move before the crowd suspected we were too afraid to fight. *Let's get this over with.* If I was going to die, I didn't want to continue dreading it. I wanted to walk with my head held high, not run like the other three, but accept my destiny.

Ladies first, he replied, allowing me to be the first royal in view.

I stepped through the shimmery outline, and the sound of the crowd disappeared. My wings exploded from my back. The manticores were focused on the first three as Curry slipped between two oak trees, Rowan and the silent man a few feet behind. The first manticore swooped down and attacked them.

The hairs on the nape of my neck rose from Kieran's attention behind me. He was keeping an eye on me as well as on the monsters. He would have to trust me to hold my own. I reached for my dagger.

Three of the manticores peeled off, chasing after Curry, while three prepared to fight Rowan and the other fae. That left four racing right at us.

Use the sword, Kieran commanded. *It'll have more length to stab them with.*

I flinched, though I didn't alter my stride. This wouldn't go over well. *When you said we couldn't be seen as allies, I left your sword in the room.*

His frustration slammed into me like a punch to the gut. He replied, *I said that before we completed the bond, Alina.*

The oak tree was only a few feet from me, but I pivoted right toward Rowan and the silent man. In the woods, our competitors could use the cover of the trees and their magic to sneak up and attack us, so I didn't want to chance following the same route.

The sound of wings beating grew closer. I waited for a second, readying for the right time.

Alina, Kieran shouted in my head, making my ears ring. His fear surged through me.

I dropped to my knees, the dirt kicking up around me, and rolled onto my back, swinging my dagger and hoping to stab the manticore in its stomach. The manticore's claws swiped where I'd been a moment ago, the dirt hiding me enough for it not to counter my move quickly, but my dagger was too short, and I missed its underside.

I couldn't see behind me in the dust, but I was only five feet from some oaks, so I rolled until the edge of my wing hit a trunk. I jumped to my feet. A manticore swung its tail at Kieran, and the second monster swiped at him.

The drafty had stayed behind to distract them from me.

As I removed my bow, Kieran swung his sword, blocking the tail, then spun away, barely avoiding the second manticore's claws.

I snatched an arrow from the quiver and loaded my bow. The second manticore lifted a bit higher in the air, his front half rising to strike at Kieran again. Kieran's back was turned toward it as he swung his blade at the neck of the one striking him with its tail.

What in the icicle hell was he doing? I let the arrow go, and it sailed into the second manticore's stomach as Kieran's sword sliced into the neck of the other monster. Brown blood squirted from the sword's cut, splattering Kieran's armor and face.

A whizzing noise came from my left and I yelped as a quill lodged into my hand. A sharp pain exploded as it went all the way through, and I hissed and rolled between two oak trees, needing a layer of protection.

I'll be right there, Kieran vowed from his spot out in the open.

I could hear the whooshing of more quills and knew that the manticore was shooting them at Kieran. I glanced at my hand. Blue blood poured from the wound, and wisps of pink magic swirled from it. I wiggled my fingers, shooting pain through my arm.

Even though removing it wasn't smart, I'd die if I didn't. Not wanting to overthink it, I dropped the bow and gripped the quill. Gritting my teeth, I yanked it out. Agony shot through me, and acid lurched in my stomach, burning my throat. Clutching my hand to my chest, I rocked back and forth, waiting for the pain to subside. Crisp magic flowed through my hand, mixing with the pain and easing it enough for me to pay attention to everything going on.

Between the various roars and hisses of the manticores, I finally understood what humans meant when they claimed to be in a living hell. That was exactly what this was, and I was certain the other four would agree with me.

I had to get moving before a manticore tracked me down.

My head said to go farther in the woods, but my heart wouldn't contemplate leaving Kieran. Legs in tune with my heart, I snatched the bow off the mulchy ground and went back toward the exposed dirt.

Before I could exit the woods, I slammed into Kieran's chest. His arms wrapped around me, and he scooped me up and sped deeper into the woods. *I'm sorry, but the manticore you were fighting, I struck its tail and forced it back out into the dirt, then took off to check on you. We need to put distance between us and them before I slow down.*

I shouldn't have allowed him to carry me, but I didn't want to fight while we were in danger. When I turned into his chest, I smelled something rancid. I jerked my head back to see it was the manticore's blood. There was no blue mixed in with it.

After a few minutes, Kieran slowed and set me down in the middle of some brush. The two of us burrowed into the greenery, and I found it sort of chilly, watching a man his size hiding in cover so small, but he made it work.

He took my hand, and his forehead creased. *I thought it struck you. I felt your pain, and I can see the blood.*

Of course it ... I looked down, and my breath caught. There was still blood on my hand, but there was also a scab. That shouldn't have been possible. *I ... I don't know.*

A shrill scream came from fifty yards away then promptly cut off. The world tilted underneath me. There was only one female other than me, and I had no doubt she had died.

Tears burned my eyes as I wrapped my arms around my legs. Rowan had saved me during the last trial, and even though we hadn't been close, I hated that someone who'd tried to do the right thing had been lost. Curry was more deserving of death.

Your empathy astounds me, Kieran said as he stared at my face. *I know of no fae other than Brianne who would feel that way about someone from the other court, but you truly care.*

Multiple sets of flapping wings caught my attention. I peeked through the brush to see two manticores flying directly at us. I froze … and heard the sound of heavy breathing.

I spun around to find two more manticores behind us. They were sniffing the air and heading our way.

We were being hunted.

I removed my bow, ready to use my arrows, but it snagged on a branch. The heavy breathing stopped, and a chill ran down my spine. They knew where we were. I had to do something fast. Now that they were in the forest, I could use my magic more easily.

I lifted a hand, and vines sprouted from the ground, encircling the two behind us.

I'll take the other two, Kieran said as he jumped to his feet and raised his hands. We stood side by side, facing opposite directions. I could feel his magic flowing through him as he shot ice at the two manticores behind me.

My vines wrapped around the four legs and moved to capture the tails. Both manticores struck with their tails. The sharp points sliced through the vines while the monsters' legs ripped the vines from the ground.

My magic wasn't working against them, but it was slowing them down.

Kieran's determination flared. *My ice is barely affecting them.*

Same here. I glanced around, unsure what else to do. I could shoot arrows, but I couldn't take down all four before they reached us.

Fly away. I'll fight all four. Kieran unsheathed his sword as he continued to shoot ice with his other hand.

Like I would ever do that. But that was the problem. I was thinking like Alina—thinking I had to choose one thing or the other. Now was the time I needed to lean on Ivy ... and just like that, I had a plan.

Thirty

MY HEART CLENCHED, and I prepared my wings for what came next.

Fly now, Kieran commanded, his urgency surging between us, sending adrenaline pumping through my body.

I wanted to snap at him but gritted my teeth. He was trying to protect me. *Shoot your ice magic at one instead to hold it off while we fight the ones charging at us.* We were dividing our magic, trying to drive both away instead of thinking strategically.

Taking my own instructions, I focused all my Earth magic on the farthest one. The vines doubled, taking hold of its paws, and even though the monster continued to yank, it wasn't having as easy of a time breaking through.

The other manticore didn't hesitate; it charged.

Alina, if we survive this, I may kill you myself. He growled, his hot anger surging between us.

Despite not actually meaning the words, there was truth behind them. If we were the last competitors standing, what would happen? I couldn't kill him. The thought alone had my heart experiencing a level of agony I would never recover from. But I also couldn't fathom standing here and letting him kill me. I didn't want to die either. I'd been avoiding thinking about the possibility of us being the final two without considering what it meant if we weren't.

The manticore was ten feet away, its mouth wide, its razor-sharp teeth protruding and claws extending. With the slight tilt of its tail, I knew the monster would attack me in full force.

As I prepared for either the smartest or dumbest thing I could possibly do, something hot boiled in my magic, a strange sensation I'd never experienced before. With my memories restored, my magic swirled inside me and funneled through my hands and body to stream toward the manticore I was keeping at a distance.

I leaped forward, ignoring the brush biting into my skin as I landed at the bottom of the forest cover and flipped onto my back. The monster soared over my head. The manticore slowed and sniffed, searching for me. Then it roared, looking under its front legs. As its back legs moved, I thrust my dagger into its sensitive belly.

The monster shrieked at a higher pitch than I'd have thought possible. Its rancid blood poured over me, filling my mouth and covering my face and chest. I gagged from the putrid taste and horrible smell. The animal bucked and twisted, and its claw stabbed my shoulder and thrashed my skin as it tried to keep its balance.

Sharp pain shot through me when I rolled underneath the leg just before the monster crashed to the ground with an agonizing scream. The ground shook from the impact, and cold terror strangled me. If I hadn't moved, I would be dead.

"Alina!" Kieran shouted, his concern slamming into me.

He must have been able to feel my disgust and horror. The last thing I wanted was for him to be distracted from his own battle. *I'm fine. I killed one of the manticores.*

As if Fate wanted to reassure him, the manticore moaned as it collapsed completely with one last wheezy breath.

His relief made me woozy. Or that might have been from my blood loss. I glanced at my shoulder and saw where its claw had punctured my armor. My blood trickled from the wound, not as fast as I'd expected, and pink wisps of magic drifted from it. A crisp, prickling sensation of magic rushed to my shoulder while a smaller amount tingled at a lesser level on my injured hand.

I must have turned into a drama queen since joining this trial because the injury hurt a whole lot more than what I expected from looking at it. There was no telling what I might find underneath the armor.

Kieran grunted, and I glanced over my shoulder to see a manticore's mouth open wide, about to swallow him whole. My heart clenched, and I stretched out my hand to help him, my shoulder screaming as Kieran shoved his sword between the monster's teeth and through the back of its mouth.

No! I yelled through our connection.

My magic faltered. The manticore I'd bound had broken through all the vines restraining it, but I didn't give a damn. Kieran was about to be mincemeat.

Then his manticore stumbled back, and Kieran yanked his sword from its mouth. Brown blood coated the sword to the hilt, but Kieran somehow kept a firm grip.

The monster dropped, and I wanted to cry in relief. I hadn't heard of sticking a blade through the back of its mouth as a kill method, but I imagined very few people had tried and lived to tell the story.

Feeling better about Kieran's chances, I focused on my second monster. It was closing in. Without my dagger, I had one option.

I pumped my wings, darting to the side, and the monster swatted at me. I leaned back, my back muscles churning to power my wings. The tips of a claw hit my face just as the creature swung its massive scorpion tail toward me. It was so huge that I hadn't thought this strategy through, and one of its sharp quills rammed into me.

My body jerked, and my back hit the ground hard, bending my wings uncomfortably as my head hit a tree trunk. My temples throbbed, but I didn't have time to focus on the pain because the manticore was on top of me.

For Summer's sake, why were you so hotheaded about bringing my sword? Kieran's fear and frustration leaked through as I watched him channel his frozen magic into the manticore near him and then run toward me.

Stay. I'll figure something out. I channeled my magic again. I used both hands, trying to focus while my head seemed to split in two. The limbs of the oaks nearby snaked out and wrapped around the manticore's neck as brush and vines from underneath held it in place. *See,* I added through our bond so he wouldn't keep attempting to reach me.

Fine, but I'll be there soon, he rasped in my head. *I can feel your pain.*

My stomach fluttered, and it had everything to do with his determination to protect me. I pushed the thought aside and searched for something … *anything* to fight off the impending threat. My magic wouldn't hold the manticore for long, though the oak branches tightened around the monster's neck.

When I sat up, my head swam, and my body wanted to keel over. Between that and how much it hurt to fill my lungs, I thought I might pass out, but that would be my death warrant, and I refused to give up that easily.

Placing both hands on the ground to steady myself, I stood slowly. The manticore hissed and swung its tail around its body. I watched as the quills shivered, as if they were about to be released one by one.

Moving my feet, I got behind the large oak as it fired its quills. Several flew to the sides of the tree as I pressed my back against the trunk, protecting myself. I hated that the tree was sustaining injuries because of me, but it would heal, unlike me, if a quill hit the right spot.

With no other weapon, I removed my bow from my body, my shoulder screaming. I clenched my jaw and grabbed an arrow from the quiver. The quill fire ceased, and I peeked around the trunk, aimed at the monster's stomach, and fired.

I overshot. The arrow missed its mark, hitting the manticore in the upper leg. It hissed, the quills shivering in its tail again.

Shifting back behind the tree, I heard a snap, and the strength of my magic weakened. The other manticore was freeing itself.

The next time I fired, I couldn't miss, or I would be the monster's first meal of the day.

The quills whistled past me and struck the ground with louder thuds than last time. The monster was getting angrier. I had to figure a way out of this and fast.

Stay where you are. I'll take care of this one too, Kieran said, and I heard feet racing toward the manticore.

My heart caught in my throat as the quills continued to soar past me. Even though the manticore was distracted, it had excellent senses.

The quills stopped, and I jumped out from my spot just as Kieran swung his sword at the manticore's neck. I watched in horror as the monster's tail whipped around, aiming for Kieran's head. Even if Kieran landed a deadly blow, it wouldn't matter.

The heat that added to my magic exploded, and pink flames erupted from my hands. The magic soared past Kieran, who halted and hit the manticore right in the chest. Its reddish fur sparked, and pink flames flickered and spread along its body. I gaped and stared at my hands in disbelief.

The tail stopped short, barely missing Kieran, as the monster tried to get away from us.

The vines pulled back from the fire, and the flames brightened. Kieran stumbled away from the tail, and his wide-eyed stare flicked to me.

You have fire magic? His surprise and betrayal flowed through me, tightening my chest.

I studied my hands, ignoring the way my shoulder ached, and noticed that the wound where the quill had gone through my hand was completely healed.

Strange.

I didn't know I had it. This was all bizarre and should've been impossible. Fae had only one magical affinity, not two. *This is brand-new information to me as well.*

Thank the shadows you have it. Kieran headed toward me, not even glancing at the monster, which wailed as the flames burned it to a crisp. *I would've been dead if not for you.* But then his face turned strained as he realized what we had done.

We'd saved each other.

I didn't think I could ever consider him my enemy. I'd struggled with it in my previous life when he'd rejected me, but in this life, there was no way I could see him as someone other than the person I loved.

Love.

What a dangerous and amazing word, especially during the Comortas.

When he reached me, he didn't hesitate to take me into his arms despite the disgusting blood covering my face and armor and coating the front of my hair. He held me close, his arms tight, like a vise I never wanted to be released from.

"I stink," I said, not wanting him to pass out from the smell. "And so do you."

"You've smelled worse." The corners of his mouth tipped upward.

I laughed, which startled me. In this dire situation, he could still make me smile. This wasn't a time for laughter, but his being safe made me a little giddy. "I'm pretty sure you're smelling your upper lip, not me."

His brows creased as he leaned back. "What does that mean?"

"It means it's you." Earth jokes didn't perform as well in Talamh. I needed to keep that in mind going forward, but there were some recent sayings that were hard to break.

He shook his head. "Then why not just say that?"

A loud shriek cut off our conversation, reminding us of where we were.

Kieran frowned and released me. He took my hand, tugging me away from the oak's support, and scanned me. "Are you okay to keep going? We need to move in case the other manticores come here to investigate their friends' deaths."

As if I had a choice in the matter. They wouldn't let me out of a trial because of shoulder and head injuries. If anything, they'd cut me so I bleed more. "Let's move." I didn't want to be here for the other monsters' return. I'd like a moment to shake off the last fight before we fought again.

Though my head hurt, it was more manageable. The ground didn't shift with each step like before, so that had to count for something.

I stretched out my wings as Kieran and I moved quietly through the woods, listening for any hints of the monsters and other contestants.

A roar came from a quarter mile away, and Kieran and I ducked under a tight group of three oaks as two manticores flew overhead. They headed in the direction we'd come from, and I wondered if they were, in fact, searching for their friends.

After a few beats, Kieran and I continued and soon heard blades clanging through the woods.

That had to be Silent Man and Curry.

Kieran nodded in that direction. *We should watch the fight and see who the survivor is.*

My stomach roiled. He was right. It would help to know who we were up against, but that meant Kieran and I would be two of the last three survivors. The inevitable that I kept pushing from my mind couldn't be ignored for much longer.

Would Fate be so cruel as to pit Kieran and me against one another?

Hey, everything will be all right, Kieran assured me as he squeezed my hand.

The clanking of metal grew louder, and I couldn't believe there weren't any manticores there. The noise alone should've attracted them, but when a mourning wail filled the air from where we'd killed four of the monsters, I realized what was taking place. Maybe these monsters weren't heartless and had a lion's pride mentality.

With that thought, we stepped around a tree, and the two men came into view.

Curry and Silent Man fought in the center of a small clearing, their swords clanging and glinting as they danced around each other. Kieran and I paused. There wasn't an easy place to hide and watch, but that would be futile anyway.

If we hid, the winner of the match would hunt us down.

With each block Silent Man made, Curry pushed him back. Silent Man stumbled a step but managed to stop a blow to his head. Curry put pressure on the man's sword, trying to power through and slice his face, but Silent Man kept holding on.

Part of me wanted to help Silent Man. I didn't know why since he was as likely to kill me as Curry, but he hadn't done anything horrible to me or anyone else in the games, as far as I knew.

I'd stepped forward to help him when Kieran wrapped an arm around my waist.

What do you think you're doing, Alina? Kieran asked, concern rushing into me.

It was a valid question, but I had no reason not to join the fight. Three people would die, and I damn well wanted to make sure Curry was one of them. *Ending this,* I answered, slipping from his hold and racing toward the other men.

As I stepped out into the clearing, I lifted out my hand, the vines listening to my call. A vine snaked from the ground, wrapping around Curry's sword hand.

Snarling, Curry kicked Silent Man in the chest, and the man fell back as Curry turned to face me. He grabbed a knife from his side and sliced through the vine. I conjured more earth magic as he rushed toward me, dodging each and every one. He held his sword high and readied to attack.

Letting my fire magic pulse out, I shot a stream of flames at him, which he countered with his water magic and a shocked shout. Steam hissed from the two clashing elements as he barreled toward me.

I'd just lifted my other hand to send pulses of the earth magic to capture Curry again when Silent Man stood and ran toward me.

Clearly, I shouldn't have felt obligated to help him. The prick.

I went back to focusing my earth magic against Curry, wishing like hell I'd removed the dagger from the manticore's stomach when it had fallen. This was all I had.

I'll take Curry. You fight Daniel, Kieran said as he came to my side. *Take my sword.*

I'm fine. I'll use my magic against him, I replied, pouting. *I want Curry.*

Curry's harassed you, and I'd honestly rather not fight one of my own. Besides, you've been injured, and Curry is a damn good swordsman. Daniel has a weak spot on his left shoulder. If you strike him there, he'll be caught in an unexpected heat wave.

I hated to take the easy way out, but if it would help Kieran fight to win, I'd gladly make the sacrifice. My shoulder was still bothering me, though I could move it without excruciating pain. Not wanting to argue, I turned my focus on Daniel.

Water from Curry splashed over me, rinsing off the manticore blood, and for one bizarre moment, I was super thankful to him.

I watched as Kieran froze Curry's feet and stopped his advance.

That was a great use of ice powers.

Daniel has wind magic, so be careful, Kieran alerted me.

I stilled. He'd just told me something about one of his own people to protect me.

That moment of hesitation was all Daniel needed. A sudden, big gust of wind swirled around me, lifting me off the ground.

I spread my wings to catch the wind and shot up vines to wrap around my legs to anchor myself. I was twenty feet in the air, but that prevented Daniel from reaching me with his sword.

Thinking I was safe, I glanced below to find Kieran and Curry fighting.

The manticores screeched with a rage that rattled my bones even in a tornado. We'd killed five, and from what I could tell, there were five individual screeches of agony.

This wouldn't go well.

I glanced down at Kieran just as he shoved his sword into

Curry's neck. The blade exited from the bottom of his head, and there was no doubt Curry had died.

Now, there were only three.

The wind stopped, and my body crashed to the ground before I could counter it.

"Alina!" Kieran screamed, not even ten feet away, as I landed on my front. My breath was knocked out of me, and Daniel appeared at my side, sword raised.

At least it isn't Kieran who kills me, I thought as I desperately called my fire magic, but I didn't have enough time.

His blade swung down, and then Kieran's body covered mine. His face filled my gaze ... and the sickening sound of a blade slicing through skin filled the air.

Pain exploded through me, but it wasn't mine. Blood trickled onto the grass all around me.

My heart stopped. What had Kieran done?

Thirty-One

MY AGONY and fear mixed with Kieran's relief. I rolled him onto his back, away from Daniel, and stood to face the silent Winter fae.

He wouldn't hurt Kieran again. I'd make sure of it.

Daniel tried to rush past me, and I blocked him. Then he dropped to his knees and gripped the hilt of his sword. "My King, *no*."

My gaze flicked to Kieran, and I finally understood his fear. The wound in Kieran's neck bled so freely that Daniel must have nicked an artery.

Tears burned my eyes. Kieran had thrown himself over me to protect me from the fatal blow.

Kieran commanded, "Now stand up and finish me."

"What?" Daniel huffed. "I can't, My King. I was here to ensure *you* won, and now I've killed you myself."

"Do as I command," Kieran rasped. "Or be a traitor to your own kind."

Even though we couldn't see or hear the audience, they could hear us.

Oh, summer had officially frozen over if he thought I was going to stand by and let this prick kill him faster. There had to be something I could do to help Kieran—I just needed to eliminate the man who'd damn near slit his throat.

Daniel's jaw twitched as he nodded. "Please forgive me, Your Majesty." Then he lifted his sword.

Roars shook the ground as the manticores arrived. But I didn't care. All I wanted to do was finish the man who planned on hurting my fated mate. I called a vine and caught Daniel's hand before he could strike then called another to retrieve Kieran's sword and bring it to my hand.

This prick would die the way he'd killed my fated mate—throat slit by Kieran's sword.

Eyes widening, Daniel turned to me, noticing me for the first time since he'd injured his king.

Alina, a manticore is targeting you, Kieran said, his fear palpable.

The sound of beating wings rained down on me, but I didn't give a shit. There was one person I needed to end. One person who would die by my hand.

I released Daniel's arm as the manticore's growl rang in my ears. I lifted my other hand, and a streak of fire shot from my palm, hitting the beast. It shrieked like its friends had.

The monster jerked its head back, and the other four circled, giving me time to focus solely on *him.*

I swung the sword, and Daniel recovered enough to block the hit. I wanted his death to be quick, so I would have to do better than that.

Daniel advanced on me, and I stepped back happily. I didn't want us anywhere near Kieran. I could see him dragging himself toward us as if he wanted to get involved in the fight.

Stay put, I said as I crossed blades with Daniel. *The last thing I need is you getting trampled, and I swear, Kieran, if you ask him to kill you again, I will make your life a living summer.*

Despite the pain swirling through him, I felt the warmth my threat gave him ... something else ... something strange, as if he was getting dizzy.

He was losing too much blood.

Clenching my teeth, I swung the sword, my shoulder aching from the discomfort. Between the vibrations of each block, I tried to grit my way through the pain of the worsening wound. I jabbed, trying to catch Daniel off guard, but he easily swiped the blade away.

Panting, I almost dropped the sword, and he kicked me in the chest. I flew backward, losing the sword, and rammed into a thick oak. Daniel turned to Kieran, who had stopped moving and was ghostly pale. He hurried to him, and I knew without a doubt what he was trying to do.

Obey his king.

Vines shot from the nearest tree, locking him in place as the four manticores descended upon us. Kieran's time was running out, and I had to handle this so I could save him. I didn't care about the manticores—they were keeping their distance from me, but Kieran and Daniel were in their sights.

As a manticore swooped down, I shot fire at it, hitting the tips of the monster's toes while pushing myself even harder. I got my feet under me and readied my weapon.

Wind churned around me, indicating that Daniel was channeling his magic. This time, I was more prepared, and I focused the brunt of my magic on the ground. Vines snaked around my feet. The magic within me blared to life stronger than I'd ever experienced. As I stepped forward, the vines on one leg loosened, and new vines took root, propelling me toward them.

My connection to Kieran grew fuzzy. My heart pounded harder, and I screamed, *You better stay awake!*

Mo fhlùr, our time together is ending. Even in thought, he slurred like someone who had drunk too many spirits.

It better not be. I couldn't lose him, *not like this.*

Hissing came from the other three manticores. Each time they hissed, they launched their quills. I stopped and placed my hands on the ground, then channeled all my magic into the earth. Vines sprouted and covered Kieran just as I raised my left hand.

Quills whistled through the air, but Daniel's wind changed their direction, and they didn't hit me. When the wind died down, I tapped into my fire magic, sprouting flames from my palms into the air. I screamed, needing this to be *over*, the flames pouring from me.

The three manticores all caught fire, and they screeched as they dropped to the ground and writhed in the flames.

I untangled the vines from Kieran and myself and turned to find Daniel choking, a quill protruding from his neck and eye. The impact had knocked him onto his back, his body sprawled at awkward angles and two puddles of blood seeping from underneath him.

I looked at Kieran, who was only ten feet away from Daniel. His face was paler than ever and sweat beaded on his forehead. Blood trickled from one corner of his lips.

The world shifted underneath me as I ran to my fated mate. I took his hand, wanting him to know I was there. The jolt barely buzzed, and I missed it desperately. *Why didn't you freeze him?* If he'd had time to race over and cover me, he could have used his magic instead.

He turned his head toward me, the blood trickling faster with the movement and pressure he put on the artery. I pressed a hand on his neck to stop the bleeding, and his eyes opened, but the warmth in them was gone. They were too pale, and I knew his death was imminent. *If I had killed him, only the two of us would have been left, and we both know that wouldn't have ended well. With our bond, neither one of us can kill the other. It's impossible, so this is the only way. Only one of us can survive, and it has to be you.*

My chest constricted so hard I was certain I'd never recover. He'd protected me and allowed himself to get hurt so I could win. My whole understanding tilted, and my entire perception changed.

I'd pushed him away because he'd made a promise to someone else when he'd thought I was dead. And still, he'd given up *everything* for me at the end. I'd honestly thought he would win, and thinking of him being with another woman after I was gone had driven me crazy. *It should be* you. *I'm not made for this world, and they need you in it.* A sob built in my chest, and I couldn't hold it in as I lifted his hand to my lips. *Kieran, I don't know how to live without you. Not anymore. I can't lose you. Not after we finally found our way to one another. I refuse to live without you.*

His pain slowly vanished, and he smiled tenderly as he pushed all his love toward me. He whispered aloud, "You have to, or they win. Live a full life for me. You're the strongest person I've ever known, and there is no one better to serve on the High Council than you. This land needs someone with your heart. You cared for all fae even before you were reborn, and now you aren't afraid to show it."

I shook my head, my breathing catching. "Do ... not ... say ... goodbye." I couldn't handle this. I searched the area for something to save him. He couldn't leave me ... not like this.

I have to. His hand went limp. "And though I support my brother, Prince Nolan, taking the crown, I ask that the Winter fae people remember what you've done for both Winter and Summer Fae during the trials. That, no matter what, you tried to help both sides as the High Court is supposed to do. I'm honored to have fought alongside you." More blood trickled from his mouth, and his eyes slowly closed. Those words had taken the last bit of strength he'd had; I could feel it through our bond.

A lump formed in my throat, and my mouth dried. I was losing him.

Mo fhlùr, I'd die all over again for you because there's nothing more precious in this world. I love...

I could feel the moment his heart stopped beating.

Thirty-Two

MY CHEST CONSTRICTED as my heart imploded. All this time, I'd believed I understood loss, but nothing could have prepared me for this moment.

I clutched Kieran's hand, rocking back and forth as the strange, crisp sensation buzzed through me.

My fated mate. Dead. Right in front of me.

He *couldn't* be gone. His time wasn't up, and the High Court had caused all this suffering. For what? To prove someone could stand after having everything stripped from them?

That crisp sensation kept flowing through my hands, but the pain gripping my heart overshadowed everything.

"Princess Alina of the Summer Court is our champion," Quinley declared deadpan, her voice echoing in my ears. "Princess, please stand and acknowledge your people." The glamour spell fell away, and I expected the crowd to cheer.

Silence. Everyone was standing, and some had raised their hands as if they were ready to cheer, but instead, they were glancing around, trying to figure out what was happening. Most of the faces in the crowd were tense, and a few had placed their hands over their hearts.

If they thought I would continue this charade, plaster on a fake smile, and pretend I was ecstatic that I'd "won," they would learn otherwise.

I stayed kneeling by my fated mate, tears streaming down my face and onto his arm. I couldn't let go of his hand. If I did, it might be the last time I ever touched him.

Worse, the buzzing of our connection drifted away. I kept my hand firmly over the wound on his neck because if I moved it, I was giving up.

And I wouldn't do that.

I would respect Kieran's wish for me to continue living because I loved him that much, and he was right. The High Court would win, but I planned on changing things come summer or winter.

I barely noticed as the weird magic increased, flooding my body. I could only guess it was breaking apart our fated-mate bond. My body grew heavy, but I realized I had to address the crowd. I refused to let Kieran's death be just another one in the books of competitors who'd died in the Comortas.

I lifted my chin and spoke. "I will not *stand* as if I've *won* something," I spat. There was no joy in what happened, and losing Kieran was the worst agony this kingdom should ever know. "Nineteen people died for the High Court's merriment and yours. Yes, the High Court might be forged in blood, but that was because of *war*, not some stupid game that was concocted to justify people killing one another. Where I lived on Earth, people vote to choose their leaders. The system's not perfect by any means, but it's far more effective than *this* travesty where being ruthless and self-centered is valued more than taking care of one another and having an open heart."

I couldn't prevent the disdain from leaking into my voice, not that I wanted to. "You killed one of the best men this kingdom had —and so many other amazing people." I took the time to list each person one by one, even Curry. "None of us deserved this." Including that arrogant ass who'd thought he was better than all of us.

"Princess *Alina*," Quinley snapped. "Just because you're the winner doesn't mean you can't be punished."

"I kneel with Princess Alina."

Shocked, I looked at the stands. A woman had fallen to her knees, head bowed, and a space had cleared around her. She began to chant, and every time she repeated the phrase, others joined her.

The stadium became a roar once more, including a trickle of boos, indicating not everyone was behind me. But the majority were shouts of support as it seemed most of the common fae agreed with me.

My fingers tingled as if they were falling asleep, but there was no damn way I was ready to let go of Kieran's hand. I'd never be ready, and I didn't know what that meant for my future, but one thing was clear—I was done being a puppet for anyone here.

In my first life, I'd molded myself into what my mother wanted, and in my second life, I'd tried to stay alone to protect myself from pain and to hide. But neither version was a true reflection of who I was. I was a merging of those people, and I was determined to do whatever it took to fight for every person in Talamh, including myself.

The crisp magic pooled and flowed outward, and I didn't stop it. I grew light-headed, and my shoulders sagged with exhaustion, but I didn't care. I would keep my ass here next to Kieran, holding on to him desperately, wishing that things had been different. In both my lifetimes, we'd never managed to be together, and the fact this was our final chance was cruel.

Quinley's and Kaley's voices echoed in the arena, blending with the chants that supported me as I lowered my head, not bothering to hide my tears. I loved Kieran and missed him already, and there was no way I'd be ashamed of that. Why had we pushed each other away and hidden our love for so long?

My neck pulsed cold, and my breath caught. When I'd died before, Kieran had said he'd lost our mark. That had to be happening to me now. My fingertips buzzed, but I didn't care if my hand fell off. There was no way I was letting him go.

Something blazed through me as the crisp magic vanished from my body, and then a bright-pink light exploded from Kieran's body. I inhaled and fought to stay upright, but my body crumpled, and I found myself on my side as I lay staring at his face.

Kieran turned his head to me and opened his startling blue eyes. What?

I scrambled upright and removed my hands, staring at him. The wound in his throat wasn't there any longer. Blood still coated his neck and armor, but the skin was smooth as if he had never been injured.

Like what had happened to my shoulder and hand.

He blinked, and my heart started beating once more.

"Kieran?" I squeaked. The arena had fallen deathly silent. "But ... I felt your heart stop beating." This was impossible ... like a dream come true, though I struggled to stay awake. My damn eyes were closing as exhaustion set in despite the disbelieving joy flaring in my heart.

"I know." He sat up and almost keeled over. He righted himself and took my hand in his. "I died. I know I did. But something pulled me back here. Something healing." He glanced at my hand and then my shoulder. "And I'm pretty sure you brought me back to life." His brows furrowed. "I can feel that you're exhausted and not feeling right."

Kieran could feel me, so I couldn't lie. But at the same time, I didn't want him to worry. *Sleepy.* That was all I managed to reply.

Had I been healing myself all along? And ... I'd healed Kieran? That was the only thing I could fathom.

Shakily, Kieran stood and lifted me into his arms, cradling me to his chest. His worry was palpable as he kissed my forehead and replied, *Sleep.*

His crisp winter scent and minty breath filled my senses and soothed me as my body buzzed wherever we touched.

Kieran was alive and holding me, and that brought me peace.

The last thing I heard was the crowd's screams, and then I drifted off to sleep.

* * *

When I found myself standing in the sacred pool of water with the seven other women, I immediately knew it was a dream. The eight of us stood before the sacred tree, its branches draining our magic as the limbs covered us.

My heart hammered, and my thoughts centered around Kieran. He'd told me he didn't want me, but the knowledge that there would be no chance for him to change his mind twisted my heart, resulting in excruciating pain.

I didn't have a choice, not when it came to saving all of Talamh and Terrea as well. Each girl had come here to sacrifice her life and magic to restore the balance of our realm because a greedy and malicious vampire had tried to take over all eight kingdoms.

The crisp magic of the pond's healing properties circled within me, its freshness reminding me of Kieran's new-snow scent and adding to my heartbreak. Even the healing magic of the pond couldn't restore the damage unleashed within my heart and soul.

My eyes grew heavy, and I didn't have the energy to lift my head anymore.

"And when you return to your home, you'll be blessed with an extra gift," said a warm, magical voice that swirled around me.

Then I succumbed to darkness.

* * *

"Alina, come back to me." Kieran's voice was so low and gravelly. "I can't do this without you. Not a second time."

"What do you mean, a second time?" Brianne asked from somewhere across the room.

I tried to open my eyes, but the lids were so heavy. *Kieran?* My chest expanded uncomfortably, and I realized he was here with me.

We were both alive.

Mo fhlùr, he replied, his relief soaring into me, followed by the warmth of his happiness. *I was so worried that, when you healed me, you died in my place. I refuse to live in a world without you in it again.*

At least our story hadn't turned out like Romeo and Juliet, where we sacrificed ourselves thinking the other was dead. *I'm not dead, but the healing magic isn't kicking in and healing me.*

Why didn't you tell me you could heal? Kieran asked and squeezed my hand. *No wonder you kept getting better so quickly.*

I ... I didn't know. I thought the fae just healed fast and that I wasn't hurt as badly as everyone thought. I tried to open my eyes again, but they only fluttered. *I think I got the healing power when I sacrificed myself in the sacred pond. And Mother Terrea blessed me with another gift the moment I passed, which explains the fire.*

Then, when you used it on me, you expelled the residual magic left behind. He sighed, then lifted my hand to his mouth and kissed each fingertip. *I'm damn grateful you had it so you could heal yourself to win the Comortas and bring me back before I was dead for too long.*

Maybe Fate was watching over us after all. *Then I'm glad to be rid of that magic as long as we are together.*

"Her eyes."

Orla's voice startled me, and adrenaline pumped through me enough that I managed to open my eyes. I gasped. I hadn't expected to wake up in Kieran's tower bedroom with Orla, Dallas, Maeve, Brianne, and Nolan around me.

My sister sat on my other side, her frost-blue chair set by the bed. Dallas stood behind her, his face lined with concern. Maeve guarded the bedroom door as if waiting for an attack while Brianne and Nolan sat at the end of the bed, both with grim expressions.

"You're awake." Orla took my free hand. "Thank a warm sunny day."

I smirked. "Three Summer Fae and three Winter fae all in one room without hurting one another. Who would've thought?"

Kieran laughed, the sound warm and carefree. "You, mo fhlùr. You've wanted this the entire time and knew it could happen."

He was right. I had, and even my younger version in my first life embraced that dream. Though the realm wouldn't change overnight, given the resistance of the High Fae who'd had it easy for so long, I had no doubt all the people in this room would make the change happen, especially with Brianne being connected to both courts.

"And when the Winter King loves my sister, who am I to hold a grudge that was never my own?" Orla leaned over and kissed my cheek. "Besides, it's not like I can get rid of him. With marks like that, the two of you won't ever be apart." She pointed at my neck and then at Kieran's.

I'd been so transfixed by his eyes that I hadn't glanced at his mark. Now I saw that the half sun and snowflake weren't only white outlines anymore but glimmered with bright-pink magic that resembled the flames I'd called from my hand. I glanced down where I could just see the bottom of my mark and found shadowy blue swirls emanating from it.

Our marks were gorgeous, and the coolness of Kieran's magic ran through me as naturally as my own.

Dallas huffed. "Alina, if befriending some frosties doesn't prove how much I love you, I don't know what will."

A deep, menacing growl emanated from Kieran, and I pushed my love and calm toward him. I glared at Dallas and said, "Stop flirting. You're married, and I'm—"

"Taken, engaged, and the future queen of the Winter Court," Kieran interjected, claiming me in every way.

And I *loved* it. "You never asked a rather important question," I teased, focusing back on my mate.

"Believe me, when everything is settled, the question will be asked, and I expect a firm yes." He reached out and stroked my fated-mate mark. Heat flooded through me. *Or I might have to punish you, and you can't heal yourself anymore.*

I wasn't sure anything he did to me could be a punishment as long as his hands were the ones on me.

"If Alina is up to it, the High Court is waiting for us." Nolan cleared his throat and averted his gaze to the floor as if he knew exactly what was happening between us.

Dallas coughed. "I agree because the way they're looking at each other is very discomfiting."

"Says the obnoxious flirt," Maeve muttered from the door.

"I think someone is jealous," Dallas singsonged, glancing at the warrior, and the smirk fell from her face.

I wanted to enjoy the moment, but the mention of the High Court concerned me. "How long have I been out?"

"Just a few hours. It's nearing dinnertime, so we should go down if you're able." Orla nodded.

Kieran shook his head. "No. She was unconscious for some time after using a ton of magic. They can—"

I want to go home, I interjected through the connection. *To your home, away from here. I want to immerse myself in the Winter Court.*

My stomach dropped as another realization dawned. He was talking about marriage and a future, but he was promised to Quinley.

My joy deflated, and I tried to push the thought away. That was something we could deal with another day.

Now, taking you home is something I can get behind. Kieran stood and helped me upright.

Something changed in him, my chest tightening more as he worried. Of course he'd felt the shift in me when I'd thought of Quinley, but I didn't want to ruin the moment by bringing it up. There wasn't a damn thing I could do to change it.

"Wait." There was something that still didn't make sense to me. "If Daniel was put into the tournament to protect you, why did he win the first trial and also finish the second before we made it through the maze?"

Kieran's brows furrowed. "I hadn't thought of that. During the first trial, he stayed by my side. When I heard the crowd's reaction to you catching Ginerva, I spun around and saw you in a precarious situation close to the finish line. He grabbed my arm and dragged me across the line, effectively finishing first. But you're right. The second trial ..."

"I can answer that." Dallas arched a brow. "He was watching you from a distance, and when you made it past the mirrors and it looked like Curry wouldn't make it, he finished quickly, likely so no one would suspect why he'd been included in the Comortas."

My heart ached. Even though the man had tried to kill me, he'd also tried to save my fated mate. I glanced at Nolan. "Thank you for protecting your brother."

"I wish I could take the credit, but I can't." Nolan shrugged. "If I'd done that, Kieran would kill me right now. That was the first thing he asked me about after he took care of you."

I flinched, remembering all the blood and gore. I glanced down, but I was wearing an elegant pale-pink dress. My stomach clenched.

I bathed and changed you alone, Kieran answered my unspoken question. *I just wanted to make you comfortable.*

My throat tightened. He'd cleaned me up and ensured I looked the part I was about to play, and he'd changed into formal clothing as well, including a pink cravat that matched my dress.

"If not Nolan, then who?" Orla asked, but I already knew the answer.

Kieran said it before me. "Quinley. She wanted to make sure she became queen." He laughed bitterly.

That was enough to make me want to get up and face the woman down. Although ... maybe, this one time, I didn't hate her for her decision.

Eager to leave, I stood up. I wobbled a bit, but with Kieran supporting me, the eight of us made our way down to the dining hall.

The members of the High Court were indeed assembled there. They watched as Kieran helped me to the Summer table and into the seat to the right of the one I'd sat in throughout the trial. Orla took the seat I'd been sitting in, and Dallas sat across from me. Prince Nolan sat next to Dallas with Brianne on his other side. Maeve took up her usual station in the corner of the room.

The High Court members scowled from where they'd gathered

in the open space where the buffet had sat earlier. Quinley's scowl was so deep I feared it would be permanent.

Okay, I didn't fear; I hoped, and maybe that made me a bad person, but I didn't care. The bitch hadn't been happy about Kieran returning from the dead or my impromptu speech that so many of the fae had latched on to.

"This is going to warm everything." Quinley grimaced. "Alina should apologize to the people. Say she spoke from a misplaced sense of heartbreak."

I snorted, sounding ever so classy. "First off, it was not misplaced."

"It was even if just for appearances." She stopped and pointed a finger at me. "You two may be *fated mates*," she said the two words like they were garbage, "but he's my future husband."

"There's no way I'd *ever*—" I started.

Kieran cut me off. "First of all, it's *Princess Alina* to you. You may be High Court, but you are *not* royalty, which brings me to a more important point. You *never* will be." He placed our joined hands on the table, making sure they were in view of everyone.

"*What?*" Quinley's head jerked back. "You made a *promise*—"

"And I died, even after you tried to make sure it didn't happen." Kieran smirked. "You know I did because you announced Alina as the winner, and I know I did because I felt my magic drift from my body. I was called back before it had gone too far to return. But my vow to you is null and void, and I will not be making it again. I have someone far more suited to the role I have in mind." He looked at me, squeezing my hand.

My cheeks hurt, and I realized I was smiling. I tilted my head and winked. *At least one good thing came of you dying.*

He laughed, the sound unusually carefree, and everyone stared at us.

Brianne leaned forward so she could see Kieran and me and asked, "Can you two speak telepathically? I've heard that fated mates can do that."

I bit my lip as Kieran nodded.

Leanna and Caden glanced at each other while Kaley and Eamon moved to the spot between Dallas and Orla. "Your Majesties, you can't entertain approving this relationship."

"Alina is older than me." Orla shrugged. "Therefore, I don't have a say in the matter, but as her sister and queen, I approve of whatever my sister chooses."

I took her hand in mine, so relieved that the two of us had found each other once more.

Dallas steepled his hands. "Since I'm taken, Alina will have to settle for second best. Might as well be *him*. But he better step up and begin defending her honor since I'm the one who gave Curry the black eye."

I figured it'd been him.

"I allowed myself to die for her to live." A low growl came from Kieran.

I glared at Dallas and said to Kieran, *He's just trying to make you angry.*

It worked. He's not dead because he's the one who brought you back to Terrea. I don't care that he's the king consort of Summer.

Dallas beamed, no doubt noting the way Kieran's nostrils flared, but he said, "True. So, that's why I'm okay with her choosing *you*."

"Well, the High Court doesn't agree with the union." Quinley stood ramrod straight. "Since it's across territories, you need our approval."

The bitch wanted Kieran, but I refused to give her what she desired. I batted my eyes and glanced at my fated mate. "I'm assuming you can accept a new resident into your land. Since Orla is queen, I don't need to stay part of the Summer Court."

His brows shot upward. *You'd move to Winter Court for me? Leave the warmth of your heritage lands behind?*

If it means I can be yours in every way, of course I will. I was tired of all the excuses for why we couldn't be together. If being declared Winter was what I needed to do, so be it. "I'll become Winter fae, or maybe the royals of Summer and Winter can acknowledge me as one of their own, and thus, I'd have a dual territoryship." I was using my dual citizenship knowledge from Earth to my advantage, trying to implement it here as well.

Orla sighed with relief. "I can support that if King Kieran can too."

"Anything that will make you happy," he said out loud as he cupped my cheek with his other hand. "I will gladly accept you as Winter under any terms."

Prince Nolan chuckled. "It sounds like there's no need for the High Court's approval since each territory has resolved the matter in its own right."

The fact that Prince Nolan was behind us as well made the situation even sweeter. If I could have dual court status, we could make it work for Brianne as well. Then, she and I would be part of Summer and Winter.

"I guess everything is settled." Kieran stood and pulled me to my feet. "I would really like to take my mate, brother, and sister back to Geimhreadh Castle so we can get Alina acclimated."

I couldn't ask for anything better than that.

Everyone else stood from the table. Eamon and Kaley came to our end to speak to Orla and Dallas while Leanna, Caden, and Quinley glared at Kieran. The decision to grant me a dual territory-ship gave both courts leverage, indicating there were workarounds if the High Court tried to abuse its power.

Not wanting to seem ungracious, I shook each High Court member's hand and smiled. "I can't wait for our first official High Court meeting."

When I reached Orla, I threw my arms around her and whispered in her ear, "In three nights, let's meet at Dath Waterfalls." It was something we'd done when we were younger, and it seemed right that we would do it again now that I had returned.

As I pulled away, she nodded. "Wouldn't miss it even if I had to travel to a warmthless climate to visit you."

Dallas hugged me, and though Kieran groaned behind me, he remained a good sport. Then I hurried over to Maeve, catching her off guard with the same show of affection. Hugging her close, I whispered, "I'm counting on you to take care of Orla. You're the only one I trust for that job."

"Of course, Your Highness." She winked at me.

Then Kieran took my hand, leading me out the door and starting our journey home.

* * *

One month later

My life was better than I could have imagined. Earlier tonight, Kieran and I had married. We'd decided to celebrate our wedding outside of Rioghail Tower, in the center of both territories, to further emphasize that both sides would be working together from here on. The High Court had been in attendance, despite their constant frowning, along with our families and witnesses from both territories.

I had chosen a white dress made of lace and cut low, emphasizing my curves, with snowflake designs woven into the dress and puffy, thin sleeves. I'd worn my Summer crown, its warm blaze of colors against the snow-white dress, emphasizing I was both Summer and Winter. The crown was made of vines and flowers that reminded me of Earth's sunflowers but in pinks, blues, and purples, along with yellows. And, of course, I'd had the three women who had helped me get my feet under me when I'd arrived, dress and style me for the wedding.

Lilidh, Cara, and Enid had been ecstatic, not only to be part of my wedding day but to have a hand in the largest, most important wedding Talamh had ever seen. And they'd been even happier that I finally remembered them.

Sunfire blossoms had lined the streets, and with the fall and spring trees blending together in the background, we'd had the perfect backdrop. Orla and Brianne had been my bridesmaids, with Nolan as Kieran's groomsman. Maeve had performed the ceremony,

337

and nothing could have made the day more perfect with one exception.

Stan.

I still missed my mentor. He'd taught me so many things to help me become who I was today. At least he didn't remember me and had peace, and I had my memories of him to hold on to and give me strength when I needed a reminder.

Now I stood at the window of our bedroom, watching snow fall. Once upon a time, I never thought I'd want to be near snow, but now the thought of not living here with Kieran was unfathomable.

Behind me came the beautiful sound of Kieran removing his jacket and tossing it on the matching chair. Though I didn't see him do it, I'd become perfectly attuned to him.

This is the most beautiful sight I've ever seen. My wife, my fated mate, in her wedding gown of snowflakes with summer flowers in her hair, standing in front of our window with the snow falling behind her. I want to live in this moment forever, my new husband said in my head, the magnitude of his love flowing through me.

I turned to him with a smirk on my face. His white shirt did nothing to hide the curves of his muscles. I reached behind my dress and began to unfasten it. "I can think of one thing that might change your mind."

His breath caught as the dress fell to the floor, leaving me in nothing but my crown, bra, and panties. I could see the growing bulge in his pants, and I felt even more empowered. I shrugged. "Unless I'm wrong. I can put some clothes on."

"Don't you dare," he growled, striding toward me and lifting me into his arms. He carried me like a princess to the bed and laid me on pink sheets he said reminded him of me. I gazed up at the large icicle chandelier centered over the bed, the glass intertwined with twilight orchids that were to signify my summer heritage.

My fingers eagerly lifted his shirt. I was desperate to consummate our union as his wife and fated mate. Within seconds, we were naked, and he trailed his fingers up my stomach, spreading goose bumps over my skin as he devoured my mouth.

He peppered kisses over my face and down my throat, and I whined, his lips sending amazing sensations shivering through me. I knew where he was heading. When he nipped and licked my nipple, I let out a gasp, and my head fell back.

He rolled his tongue over my nipple, and I tangled my hands in his hair, tugging gently, wanting more of everything. His free hand caressed my other breast in rhythm with his tongue, igniting a spark inside me. "Kieran," I moaned.

I traced the curves of his muscles, pressing him to me, seeking more contact. My body was on fire, my need for him more intense than before. He lowered his hand between my legs, and my stomach clenched tight with need. His hand gently spread my legs apart, and a deep growl vibrated in his chest as he slipped his fingers inside me and began thrusting gently.

Ecstasy exploded within me, and my insides clenched. I moved my hips through the crest of pleasure, grinding as he kept up with my body's tempo.

Even when the pleasure eased, it left me with a more urgent need. Nothing compared to feeling him inside me. I met his gaze to find he'd been watching me fall apart.

"Mo fhlùr, you are my undoing." He smirked and circled his fingers over my core.

Need knotted in my stomach, but I pushed him away. He'd gotten me ready—now it was my turn to satisfy him. "Lie down," I commanded.

"But ..." He pouted until I stroked him.

His eyelids drooped, and he lay beside me and captured my lips with his. Our tongues touched and melded in sync with my pace as I stroked him. His hips jerked, and his hands cupped my breasts. We caressed each other, lost in the moment. Nothing existed outside of him and me, and I never wanted that to change.

"Stop," he rasped and grabbed my hand. "This isn't how I want to finish." He rolled me onto my back and kneeled before me.

He'd always been handsome, but to see him like this—naked and aroused for me—was hotter than anything I'd ever seen. Every inch of him was hard and perfect.

I scooted back to give him room, and he positioned himself between my legs and guided himself to my opening. I arched against him, and he slid inside me. He hissed, his body shuddering, then he drove in deeper. I moaned. My body was already thrumming and ready for my next release.

My fingers dug into his back as I wrapped my legs around his waist, pulling him deeper. He thrust faster as my mouth captured his. I wanted to taste, touch, and feel him. I wanted to be surrounded by him, especially after how I'd almost lost him.

The pleasure built, and he tore his mouth from mine and kissed the mark on my neck. His body tensed as he moved faster, both of us nearing ecstasy.

But I needed *more*. This wasn't enough. I rolled us over and pushed him onto his back as I climbed on top of him.

He grinned, watching me sink onto him as he thrust deeper inside me. His approval had my body coiling tighter as I rode him slow and sweet, marking the occasion between us. An orgasm rocked us both, our desires melding together now that we were one.

As our pleasure continued to peak, I didn't break my rhythm, wanting to keep the sensations rolling between us for as long as possible.

When the pleasure eased, I lay across his chest. He wrapped his arms around me, hugging me close despite our sweaty bodies.

"I love you," he said and kissed the top of my head. "Not even that describes the depths of what I feel for you."

I nuzzled into his chest, listening to his heartbeat. *I love you too. More than anything else. And our future will be spent together, righting all the wrongs of the past.*

With lots of sex, he added, and I laughed.

For the first time ever, I felt content.

We had already begun to unify our people and bridge the gap between the two courts and the classes within.

Best of all, we were doing it together. I would've never dreamed that my own perception would change from the moment I woke up here after being taken from the party. I'd always been expecting the worst, and I never would've thought that being kidnapped would be the best thing to ever happen to me.

Though I missed parts of Earth, Talamh was my true home. Here, with my sexy, smart, self-sacrificing fated mate who lay right next to me, was where I belonged.

OF SHADOWS AND FAE
PRONUNCIATION GUIDE

Talamh	TAL-AHV
Alina	AH-LEEN-UH
Kieran	KEER-AN
Sambradh	SAM-BRUH
Deigh	DAY
Geimhreadh	GEYV-ROO
Beatha	BAY-UH
Rioghail	REE-UH-UHL
Dath	DAH
Comortas	KUH-MOR-TUSS
Brianne	BREE-UHN
Kaley	KAH-LEE
Caden	KAJ-EN
Leanna	LAN-UH
Quinley	KWIN-LEE
Eamon	EH-MUHN
Lilidh	LEE-LEE
Maeve	MEHV
Cara	KAHR-UH
Moire	MOY-RUH

Forgotten Kingdoms
Pronunciation Guide

Terrea (World Name)	**Ter-Ay-Yuh**
Havestia (Festival when the veil between worlds opens)	**Hav-Est-Ee-Uh**
Aelvaria	**El-Vahr-Ee-Uh**
Ember	Em-Burr
Hadeon	Hay-Dee-On
Draconia	**Drah-Cone-Ee-Uh**
Saphira	Sa-Fee-Ruh
Ryker	Rye-Kurr
Isramaya	**Is-Ruh-My-Uh**
Rhodelia	Row-Del-Ee-Uh
Varan	Vair-En
Isramorta	**Is-Ruh-Mor-Tuh**
Morgana	Mor-Gahn-Uh
Avalon	Av-Uh-Lahn
Magiaria	**Mayj-Air-Ee-Uh**
Adira	Ah-Deer-Uh
Kage	Kayj
Sepeazia	**Seh-Pee-Zee-Uh**
Stella	Stel-Uh
Brandt	Brant
Talamh	**Tal-Ahv**
Alina	Ah-Leen-Uh
Kieran	Keer-An
Vargr	**Var-Gur**
Evera	Eh-Veer-Uh
Axel	Ax-El

Of Elves & Ember
Chapter One

I didn't belong here.

Of course, that feeling was nothing new. Even as a child, when I still had parents who were alive and adored me, there had been a persistent sense of being other. While the other children played and made friends, I stayed indoors alone to draw things that only existed in my mind, never quite able to escape the restless, empty feeling that plagued my soul.

Then my parents died, and that feeling only intensified.

Tonight was different, though. My skin itched with an almost eerie feeling, contributing to what was more of a pervasive insistence that I was out of place than the normal vague intuition. Then again, this wasn't exactly my scene.

Smoke clung to every surface of the crowded casino in the middle of the Vegas strip. It was bad enough on a normal day, but intolerable on Halloween. Bodies crushed against each other, the masks and costumes making everyone even bolder than usual.

I could barely breathe in here. All I wanted to do was go back up to the relative quiet of the rooftop where I could see the stars. One look at my best friend's wide grin and bright brown eyes as she took in the fairy-themed bar, though, reminded me of why I had left my solitude to begin with.

Isa excitedly pointed at the careful details of the gazebo. It was covered in flowers and vines while artificial stars lit up the ceiling and smoke machines made it look like the partygoers were dancing on clouds.

It was pretty cool, I supposed. For a crowded club full of drunk assholes.

The hair stood on the nape of my neck, and I spun to find someone's eyes on me. That wasn't unusual, in and of itself. My fiery ombre hair tended to catch attention, even when I wasn't wearing a black dress and combat boots, dressed like a shadow in a sea of sparkles.

But this man smiled at me like we were already friends. I narrowed my eyes, trying to figure out if he was drunk or hitting on me or just a rare genuine person, trying to decipher the odd melancholy that surged in my chest when I took in the details of his costume.

Before I could make sense of it, my best friend stepped between us.

"Mira, Mami. I'm going to give you a pass for taking your ears off again since I know you didn't want to come." She pointedly glanced at the headband with glittering cat ears that was wrapped around the strap of my purse instead of on my head. "But at least come get a drink with me."

Isa's brown eyes widened like some sort of anime character, her full lips pursed in a delicate pout that had me rolling my eyes.

I knew she wasn't pleading for her sake, but for mine. She had wanted me to take a break so badly, from life and work and the restless energy that made me want to sell my shop, pick up in a new town, and start all over until I finally found somewhere that felt like home.

When I got the literal golden ticket announcing an all-expenses-paid trip to Vegas this weekend for two, I had already been strangely tempted to accept. That was weird, in itself, because I didn't like casinos or crowds or Halloween. Hell, the entire thing felt like a scam, but I had called to verify the details through the airline and the hotel, and everything was confirmed.

Still, I normally would have declined, but instead I had an inexplicable urge to accept. Then my only other friend, Ivy, received the same ticket. She shouldn't have wanted to go, either, but Isa had insisted it was a sign, from the universe or whatever powers that governed our lives. And of course, she insisted on joining us.

That's how I found myself here on one of the busiest weekends for my burgeoning tattoo shop, instead of losing myself in an endless line of clients gushing over the new psychedelic inks for the fantastical creatures that I was quickly becoming known for.

But Isa was a better friend than I deserved. Open and kind where I was distant and closed off. For her sake, I put the ears back on my head and made an effort to smile.

"All right, let's go."

She let out a squeal of excitement, linking her arm in mine as she dragged us to the fairytale-like bar.

The counter was carved to look like a fallen tree, while branches wrapped around to form shelves behind the bartenders. Twinklelights lit up the bottles of liquor while blue and pink flowers covered dark green vines that stretched around and between the shelves, giving it the feel of a real enchanted forest.

Isa took in every detail while I studied the menu, finally ordering something called Faerie Fire for her and a whiskey on the rocks for myself.

The frazzled bartender nodded, disappearing to take several more orders before he got to making the drinks. I diverted my attention to the sea of dancers.

"You should go."

"I said I wouldn't leave your side, and I won't. I'm still holding out that you'll want to dance after two or three more of those whiskeys," she said with a wink.

It wasn't completely outside of the realm of possibility. I did like to dance, and I had a dagger in my combat boot for anyone who got too handsy with either of us.

The sound of two drinks sliding across wood pulled my attention back to the bar. Two glasses sat in front of us, holding identical red concoctions that were very much not whiskey. I looked up to tell the bartender he had gotten it wrong, but he was already well away from us with his back turned.

Another masked, drunken moron bumped into me.

"Meow, kitty cat." He slung an arm around me.

My hand twitched toward my dagger, but Isa was already there, using all hundred pounds of her weight to shove him off me.

"Chinga te, Pendejo. Not tonight," she cursed him in Spanish, and I might have laughed if I hadn't been so irritated.

He put his hands up and backed away. I ripped the ears off my head, and Isa tucked them back around my purse strap with an apologetic look. She shoved my drink a little closer to me.

I eyed it dubiously, noting the bartender was still an ocean away and not so much as glancing in our direction.

To be buzzed on whatever disgustingness was in this cup, or to be sober? They set the strobe lights to pulsating, and my decision was made.

I took a sip, nearly gagging at the sickly-sweet taste of it. It was like raspberries had a vodka-and-rum-soaked baby with some lemons in a gallon of sugar. Isa, however, looked delighted while she drank hers, nearly downing it in one go.

Gross.

Then again, it was the only alcohol I had at my disposal to dull the throbbing bass and strobing lights wreaking hell on my cranium. The urge to take another sip overwhelmed me. So I did.

It was...better. Maybe?

The man who had been looking at me earlier, leaned over to whisper something to Isa. She giggled before turning to me.

"The dance floor misses me," she said with a half apology.

Then she flounced off into the crowd. What the hell?

That drink must have hit her fast. I surveyed her steady movements for signs that I should go after her. She appeared to be okay, just buzzed, so I kept my seat, making sure her bouncy black ponytail and sparkly cat ears were in sight.

"You don't like to dance?" The man who had spoken to Isa, the one who had been watching me, asked in a lightly accented voice.

British? Australian? It was too loud for me to try to narrow it down when I could barely hear him.

His deep brown skin had undertones of blue that only highlighted the pale glowing blue runes painted on his arms and face. Silver hoops lined the tips of his pointed ears that looked far more real than they should have.

When they began swimming in my vision, I realized I had been staring for far too long. I blinked and shook my head.

"It's more that I don't like people," I said a bit bluntly.

My words felt further away than they should have. I took another sip of my drink, almost taking comfort in the fruity flavor I couldn't quite place.

He chuckled. "Fair enough. I'm Kallius, by the way."

He scooted closer, so I leaned away.

"Ember." I didn't want to encourage him, but whatever courtesy lessons my parents had instilled in me in the brief decade they'd been with me had stuck. There was no need to be rude to him. Yet.

In truth, he had a kind, open face and a genuine smile. He looked at me like he already considered me a friend, with none of the lewdness I had come to expect from men. Something in me wanted to trust him, which sent up immediate alarm bells, making me go the other way.

Appearances could be deceiving. Anyone who has lived on the streets learns that fast.

"How's the drink?" He tilted his head and took a step back, taking my cue to give me some space.

"Disgusting." I scowled.

He pursed his lips and arched a dark eyebrow.

"Is that why it's halfway gone?" Kallius teased.

A laugh bubbled out of me, unexpected and loud.

I tilted my head, studying the lines of his face as he grinned. In another life, I wondered if I would have found him attractive.

But I didn't have it in me to be deeply attracted to anyone, as I had discovered the hard way in one too many failed relationships. I always hit a wall, and I was tired of feeling like a failure, an outsider, like there was something wrong with me. Tired of feeling the constant disappointment emanating from the other person when I had no desire to rip their clothes off with reckless abandon.

After several lackluster relationships, paired with underwhelming experiences in the bedroom, I had stopped trying. I only clumsily shook my head at his teasing, pulling my phone out of my small leather purse to text Ivy.

Where was she, anyway?

I tried to ask her, forcibly tapping letters on the glass screen, to tell her that Isa had left me here. Which was still...strange. Wasn't it?

My head was light, each of my thoughts dancing just out of reach. Everything felt off right now.

I scanned the crowd. Finding the familiar ponytail took me longer than it had before. Isa was laughing and dancing in a sea of other women dressed in animal costumes.

Looking back down, I stared at the blurring words on my screen, but I managed something almost coherent. Hopefully.

"We should go somewhere quieter, so we can talk." The man's voice was loud, almost like it was resounding in my head. I started, nearly dropping my phone.

I went rigid, clutching my grossly addicting drink in my fist with one hand while I tucked my phone away with the other. "No, we shouldn't."

I had to work harder than I should have to enunciate the words. This drink really was strong. The thought should have made me stop, slow down. A buzz was one thing, but I never let myself get drunk in front of strangers.

Instead, I took another long sip.

"She doesn't even know you, Kallius. How did you think she was going to take that?" a lighter voice hissed.

All at once, the man disappeared, replaced by a woman who looked startlingly like him. Had I seen her before tonight?

"I'm Celani, by the way," she said, leaning against the bar.

I mumbled something that sounded vaguely like Ember while she ordered a drink for herself from the bartender.

The light reflected off her silver cloak, highlighting similar rune tattoos her brother had painted on. Her whole Vikings-meets-Lord-of-the-Rings costume was epic, and the silver-white hair peeking out from her hood gave her even more of an ethereal appearance.

The dye job was excellent. So good that it almost looked natural. It had me thinking about every single time someone asked me about mine, the way my roots faded from a deep red down to a faint orange and golden blonde tips. Like I had a head of fire.

No matter how many times I tried to dye over it, the color peeked through within days. No one believed me when I told them it was that way naturally, and I didn't push, not wanting yet another thing to make me feel other.

"My brother's an idiot," the woman continued when I didn't respond. "He isn't trying anything untoward."

Untoward? The old-fashioned word went with her medieval costume and her polished accent, something that sounded close to British but maybe not quite. My shoulders relaxed without my permission, but I still raised an eyebrow. Or tried to. My face felt funny. Numb.

"Of courshhh not." My efforts to enunciate were less successful this time. "Men always say that with...noble intenshions."

The corner of her mouth tilted up in a knowing grin.

"Just ignore him. You don't want to dwell on that anyway. You want to go look at the paintings in the corner." Her voice reverberated in my head, stronger than her brother's had.

Did I? My attention turned to the massive, floor-to-ceiling canvases in the corner. One was of a sunny spring day with an open forest filled with wildflowers. It was bright, and lovely, and everything I was decidedly not.

The other, though, held snow-capped mountains under a night

sky. Silvery blue flowers peppered the snow while serene waterfalls cascaded from the cliffs into a glimmering pond.

Then there were the stars, painted so realistically that they seemed to be twinkling.

That was probably just my blurry vision, though. Surely.

Still, Celani was right. I did want to get a closer look.

I needed to.

I stumbled over there, drawn to the artwork with a magnetism I didn't understand, while Celani waited patiently next to me. I stared for minutes — or hours, maybe — transfixed, until Ivy's familiar voice sounded behind me.

"Not drinking whiskey, huh?"

Celani muttered a soft dammit as I spun around to find my friend. Or at least, a blurry shape that looked like her, wearing a pig onesie.

When my eyes focused again, I thought about how unfair it was that she looked pretty, even dressed in that.

Her strawberry-blonde hair glittered like a freaking halo around her head, and her pale green eyes reminded me of the spring painting behind us.

I turned to introduce her to Celani, but the Elven-dressed woman was gone.

Shaking my head, I remembered my text to Ivy and how long she had taken to show up.

"You. Bishhhhh," I gritted out, but my voice was far away to my own ears.

"Well, you did tell me to join you at farty bar. So, you know, shit happens." She gave me an unapologetic shrug.

I cringed, wrinkling my nose in disgust.

"Ew. No way. I said...Fairy Bar." Probably. I wasn't even sure I said it now.

Then I caught a whiff of her, a floral shampoo mixed with the heady scent of sweaty armpits, and I wondered all over again why she was wearing the onesie.

"A costume." She answered what I had apparently spoken out loud. "Unlike you."

"Don't celebrate," I reminded her. She knew I hated this time of year. A lifetime on the streets had taught me that people were even more unpredictable when they had masks to hide behind.

Something twisted inside of me at the thought.

I suddenly found myself in need of another drink. I shoved my glass into her hand and took off toward the bar, trying not to think about the way the crowd of people made me feel even more alone. The way all of the bad memories were creeping in. The way the painting had stirred in me an odd mix of nostalgia and longing and pain.

I stumbled against the wall, and a face appeared in my vision. It was a woman dressed as a guard, but she was the most beautiful person I had ever seen. Amethyst waves framed a face that was practically glowing in its perfection.

Her plump lips pursed into a concerned frown, and a gentle hand came to brush the hair off my forehead that was suddenly too hot.

"It will be better soon, Child," she said in a voice like wind chimes. With a last maternal look, she placed the cat ears that were hooked around the strap of my bag back on my head.

I opened my mouth to tell her I hadn't been a child in a long time, but she was already gone.

My head spun, and I wondered if I'd imagined the entire thing.

Somehow, I made it back to the bar. At least, I thought so. The woman was there, giving me a perplexed look while ethereal silver markings winked in and out of existence in my field of vision.

"I need another...drrrrink."

"I don't think you do. Stars, I didn't realize how human you would be."

I must have been even drunker than I realized, because that made no sense.

"You don't want another drink, Ember. You want to come with me."

I nodded, my eyes fixed on hers. Of course I did. Why wouldn't I? She was a beautiful moon fairy elf queen. I must have spoken the thought aloud, because she looked at me askance.

"Yes, you've had plenty," she muttered, amusement coloring her tone.

She led me back past the gyrating crowd toward the painting, supporting my weight. Ivy was gone. Where was she? And Isa was... still dancing? The thought sobered me slightly. I should find them.

"I need to find...friends."

"No, you don't. You need to come with me." Her voice dipped lower into a whisper, something earnest like a promise. "The shadow king is waiting for you."

Goosebumps lined my skin, and my eyes snapped to hers. Those words stirred something inside me.

A warning.

Dread.

Pain.

Some small part of my mind rebelled, but it wasn't strong enough to combat the soul-deep yearning I had to follow Celani. So I followed.

Right through the painting.

About the Author

Jen L. Grey is a *USA Today* Bestselling Author who writes Paranormal Romance, Urban Fantasy, and Fantasy genres.

Jen lives in Tennessee with her husband, two daughters, and two miniature Australian Shepherds. Before she began writing, she was an avid reader and enjoyed being involved in the indie community. Her love for books eventually led her to writing. For more information, please visit her website and sign up for her newsletter.

Check out her future projects and book signing events at her website.
www.jenlgrey.com

Also by Jen L. Grey

Twisted Fate Trilogy

Destined Mate

Eclipsed Heart

Chosen Destiny

The Forbidden Mate Trilogy

Wolf Mate

Wolf Bitten

The Marked Dragon Prince Trilogy

Ruthless Mate

Marked Dragon

Hidden Fate

Shadow City: Silver Wolf Trilogy

Broken Mate

Rising Darkness

Silver Moon

Shadow City: Royal Vampire Trilogy

Cursed Mate

Shadow Bitten

Demon Blood

Shadow City: Demon Wolf Trilogy

Ruined Mate

Shattered Curse

Fated Souls

Shadow City: Dark Angel Trilogy

Fallen Mate

Demon Marked

Dark Prince

Fatal Secrets

Shadow City: Silver Mate

Shattered Wolf

Fated Hearts

Ruthless Moon

The Wolf Born Trilogy

Hidden Mate

Blood Secrets

Awakened Magic

The Hidden King Trilogy

Dragon Mate

Dragon Heir

Dragon Queen

The Marked Wolf Trilogy

Moon Kissed

Chosen Wolf

Broken Curse

Wolf Moon Academy Trilogy

Shadow Mate

Blood Legacy

Rising Fate

The Royal Heir Trilogy

Wolves' Queen

Wolf Unleashed

Wolf's Claim

Bloodshed Academy Trilogy

Year One

Year Two

Year Three

The Half-Breed Prison Duology (Same World As Bloodshed Academy)

Hunted

Cursed

The Artifact Reaper Series

Reaper: The Beginning

Reaper of Earth

Reaper of Wings

Reaper of Flames

Reaper of Water

Stones of Amaria (Shared World)

Kingdom of Storms

Kingdom of Shadows

Kingdom of Ruins

Kingdom of Fire

The Pearson Prophecy

Dawning Ascent

Enlightened Ascent

Reigning Ascent

Stand Alones

Of Shadows and Fae

Death's Angel

Rising Alpha